D1053120

Katharine Kerr's
Novels of Deverry,
The Silver Wyrm Cycle

Now available from DAW Books:

THE GOLD FALCON (#1)

Forthcoming from DAW:

THE SPIRIT STONE (#2)

THE SHADOW ISLE (#3)

THE GOLD FALCON

Book One of *The Silver Wyrm*

Katharine Kerr

DAW BOOKS, INC.

DONALD A. WOLLHEIM, FOUNDER
375 Hudson Street, New York, NY 10014
ELIZABETH R. WOLLHEIM
SHEILA E. GILBERT
PUBLISHERS
http://www.dawbooks.com

First Printing, July 2006

1   2   3   4   5   6   7   8   9

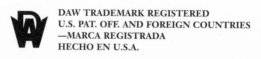

For Peg Strub, M.D.,
whose sharp eyes saved my life.

AUTHOR'S NOTE

I seem to have inadvertently caused some confusion among readers of this series by my system of subtitles for the various volumes in it. All of the Deverry books are part of one long story, divided into four "acts," as it were. Here's the correct order:

Act One: *Daggerspell, Darkspell, The Bristling Wood, The Dragon Revenant.*

Act Two, or "The Westlands": *A Time of Exile, A Time of Omens, Days of Blood and Fire, Days of Air and Darkness.*

Act Three, or "The Dragon Mage": *The Red Wyvern, The Black Raven, The Fire Dragon.*

Act Four, or "The Silver Wyrm": *The Gold Falcon,* which is the book you have in hand. Yet to be published: *The Spirit Stone* and *The Shadow Isle.*

THE POISONED ROOT OF IT ALL

I N THE YEAR 643, deep in the Dark Ages of the kingdom of
Deverry, a loose coalition of clans, allied with the few merchants and craft guilds of that time, put a new and unstable
dynasty on the throne of the high king. In those wars the Falcon
clan lost most of its men, noble-born and commoners both. In
gratitude, the king betrothed his third son, Galrion, to the last
daughter of the Falcon, Brangwen. But her brother, Lord Gerraent, loved her far more than a brother should, and Prince Galrion
loved the magical dweomer power more than he did his betrothed.
When Galrion broke off the betrothal, his father the king banished
him from the royal line forever. The prince took the name of
Nevyn, which means "no one" in the Deverrian tongue, and went
off to study the dweomer with the master who had hoped to teach
his craft to Galrion and Brangwen both.

As for Brangwen, left heartsick and shamed, she fell into her
brother's arms and bed. Soon enough, she was with child. Only
then did Nevyn realize how greatly he loved her and how badly
he'd failed her. Although he tried to get her away from her brother,
he failed to stop the inevitable tragedy. When she drowned herself
in shame, at her grave he swore a rash vow. Once she was reborn
again on the wheel of life and death, he "would never rest" until he

put right the evil he'd done by bringing her to the dweomer power which should have been hers. Little did he realize that fulfilling this vow would take him four hundred years of a single dweomer-touched lifetime, while the other actors in their tragedy were reborn and died again and again.

During his long life other souls would find themselves tangled in the chains of his and Brangwen's wyrd (fate or karma). Some were people he helped; others became his enemies. Nevyn took apprentices, such as Aderyn and Lilli, and made contact with other masters of the dweomer, such as Dallandra, one of the Westfolk, elven nomads who wander the plains to the west of Deverry proper.

Eventually Brangwen was reborn as Jill, the daughter of a mercenary soldier named Cullyn of Cerrmor and Seryan, a tavern lass. After more than a few adventures she finally saw her true destiny and went with Nevyn to study the dweomer as she should have done all those years before. Only then could Nevyn die.

Jill outlived him by many years. With the help of the elven dweomermaster, Dallandra, and her bizarre lover, Evandar, a powerful soul who had never been incarnated at all, Jill captained the first war against the savage Horsekin and their so-called goddess, Alshandra. In truth, Alshandra was a mortal spirit, though one of immense magical power, and in the end Jill managed to kill her, though she went to her death as well. One of those Jill left behind was the man she'd loved in her youth, the half-mad berserker Rhodry Maelwaedd, whose wyrd turned out to be something stranger than even a great master of the dweomer could have imagined.

For over fifty years, Dallandra and the Westfolk have stayed on guard against the Horsekin and the cult of their false goddess. Although Alshandra is dead, the religion she left behind lives on. Dallandra has also been doing her best to shepherd the other souls bound by wyrd to her and ultimately to Jill and Nevyn while she continues her own dweomerwork of serving her own people. But now, on the border between Deverry and the Westfolk lands, the winds of change are blowing, and they are ill winds indeed. . . .

ARCODD PROVINCE
SUMMER, 1159

The ancient Greggyn sage, Heraclidd, tells us that no man steps in the same river twice. Time itself is a river. When a man dies, he leaves the river behind, only to cross it again at the moment of birth. But betwixt times, the river has flowed on.

—*The Secret Book of Cadwallon the Druid*

NEB STRODE ACROSS the kitchen and stood next to the window, no more than a hole cut in the wall, open to the smell of mud and cows. Still, he found the air cleaner than that inside. Smoke rose from damp wood at the hearth in the middle of the floor and swirled through the half-round of a room before it oozed out of the chinks and cracks in the walls. Aunt Mauva knelt at the hearth and slapped flat rounds of dough onto the griddle stone. The oatcakes puffed and steamed. Neb heard his stomach rumble, and Clae, his young brother, took a step toward their aunt-by-marriage.

"Wait your turn!" she snapped. Her blue eyes narrowed in her bony face, and strands of dirty red hair stuck to her cheeks with sweat. "Your uncle and me eats first."

"Give that batch to the lads." Uncle Brwn was sitting at the plank table, a tankard of ale in his hand. "They've been pulling stones out of the west field all day, and that watery porridge you dished out this morning was scant."

"Scant? Scant, was it?" Mauva turned and rose in one smooth motion. "You've got your bloody gall! Dumping more mouths to feed into my lap—"

Brwn slammed the tankard down and lurched to his feet. "You

miserly barren slut! You should thank the gods for sending you my nephews."

Mauva squealed and charged, waving her fists in the air. Uncle Brwn grabbed her by the wrists and held on until she stopped squirming. He pushed her back, then set his thick and callused hands on his hips, but before he could speak, she shoved her face up under his, and they were off again, screaming at each other, sometimes with curses, more often with meaningless grunts and squeals. Neb knelt down by the hearth, found a thin splint of wood, and flipped the oatcakes over before they burned.

"Get somewhat to carry these," he hissed at Clae.

Clae glanced around the kitchen. On the sideboard stood an old flat basket; he grabbed it and held it up. Neb nodded, and Clae brought the basket over. Neb flipped the cooked cakes into the basket—three apiece. Little enough, but they would have to do. His screeching kin might quiet down before he could cook another batch. He stood up, grabbed the basket from Clae, and slipped out the back door. Clae followed, and together they slogged across the muddy farmyard and dodged around the dungheap. Skinny chickens came clucking, heads high and hopeful.

"Forgive me," Neb said. "There's barely enough for us."

A packed earth wall surrounded house, barn, and farmyard. They hurried through the gate and trotted around the outside of the wall, where an apple tree stood to offer them some shade. They sat down, grabbed the still-warm cakes, and gobbled them before Mauva could come and take them back. Above them little apples bobbed among the leaves, still too green, no matter how hungry they were. Clae swallowed the last bit of cake and wiped his mouth on his sleeve.

"Neb?" he said. "I wish Mam hadn't died."

"So do I, but wishing won't bring her back."

"I know. Why does Uncle Brwn put up with Mauva?"

"Because she lets him drink all the ale he wants. Are you still hungry?"

"I am." Clae sounded on the edge of tears.

"Down by the river we can find berries."

"If she finds us gone, she'll make Uncle beat us."

"I'll think of some way to get out of it. If we get back late enough, they'll both be drunk."

Brwn's farm, the last steading on the Great West Road, lay a mile beyond the last village. No one saw the boys as they hurried across the west field and jumped over the half-finished stone wall into wild meadow. It was a lovely warm afternoon, and the slanted light lay as thick as honey on the green rolling pasture land. Tinged with yellow clay, the river Melyn churned and bubbled over boulders. All along its grassy banks stood mounds of red-berry canes, heavy with fruit, sweet from a long hot day. The boys gorged themselves, drank river water, and stuffed in a few more handfuls of berries. Clae would have eaten still more, but Neb stopped him.

"You don't want the runs, do you?"

"I don't, truly, but oh, it's so good not to be hungry."

They sat down in the warm grass and watched the river gleam like gold in the afternoon light, gliding along south to join the great rivers of the kingdom of Deverry—or so they'd always been told. They'd spent their entire lives here in Arcodd province. Off to the east stretched half-settled farmland; to the west and north, wild country. Far away south from their rough frontier lay the rich fields of the center of the kingdom and the fabled city of Dun Deverry, where the high king lived in a reputedly splendid palace.

When Neb turned to the north, he could see, about half a mile away, the smooth rise of pale tan cliff that separated this valley from the high plateau beyond. The river tumbled down in a spray of white laced with rainbows. Above, the primeval forest, all tangled pines and scruffy underbrush, stood poised at the cliff edge like a green flood, ready to pour over the valley.

"Neb?" Clae said. "Can we go look at the waterfall? Can we go up to the top?"

"I don't think so. We don't want to be caught up there in the dark."

"I guess not. Well, maybe Aunt Mauva will be drunk soon."

Materializing as silently and suddenly as always, the Wildfolk appeared. Knee-high gray gnomes, all warts and spindly limbs, clustered around the two boys. In the air blue sprites flew back and forth, wringing their tiny hands, opening tiny mouths to reveal their needle-sharp fangs. At the river's edge undines rose up, as sleek as otters but with silver fur. The gnomes grabbed the sleeves of Neb's torn shirt and pulled on them while the sprites darted back and forth. They would start north toward the waterfall, then swoop back to buzz around the lads like flies. A big yellow gnome, Neb's favorite, grabbed his hand and tugged.

Clae saw none of this, because he was pawing through the grass. Finally, he picked out a bit of stick and began chewing on it.

"Get that out of your mouth," Neb said. "And come on, we're going to have a look at the waterfall after all."

Clae grinned and tossed the stick into the river. An undine caught it, bowed, and disappeared into foam.

In a crowd of Wildfolk the two boys headed upstream, following a grassy path beside the noisy river. Now and then Clae seemed to feel the presence of the gnomes. When one of them brushed against him, he would look down, then shrug as if dismissing the sensation. For as long as he could remember Neb had seen the Wildfolk, but no one else in his family had the gift of the Sight. He'd learned early to keep his gifts to himself. Any mention of Wildfolk had exasperated his literal-minded mother and made the other children in town mock and tease him.

The two boys followed the river to the white water churning around fallen boulders. They panted up the steep path that zigzagged along the cliff face, then turned to look back. Under a black plume the distant village was burning. Neb stared, unable to comprehend, unable to scream, merely stared as the bright flower of flame poured black smoke into the sky. Little people, the size of red ants from their vantage point, scurried around and waved their arms. Larger ants chased them and waved things that winked metallic in the sun. A cluster of horses, the size of flies, stood on the far side of the village bridge. The farm—it too burned, a blossom of deadly gold among the green meadows. Two horses and riders circled the earthen wall.

"Raiders!" Clae's voice was a breathy sob. "Oh, Neb! Horsekin!"

Overhead a raven shrieked, as if answering him. The two riders suddenly turned their horses away from the farmstead. They broke into a gallop and headed upstream for the waterfall.

"Into the forest!" Neb said. "We've got to hide!"

They raced across the grassy cliff top, plunged into the forest, and ran panting and crashing through the underbrush among the pines and brambles. Twigs and thorns caught and tore Neb's shirt and brigga, but he drove his brother before him like a frightened sheep until at last they could run no more. They burrowed into a thick patch of shrubs and clung together. If the slavers caught them, they would geld Clae like a steer. *And they'd kill me,* Neb thought. *I'm old enough to cause trouble.*

Neb could see nothing in the tangled mass of forest. He could hear only the waterfall, plunging down over rock. Had they run far enough? Voices—Neb thought he heard voices, deep ones, muttering in what sounded like anger, then a crash and a jingle, very faint, as if someone had dropped something metallic on to a rock. He did hear a shout that turned to a scream. Clae stiffened and opened his mouth. Neb clapped a hand over it before he could speak.

Whether voices or not, the sounds died away, leaving only the chatter of the waterfall to disturb the silence. Slowly the normal noises of a forest picked up, the distant rustles of small animals, the chirping of birds. The yellow gnome appeared to perch in a nearby bush and grin. It patted its stomach as if pleased with itself, then disappeared. Slowly, too, the gray twilight deepened into a velvety night. They were safe for now, but on the morrow in the sunlight the Horsekin might return to search the woods. Neb realized that he and Clae had best be gone as soon as it was light enough to see.

Eventually Clae squirmed into his brother's lap like a child half his size and fell asleep. Neb drowsed, but every snap of a twig, cry of an owl, or rustle of wind woke him in startled terror. When at last the gray dawn came, he felt as stiff and cold as an old man. Clae woke in tears, crying out at his memories.

"Hush, hush," Neb said, but he felt like weeping himself. "Now we have to think. We don't have a cursed bite to eat, and we'd best find something."

"We can't go down to the river. If the Horsekin are still there, they'll smell us out."

"They'll what?"

"Smell us out. They can do that."

"How do you know?"

Clae started to answer, then looked away, visibly puzzled. "Someone must have told me," he said at last.

"Well, we've heard plenty of tales about the Horsekin, sure enough. Speaking of noses, wipe yours on your sleeve, will you?"

Clae obliged. "I never thought I'd miss Uncle Brwn," he said, then began to weep in a silent trickle of tears. *Our uncle's dead,* Neb thought. *The last person who would take us in, even if he was a sot.*

"We're going to walk east," Neb said. "We'll follow the rising sun so we won't get lost. On the other side of the forest, we'll find a village. It's a long way, so you'll have to be brave."

"But, Neb," Clae said, "what will we eat?"

"Oh, berries and birds' eggs and herbs." Neb made his voice as strong and cheery as he could. "There's always lots to eat in summer."

He was, of course, being ridiculously optimistic. The birds' eggs had long since hatched; few berry bushes grew in forest shade. At every step the forest itself blocked their way with ferns and shrubs, tangled between the trees. They had to push their way through, creeping uphill and hurrying down as they searched for the few herbs that would feed, not poison them. Water at least they had; they came across a good many rivulets trickling down to join the Melyn. By sundown, Clae could not make himself stop weeping. They made a nest among low-growing shrubs, where Neb rocked him to sleep like a baby.

As he watched the shadows darken around them, Neb realized that they were going to die. He had no idea how far the forest stretched. Were they going straight east? Trying to follow the sun among trees might have them wandering around in circles. *You can't give up,* he told himself. He'd promised his dying mother that he'd keep Clae safe. The one concern he could allow himself now was keeping them both alive. He fell asleep to dream of sitting at his mother's table and watching her pile bread and beef onto the trencher he shared with Clae.

In the morning, Neb woke with a start. A gaggle of gnomes stood around them as if they were standing guard, while sprites floated overhead. The yellow gnome materialized and stood pointing to its stomach.

"Do you know where there's food?" Neb whispered.

The gnome nodded and pointed off into the forest.

"Can you show me where it is?"

Again the gnome nodded. When Neb shook him, Clae woke with a howl and a scatter of tears. He slid off Neb's lap and screwed his fists into his eyes.

"Time to get on the road," Neb said with as much cheer as he could muster. "I've got the feeling we're going to be lucky today."

"My feet hurt. I can't walk anymore." Clae lowered his hands. "I'll just die here."

"You won't do any such thing. Here, stick out your legs. One at a time! I'll wrap the swaddling for you."

With the rags bound tight against his feet, Clae managed to keep walking. As they beat their way through fern and thistle, the Wild-folk led the boys straight into the forest, dodging around the black-barked pines and trampling through green ferns. Neb was beginning to wonder if the gnomes knew where they were going when he realized that up ahead the light was growing brighter. The trees grew farther apart, and the underbrush thinned. A few more yards, and they stepped out into a clearing, where a mass of red-berry canes grew in a mound. Clae rushed forward and was already stuffing his mouth when Neb caught up with him. Neb mumbled a prayer of thanks to the gods, then began plucking every berry he could reach.

Red juice like gore stained their hands and faces by the time they forced themselves to stop. Neb was considering finding a stream to wash in when the yellow gnome appeared again. It grabbed his shirt with one little hand and with the other pointed to the far side of the clearing. When Neb took a few steps that way, he realized that he could hear running water.

"There's a stream or suchlike over yonder," Neb said to Clae. "We'll go that way."

The gnome smiled and nodded its head. Other Wildfolk appeared and surrounded them as they crossed the clearing. They worked their way through forest cover for about a hundred yards before they found the stream, and just beyond that, a marvel: a dirt road, curving through the trees. When Neb sighted along it, it seemed to run roughly east.

"I never knew this road was here," Clae said.

"No more did I," Neb said.

"I wonder where it goes to? There's naught out to the west of here."

"Doesn't matter. We can walk faster now, and a road means people must have made it."

"But what about the raiders?" Clae looked nervously around him. "They'll follow the road and get us."

"They won't," Neb said firmly. "They've got those huge horses, so they can't ride through the wild woods. They'll never get as far as this road."

Neb insisted they wash their hands before they scooped up drinking water in them. When they finished, he pulled up a handful of grass, soaked it, and cleaned the snot and berry juice off Clae's face.

All that day they tried to ignore their hunger and make speed, but now and again the road dipped into shallow ravines or swung wide around a mound or spur of naked rock—no easy traveling. As far as Neb could tell, however, it continued to run east toward safety. Around noon, the forest thinned out along a stream, where they found a few more berries and a patch of wood sorrel they could graze like deer. Then it was back on the road to stumble along, exhausted. Neb began to lose hope, but the sprites fluttered ahead of them, and the yellow gnome kept beckoning them onward.

Toward sunset, Neb saw thin tendrils of pale blue smoke drifting far ahead. He froze and grabbed Clae's arm.

"Back into the trees," he whispered.

Clae took a deep breath and fought back tears. "Do we have to go back to the forest? I'm all scratched up from the thistles and suchlike."

The yellow gnome hopped up and down, shaking its head.

"We can't stay on the road," Neb said.

"Oh, please?"

The gnome nodded a violent yes.

"Very well." Neb gave in to both of them. "We'll stick to the road for a bit."

"My thanks," Clae said. "I'm so tired."

The gnome smiled, then turned and danced along the road, leading the way. In about a quarter of a mile, off to the left of the road, the forest gave way to another clearing. In the tall grass two horses grazed at tether, a slender gray like a lady's palfrey and a stocky dun packhorse. Beyond them the plume of smoke rose up. Neb hesitated, trying to decide whether to run or go forward. The wind shifted, bringing with it the smell of soda bread, baking on a griddle. Clae whimpered.

"All right, we'll go on," Neb said. "But carefully now. If I tell you to run, you head for the forest."

A few yards more brought them close enough to hear a man singing, a pleasant tenor voice that picked up snatches of songs, then idly dropped them again.

"No Horsekin would sing like that," Neb said.

The yellow gnome grinned and nodded his agreement.

Another turn of the road brought them to a camp and its owner.

He was hunkering down beside the fire and baking bread on an iron griddle. On the tall side, but slender as a lad, he had hair so pale that it looked like moonlight and a face so handsome that it was almost girlish. He wore a shirt that once had been splendid, but now the bands of red and purple embroidery were worn and threadbare, and the yellow stain of old linen spread across the shoulders and back. His trousers, blue brigga cut from once-fine wool, were faded, stained, and patched here and there—a rough-looking fellow, but the gnomes rushed into his camp without a trace of fear. He stood up and looked around, saw Neb and Clae, and mugged amazement.

"What's all this?" he said. "Come over here, you two! You look half starved and scared to death. What's happened?"

"Raiders," Neb stammered. "Horsekin burned my uncle's farm and the village. Me and my brother got away."

"By the gods! You're safe now—I swear it. You've got naught to fear from me."

The yellow gnome grinned, leaped into the air, and vanished. As the two boys walked over, the stranger knelt again at the fire, where an iron griddle balanced on rocks. Clae sat down nearby with a grunt of exhaustion, his eyes fixed on the soda bread, but Neb stood for a moment, looking round him. Scattered by the fire were saddlebags and pack panniers stuffed with gear and provisions.

"I'm Neb and this is Clae," Neb said. "Who are you? What are you doing here?"

"Well, you may call me Salamander," the stranger said. "My real name is so long that no one can ever say it properly. As to what I'm doing, I'm having dinner. Come join me."

Shamelessly, Neb and Clae wolfed down chunks of warm bread. Salamander rummaged through saddlebags of fine pale leather, found some cheese wrapped in clean cloth, and cut them slices with a dagger. While they ate the cheese, he bustled around, getting out a small sack of flour, a silver spoon, a little wood box of the precious soda, and a waterskin. He knelt down to mix up another batch of bread, kneading it in an iron pot, then slapped it into a thin cake right on the griddle with his oddly long and slender fingers.

"Now, you two had best settle your stomachs before you eat anything more," he said. "You'll only get sick if you eat too much after starving."

"True spoken," Neb said. "Oh ye gods, my thanks. May the gods give you every happiness in life for this."

"Nicely spoken, lad." Salamander looked up, glancing his way.

His eyes were gray, a common color in this part of the country, and a perfectly ordinary shape, but all at once Neb couldn't look away from them. *I know him*, he thought. *I've met him—I couldn't have met him.* Salamander tilted his head to one side and returned the stare, then sat back on his heels, his smile gone. Neb could have sworn that Salamander recognized him as well. The silence held until Salamander looked away.

"Tell me about the raid," he said abruptly. "Where are you from?"

"The last farm on the Great West Road," Neb said, "but we've not lived there long. When our mam died, we had to go live with our uncle. Before that we lived in Trev Hael. My da was a scribe, but he died, too. Before Mam, I mean."

"Last year, was it? I heard that there was some sort of powerful illness in your town. An inflammation of the bowels, is what I heard, with fever."

"It was, and a terrible bad fever, too. I had a touch of it, but Da died of it, and our little sister did, too. Mam wore herself out, I think, nursing them, and then this spring, when it was so damp and chill—" Neb felt tears welling in his voice.

"You don't need to say more," Salamander said. "That's a sad thing all round. How old are you, lad? Do you know?"

"I do. Da always kept count. I'm sixteen, and my brother is eight."

"Sixteen, is it? Huh." Salamander seemed to be counting something out in his mind. "I'm surprised your father didn't marry you off years ago."

"It wasn't for want of trying. He and the town matchmaker just never seemed to find the right lass."

"Ah, I see." Salamander pointed and smiled. "Look, your brother's asleep."

Clae had curled up right on the ground, and indeed he was asleep, openmouthed and limp.

"Just as well," Neb said. "He'll not have to listen to the tale this way."

Neb told the story of their last day on the farm and their escape as clearly as he could. When he rambled to a stop, Salamander said nothing for a long moment. He looked sad, and so deeply weary that Neb wondered how he could ever have thought him young.

"What made you go look at the waterfall?" Salamander asked.

"Oh, just a whim."

The yellow gnome materialized, gave Neb a sour look, then climbed into his lap like a cat. Salamander pointed to the gnome with his cooking spoon.

"It's more likely he warned you," Salamander said. "He led you here, after all."

Neb found he couldn't speak. Someone else with the Sight! He'd always hoped for such. The irony of the bitter circumstances in which he'd had his hope fulfilled struck him hard.

"Did anyone see you up on the cliff?" Salamander went on.

"I think so. Two Horsekin rode our way, but they were too far away for me to see if they were pointing at us or suchlike. We ran into the forest and hid." Neb paused, remembering. "I thought I heard voices, but the waterfall was so loud, it was hard to tell. There was a scream, too. It almost sounded like someone fell off the cliff."

The yellow gnome began to clap its hands and dance in a little circle.

"Here!" Salamander said to it. "You and your lads didn't push that Horsekin down the cliff, did you?"

The gnome stopped dancing, grinned, and nodded. Salamander, however, looked grim.

"Is he dead?" Salamander said.

The gnome nodded yes, then disappeared.

"Ye gods!" Neb could hear how feeble his own voice sounded. "I always thought of them like little pet birds or puppies. Sweet little creatures, that is."

"Never ever make that mistake again!. They're not called the *Wild*folk for naught."

"I won't, I can promise you that!" Neb paused, struck by his sudden thought. "They saved our lives. If that Horsekin had gotten to the top of the cliff . . ." His voice deserted him.

"He would have found you, truly. They have noses as keen as dogs'."

"Well, that's one up for Clae, then. He told me that. But sir, the Wildfolk—what are they?"

"Sir, am I?" Salamander grinned at him. "No need for courtesies, lad. You have the same odd gift that I do, after all. As to what they are, do you know what an elemental spirit is?"

"I don't. I mean, everyone knows what spirits are, but I've not heard the word elemental before."

"Well, it's a long thing to explain, but—" Salamander stopped abruptly.

With a whimper Clae woke and sat up, stretching his arms over his head. Conversation about the Wildfolk would have to wait. Salamander flipped the griddle cake over with the handle of the spoon before he spoke again.

"May the Horsekins' hairy balls freeze off when they sink to the lowest hell," Salamander said. "But I don't want to wait that long for justice. Allow me to offer you lads my protection, such as it is. I'll escort you east, where we shall find both safety and revenge."

"My thanks! I'm truly grateful."

Salamander smiled, and at that moment he looked young again, barely a twenty's worth of years.

"But, sir?" Clae said with a yawn. "Who are you? What are you really?"

"Really?" Salamander raised one pale eyebrow. "Well, lad, when it comes to me, there's no such thing as really, because I'm a mountebank, a traveling minstrel, a storyteller, who deals in nothing but lies, jests, and the most blatant illusions. I am, in short, a gerthddyn, who wanders around parting honest folk from their coin in return for a few brief hours in the land of never-was, never-will-be. I can also juggle, make scarves appear out of thin air, and once, in my greatest moment, I plucked a sparrow out of the hat of a fat merchant."

Clae giggled and sat up a bit straighter.

"Later," Salamander went on, "after I've eaten, I shall tell you a story that will drive all thoughts of those cursed raiders out of your head so that you may go to sleep when your most esteemed brother tells you to. I'm very good at driving away evil thoughts."

"My thanks," Neb said. "Truly, I don't know how I'll ever repay you for all of this."

"No payment needed." Salamander made a little bob of a bow. "Why should I ask for payment, when I never do an honest day's work?"

Just as twilight was darkening into night, Salamander built up the fire and settled in to tell the promised story, which fascinated Neb as much as it did young Clae. Salamander swept them away to a far-off land where great sorcerers fought with greedy dragons over treasure, then told them of a prince who was questing for a gem that had magic, or dweomer, as Salamander called it. He played all the parts, his voice lilting for the beautiful princess, snarling for the evil sorcerer, rumbling for the mighty king. Every now and then, he sang a song as part of the tale, his beautiful voice harmonizing with the wind in the trees. By the time the stone was found, and the prince and princess safely married, Clae was smiling.

"Oh, I want there to be real dweomer gems," Clae said. "And real dweomermasters, too."

"Do you now?" Salamander gave him a grin. "Well, you never know, lad. You think about it when you're falling asleep."

Neb found a soft spot in the grass for his brother's bed. He wrapped Clae up in one of the gerthddyn's blankets and stayed with him until he was safely asleep, then rejoined Salamander at the fire.

"A thousand thanks for amusing my brother," Neb said. "I'd gladly shower you with gold if I had any."

"I only wish it were so easy to soothe your heart," Salamander said.

"Well, good sir, that will take some doing, truly. First we lost our hearth kin, and now our uncle. It was all so horrible at first, it had me thinking we'd escaped the raiders only to live like beggars in the streets."

"Now here, the folk in this part of the world aren't so hard-hearted that they'll let you starve. One way or another, we'll find some provision for you and the lad."

"If I can get back to Trev Hael, I can make my own provision. After all, I can read and write. If naught else, I can become a town letter-writer and earn our keep that way."

"Well, there you go! It's a valuable skill to have." Salamander hesitated on the edge of a smile. "Provided that's the craft you want to follow."

"Well, I don't know aught else but writing and suchlike. I'm not strong enough to join a warband, and I wouldn't want to weave or suchlike, so I don't know what other craft there'd be for me."

"You don't, eh? Well, scribing is an honorable sort of work, and there's not many who can do it out here in Arcodd."

Neb considered Salamander for a moment. In the dancing fire-light it was hard to be sure, but he could have sworn that the gerth-ddyn was struggling to keep from laughing.

"Or what about herbcraft?" Salamander went on. "Have you ever thought of trying your hand at that?"

"I did, truly. Fancy you thinking of that! When my da was still alive, I used to help the herbwoman in Trev Hael. I wrote out labels for her and suchlike, and she taught me a fair bit about the four humors and illnesses and the like. Oh, and about the four elements. Is that what you meant by elemental spirits?"

"It is. The different sorts of Wildfolk correspond to different elements. Hmm, the herbwoman must have been surprised at how fast you learned the lore."

"She was. She told me once that it was like I was remembering it, not learning. How did you—"

"Just a guess. You're obviously a bright lad."

Salamander was hiding something—Neb was sure of it—but probing for it might insult their benefactor. "Govylla, her name was," Neb went on. "She lived through the plague. Huh—I wonder if she'd take us in, Clae and me, as prentices? Well, if I can get back there. Some priests of Bel were traveling out here, you see, and so they took us to our uncle."

"And some might well be traveling back one fine day. But for now, we need to get the news of raiders to the right ears. I happen to have the very ears in mind. I've been traveling along from the east, you see, and the last place I plied my humble trade was the dun of a certain tieryn, Cadryc, noble scion of the ancient and con-joined Red Wolf clan, who's been grafted upon the root of a new demesne out here. When I left, everyone begged me to come back again soon, so we shall see if they were sincere or merely courteous. I have a great desire to inform the honorable tieryn about these raiders. Oh, that I do, a very great desire, indeed."

As he stared into the fire, Salamander let his smile fade, his eyes darkening, his slender mouth as harsh as a warrior's. In that moment Neb saw a different man; cold, ruthless, and frightening. With a laugh the gerthddyn shrugged the mood away and began singing about lasses and spring flowers.

Down the hill behind Tieryn Cadryc's recently built dun lay a long meadow, where the tieryn's warband of thirty men were amusing themselves with mock combats in the last glow of a warm afternoon. Two men at a time would pick out wooden swords and wicker shields, then face off in the much-trampled grass. The rest of the troop sat in untidy lines off to either side and yelled comments and insults as the combat progressed. Gerran, the captain of the Red Wolf warband, sat off to one side with Lord Mirryn, Tieryn Cadryc's son. Brown-haired and blue-eyed, with a liberal dusting of freckles across his broad cheekbones, Mirryn was lounging at full length, propped up on one elbow, and chewing on a long grass stem like a farmer.

"One of these days our miserly gwerbret's bound to set up a proper tourney," Mirryn said. "Although everyone knows you'd win it, so I doubt me if I can get anyone to wager against you."

"Oh, here," Gerran said. "It's not that much of a sure thing."

"Of course it is." Mirryn grinned at him. "False humility doesn't become you."

Gerran allowed himself a brief smile. Out in the meadow a new fight was starting. The rest of the warband called out jests and jeers, teasing Daumyr for his bad luck in drawing his sparring partner. Daumyr, the tallest man in the troop at well over six feet, stood grinning while he swung his wooden sword in lazy circles to limber up his arm. His opponent, Warryc, was skinny and short—but fast.

"Ye gods, Daumyr's got a long reach!" Mirryn said. "It's truly amazing, the way Warryc beats him every time. Huh—there must be a way we can use this at the next tourney."

"Use it for what?" Gerran said.

"Acquiring some hard coin, that's what, by setting up a wager, getting some poor dolt to bet high on Daumyr."

"The very soul of honor, that's you."

Gerran was about to say more when he heard hoofbeats and shouting. A young page on a bay pony came galloping across the meadow.

"My lord Mirryn! Captain Gerran!" the page called out. "The tieryn wants you straight away. There's been a raid on the Great West Road."

Mirryn led the warband back at the run. Up at the top of a hill, new walls of pale stone, built at the high king's expense, circled the fort to protect the tall stone broch tower and its outbuildings. The men dashed through the great iron-bound gates, stopped in the ward to catch their collective breath, then hurried into the great hall. Sunlight fell in dusty shafts from narrow windows, cut directly into stone, and striped the huge round room with shadows. Gerran paused, letting his eyes adjust, then picked his way through the clutter of tables and benches, dogs and servants. The warband followed him, but Mirryn hurried on ahead to his father's side. When he saw Gerran lingering behind, Mirryn waved him up with an impatient arm.

By the hearth of honor, Cadryc was pacing back and forth, a tall man, tending toward stout, with a thin band of gray hair clinging to the back of his head and a pair of ratty gray mustaches. Perched on the end of a table was the gerthddyn, Salamander. Mirryn and Gerran exchanged a look of faint disgust at the sight of him, a babbling fool, in their shared opinion, with his tricks and tales. When Gerran started to kneel before the tieryn, Cadryc impatiently waved him to his feet.

"Raiders," Cadryc said. "Didn't the page tell you? We're riding tomorrow at dawn, so get the men ready."

"Well and good, Your Grace," Gerran said. "How far are they?"

"Who knows, by now?" Cadryc shook his head in frustrated rage. "Let's hope they're still looting the village."

"Bastards," Mirryn said. "I hope to all the gods they are. We'll make them pay high for this."

"You're staying here, lad," Cadryc said. "I'm not risking myself and my heir both."

Mirryn flushed red, took a step forward, then shoved his hands into his brigga pockets.

"For all we know, the raiders have set up some sort of ruse or trap," Cadryc went on. "I'll be leaving you ten men to command on fort guard. Your foster brother here can handle the rest well enough."

"Far be it from me to argue with you," Mirryn said. "Your Grace."

"Just that—don't argue," Cadryc snapped. "And don't sulk either."

Mirryn spun on his heel and stalked off, heading back outside.

Cadryc muttered a few insults under his breath. Gerran decided a distraction was in order and turned to the gerthddyn.

"Little did I dream our paths would cross so soon," Salamander gave him a fatuous smile. "An honor to see you, Captain."

"Spare me the horseshit," Gerran said. "Did you see this raid or only find a burned village or suchlike?"

"Ah, what a soul of courtesy you are." Salamander rolled his eyes heavenward. "Actually, I found refugees, who escaped by blind luck."

When Salamander pointed, Gerran noticed for the first time a tattered dirty lad and an equally ragged little boy, kneeling by the corner of the massive stone hearth. Dirt clotted in hair that was most likely mousy brown, and they shared a certain look about their deep-set blue eyes that marked them for close kin. Skinny as a stick, the older lad was, with fine, small hands, but the younger, though half-starved from the look of him, had broad hands and shoulders that promised strong bones and height one day.

"They lost everything in the raid," Salamander said. "Kin, house, the lot." He pointed. "Their names are Neb and Clae."

"We'll give them a place here." Tieryn Cadryc beckoned to a page. "Go find my wife and ask her to join us."

When the page trotted off, Neb, the older lad, watched him go with dead eyes.

"How many of them were there?" Gerran asked him. "The raiders, I mean."

"I don't know, sir," Neb said. "We were a good distance away, up by the waterfall, so we could see down into the valley. We saw the village burning, and our farm, and then a lot of people just running around."

"Cursed lucky thing you were gone."

The lad nodded, staring at him, too tired to speak, most likely.

"The raiding party won't be traveling fast, not with prisoners to drag along," Cadryc broke in. "I've sent a message to Lord Pedrys, telling him to meet us on the road with every man he can muster. I'd summon the other vassals as well, but they live too cursed far east, and we've got to make speed."

"Your Grace?" Gerran said. "Wasn't there a lord near this village?"

"There was. What I want to know is this: is there still?"

Neb watched the captain and the tieryn walk away, talking of their plans, both of them tall men, but red-haired Gerran was as lean as the balding tieryn was stout. Neither would be a good man to cross, Neb decided, nor Lord Mirryn either. Salamander left his perch on the table and joined the two boys.

"Well, there," the gerthddyn said. "Your uncle will be avenged, and perhaps they'll even manage to rescue your aunt."

"If they do," Clae said, "we won't have to go back to her, will we?"

"You won't. Judging from what you told me on our journey here, she doesn't seem to be a paragon of the female virtues, unlike the tieryn's good wife." Salamander glanced over his shoulder. "Who, I might add, is arriving at this very moment."

Salamander stepped aside and bowed just as the lady hurried up, a stout little woman, her dark hair streaked with gray. She wore a pair of dresses of fine-woven blue linen, caught in at the waist by a plaid kirtle in yellow, white, and green. Two pages trailed after her, a skinny pale boy with a head of golden curls and a brown-haired lad a few years older.

"My lady, this is Neb and Clae," Salamander said. "Lads, this is the honorable Lady Galla, wife to Tieryn Cadryc."

Since he was already kneeling, Neb ducked his head in respect and elbowed Clae to make him do the same.

"You may rise, lads," she said. "I've heard your terrible story from young Coryn, here." She gestured at the older, brown-haired page. "Now don't you worry, we'll find a place for you in the dun. The cook and the grooms can always use an extra pair of hands."

"My thanks, my lady," Neb said. "We'll be glad to work for our keep, but we might not be staying—"

"My lady?" Salamander broke in. "Luck has brought you some-one more valuable than a mere kitchen lad. Our Neb can read and write."

"Luck, indeed!" Lady Galla smiled brilliantly. "My husband's had need of a scribe for ever so long, him and half the noble-born in Arcodd, of course, but what scribe would be wanting to travel all the way out here, anyway, if he could find a better place down in Deverry? Well and good, young Neb, we'll see how well you form your letters, but first you need to eat, from the look of you, and a bath wouldn't hurt either."

"Thank you, my lady." Clae looked up with wide eyes. "We've been so hungry for so long."

"Food first, then. Coryn, take them to the cookhouse and tell Cook I said to feed them well. Then do what you can about getting them clean. Clothes—well, I'll see what I can find."

The food turned out to be generous scraps of roast pork, bread with butter, and some dried apples to chew on for a sweet. The cook let them sit in the straw by the door while she went back to work at her high table, cracking dried oats with a stone roller in a big stone quern. Coryn helped himself to a handful of apples and sat down with them. He seemed a pleasant sort, chatting to the brothers as they wolfed down the meal.

"I do like our lady," Coryn said. "She's ever so kind and cheer-ful. And our lord's noble and honorable, too. But watch your step around Gerran. He's a touchy sort of man, the Falcon, and he'll slap you daft if you cross him."

"The Falcon?" Neb said with his mouth full. "What—"

"Oh, everyone calls him that. He's got a falcon device stamped on his gear and suchlike."

"Is it his clan mark?"

"It's not, because he's not noble-born." Coryn frowned in thought. "I don't know why he carries it, and he probably shouldn't, 'cause he's a commoner."

The cook turned their way and shoved her sweaty dark hair back from her face with a crooked little finger. "The mark's just a fancy of Gerran's," she said. "After all, he was an orphan, and it's a comfort, like, to pretend he's got a family."

"Still," Coryn said, "it's giving himself airs."

"Oh, get along with you!" The cook rolled her eyes. "It comes to him natural, like. He was raised in the dun like Lord Mirryn's brother, wasn't he now?"

"Why?" Clae said with his mouth half full.

The cook glared, narrow-eyed.

"Say please," Neb muttered.

"Please, good dame," Clae said. "Why?"

"That's better." The cook smiled at him. "When Gerran was but a little lad, his father was killed in battle saving the tieryn's life, and the shock drove his poor mother mad. She drowned herself not long after. So our Cadryc took the lad and raised him with his own son, because he's as generous as a lord should be and as honorable, too."

"That's truly splendid of him," Neb said. "But I can see why Gerran's a bit touchy." He wiped his greasy mouth on his sleeve. "I'll do my best to stay out of his way."

"Now you've got dirt smeared in the grease." Coryn grinned at him. "We'd better get you that bath."

Rather than haul water inside to heat at the hearth, they filled one of the horse troughs and let it warm in the hot sun while Coryn pointed out the various buildings in the fort. Eventually Neb and Clae stripped off their clothes and climbed into the water. Neb knelt on the bottom and kept ducking his head under while he tried to comb the worst of the dirt and leaves out of his hair. They were still splashing around when Salamander came strolling out of the broch with clothing draped over his arm.

"Well, you look a fair sight more courtly," the gerthddyn said, grinning. "Lady Galla's servant lass has turned up these." He held up a pair of plain linen shirts, both worn but not too badly stained, and two pair of faded gray brigga. "She says you're to give her the old ones to boil for rags."

"My thanks," Neb said. "Our lady's being as generous as the noble-born should be, but truly, I'd rather go back to Trev Hael."

"Ah, but here is where your wyrd led you. Who can argue with their wyrd?"

"But—"

"Or truly, wyrd led you to me, and I led you here, but it's all the same thing." Salamander gave him a sunny smile. "Please, lad, stay here for a while, no more than a year and a day, say. And then if you want to move on, move on."

"Well and good, then. You saved our lives, and I'll always be grateful for that."

"No need for eternal gratitude. Just stay here for a little while. You'll know when it's time to leave."

"Will I?" Neb hesitated, wondering if his benefactor were a bit daft. "You know, I just thought of somewhat. The lady wants to see my writing, but I've got no ink and no pens either. I saw some geese over by the stables, but the quills will take a while to cure."

"So they will, but I've got some reed pens and a bit of ink cake, too."

"Splendid! You can write, too?"

"Oh, a bit, but don't tell anyone. I don't fancy having some lord demand I stay and serve him as a scribe. Me for the open road."

"I've been meaning to ask you a question, truly. Why have you come all the way to Arcodd? There's not a lot of folk out here, and most of them are too poor to pay you to tell them tales."

"Sharp lad, aren't you?" Salamander grinned at him. "Well, in truth, I'm looking for my brother, who seems to have got himself lost."

"Lost?"

"Just that. He was a silver dagger, you see."

"A what?" Clae broke in. "What's that?"

"A mercenary soldier of a sort," Salamander said. "They ride the countryside, looking for a lord who needs extra fighting men badly enough to pay them by the battle."

Clae wrinkled his nose in disgust, but Neb leaned forward and grabbed his arm before he could say something rude. "Your hair's still filthy," Neb snapped. "Wash it out." He turned to Salamander. "I'll pray your brother still rides on the earth and not in the Otherlands."

"My thanks, but I truly do believe he's still alive. I had a report of him, you see, that he'd been seen up this way."

Neb found himself wondering if Salamander were lying. The gerthddyn was studying the distant view with a little too much attention and a fixed smile. He refused to challenge the man who'd saved his life. Besides, having a silver dagger for a brother was such a shameful thing that he couldn't begrudge Salamander his embarrassment.

"I'll just be getting out," Neb said. "Come on, Clae. We'll have to help the stableman empty this trough. Horses can't drink dirty water."

Neb hoisted himself over the edge and dropped to the ground. He shook himself to get the worst of the water off, then, still damp, put on the clothes Salamander handed him. The baggy wool brigga fit well enough, but when he pulled the shirt over his head, it billowed around him. The long sleeves draped over his hands. He began rolling them up.

"We can find you a bit of rope or suchlike for a belt," Salamander said. "And, eventually, a better shirt."

Later that afternoon, with pen and ink in hand, Neb went into the great hall and found Lady Galla waiting, sitting alone at the table of honor. She'd gathered a heap of parchment scraps, splitting into translucent layers from hard use. A good many messages had been written upon them, then scraped off to allow for a new one.

"Will these do?" Galla was peering at them. "I looked all over, because I did remember that I had the accounts from our old demesne in a sack or suchlike, but I couldn't find it. These turned up lining a wooden chest."

"I'm sure they'll do, my lady." Neb searched through them and found at last a scrap with a reasonably smooth surface. "Now, what would you like me to write?"

"Oh, some simple thing. Our names, say."

Neb picked the script his father had always used for important documents, called Half-inch Royal because the scribes of the high king's court had invented it. Although she couldn't read in any true sense of the word, Galla did know her letters, and she could spell out her name and Tieryn Cadryc's when he wrote them.

"Quite lovely," she announced. "Very well, young Neb. As provision for you and your brother, you shall have a chamber of your own, meals in the great hall, and a set of new clothing each year. Will that be adequate?"

Neb had to steel himself to bargain with the noble-born, but he reminded himself that without tools, he couldn't practice his craft. "I'll need coin as well, for the preparing of the inks and suchlike. I could just mix up soot and oak gall, but an important lord like your husband should have better. A silver penny a year should be enough. I hope I can find proper ink cakes and a mixing stone out here."

"The coin we have, thanks to the high king's bounty." Galla thought for a moment. "Now, I think you might find what you need in Cengarn. His grace my husband has been talking about riding to the gwerbret there, and so if he does, you can go with him."

"Splendid, my lady, and my thanks. But then there's the matter of what I'm going to write upon. Fine parchments cost ever so much if you buy them, and I don't know how to make my own. Even if I did, could you spare the hides? You can only get two good sheets from a calfskin, and then scraps like these."

"Oh." Galla paused, chewing on her lower lip. "Well, I'd not thought of that, but if you can find parchment for sale, I'm sure we can squeeze out the coin to buy some, at least for legal judgments and the like."

"We can use wax-covered tablets for ordinary messages, if you have candle wax to spare. I can write with a stylus as well as a pen."

"Now that I can give you, and a good knife, too, for cutting your pens." Much relieved, Galla smiled at him. "I've got a very important letter to write, you see. My brother has a daughter by his first wife, who died years and years ago. So he remarried, and now he and his second wife have sons and daughters of their own. The wife—well. Let's just say that she's never cared for her stepdaughter. There's only so much coin at my brother's disposal, and she wants to spend it on her own lasses. The wife wants to, I mean, not little Branna. That's my brother's daughter, you see, Lady Branna, my niece. So I'm offering to take the lass in, and if we can't find her a husband, then she can live here as my servingwoman." Lady Galla paused for a small frown. "She's rather an odd lass, you see, so suitors might be a bit hard to find. But she does splendid needlework, so I'll be glad to have her. It's truly a marvel, the way she can take a bit of charcoal and sketch out patterns. You'd swear she was seeing them on the cloth and just following along the lines, they're so smooth and even. And—oh here, listen to me! A lad like you won't be caring about needlework. You run along now and make those tablets. I'll have Coryn bring you wax and knives and suchlike."

"Very well, my lady, and my thanks. I'll go hunt up some wood."

Neb took Clae with him when he went out to the ward, which, with the dun so newly built, lacked much of the clutter and confusion of most strongholds. Behind the main broch tower stood the round, thatched kitchen hut, the well, and some storage sheds. Across an open space stood the smithy, some pigsties and chicken coops, and beyond them the dung heap. A third of the high outer wall supported the stables, built right into the stones, with the ground level for horses and an upper barracks for the warband and the servants.

"Neb?" Clae said. "We've found a good place, haven't we?"

"We have." Neb looked at him and found him smiling. "I think we'll do well here."

"Good. I want to train for a rider."

"You what?"

"I want to learn swordcraft and join the tieryn's warband."

Neb stopped walking and put his hands on his hips. Clae looked up defiantly.

"Whatever for?" Neb said at last.

"Because."

"Because what?"

"You know." Clae shrugged and began scuffing at one of the cobbles with his bare toes. "Because they killed everyone."

"Ah. Because the raiders destroyed our village?"

Clae nodded, staring at the ground. *Ye gods!* Neb thought. *What would Mam say to this?*

"Well, I can understand that," Neb said. "I'll think about it."

"I'm going to do it."

"Listen, I'm the head of our clan now, and you won't do one wretched thing unless I say you may."

Clae's eyes filled with tears.

"Oh, ye gods!" Neb snapped. "Don't cry! Here, it's all up to the captain, anyway. The Falcon. What's-his-name."

"Gerran." Clae wiped his eyes on his sleeve. "He's too busy now. I'll ask him when they get back."

"Very well, but if he says you nay, there's naught I can do about it."

"I know. But he lost his mam and da, didn't he? I bet he'll understand."

"We'll see about that. Now help me find the woodpile and an ax."

They found the woodshed behind the cookhouse and an ax as well, hanging inside the door. Neb took the ax down and gave it an experimental swing. In one corner lay some pieces of rough-hewn planks, all of them too wide and most too thick, but Neb couldn't find a saw. He did find a short chunk of log, some ten inches in diameter, that had the beginnings of a split along the grain.

"Here!" A man's voice called out. "What do you think you're doing?"

Neb turned around and saw a skinny fellow, egg bald, hurrying toward them. Above his bushy gray beard his pale blue eyes were narrowed and grim.

"My apologies, sir," Neb said. "But I'm about Lady Galla's business."

"If she wanted a fire," the fellow said, "she could have sent a servant to ask me. My name is Horza, by the by, woodcutter to this dun."

"And a good morrow to you, sir. I'm Neb, and this is my brother, Clae. I'm the new scribe, and I need wood for tablets. Writing tablets, I mean. They need to be about so long and—"

"I know what writing tablets look like, my fine lad. Hand me my ax, and don't you go touching it again, hear me?"

"I do. My apologies."

Horza snorted and grabbed the ax from Neb's lax grasp. For a moment he looked over the wood stacked in the shed, then picked up a short, thin wedge of stout oak in one hand. He set the thin wedge against the crack in the log and began tapping it in with the blunt back of the ax head. His last tap split the dry pine lengthwise. He let one half fall, then flipped the ax over to the sharpened edge and went to work on the other half. A few cuts turned it into oblongs of the proper length and thickness.

"I'll make you two sets, lad." Horza picked up the remainder of the log. He treated it the same while Neb watched in honest awe at his skill.

"These'll have to be smoothed off and then scoured down with sand," Horza said. "That's your doing."

"It is, and a thousand thanks!" Neb took the panels with a little bow. "You're a grand man with an ax."

"Imph." Horza tipped his head to one side and looked the boys over. "Scribe, are you? What sort of name is Neb, anyway? Never heard it before."

"Well, it's short for somewhat. My father was a man of grand ideas. He named me Nerrobrantos, for some Dawntime hero or other. And my brother's name is truly Caliomagos."

"Or Neb and Clae, and the shorters are the betters, true enough. Now run along, lads. I've got work to do."

"My thanks. I'll take these back to the great hall and work on them there."

As soon as Horza was out of earshot, Clae turned to Neb. "He's got his gall talking about our names," he said. "What kind of a name is Horza, anyway?"

"A very old one," Neb said, smiling. "His ancestors must have been some of the Old Ones, the people who already lived here when our ancestors arrived."

"Well, it sounds like a lass's name."

"Their language must have been a fair bit different from ours, that's all."

"Oh." Clae considered this information for a moment, then shrugged. "Can I go play White Crow with the pages? Coryn asked me."

"By all means. I'll not need any help with this, anyway."

Neb took his tablets to a table by the servants' hearth, where a bucket of sand stood ready to smother any sparks that found their way onto the straw-covered floor. He fetched some water in a pottery stoup, helped himself to a handful of sand, grabbed some straw from the floor, and set to work. He sprinkled the sand on the wood, then wet down the straw and used it to scour the splinters away.

As he worked, he found himself wondering about this lass, Branna, whose life was going to be decided by the letter he would write on these tablets. Would anyone ask her opinion about being packed off to the rough border country? No doubt she'd have no more choice about it than he and Clae had had about Uncle Brwn's farm. He felt a sudden sympathy for her, this lass he didn't know, and found himself wondering if she were pretty.

That night Neb and Clae shared a comfortable bed in a wedge-shaped room high up in the broch tower. They also had a wobbly table and two stools, a carved wooden chest to store whatever possessions they might someday have, and a brass charcoal brazier for the winter to come. The curved arc of the stone outer wall sported a narrow window, covered by a wooden shutter. In Arcodd at that time, these furnishings all added up to a nicely appointed chamber, suitable for an honored servitor to the noble-born.

Although Clae fell asleep immediately, Neb lay awake for a little while and considered this sudden truth: he was indeed a tieryn's servitor now, the head of what was left of their family and a man who could provide for that family, as well. He only wished that Uncle Brwn's death hadn't been the price. *If they rescue Mauva,* he thought, *I'll see if I can get her a place in the kitchen. Brwn would like that, knowing I'd taken care of her.*

When he fell asleep, he dreamed of Lady Branna, or rather, of a beautiful lass that his dream labeled Lady Branna. He could see her clearly, it seemed, in the great hall of some rough, poor dun. She sat in a carved chair near a smoky hearth, her feet up on a little stool to keep them from the damp straw covering the floor. A little gray gnome crouched by her chair. In the dream some man he couldn't see announced, "the most beautiful lass in all Deverry." Neb moved closer, smiling at her. She looked up, saw him, and smiled in return.

"My prince, is it you?"

Her voice sounded so real that he woke, half sitting up in bed. In the darkness Clae muttered to himself and turned over, sighing. Neb lay down again, and this time when he slept, he dreamed of nothing at all.

Gerran woke well before dawn. Since he'd laid out his clothing the night before, he could dress by the faint starlight coming through the window. Even though he would have preferred sleeping out in the barracks with the other common-born riders, Tieryn Cadryc had insisted on giving him a chamber in the broch tower. Gerran was just buckling on his sword belt when he saw a crack of light beneath his door. Someone knocked.

"Gerro?" Mirryn said.

"I'm awake, truly." Gerran swung the door open. "I wondered if you'd be up and about."

Mirryn gave him a sour smile. He carried a pierced tin candle lantern inside, then put it down on top of the wooden chest that held the few things Gerran owned. Neither of them spoke until Gerran had shut the door again.

"I know it aches your heart," Gerran said. "But I can understand why your father's making you stay behind."

"Oh, so can I, but it doesn't lessen the ache any." Mirryn leaned against the curve of the wall. "The men are going to start thinking I'm a coward."

"Oh, here, of course they won't! They heard your father give the order."

Mirryn cocked his head and considered him for a moment. "It's an odd thing, the way you say that. *Your* father. He's yours, too, a foster father truly, but—"

"I'm not noble-born, and that makes all the difference in the world. It was an honorable fancy of the tieryn to treat me like one of his own when I was a lad, but I'm grown now."

"You're still my brother in my eyes."

"And you in mine." Gerran hesitated, then merely shrugged. "I'm grateful for that, but—"

"But in the eyes of everyone else," Mirryn said, "you're not?"

"Just that. Which is why your father will risk my life but not yours."

"I know that, and I suppose everyone else does, too, but ye gods, Gerro! What's going to happen when I inherit the rhan? If I've never ridden to war, who's going to honor me?"

"It's too cursed bad the gods saw fit to give you naught but sisters."

Mirryn laughed with a shake of his head. "I've never known anyone who could parry questions like you can." He glanced out of the window. "Sky's getting gray."

"I'd best get down to the stables. It's not truly my place, but if I'm given the chance, maybe I can have a few words with his grace."

"Talk some sense into him." Mirryn looked away with a sigh. "I might as well be another useless daughter if he's going to keep me shut up in the dun."

By the time that Gerran saddled his horse, twenty men from the warband had begun to assemble in a ward flaring with torchlight. Gerran rode through the mass of men and horses, sorted out the riding order, and decided which men would lead the packhorses with the supplies. Behind them would come oxcarts with full provisions, but the carts traveled so slowly that they would doubtless only catch up to the troop in time to provision their ride home. Gerran was just telling the head carter about the route ahead when he saw the gerthddyn, mounted up and walking his horse into line. Gerran assigned him a place at the end of the riding order, and Salamander took it cheerfully with a small bow from the saddle. Gerran jogged back up the line and fell in next to Cadryc.

"Your Grace?" Gerran said. "What's that magpie of a minstrel doing along?"

"Cursed if I know," Cadryc said. "He begged me to let him ride with us for vengeance. Must be a good heart in the lad, for all he dresses like a stinking Deverry courtier."

"Vengeance? For what?"

"Now, that's a good question." Cadryc paused, chewing on his mustaches. "He must have lost kin or suchlike to the raiders." He shrugged the problem away. "I don't see your foster brother anywhere. I thought he'd have the decency to come see us off at least."

"Well, your Grace," Gerran said, "suppose he'd been happy to stay behind? Wouldn't that have ached your heart?"

Cadryc turned in the saddle, stared at him for a moment, then laughed, a rueful sort of mutter under his breath. "Right you are, Gerro," the tieryn said. "Let's get up to the head of the line. Sun's rising."

Panting, swearing, the ten men left behind on fort guard hauled on the chains that opened the heavy gates. With one last heave and a curse, they swung them ajar, then dropped the chains and ran out of the way. Cadryc yelled out a command and waved his men forward at the trot.

The warband traveled south through the tieryn's rhan, that is, the vast tract of half-wild country under his jurisdiction, within which he could bestow parcels of land in return for fealty and taxes.

Near the dun, the freeholds of the local farmers stood pale green with wheat, but ahead lay the pine forests, covering the broken tablelands of Arcodd province and beyond. The plateau itself stretched for nearly two hundred miles. To the west, it sloped down into lands marked on no Deverry map. To the north it steadily rose until it became the foothills of the Roof of the World.

To the south, where the warband was heading, lay the rich farmland of the Melyn Valley, but once the men reached the edge of the forest cover, they turned west onto the dirt road that had so surprised Neb. Cadryc had levied a labor tax on his farmers to hack it out of the forest. No one had grumbled. They could see that its purpose was their safety.

A few hours before sunset, the warband rode up to an open meadow. Cadryc called a halt, then leaned over his saddle peak to stare at the trampled grass.

"Someone's been here recently," the tieryn said. "Ye gods! If the raiders have found this road—"

"Your Grace?" Salamander trotted his horse up to join them. "Allow me to put your mind at rest. I'm the culprit. It was on this very spot, it was, that Neb and Clae found me."

"Ah. Well, that's a relief!" Cadryc turned in the saddle. "Gerran, have the men make camp."

They'd just gotten settled when Lord Pedrys, one of Cadryc's vassals, rode in to join them. He brought ten men and supplies with him, and as usual, the young lord was game for any fight going. When Cadryc, Pedrys, and Gerran gathered around the tieryn's fire to discuss plans, Pedrys had an inappropriate grin on his blandly blond face.

"I wonder if we'll catch them?" Pedrys said. "If the bastards are this bold, we've got a chance."

"Just so," Cadryc said. "If nothing else, we can see if Lord Samyc's still alive. He's only got five riders in his warband, but I can't see him sitting snug in his dun while scum raid his lands."

"True spoken," Pedrys said. "Five riders! And you've got thirty all told, and me fifteen, and we can't even spare all of them for rides like this. How, by the black hairy arse of the Lord of Hell, does our gwerbret expect us to defend the valley?"

Cadryc shrugged and began chewing on the edge of his mustache. "We're going to have to ask him just that. We need help, and that's all there is to it."

"It's all well and good to say that, Your Grace, but what can he do without an army?"

"He's going to cursed well have to send messengers down to Dun Deverry and beg the high king for more men." Cadryc slammed one fist into the palm of his other hand. "I don't give a pig's fart if it aches his heart or not."

"I don't understand why it does." Pedrys sounded more than a little angry. "Ye gods, his own father was killed by Horsekin!"

"True spoken. But the gwerbrets of Cengarn used to rule Arcodd like kings, didn't they? Oh, they sent taxes to the high king's chamberlain, and they made a ritual visit to court once a year, but still—" Cadryc shrugged. "The king never cared what they did out here. Now—well, by the hells! Everything's changed."

Both Pedrys and Gerran nodded their agreement.

Some thirty years before, the high king had begun encouraging his subjects to settle the rich meadowlands of south-western Arcodd. Doing so meant creating many a new lordship and marking out many a new rhan. Technically, of course, all these new lords owed direct fealty to the gwerbrets of Cengarn, but it was the high king, not the gwerbret, who produced the coin and the men to turn these holdings into something more than lines on a map. Royal heralds had traveled throughout Deverry, offering freehold land to farmers and craftsmen if they would emigrate to Arcodd. A good many extra sons, who stood no chance of inheriting their father's land or guild shop, were glad to take up the challenge, and a good many extra daughters, whose dowries were doomed to be scant, were glad to marry them and emigrate as well.

Men who could ride in a warband were harder to come by, but the lords put together the biggest troops they could. Everyone remembered the Horsekin, who years before had ridden out of nowhere to besiege Cengarn itself. Yet at first, the settlement of the Melyn Valley proceeded so easily that it seemed the Horsekin had forgotten about Deverry. Farms spread out, villages grew among them. The virgin land produced splendid crops and the farmers, plenty of children. It seemed that the gods had particularly blessed the valley and its new inhabitants.

Then, some fifteen years before Neb and his brother came staggering out of the forest, the raiders struck at a village near Cengarn in the first of a series of raids. Each time they slaughtered the men, took the women and children as slaves, looted, and burned what they couldn't carry off. Finally the gwerbret in Cengarn and his loyal lords had caught them and crushed them. Gerran's father had come home from that battle wrapped in a blanket and slung over his saddle like a sack of grain. Gerran could remember rushing out into the ward and seeing two men lifting the corpse down. His mother's scream when she saw it still seemed to ring out, loud in his memory.

"What's wrong with you, Captain?" Pedrys said abruptly. "You look as grim as the Lord of Hell himself!"

"My apologies, my lord," Gerran said. "I was just thinking about the raiders."

"That's enough to make any man grim, truly," Cadryc said, then yawned. "We'd best get some sleep. I want to be up at dawn and riding as soon as we can."

"Very well, Your Grace." Gerran stood up. "I'll just take a last look around the camp."

Scattered across the meadow, most of the men were asleep in their blankets by dying campfires. The warm night was so achingly clear that the stars hung close like a ceiling of silver. Nearby, guarded by a pair of sentries, the horses stood head-down and drowsy in their hobbles. Gerran was starting out to have a word with the sentries when he saw someone coming toward him. He laid his hand on his sword hilt, but it was only the gerthddyn, his pale hair strikingly visible in the dark.

"Lovely night, isn't it?" Salamander said.

Although Gerran had been thinking just that, hearing this unmanly sentiment voiced annoyed him.

"Warm enough, I suppose," Gerran said. "Tell me somewhat. What made you ride with us?"

"I'm not truly sure," Salamander said.

"You told our lord that you wanted vengeance."

"Well, that's true enough. The Horsekin killed a good friend of mine some years ago. And I'm looking for my brother, of course. You may remember that when I last passed your way, I told you—"

"—about your brother the silver dagger. What is this? Do you think you're going to find him just wandering around the countryside?"

"Imph, well, you never quite know where he'll turn up."

Gerran waited, then realized that Salamander was going to tell him no more unless he pried.

"Well, now that you're here, you're riding under my orders," Gerran said instead. "I want you to stay well back out of the way if it comes to battle."

"Fair enough." Salamander bowed, took a few steps away, then suddenly stooped down and picked something up from the grass. "One of the lads is getting careless. I wonder whose bridle this belongs on?"

When he held up a brass buckle, Gerran could barely see it. Salamander pressed it into his hand, then walked on with a cheery good night. Gerran rubbed the buckle between his fingers as he watched him go. *So,* he told himself, *that's why he's so cursed odd! There's Westfolk blood in his veins.*

Around noon on the morrow, the combined warbands reached a stone marker beside the road. The tieryn called a halt to rest the horses and let the men eat a scant meal from their saddlebags. Although the cairn, a mere heap of gray stones, carried no inscriptions, those who had been let in on its secret knew that a shallow canyon nearby led straight south. The road itself ended at the marker, because extending it south would have given their enemies an easy path to the tieryn's lands.

At the head of the canyon, a small waterfall trickled down over ragged shelves of dark rock, fringed at the edges with long streamers of ferns. The men dismounted and led their horses down a narrow path to the reasonably flat floor of the canyon, where a faint trail led along the edge of a stream through pine forest. After a mile or so of this difficult traveling, the canyon walls grew lower and began to splay out. The trail widened just enough to allow the men to mount up and ride single file. They could see bright sunlight and open space ahead through the trees where the trail widened once again. Gerran yelled at his men to fall into their regular riding order, two abreast and ready for trouble, as he remarked to Lord Pedrys.

"Do you think the Horsekin would lay an ambuscade?" Pedrys said.

"I don't know, my lord, but I wouldn't put it past them."

In dappled sunlight the men rode through the last of the pines. No one spoke; everyone kept one hand on his sword hilt and the reins of his horse in the other. Cut stumps appeared among the grasses and weeds of second growth. One last bend in the trail brought them to the long broad valley, green with ripening wheat and meadowland. A couple of miles off to the west the Melyn ran, a thin sparkling line at their distance. Gerran could just make out a patch of black beside it—Neb's farm, he assumed.

"I don't see any Horsekin," Cadryc remarked. "Don't see much of anything but grass."

"True spoken, Your Grace," Gerran said. "Most likely the bastards are long gone."

"We've got to get more fighting men down here. All there is to it!"

"Or else stop these cursed raids once and for all, Your Grace," Gerran said. "If the king would lend us an army—"

"That's in the laps of the gods," Cadryc said. "We'll worry about the grand schemes later. We've got a hard job to do right now."

With a wave of his arm the tieryn led them forward. They rode on down to the smoking tangle of wood and ashes that had once been Brwn's farm. The fire had leaped to the apple tree outside the earthen wall and left it as black and gaunt as a dead sentry, but the damp grass still grew green beyond. Nearby lay the corpse of a tall, burly man, his head torn half off his shoulders. In the hot sun he lay swollen and stinking. Birds and foxes had eaten a good bit of him. Salamander rode up to join Gerran and the noble-born.

"Neb's uncle," Salamander said. "What's left fits the description anyway."

"Let's get him buried," Cadryc said. "There's naught else to do for him."

"We might as well wait and dig one long ditch," Pedrys said. "I'll wager there's more dead men ahead of us."

Unfortunately, Pedrys had spoken the truth. When they rode up to the ruins of the village, they found the first corpses about three hundred yards from the bridge. Four men lay in a straggling line, cut down as they tried to flee. Another twelve lay in the village square, either rotting and spongy or half-burned. The latter had most likely been killed in their houses, then caught under burning beams and walls.

"But who pulled them free?" Pedrys said. "What is this? Did the raiders want to count their kills?"

"Most likely they just wanted to make sure they'd slaughtered the lot," Gerran said.

"If so, they did a bad job of it," Salamander said. "Neb told me how many men and lads were in the village, you see. The women and children are long gone by now, of course, prize booty, all of them. So there should be twenty dead, not counting Neb's uncle."

"Then that leaves four men missing," Pedrys said. "Maybe they got away in time."

But three of the men turned up lying dead, clustered together by the village well where, apparently, they'd tried to make a stand. One corpse still clutched a hay rake.

"Why didn't the raiders put these men with the others?" Salamander said. "I wonder if someone interrupted them?" He looked up as if he were studying the sky.

"I doubt me if the gods came down to help," Gerran said. "Come along. There's one villager still missing."

Although the men searched the village thoroughly, they never found that last corpse. By the time they'd finished, the younger men in the warband had turned white-faced and shaky; a few had rushed off to vomit. It was the pity of it more than the stench and rot that troubled Gerran: peaceful farmers, slaughtered like their own hogs as they tried to defend themselves and their women with sticks and axes against swords and spears.

Yet even though they'd lost the fight in the end, the farmers had gained one small victory. Pinned under a half-burned roof beam lay the charred corpse of a Horsekin warrior. Gerran found him as he searched the ruins of the village smithy. At his shout Daumyr strode over with Warryc trotting after. The three of them fell silent, staring at the corpse.

Like most of his kind, he was well over six feet tall, broad in the shoulders, long in the arms. What was left of his skin was milk white, but heavily decorated with blue-and-black tattoos. Some designs portrayed animals; others seemed to be letters of some sort. He sported a huge mane of dark hair, braided into many strands, tied off with amulets and studded with charms, but the magicks had failed to protect him. Daumyr picked up a nearby plank and used it as a lever to turn him over. He'd been killed by the thrust of three sharp prongs—a pitchfork, Gerran assumed—into the middle of his back.

"Haul him out," Gerran said. "We'll leave him for the ravens."

"Good idea!" Daumyr tossed the plank back down. "May he freeze to the marrow in the deepest hell."

Warryc stooped, brushed away cinders with one hand, grabbed something from the rubble, then stood back up, clutching his prize. "This must have fallen off the bastard's jerkin." Warryc opened his hand to show a golden arrow, about four inches long and backed with a heavy pin. "I've seen somewhat like it before, somewhere."

"A clan marker?" Gerran said. "Maybe a troop badge?"

Warryc shook his head and studied the arrow; his narrow dark eyes narrowed further, nearly to slits. "Somewhat to do with their religion," he said at last. "The cursed Horsekin, I mean."

"Well, hand it over," Gerran said. "The tieryn might know."

Gerran set the warband to digging a long mass grave outside the earthwork, then rejoined the tieryn, who was standing by the line of corpses and talking with Salamander. Gerran was honestly surprised to see the gerthddyn so calm in the midst of so much death. His opinion of Salamander rose.

"We never found that last man," Cadryc said. "Well, we'll be riding downriver to Lord Samyc's dun. If he's hiding somewhere, perhaps he'll hear or see us and come running."

"We can hope, your Grace," Salamander said. "I'm more afraid of what else might appear along the way."

"Naught good or so I'd wager." Gerran fished the gold arrow out of his pocket and held it out. "One of the men found this. He was thinking it had somewhat to do with the Horsekin's wretched gods."

Cadryc held out empty hands to show his ignorance, but the gerthddyn took the arrow and weighed it in his palm.

"It most assuredly does," Salamander said. "It's the token of a goddess, actually, Alshandra, Huntress of Souls, the archer who dwells beyond the stars, the hidden one."

"I've heard of her before," Cadryc said. "It's a pity she's not a fair bit more hidden than she is."

"Oh, absolutely. Her worshipers, alas, are both conspicuous and near to hand." Salamander glanced at Gerran. "Does the fellow who found this want it?"

"Probably. For the gold, most likely."

"I think I'll ask him to sell it to me. Somewhat tells me that I should keep it. Might be useful, like."

"Useful for what?" Cadryc snorted.

"I know not, but I have a feeling, a deep hunch, hint, or portent that I should own this little bauble. Which man was it, Captain, if you don't mind me asking?"

"Not at all." Gerran pointed to the men digging the trench. "It's Warryc, the skinny short fellow with the brown hair down at the very end. Next to the tall blond fellow, Daumyr his name is."

Salamander trotted off, and Gerran and the tieryn followed more slowly. The warband swung the remains of the villagers into the trench, then covered it over with earth, a brown scar in the green meadow. They finished just at sunset, and off to the cloudy west the light blazed red like a funeral fire. For lack of a priest, the tieryn tried to say a few reverent words. For a long moment he stood at the head of the trench and struggled with this unfamiliar activity while the men watched in silence.

"Ah, horseshit," Cadryc said at last. "There's only one thing to say: vengeance!"

The warband shouted back the word. "Vengeance!" rolled across the farmlands to echo back from the distant cliffs.

As they walked back to their horses, they passed the corpse of the Horsekin warrior, left sprawled in the open air for the ravens as a final insult. Salamander paused for a moment to contemplate him, and Gerran stopped to see what the gerthddyn was up to.

"Doesn't this strike you as odd, Captain?" Salamander said. "The Horsekin never leave their dead behind."

"So I've heard, truly," Gerran said. "He was killed by a farmer, though. Maybe they see that as a dishonor."

"Maybe, but I have my doubts. And then they didn't finish searching the village. I wonder, I truly do."

"Searching?"

"Why else line up the dead? Were they trying to make sure they'd killed everyone or was it mayhap a certain person they wanted dead? I don't know, mind. I'm merely considering possibilities."

The warband camped that evening a spare mile downriver from the ruins, just far enough to leave the smell of the dead village behind. The missing villager never appeared, even though they built campfires in the hopes of drawing his attention should he be hiding nearby. On the chance that the raiders were lingering out to the west, Gerran doubled the usual number of sentries. He also had his men hobble their horses as well as tethering them, a precaution that proved wise on the morrow.

Toward dawn Gerran woke abruptly. He could have sworn that he'd heard someone calling his name. He sat up in his blankets and looked around, but in the cold gray light of first dawn he saw nothing but the sleeping camp. He pulled on his boots and got up, buckling on his sword belt. He was planning on relieving the sentries out by the tethered horses, but when he glanced at the river, he saw Salamander standing on the bank. He picked his way through the sleeping men and walked down to join the gerthddyn.

"You're up early," Gerran said.

"I am, and so are you." Salamander glanced at him and smiled, then returned to staring out across the river.

"Someone out there?"

"Not a Horsekin in sight, but look, there's some odd thing in the sky. A flock of ravens perhaps, most deeply grieved with us for burying their gruesome feast."

Gerran looked up to see, far off to the west, a flock of birds flying toward them in the brightening dawn. Or was it a flock? He heard a distant sound, a thwack and slap like a hand hitting a slack leather drum. The supposed flock looked remarkably like one bird, one enormous bird, flying steadily on huge silver wings. The sound swelled into a boom as the enormous wings carried the creature straight for them. He could see its long neck, its massive head with flaring nostrils and deep-set eyes, the silver scales touched about the head and spiked tail with iridescent blue, glimmering in the rising sun.

"It can't be," Gerran muttered. "Ye gods, it is! It's a dragon!"

Behind him the camp exploded with noise—men yelling and cursing, horses whinnying in terror. Gerran knew he should turn and rush back, should impose some kind of order or at the least guard the horses, but he stayed, staring at the huge silver wyrm. It was so strong, so powerful, and beautiful, as well, in his warrior's eyes, with the sun glistening on its smooth skin, stretched and supple over immense muscles. It reached the river, dipped one wing, then sheared off, heading north. On its side, just below the wing's set, Gerran saw a smear of reddish black—old blood from a wound.

"Rhodry!" Salamander started yelling at the top of his lungs. "I mean, blast it, Rori! It's me, Ebañy! Rori, come back! Rhod—I mean Rori! Wait!"

Screaming like a madman, waving his arms, Salamander raced down the riverbank, but the dragon flapped his wings in a deafening drumbeat and rose high, banking again to head back west. Gerran set his hands on his hips and glared as the gerthddyn came jogging back to him.

"And just how did you know its name?" Gerran said.

Salamander winced, tried to smile, and looked away. "Actually, you see, well, um, er—that's my brother. He was a silver dagger named Rhodry, but now that he's a dragon, he's known as Rori. I keep forgetting to use the right name."

Gerran started to speak, but his words twisted themselves into a sound more like a growl.

"I'm not a dragon," Salamander said hastily. "Neither was he originally."

"What? Of all the daft things I've ever heard—"

"Scoff all you want. He was turned into a dragon by dweomer."

"Dafter and dafter! What are you, a drooling idiot? There's no such thing as dweomer, and a witch could never have done aught as that."

"I should have known you'd take it this way." Salamander looked briefly mournful. "I'm telling you the exact truth, whether you believe it or no. So I thought I'd best find him and see how he was faring and all that. It seemed the brotherly thing to do."

"Daft." Gerran was finding it difficult to come up with any other word. With a last angry shrug he turned on his heel and ran back to camp.

It took till noon for Gerran and the two lords to transform the warbands from a frightened mob of men and horses into an orderly procession. Even then, as they rode south along the riverbank, the men kept looking up at the sky, and the horses would suddenly, for no visible reason, snort, toss their heads, and threaten to rear or buck until their riders calmed them. To set a good example, Gerran kept himself from studying the sky, but he did listen, waiting for the sound of wings beating the air like a drum.

In midafternoon they stopped to water their horses at the river. As soon as his horse had finished drinking, Salamander handed its reins to one of the men and went jogging eastward into the meadowlands.

"What in all the hells does he think he's doing?" Gerran said. He tossed his reins to Warryc and ran after the gerthddyn.

Not far off a small flock of ravens suddenly sprang into the air, squawking indignantly. With his Westfolk eyes, Salamander must have seen them from the riverbank, Gerran realized, and sure enough, he found the gerthddyn standing by the scattered remains of the ravens' dinner, a dead horse, or to be precise, the mangled bones, tail, and a few scraps of meat of what had once been a dead horse. Lying around it in the tall grass were torn and broken pieces of horse gear. Salamander nudged a heavily painted leather strap, once part of a martingale, perhaps, with his toe.

"Horsekin work," Salamander said. "They decorate all their horse gear. I think we now know what disturbed the raiders at their foul, loathsome, and heinous work."

"The dragon?" Gerran said.

"Exactly. Their horses doubtless panicked as ours did at the thought of ending up in a great wyrm's stomach. I wonder if dragons follow the Horsekin around? Where else are you going to find heavy horses like theirs?"

"The best meal going, eh? It could well be, but come along, we've got to keep moving today."

When the sun was getting low, the warband came to another burned village, a tangled heap of ruins spread out over a charred meadow. Once again the horses began snorting and trembling. Swearing under their breaths, Cadryc, Pedrys, and Gerran dismounted some distance away and walked over to the ruin, expecting the worst, but they found no corpses, not even a dead dog, among the drifting pale ash.

"Well and good," Cadryc said. "I'll wager they got to Lord Samyc's dun in time."

"And I'll wager they're still there, Your Grace," Gerran said. "One way or another."

"Just so. Let's get on the road."

Lord Samyc's dun stood on a low artificial hill, guarded by a maze of earthworks on the flat and a stone wall at the top. Not far away lay a patch of woodland. As the warbands rode up to the earthworks, Gerran saw a straggle of farmers leaving the trees with a cart full of firewood and an escort of two mounted men. When Tieryn Cadryc rose in his stirrups to hail them, the riders whooped with joy and galloped straight for the warbands waiting on the flat. One man dismounted and ran to grab Cadryc's stirrup as a sign of fealty. A dark-haired young lad, he grinned from ear to ear.

"Ah thank every god, Your Grace," the rider said. "How did you get the news?"

"Someone from the farther village escaped," Cadryc said. "How fares your lord?"

"That's a tale and a half, my lord. Here, the farmers from our village got to the dun in time. One of the lads was out looking for a lost cow, so he saw the Horsekin coming and raised the alarm."

"That's good to hear."

"Truly, Your Grace. So, the first thing we knew about it was when the whole cursed village comes charging up to the gates and yelling about raiders. So we let them in, and Lord Samyc wanted to ride out, but his lady begged him not to. There's a woman for you, but anyway, cursed if the whole stinking village didn't take her side." The lad looked retrospectively furious. "They stood in front of the gates, and our lord was yelling and swearing, but they wouldn't move, and all for her ladyship's sake. So in the end Lord Samyc gave in."

"It gladdens my heart to hear that," Cadryc said. "This raiding party must have been a large one."

"It was, Your Grace. Cursed if thirty Horsekin didn't ride up to the maze here." The lad gestured at the earthworks. "We could see them from the top of the wall, and they were yelling back and forth in that cursed ugly language of theirs, as bold as brass they were."

Cadryc glanced Gerran's way with troubled eyes.

"We've not seen that many in a long time, Your Grace," Gerran said.

"Indeed." Cadryc raised one hand to get everyone's attention. "All right, men, let's get this wood up to the dun."

The villagers had turned Lord Samyc's small ward into a camp, crammed with their cows, children, poultry, dogs, and heaps of household goods. When the warbands rode in, the men and horses filled the last available space. As he dismounted, Gerran saw a pair of hysterical servants rushing around and yelling back and forth about trying to feed so many guests. Red-haired, freckled, and a fair bit younger than Gerran, Lord Samyc ran out of the broch and knelt before the tieryn.

"It gladdens my heart to see your grace," Samyc said. "Even though you have every right to despise me for my dishonor."

"Suicide brings little honor, my lord," Cadryc said. "Now get up and stop brooding about it."

Startled, Samyc scrambled to his feet and glanced over his shoulder. In the doorway of the broch, a young woman, so great with child that she'd slung her kirtle over one shoulder rather than wrapping it round her middle, stood watching the confusion in the ward. Gerran was surprised that Lord Samyc's lady hadn't delivered under the stress of the raid. She needed the help of a servant girl to curtsy to the tieryn.

"Have I done a wrong thing, Your Grace?" she said. "Have I truly ruined my husband's whole life by refusing to let him die?"

"Oh, horse—oh, nonsense," Cadryc said. "He'll get over his sulk in time."

Since Lord Samyc had no room to shelter everyone, Lord Pedrys and Tieryn Cadryc stayed in the broch while Gerran led the warbands down to the riverbank to camp. On the off chance that the raiders would try a night strike, Gerran posted guards. When the gerthddyn offered to stand a watch, Gerran's first impulse was to turn him down, but then he remembered Salamander's formidable eyesight. Gerran gave him the last watch and decided to stand it with him.

Some while before dawn, they walked down to the river together. Flecked with starlight, the water flowed broad and silent. Off to the west the rolling meadowlands lay dark. Somewhere out there the Horsekin were camping with their miserable booty.

"On the morrow, Captain," Salamander said, "do we ride after the raiders?"

"I hope so," Gerran said. "We doubtless don't have a candle's chance of warming hell, but it would gladden my heart to get those women and children back. Better a free widow than an enslaved one."

"True spoken. You know, there's somewhat odd about this raid, isn't there? At least thirty fighting men and their heavy horses— that's not an easy lot to feed on a long journey. And they've traveled all this way to glean a handful of slaves from a couple of poor villages?"

"Huh. I'd not thought of it that way before. I suppose they brought a good number of men because they knew we'd stop them if we could."

"Mayhap. But why run the risk at all? Now, far to the south, down on the seacoast, there are unscrupulous merchants who'll buy slaves at a good price, transport them in secret, and sell them in Bardek. But that's a wretchedly long way away, and how could the Horsekin move a small herd of slaves unnoticed? They'd have to ride through Pyrdon and Eldidd, where every lord would turn out to stop them, or else travel through the Westfolk lands. The Westfolk archers would kill the lot of them on sight. They hate slavery almost as much as they hate the Horsekin."

"So they would. I've got a lot of respect for their bowmen. Your father's folk, are they? Or your mother's?"

Salamander tipped his head back and laughed. "My father's," he said at last. "You've got good eyes, Captain."

"So do you, and that's what gave you away. But here—" Gerran thought for a moment. "The Horsekin have plenty of human slaves already, from what I've heard, and they let them breed, to keep the supply fresh, like. They don't need to raid. You're right. Why are they risking so much for so little?"

"It's a question that strikes me as most recondite, but at the same time pivotal, portentous, momentous, and just plain important. Tell me somewhat. These raids, they started when farmers began to settle the Melyn river valley, right?"

"A bit later than that. When the farms reached the river."

"Oho! I'm beginning to get an idea, Captain, but let me brood on it awhile more, because I might be wrong."

At dawn, Gerran joined the noble-born for a council of war over breakfast in Samyc's great hall. The three lords wanted to track the raiders down, but they ran up against a hard reality: they lacked provisions for men and horses alike. The crop of winter wheat was still two weeks from harvest. After a bit of impatient squabbling, someone at last remembered that the farther village's crops would be milk-ripe and of no use to the poor souls who'd planted them.

"Here, what about this?" Lord Samyc said. "I'll give you what supplies I've got left from the winter. Then my farm folk can go harvest the milk-ripe crops to feed my dun when I get back to it."

Cadryc glanced at Gerran. Over the years, whether as father and stepson or tieryn and captain, they'd come to know each other so well that they could exchange messages with a look and a gesture. Gerran, being common-born, had no honor to lose by suggesting caution, and since he was the best swordsman in the province, no one would have dared call him a coward. The other two lords were also waiting for him to speak, he realized, though no doubt they would have denied it had anyone pointed it out.

"Well, my lord," Gerran said, "Didn't Lord Samyc's man tell us that thirty Horsekin rode to the dun?"

"He did," Cadryc said.

"So I'll wager their warband numbers more than that. Someone must have been guarding the prisoners from the first village while the raiders rode to the second one. We've got thirty men ourselves, and Lord Samyc can give us only a few more."

"Ah!" Samyc held up one hand to interrupt. "But some of my villagers have been training with the longbow."

"Splendid, my lord!" Gerran said. "How many?"

"Well, um, two."

"Oh."

"We're badly outnumbered." Pedrys leaned forward. "Is that it, Captain?"

"It is, my lord, though it gripes my soul to admit it. We've all faced the Horsekin before. They know how to swing a sword when they need to. If we had more than two archers to call upon, the situation would be different."

The three lords nodded agreement.

"So, I don't think it would be wise to follow them, your grace," Gerran said. "What if they have reinforcements waiting farther west?"

Cadryc stabbed a chunk of bread with his table dagger and leaned back in his chair to eat it.

"It gripes my soul," Pedrys snarled, "to let them just ride away with our people."

"It gripes mine, too," Cadryc said, swallowing. "But what good will it do them if we ride into a trap? We've got to think of the rest of the rhan, lads. If we're wiped out, who will stand between it and the Horsekin?"

"That's true," Samyc said. "Alas."

Cadryc pointed the chunk of bread at the two lords in turn. "We need more men, that's the hard truth of it. I know I've said it before, but it's the blasted truth."

"Just so, Your Grace," Gerran said. "It's too bad we don't have wings like that dragon."

"Indeed." Cadryc glanced at Samyc. "Do you know you've got a dragon in your demesne?"

"It's not mine, exactly," Samyc said with a twisted grin. "It comes and goes as it pleases."

"When did you first see it, my lord?" Gerran said. "If I may ask."

"Well, it was a bit over a year ago, just when the snow was starting to melt. It came flying over the dun here, bold as brass. I'd heard of dragons before, of course, but seeing a real one—ye gods!"

"Truly," Cadryc said. "I don't mind admitting that the sight was a bit much excitement at the start of a day."

"Let's hope it likes the taste of Horsekin," Gerran said.

Cadryc laughed with a toss of his head. "I've got a scribe now," he said with a nod at the two lords. "So I'll send a letter to the gwerbret and see what kind of answer he has for us. Get the warbands ready to ride, Gerro, will you? We're going home."

"I will, Your Grace," Gerran said. "One thing, though, that last man from Neb's old village." He looked Samyc's way. "Did he take shelter with you, my lord?"

"Not that I know of. Did someone escape, you mean?"

"Just that. I'd like to hear what he has to say. Any information we can get about the raid is all to the good." Gerran stood up. "I'll ask around out in the ward."

Unfortunately, no one, not farmer nor member of the warband, had seen any escapee arrive at the dun, nor had the woodcutting expedition turned him up that morning in the coppice. It was possible, one farmer pointed out, that the man or lad was hiding in the wild woods across the river to the west.

"They're not far, about three miles," Gerran told Cadryc. "Do you think it's worth a look?"

"I do," Cadryc said. "I want to hear what he can tell us."

When they rode out, the warbands clattered across Lord Samyc's bridge, then headed out into the meadowland on the western side of the river. They found the last man from the village long before they reached the wild wood, along with the site of what must have been one of the raiders' camps, judging from the trampled grass, fire pits, scattered garbage, and the like.

The villager, however, could tell them nothing. About a hundred yards west of the camp, they found a lumpish low mound covered with blankets that had been pinned down at each corner with a wooden stake. They all assumed that it was a dead Horsekin, covered to protect him from scavengers. With a dragon hunting their mounts, the Horsekin would have had no time for a proper burial.

"Let's take those blankets off," Cadryc said. "Let the ravens pull him to pieces."

Gerran dismounted, and Salamander joined him. Together they pulled up the wood stakes and threw back the blankets. Flies rose in a black cloud of outraged buzzing. For a moment Gerran almost vomited, and Salamander took a few quick steps back.

The corpse was human, naked, lying on his back, and he'd been staked out with thick iron nails hammered through the palm of each hand and the arch of each foot. Judging from the amount of dried blood around each stake, he'd been alive for the process and perhaps for a little while after. He was bearded in blood, too, because he'd gnawed his own lips half away in his agony. Where his eyes had been black ants swarmed. At some point in this ghastly process the Horsekin had slit him from breech to breastbone and pulled out his internal organs. In a pulsing mass of ants they lay in tidy lines to either side of him, bladder, guts, kidneys, liver, and lungs, but the heart was missing.

"What—who in the name of the Lord of Hell would do such a thing?" Gerran could only whisper. "Ye gods, savages! That's all they are!"

"In the name of Alshandra, more likely." Salamander sounded half-sick. "I've heard about this, but I've never seen it before, and I thank all the true gods for that, too."

"What have you heard?"

"That they do this to selected prisoners, always men, and usually someone who's been stupid enough to surrender. They send them with messages to Alshandra's country. That's somewhere in the Otherlands, I suppose." Salamander paused to wipe his mouth on the sleeve of his shirt. He swallowed heavily, then turned away from the sight. "As the prisoner's dying, they tell him he's lucky, because their goddess will give him a favored place in her land of the dead."

"I hope to every god that he lied when he got there."

"That's why they keep the heart. If he lies, they say, they'll torture it, and he'll feel the pains in the Otherlands."

Gerran tried to curse, but he could think of nothing foul enough. He turned away and saw that even Cadryc had gone white about the mouth.

"Let's bury him," the tieryn said. "And then we're heading home. There's naught else we can do for him or any of the other poor souls they took."

"Good idea, your grace." Gerran pointed to a pair of riders. "You—take the latrine shovels and dig him a proper grave."

As they dismounted, Gerran heard a raven calling out from overhead. He glanced up and saw a single large bird circling—abnormally large, as he thought about it. With a flap of its wings it flew away fast, heading east. Gerran turned to mention it to Salamander, but the gerthddyn had walked some yards away and fallen to his knees. He appeared to be ridding himself of his breakfast in a noisy though understandable fashion. *And after all,* Gerran told himself, *there's naught strange about a corpse-bird come to carrion.* He put the matter out of his mind.

Everyone was very kind. Perhaps that was the most painful thing of all, this unspoken kindness, or so Neb thought. None of the other servants resented his sudden arrival into a position of importance. They gave him things to put in his chamber—a pottery vase from the chamberlain, a wood bench from the cook, a wicker charcoal-basket from the head groom's wife. One of the grooms gave Neb a nearly-new shirt embroidered with the tieryn's blazon of a wolf rampant; his wife gave Clae a leather ball that had been her son's before he went off to his prenticeship. Neb saw every gift as an aching reminder that he'd been stripped of kin the way he stripped a quill of feathers when he made a pen.

But it's better than starving, Neb would forcibly remind himself. It was also better than being enslaved by Horsekin, but Neb did his best to keep from thinking about that. In the farming village he'd had two friends, boys his own age who were most likely dead now, and their mothers and sisters enslaved. At times, memories crept into his mind like weevils into grain, but he picked them out again. Now and then he indulged himself with the hope that at least one friend had managed to escape, but he never allowed the hope to blossom into a full-fledged wish.

To distract him, he also had work to do. With the winter wheat almost ripe for harvest, the tieryn's farmer vassals would soon owe him taxes in kind—foodstuffs, mostly, but also some oddments such as rendered tallow for candles and soap. The elderly chamberlain, Lord Veddyn, took Neb out to the storehouses, built of stone right into the dun's walls.

"I must admit that it gladdens my heart you're here," Veddyn said. "I used to be able to remember all the dues and taxes, store them up in my mind, like, but it gets harder and harder every year. I've been wishing I knew a bit of writing myself, these past few months."

"I see," Neb said. "Well, we can set up a tally system easily enough, if you've got somewhat for me to write upon. Wax on wood won't do."

"I've got a bit of parchment laid by. It's not the best in the kingdom, though."

In a cool stone room that smelled of onions, Veddyn showed him a wooden chest. Neb kicked it a couple of times to scare any mice or spiders away, then opened it to find a long roll of old vellum, once of a good quality, now a much-scraped palimpsest.

"It's cracking a bit, isn't it?" Veddyn said. "My apologies. I thought it would store better than this."

"We can split it into sheets along the cracks. It'll do."

Out in the sun Neb unrolled about a foot of the scroll and released a cloud of dust and ancient mold. He sneezed and wiped his nose on his sleeve, then held the roll up to the light.

"This must have been a set of tax tallies," Neb said. "I can just make out a few words. Fine linen cloth, six ells. Someone someone ninety-five bushels of somesort barley."

"It's from our old demesne—what's that noise?"

Neb cocked his head to listen. "Riders coming in the gates," he said. "I wonder if his grace has ridden home."

"Not already, surely!"

They hurried around the broch to find a small procession entering the ward. Four armed men with oak leaf blazons on their shirts escorted a heavily laden horse cart, driven by a stout middle-aged woman, while behind them came a person riding a gray palfrey. *Taxes*, Neb thought at first, *here early*.

As the pages and a groom ran out to take the horses, the rider dismounted with a toss of her long blonde hair, caught back in a silver clasp. A pretty lass, though not the great beauty he'd seen in his earlier dream, she was wearing a faded blue dress, caught up at her kirtled waist, over a pair of old torn brigga. The Wildfolk of Air, sylphs and sprites both, flocked around her, and perched behind her saddle was a little gray gnome, who looked straight at Neb, grinned, and waved a skinny clawed paw. The gnome looked exactly like the little creature in Neb's dream.

"It's Lady Branna!" Veddyn said. "Here, greet her and her escort, will you? Where's Lord Mirryn, I wonder? He's always off somewhere when you need him! And the pages have their hands full. I'd better go tell Lady Galla her niece has arrived."

When Neb walked up, the lady turned around and smiled at him, a distant but friendly sort of smile such as she doubtless would give to any stranger, but Neb felt his heart start pounding. Instantly he knew two things so crucial that he felt as if he had waited his entire life for this lass to appear. One, he loved her, and two, she shared all his secrets, perhaps even secrets he hadn't realized he was keeping. He tried to speak but felt that he was gasping like a caught fish on a riverbank.

Fortunately, Branna appeared just as startled. Her smile vanished, her eyes grew wide, and she stared at him unspeaking. He studied her face with a feeling much like hunger: narrow mouth, snub nose, a dusting of freckles over her high cheekbones, dark blue eyes. He had never wanted anything more than to reach out and take her hand, but someone behind them called her name and sharply. Branna flinched and looked away.

"Here, who are you?" The stout woman who'd been driving the cart came striding over. A widow's black scarf half-covered her gray hair, and she wore gray dresses, much stained. She pointed a callused finger at Neb.

"My name is Nerrobrantos, scribe to Tieryn Cadryc," Neb said. "And you are?"

"Her ladyship's servant."

"More like my guardian dragon," Branna said, then laughed. Her voice was pleasantly soft. "Don't be so fierce, Midda. A scribe may speak to a poverty-stricken lady like me." She turned back to Neb. "Do people really call you Nerrobrantos all the time?"

"They don't." Neb at last remembered how to smile. "Do call me Neb, my lady."

"Gladly, Goodman Neb. Here comes Aunt Galla, but maybe we'll meet again?"

"I don't see how we can avoid meeting in a dun this size."

She laughed, and he'd never heard a laugh as beautiful as hers, far more beautiful than golden bells or a bard's harp. For a long time after Lady Galla had led her inside, Neb stood in the ward and stared out at nothing. He was trying to understand just what had convinced him that his entire view of the world was about to change.

Mirryn brought him out of this strange reverie when the lord hurried over to the men of the lady's escort, who were waiting patiently beside their horses.

"What's this?" Mirryn said. "I see our scribe's just left you all standing here."

"My apologies, my lord," Neb said. "I don't have the slightest idea of where to take them. I've never lived in a dun before."

Mirryn's jaw dropped. Neb had never seen anyone look quite so innocently surprised. The lord covered it over with a quick laugh.

"Of course not," Mirryn said. "You're a townsman, after all, or you were."

Neb smiled, bowed, and made his escape. He carried the roll of parchment up to his chamber, where he could cut it into sheets with his new penknife, but even as he worked, he was thinking about Lady Branna.

"Now, here, my ladyship," Midda said. "I'm sure we can make you a better match than a scribe, and besides, you just met the lad."

"What makes you think I want to marry him?" Branna said.

"The way the pair of you were looking at each other. All cow-eyed, like."

Branna shrugged and went to perch on the wide windowsill of her new chamber. Lady Galla had given her a decent situation, especially for a destitute extra daughter, unwelcome in her own father's dun. The sunny chamber had its own hearth, a comfortable-looking bed, and a window that sported proper wooden shutters against possible rain. Branna had brought along her dower chest, made of plain wood and chipped around the lid— the best that her stepmother would part with. Midda was at the moment inspecting its contents to make sure they'd not suffered any damage during the journey. Branna had spent hundreds of hours working on them: two woad-blue blankets in an overshot weave and an embroidered coverlet for the marriage bed, the unassembled pieces of a heavily embroidered wedding shirt for her eventual husband, and various dresses and underclothes for herself. The little gray gnome sat on the bed and concentrated on picking at his long toenails.

"Well, I certainly don't want to marry Neb," Branna said. "He just reminds me of someone I saw once. I was surprised, is all."

"And where would you have seen the lad before?"

"If I knew, I wouldn't have been surprised, would I now?"

Midda sighed with a shake of her head, then resumed the unpacking. From a sack she took out two old, threadbare blankets, another grudged gift. When she spread them over the bed, the gnome vanished only to reappear in Branna's lap. *Neb sees the Wildfolk, too,* Branna thought. *I could see his eyes move, following them.*

"I'm off to get some firewood and the like," Midda announced. "It might be chilly tonight."

"Well and good, then. Has that chamberlain given you a decent place to sleep?"

"He has. A nice little space set off by partitions, private like, and only one other woman to share it with, and us with a mattress apiece. Much better than I had—" She paused to gesture at the room. "Than *we* had at your father's dun."

With one last snort of remembered disgust, Midda bustled out of the room. The gnome reached up a timid little paw and touched Branna's cheek.

"It is nicer," Branna said. "And I certainly can't be any more miserable than I was before. Now, if only I really had dweomer, I'd turn my stepmother into a frog, and I'd not turn her back unless she begged me."

The gnome grinned and nodded his head in agreement.

"If only I really had dweomer," Branna went on. "I say that too much, don't I? But they were such lovely tales I used to tell us. I suppose I should stop. I'm grown now and marriageable and all the rest of it."

The thought of abandoning her fantasies saddened her, because she'd told herself those tales for as long as she could remember. They had started as dreams, beautifully vivid dreams, so coherent and detailed that at times she wondered if they were actually memories.

From those wonderings she had developed a detailed fantasy

about another Then and another When, as she called it—another life somewhere that she and her gnome had lived together, when she'd been a mighty sorcerer who had traveled all over Deverry and far away, too, off to Bardek and beyond. Her favorite tale concerned a magical island far across the Southern Sea, where elven sorcerers lived and studied books filled with mighty spells. The gnome had always listened, nodding his head when he agreed with some detail, or frowning when he felt she'd got something wrong.

"Neb," she said aloud. "There was a man with a name like that in the tales, do you remember? But he was old. He can't be the same person."

The gnome scowled and wagged a long warty finger at her.

"What? You can't mean he is the same person."

The gnome nodded.

"Oh, here, that's silly. And impossible."

The gnome flung both hands into the air and disappeared. Branna was about to try calling him back when someone knocked on the door. Lady Galla opened it and hurried in, with a page carrying a folded coverlet right behind her. Branna scrambled down from the windowsill and curtsied.

"There you are, dear," Galla said. "Do you like the chamber? I found somewhat to brighten it up a bit. Now that you're here, we'll have to start on some bed curtains for you. We should be able to get them done before the winter."

"Thank you so much," Branna said. "I really really appreciate all this, Aunt Galla."

"You're most welcome, dear." Galla took the coverlet from the page. "You may go, Coryn."

The page skipped off down the hall. Together, the two women spread out the coverlet, linen embroidered with red-and-blue spiral roundels and thick bands of yellow interlace.

"It's awfully pretty," Branna said.

"And cheerful. Having somewhat cheerful's important just now,

I should think." Galla reached out and patted her hand. "And don't you worry, we'll see about finding you a proper husband."

"Tell me somewhat. Would it be horribly wrong of a lass like me to marry some common-born man, one who has some standing, I mean, like somebody who's serving a powerful lord?"

"Not at all, truly, just so long as he could provide for you properly."

"Oh, I'm used to doing without."

Galla winced and glanced away. "Your dear stepmother," she said at last. "Well, I'm sure she has her virtues."

"She popped out two sons in four years. That's all the virtue Da cares about." Branna heard the venom in her voice and tried to speak more calmly. "He never much liked me, anyway."

"Now, dear, it's hard for a true-born warrior like him to show tender feelings."

"Oh, don't try to sweeten it! You know that he blames me for my mother's death. Well, doesn't he?"

"It's a hard situation all round." Galla hesitated. "He did at the time, dear, but I tried to make him see reason." Again the hesitation. "Not that he did. Oh, it griped my very soul! You nearly died with her, you know, and your poor mother was never very strong anyway." She collected herself with a little sigh. "Well, you're here now, and I'm glad you've come to me."

"So am I. I truly am." Branna crossed to the window and looked out. She could see past the ward and over the dun wall to the green fields and the stream beyond. "It's even a lovely view. At home I could look out over the cookhouse, and the smoke really was awful."

"That woman!" Galla rolled her eyes heavenward.

Branna sat down on the broad stone windowsill and leaned out, just slightly, to look up at the sky. A solitary raven was hovering over the dun on outstretched wings. As she watched, she realized that while it looked the size of an ordinary bird, it had to be flying extremely high, because she couldn't see its eyes or the fine points of its wings. The only explanation could be that it was abnormally large. It flapped and circled, then hovered again, as if it were studying the dun below. She waited, watched, as it repeated the maneuver, but no other ravens flew up to join it, and it never made a sound. Finally, with one last flurry of black wings it flew away, heading north.

"What is it, dear?" Galla said.

Branna drew her head back inside. "Probably naught. A solitary raven, and I thought it was watching us."

"It was probably just eyeing the stables in the hopes of stall sweepings. They eat the most disgusting things, ravens."

"True spoken, but this one—I don't know why, but it chilled my heart. It seemed so large, for one thing."

"Perhaps it was a rook, not a raven at all."

"Well, that could be it. Silly of me, I know." Branna arranged a bright smile. In her chilled heart she doubted very much indeed that the bird she'd seen was a rook or any other natural animal. *Yet what else would it be?* she asked herself.

"I think we've finished here," Galla said. "Shall we go down to the great hall?"

As they were walking over to the table of honor, Branna noticed Neb, sitting on the servants' side of the room near a window. In the patch of sunlight that fell onto his table lay sheets of parchment, upon which he was scoring lines with the back of his little penknife against a strip of wood. A fat yellow gnome crouched on the table beside the parchments. It turned its head, leaped to its clawed feet, and began dancing on the parchments. Neb laid down his penknife and swatted at the gnome, who turned and pointed at Branna. Neb raised his head and looked her way. *He certainly does see the Folk!* she thought. Young, skinny, so completely different from the old man she'd often dreamed about— and yet his ice-blue eyes seemed so familiar that she nearly ran to him, nearly called him by the name she'd given him for her tales: Nevyn.

Neb raised his hand in greeting and smiled at her, as if he were hoping she'd join him, but Aunt Galla beckoned to her, and her cousin Mirryn was already sitting at the honor table. Branna risked a smile Neb's way, then hurried after her aunt.

Branna passed the afternoon pleasantly, playing Carnoic with Mirryn, chatting with Galla. Lord Veddyn joined Neb at his table and began reciting the list of taxes owed, stumbling every now and then over his faulty memory, so that the scribe could write them down. At each lapse, Galla would stand up and shout corrections Veddyn's way. Once in a while, as casually as she could manage, Branna would steal a look at Neb. Often enough, she found him looking back. They would both blush and look away again.

Since she was tired from her journey, Branna went to bed early. Unlike her old bed in her father's dun, her new mattress was soft and comfortable, and the down pillows smelled fresh, not sour. She lay down, then turned on her side to look at the sliver of starry sky visible through her window. Earlier, she'd resolved to give up her strange dreams of dweomer, but as soon as she fell asleep, a dream took her over.

She was standing at another window, looking at the sky. A full moon drifted in the field of stars. As she watched, the moon began to shrink until it turned into a gem, an opal, she thought, but it gleamed just as brightly as before. Suddenly she stood inside a chamber, and an old man, dressed in the brown tattered clothes of a poor farmer, was holding the opal out to her.

Branna woke and sat up. Judging from the wheel of stars outside her window, dawn lay a long way off. Her gnome appeared and flopped down on the bed beside her.

"Another odd dream," she told it. "Twice odd, really, because it wasn't the sort of dream I used to weave into a story, but it truly did seem more important than the usual sort of dream."

The gnome yawned, then left its mouth half-open and began to pick its teeth with one skinny fingernail.

"And of no interest to you, obviously. Humph!"

Branna lay down again, and fell back asleep almost immediately.

She had no more dreams that night, or at least, none that she remembered when she woke with the dawn.

On the day after Branna's arrival, the tieryn and his warband rode back to the dun. From the window of his tower room Neb watched them file through the gates—the horses weary, the men covered with dust from the roads. A provision cart and a couple of mules with empty packsaddles followed them, but no villagers walked behind, not a single man, woman, or child. Neb's eyes filled with tears as his last shred of hope blew away like the dust in the wind. He and Clae alone had escaped the Horsekin.

In his grief Neb decided against going down to the bustle and confusion of the great hall. He could wait to hear the grim report of what the warbands had found. When the sun had sunk low in the sky, however, Salamander came to his chamber. The gerthddyn had bathed and put on fresh clothes, including a shirt so heavily embroidered that it draped as stiffly as leather.

"I'll wager you can guess my news," Salamander said. "No one was left alive. We buried your uncle. I fear me your aunt's been taken by the Horsekin."

"And the other women, too?"

"Just that. I'm sorry."

Neb stared into empty air and fought the memories down.

"We'd best get ourselves to the great hall," Salamander went on. "They're serving the evening meal, and the tieryn wants you to write an important letter."

A spiral staircase wound down to the great hall, dim with the shadows of twilight. Near the door the men of the warband were drinking at their tables while they waited for their dinner. Across from them, near the nobles' hearth, Tieryn Cadryc sat at the head of the table of honor with his wife at his right hand. Branna was sitting next to Lady Galla. She wore a pair of clean dresses, the outer a pale blue, cut short in front and slashed at the sleeves to reveal a gray underdress. An embroidered band of interlace ran around the neck, and like a pendant hanging from a chain an embroidered dragon lay just over her collarbone. Neb felt himself blush for no particular reason, then noticed the gerthddyn staring at her, his lips half-parted as if in surprise. Or was it sexual interest? Neb wanted to slap him across the face, but the emotion shocked him so much that he managed to suppress it.

"Have you met Lady Branna before?" Neb said.

"The ice in your voice, lad, would freeze most men's blood."

Neb raised one eyebrow and considered him.

"Ye gods," Salamander said, "the look in your eyes just might do the same."

"Have you met her before?"

"I've not."

"Then you'd best mind your manners around her."

Salamander opened his mouth, then shut it again. Neb turned on his heel and strode off to the honor table, where Tieryn Cadryc waited for him.

After the meal, Salamander went up to the little room in the broch that Lady Galla had given him, a wedge of the circular floor plan defined by woven wicker partitions, but private nonetheless, because the compartments to either side held stacks of curing firewood. He spread his blankets out on the mattress on the floor, then strolled over to the unshuttered window. He could see over the dun walls to the meadows off to the east, where a quarter moon was just rising out of mist. When he boosted himself up to sit on the wide stone windowsill, the Wildfolk came to join him, a flock of sprites in the air, a gaggle of gnomes on the floor and the sill.

"Well, this is a pretty predicament, isn't it?" Salamander said to them. "I've seen my brother now, and I can't say I cared for the sight."

The Wildfolk all nodded in sad sympathy. Beyond the window the mist in front of the rising moon glowed and seemed to swirl in the distant light. Salamander focused upon it and let his mind fill with the memory of the silver wyrm, flying overhead on huge wings. In but an instant the memory turned into a vision. The silver dragon lay curled on a flat outcrop of rock among high mountains, his scales gleaming in the moonlight. He was perhaps eating something he held nestled against his side; Salamander could see the enormous head moving in a regular rhythm, licking something—licking a wound. The dragon moved restlessly, tossing his head, and Salamander could finally distinguish a dark streak on his side, oozing what appeared to be blood. In a moment the dragon went back to cleaning the wound with the only tool he had, his own tongue, a gesture so like that of a dog that Salamander felt profoundly nauseated.

His brother was living like an animal. No, his brother was an animal now, albeit a sapient creature who could speak, and in several languages at that. But he had no hands, no tools to ease his life, nothing but what his dragon form gave him. Salamander broke the vision. As if they felt his distress, the Wildfolk crowded closer.

"Ye gods, I feel sick and twice so," Salamander said. "I think me I'd best talk with my master in the dweomer."

This time, when he gazed into the moon-mist, he thought of Dallandra, his teacher and savior. At first he remembered her face; then he thought he might be seeing her face; all of a sudden he did see it. Her steel-gray eyes were narrow with concentration, and wisps of her ash-blonde hair hung untidily across her forehead and stuck to her cheeks. Yet, although the vision enlarged, the mist only thickened, swirling around her and threatening to hide her entirely.

"Dalla," he thought-spoke to her in Elvish. "Dalla, it's Ebañy. Is something wrong?"

He saw her flinch in surprise, then smile. She sat back on her heels and appeared to be looking straight at him. Through the mist he could see flickering light. Smoke and a fire?

"What do you mean, is something wrong?" she thought her answer back to him.

"I can barely see you for the smoke."

"It's not smoke. We're still on the coast. It's high tide, and the ocean's etheric veil is running high with it. Let me sharpen the image."

With that he could see her clearly. She was kneeling in front of the flickering light, which proved to be a small campfire.

"That's much better," he said. "You haven't left? I thought you'd have all started north by now."

"We had to wait for Carra to get back from Wmmglaedd. She and Meranaldar went there to talk history with the priests. We'll ride out on the morrow, most likely. Where are you?"

"In Tieryn Cadryc's dun once more. I've got strange news. I've seen our Rhodry, but I don't think he recognized me. It was down in the Melyn River valley."

"Does he look well?"

"No. I mean, by the Dark Sun herself! How could he look well in that body? He's a dragon, all scaly."

"Calmly now! Your thoughts are beginning to dance around."

"Sorry." Salamander took a deep breath. "But he seems to have hurt himself somehow. There's something that looks like a dagger's cut over one rib."

"How very odd! It couldn't still be the old wound, the one I couldn't get to staunch. On a creature the size of a dragon, it should have healed right up."

"Why would it? If it was a magical curse or suchlike—"

"But it wasn't any such thing. When it happened, I wasn't thinking clearly, so I didn't see the obvious. About a month later, when I was watching the men in my alar butcher a sheep, I realized the dagger had punctured a lung. There's a tremendous lot of blood vessels there, and most of the blood was draining into his chest cavity. He was drowning, actually, in his own blood."

For a moment Salamander nearly lost the vision in a wave of compassionate disgust. He steadied his mind and went on. "Then if it wasn't a dweomer wound, what I saw must be a fresh injury. Perhaps something he was trying to eat fought back."

"Very likely, yes. Well, there's naught I can do about it, unfortunately, unless he seeks me out, and so far, he hasn't. Do you have any other news?"

"Oh, a few small tidbits." Salamander paused for drama's sake. "I also ran across Nevyn, Jill, and Cullyn as well—or at least, I think it's Cullyn. I only saw him once or twice, and that was years ago."

"You what? Ye gods! They've all been reborn?"

"Yes, all reborn and here together, and Neb's growling like a dog with a stolen joint of mutton at anyone who casts an unseemly glance at little Branna. I wonder if Gerran's noticed the lass yet? Things could turn most unpleasant, you know, should he take a fancy to her. They're all still quite young. I'd say that Gerran's the oldest of the lot, and he seems to be about twenty. I really wish that Deverry men kept better track of things like someone's age."

"They don't have much reason to, I suppose. So Gerran is the man you think is Cullyn reborn?"

"Yes. Sorry, I wasn't being clear. The other names—"

"I could guess them, yes. Tell me about them. How did you find them?"

"It was more like they found me."

Dallandra listened intently to his tale, breaking her concentration only to feed a few sticks of wood into her little fire.

"Do Neb and Branna remember who they are?" Dalla said when he'd finished. "Or were, I should say."

"No. They do both see the Wildfolk."

"Odd. I would have thought that Neb, at least, would have memories of working dweomer."

"So would I. Of course, he may have them but be keeping them to himself."

"That's quite true." Dallandra paused briefly. "What about Neb's little brother?"

"I don't recognize him at all."

"That's interesting in itself. If you need me, I can gather an escort and ride your way."

"My thanks. I just might take you up on that. There's another thing, oh mighty mistress of magicks. The Horsekin. They've been raiding in the Melyn River valley."

"Again?"

"Again. It's most peculiar, too. They sent a sizable warband of heavy cavalry to burn two villages. For their trouble they got maybe thirty slave women and girls and two small boys. They didn't even bother harvesting the wheat in the fields. Does that make sense to you?"

"No, it certainly doesn't."

"I've been talking with the tieryn and his captain—Gerran, that is—about the raids. Their history is peculiar as well. Imagine in your mind the western flank of Deverry. Now imagine a line running from Cengarn down straight south to the sea. The Horsekin only attack settlements to the west of that line."

"I suppose the settlements farther east are too well guarded."

"Not on your life, oh, princess of powers perilous. I suspect—and as of now it's a mere suspicion only—that the Horsekin are trying to stop human settlement from spreading."

"To protect their borders?"

"Their borders are too far north for that. No, I wonder if there's something they want to hide out to the west of here."

"Hide? Such as what?"

"Such as a permanent camp set up to outflank the men of the Rhiddaer. It's the only thing I can think of, anyway."

Salamander could feel her shock as if it rode on a wave of mist, breaking over him. When her thoughts reached him, he could feel their venom as well.

"That would be just like them, wouldn't it?" Dallandra thought-spoke. "They've had forty years to lick their wounds from the last war, and now they're ready for more trouble." She paused, and her image flickered and grew thin as she withdrew her attention from scrying. In a few moments it clarified and grew bright again. "They can't attack the Rhiddaer directly—yet, I'd guess they're trying to cut it off from any possible help from Deverry."

"Perhaps that. Perhaps to cut it off from our folk, as well, or to cut us off from Deverry, or Deverry off from us. I know not, but I surmise much, none of it pleasant. I was wondering if any of our people have stumbled across this whatever it is, if indeed it exists, or if they've heard rumors, hints, clues, or even suspicions."

"I'll find out. We're on our way to the alardan for the summer festival. I'm riding with the prince's alar, and of course Calonderiel and his archers are, too."

"Excellent! Cal's just the man we need. I'd hoped to come west for the festival, but I think I'd better keep an eye on things here."

"Yes, do. How have you been faring? Your mind feels steady to me, but after what you've been through—"

"No sign of a recurrence, I assure you, oh princess of powers perilous."

"Good. Let me know at the first sign of any trouble." With a smile for a farewell, Dallandra broke the link between them.

Salamander stayed in the window and considered the view without truly registering it. *I used to call Jill the princess of powers perilous,* he thought. *Back before I went mad, back before I lost everything I loved, there in Bardek.*

No matter how carefully he thought about his return to Deverry from the southern islands, some forty years ago, he could never remember it. There had been a ship, of course—how else could he have crossed the ocean between Bardek and Deverry? How he had gotten on that ship, and why he'd left his wife and children behind, had fallen out of his memory like apples falling through a rotted sack. *The madness,* he thought. *With my mind all to pieces like that, it's a wonder I can remember anything.* He could bring up a few memory-images of landing in Eldidd, where Dallandra had been waiting to take him into her care.

Curing his madness had given Dallandra a hard ten years' work. Once his mind began healing, Salamander had devoted several years to his youngest son, who suffered from mysterious troubles, before he'd returned to Bardek. Once there, he had searched all over the islands for a good long while before he finally found the troupe of traveling acrobats led by his eldest son, a grown man by then with children of his own. Kwinto had given his truant father a cold enough welcome, too.

"Too late," Salamander said aloud. "Too late to see Marka again, too late to prove to her that I kept my promise. I did come back, my love, truly I did."

He could see her in his mind so clearly, and as always, he remembered her as a slender young woman, laughing, smiling, tossing her head of curls as she ran to greet him—so clearly that it seemed he could reach out and take her hand, but only empty air returned his grasp. *She's dead,* he reminded himself. *She died before you found them.* He leaned his head back against the cold stone and wept.

allandra smothered her little fire, then left her tent, which stood on the edge of the encampment. When she turned toward the sea, she could see the tidy whitewashed buildings of the new town, Linalavenmandra, a name that meant "sorrow but new hope," though most often its inhabitants merely called it Mandra, "hope." From her vantage point, its whitewashed square buildings seemed as pale as ghosts against the nighttime sea. Even though returning refugees from the Southern Isles had built the town over twenty years ago, it still amazed her every time she saw it: a proper town, sheltering not Deverry men but her own folk, with a town square and straight streets, trees and gardens, a town fountain and a holy spring. Beyond them, out of her immediate sight, lay farms. All her long life she'd known only wild sea grass in this spot, sea grass and rock and the winter waves that crashed and boomed on the long pale beach. The waves still crashed, but onto a rocky seawall now, jutting out into a new harbor, where a wooden pier offered docking for elven longships.

With a shake of her head, Dalla turned away and strode through the camp. Despite the new town, most of the People, as the elven

folk called themselves, still spent every spring and summer traveling in small groups, or alarli, following their herds of horses and
flocks of sheep. In this alar two dozen round tents sprawled across
a meadow near a stream. Out in the grasslands behind them, a herd
of over four hundred horses, guarded by armed riders, grazed at
tether.

In among the tents, the adults stood talking together in twos and
threes or sat around small fires, finishing the evening meal. Children ran around, playing with leather balls, chasing each other or
their dogs. Occasionally, Wildfolk materialized to join the games.
Warty little gnomes wandered between the tents; translucent
sylphs and pale sprites flitted after the children or teased the dogs,
who couldn't see them but who could feel their pinching fingers.
The dogs would bark and snap, and the Wildfolk would disappear,
only to pop up smirking somewhere nearby.

On the surface the camp seemed no different from the elven
camps Dallandra had always known. The tents were just as brightly
painted, the fires just as warm. The People lived their lives as nois-
ily as ever, in a society of ever-shifting relationships that made Deverry folk shake their heads in bewilderment. But here and there
Dalla saw the signs that everything had changed.

In front of every tent, like guests at the meal, stood longbows and
quivers. Mail shirts and other pieces of armor lay close at hand as
well. Most of the men and some of the women wore swords, even
when they were merely chatting with old friends. At the cry of birds
passing overhead the camp would fall silent; hands on sword hilts,
a few men would look up, judging whether or not the birds were ordinary creatures or magical spies, mazrakir, as the Horsekin called
shape-changers. Sooner or later, everyone knew, the same raids that
were bleeding the human farmlands were bound to ride their way.

In the middle of the camp Dallandra finally spotted the Banadar,
or warleader, of the Eastern Border, to give Calonderiel his official
title. He was sitting by himself on a dead log in front of his tent, the
second largest in camp. In the flickering firelight the deer painted
upon the tent walls seemed at moments to fling up their heads,

ready to run. Calonderiel's hair gleamed, so pale it was almost white, but shadows hid his violet eyes.

"I've spoken to Ebañy," Dallandra said. "And I see trouble coming."

Calonderiel looked up, startled. "What's he done now?"

"It's not what he's done, it's what he's found."

Calonderiel moved over to give her room to sit beside him on the log, but after a moment's hesitation, she knelt on the ground nearby. At the gesture he winced; he'd fallen in love with her all over again, and as it had before, his devotion annoyed her. Before he could speak of his feelings, she brandished Salamander's news like a shield.

"The Horsekin are raiding in Arcodd again."

"Bastards!" Calonderiel paused to spit into the fire. "I wonder if Cengarn's going to call in our alliance?"

"I don't know, but maybe Ebañy can find out. He thinks the Horsekin might be trying to hide something, a fort or armed camp, he said, near the border."

"And they're using the raids as a distraction?"

"Well, that's what he suspects. He doesn't know. I take it that seems logical to you."

"It's the first thing I thought of. If his suspicions are right, we'll have to mount some kind of attack. A Horsekin fort nearby? Ye gods, it's like a dagger at our throats!"

"That's rather what I thought, too."

"We might be the ones to call in our alliance with Cengarn, not the other way round. At least we have Mandra now. If things get desperate, we can get the prince and his family to safety there and fortify the place. If it looks like the town's going to fall, well, they have boats."

"Do you think things will get that desperate?"

"Who knows?" Calonderiel shrugged. "But we might as well plan for the worst. Which reminds me. We need to send messengers to Braemel. We're going to need every ally we have. Huh!" Cal paused to shake his head and smile. "I remember how angry I was when that Horsekin woman—Zatcheka, wasn't it?—arrived to visit you."

"You were even angrier when I went to Braemel to visit her daughter."

"Yes, I was. Well, I was wrong, wasn't I?"

"You?" Dallandra laid her hand on her forehead and feigned shock. "Wrong?"

"I deserve that, I suppose," Cal said, glowering. "But I'm glad now that you know the Gel da'Thae and their ugly language, too. Think Braemel will send us aid?"

"Yes, I do. They're as afraid of the wild Horsekin as we are. Never forget that. They may all look alike to us, but the Gel da'Thae see themselves as very different from the tribal Horsekin."

"Good." Calonderiel stared into the fire, his mouth working as he thought things through. Eventually he looked up. "Did Ebañy have any other news?"

"Yes, but only of a personal sort."

Calonderiel waited expectantly. When she said nothing more, he picked a stick up from the ground and began shredding the bark with a fingernail. Dalla longed to tell him her news, that two powerful dweomermasters had been reborn close at hand, that perhaps they might recover the lore and the power it gave them quickly, in time to aid the People in their battle with the Horsekin. But he knew nothing of the great secret, that souls lived many lives, and she was forbidden by her vows to tell anyone unless they asked her outright.

Eventually Cal tossed the stick onto the fire and looked up. "Do you remember Cullyn of Cerrmor?" he said.

"Jill's father? I never met him, but I certainly know who he was. Why?"

"I was just remembering a time long long ago, when Cullyn was the captain of another lord's warband, and we were drinking together. I saw an omen, or felt it, or something like that."

"And it was?"

"That someday we'd ride together in a war, an important war, the most significant one we'd ever fight." He tossed the stick into the fire and looked at her. "When he died, I realized that the omen must have been some silly imagining on my part." He paused to glare at the fire as if it had offended him. "It's a pity, too, because I'd love to have his sword on our side now. Ye gods! We'd better go tell the prince." Calonderiel stood up. "Trust Ebañy to be a bird of ill omen!"

But I'll wager you were right about Cullyn, Dallandra thought. *The pity is that I can't tell you so.* Suddenly she felt so cold, so frail, that she could barely speak. She started to get to her feet, but she staggered and nearly fell. Calonderiel caught her by the shoulders and steadied her.

"Are you ill?" he said.

"No, it's just the omens. I feel omens round us, thick as winter snow. I'll be all right in a bit."

"Dalla, Dalla, you pour out your life for us, don't you?"

She could see genuine concern in his dark violet eyes, a compassion far different from his usual romantic longing. When he laid the back of a gentle hand against her cheek, she let it rest there for a moment before she turned away.

"I'll be all right," she repeated. "We have to go tell the prince."

Ever since his father's death some three years previously, Daralanteriel was technically a king, the overlord of the legendary Seven Cities of the far west, but since their ruins had lain abandoned for over a thousand years, everyone referred to him as a prince. It seemed more fitting to save the title of king for a man who had something to rule. Even so, Daralanteriel tran Aledeldar, Prince of the Seven Cities and Ranadar's Heir, traveled with a retinue these days. Along with a hand-picked group of sword warriors, Dallandra with her dweomer and Calonderiel with his band of archers kept the royal family constant company. If the Horsekin should raid, they'd find the prince well guarded.

Daralanteriel's tent, the largest in the Westlands, dominated the center of the camp. The deer hides that covered the wood frame had been cut into straight panels, laced together, then painted. On the tent flap and around the opening hung painted garlands of red roses, so realistically portrayed that it seemed one might smell them. The rest of the tent sported views of Rinbaladelan in its days of glory. One panel portrayed the high tower near the harbor, another the observatory with its great stone arcs, a third the temple of the sun, so detailed that it seemed one might walk among them—not, of course, that anyone alive had ever seen the actual city to judge the accuracy of the paintings. The artist had followed the descriptions in a book belonging to Daralanteriel's scribe, Meranaldar. While the book was a copy of a work saved from the destruction of Rinbaladelan, some twelve hundred years previously, it lacked any actual drawings.

Even though they were royal, Dallandra found Dar's wife and daughter sitting on the ground in front of their tent like any other Westfolk family would do, sharing a meal of roast rabbit and flatbread. Dressed in a loose tunic over doeskin breeches, Princess Carramaena of the Westlands knelt by the fire and poked at the coals with a green twig. Some few feet away, her eldest daughter, Elessario, sat with her knees drawn up and her arms clasped around them to allow her to rest her head upon them. Superficially the two women looked much alike, both of them blonde, with pretty, heart-shaped faces. Their eyes, however, differed greatly. Elessario's eyes were a dark yellow, and cat-slit like all elven eyes. Her mother, a human being, had blue eyes and the round pupils of her kind. At the sight of the banadar, Elessario grinned.

"Cal!" Elessario said. "Where's your son?"

"Maelaber?" Calonderiel said. "Taking his turn on horse guard. Where's your papa?"

"Doing the same thing." Elessi giggled, then hid her mouth with one hand. She was a changeling, or so the People called the wild children who'd been born to them over the years. Although she was the most normal of them, her mind had stopped developing when she'd been about twelve years old.

"Then I'd best go fetch him." Calonderiel glanced at Carra. "We've had some bad news."

"I'll come, too!" Elessario scrambled to her feet.

"Say please," Carra said.

"Please, Cal? Can I come with you?"

"You may." Calonderiel gave her a smile. "But you'll have to be careful around the horses."

They hurried off, with Elessario talking all the while. Carra shook her head and sighed.

"My poor little changeling! To think we thought she'd be the queen of the Westlands one fine day." Over the years Carra had become fluent in Elvish, though one could still hear Deverry's rolled R's and Rh's in her accent. "I'm so glad we've had other children."

"So am I. You must be looking forward to seeing the girls. I'm assuming they'll come to the festival."

"They'd better, or I'll have some harsh words for them. Perra must have had her baby by now, too. I can hardly wait to see them both."

Dallandra smiled and sat down near her. "Some news—I've heard from Salamander."

"Has he found Rhodry?"

"Not to say found him, but he did see him, flying over the Melyn River. He's not sure whether or not Rhodry saw him, or heard him either. Dragons make a lot of noise when they fly."

"I remember Arzosah, yes, flapping those huge wings of hers." Carra paused, suddenly sad. "Dalla, is there anything anyone can do for him? Rhodry, I mean, to change him back again. I can't bear it, thinking of his being like that forever. He would have died for us, after all."

"In a way, he did. Unfortunately, I don't have the dweomer to bring him back. I honestly don't know if anyone does."

Carra bit her lip hard.

"Well, he may be perfectly happy," Dalla went on. "In a way, he'd stopped being human long before Evandar gave him dragon form. You saw him after battles. That berserker laugh!"

"I can hear it still, yes, whenever I think of him. If only Evandar were still alive! Do you think he could turn Rori back?"

"Oh, undoubtedly, but he's gone. I don't know if any other dweomermaster will ever match his power."

"Probably not." Carra reached up and touched her cheek, still as smooth and unlined as a young lass'. "It's because of Evandar that I've not aged, isn't it? He told me once he'd give me a gift, and it's this, isn't it?"

"Yes, indeed, you've guessed his riddle." Dallandra felt her voice waver. "He did love riddles, and his elaborate jokes."

"You still miss him, don't you?"

Dallandra nodded, fighting back tears. Over the years the true mourning had left her. Whole months would pass with never a thought of Evandar, but now and again, she would remember some detail of their time together, and the grief would stab her to the heart.

Fortunately, a distraction arrived in the person of Carra's youngest child. Followed by a pair of big gray dogs and a stream of Wildfolk, Rodiveriel came running. Laughing, he threw himself into Carra's lap. The dogs flopped down, panting, displaying wolfish fangs. They had white faces and a black stripe of coarser hair down their gray backs like wolves as well, but they were, or so Carra assured everyone, merely dogs, descendants of the loyal pet that had guarded her when Elessi was an infant.

"What's all this, Rori?" Carra said, smiling.

"Nothing." He slid off to sit on the ground near the dogs. "I'm tired, but I don't want to go to bed yet. It's not even truly dark."

"All right, then, but when it's truly dark, in you go."

He made a face at her but said nothing. He'd inherited his father's raven-dark hair, but his eyes, though a pale gray like Dar's, were human in shape. His name was a hybrid—Carra had wanted to honor Rhodry, the man who'd saved her life all those years past. And yet he was also the Marked Prince of the Seven Cities, assuming of course, that the kingdom ever came back to life. If the cities did become a prize worth fighting over, would the People accept a man with human blood as their ruler? Dallandra doubted it. *There's trouble enough to worry about without that,* she told herself. *If the*

Horsekin murder us all, no one's going to care about a dead kingdom anyway.

Late into the night the men talked of war. Dalla left them when the stars had completed half their wheel of the sky and went to her tent to sleep. Yet an omen-dream woke her in the gray light of dawn. She sat up and stared at the tent bags hanging on the wall, but in her mind she was seeing the omens.

"A silver dagger and a bone whistle." She spoke aloud to ensure that she'd remember what she'd seen. "Someone's silver dagger and a long bone whistle. Ye gods, what an odd pair of things!" Yet she'd seen them both before, she realized, and eventually she retrieved the memory. One of Alshandra's followers had tried to work evil with a dragonbone whistle during the siege of Cengarn, and Yraen's silver dagger had ended up in the hands of the Horsekin after his death. "It was never truly finished, that war," Dalla whispered. "May the Star Goddesses help us all!"

Neb was quite proud of the letter he wrote for Tieryn Cadryc. Since it was addressed to a gwerbret, he trimmed up the best piece of parchment and chose the Half-inch Royal hand for the letters. For good measure he put a line of interlace at the top and a little sketch of a red wolf, the tieryn's blazon, below the place where Cadryc would make his mark.

Neb had an odd knack when it came to drawing things: he would picture his intended images in his mind, get them clear, and then push the image out through his eyes—or so he thought of the process—onto the parchment or whatever surface he was using. All he had to do then was trace around the image, which he could see as clearly as if it were already drawn. The trick came so naturally to him that he'd never given it much thought, but as he worked, he remembered Lady Galla telling him about Branna's needlework skills. *She can do this, too,* he thought. *We're alike in this.* The words pleased him deeply: we're alike.

When the ink had dried, Neb took it up to the table of honor, where the noble-born were finishing up their breakfast. Cadryc took it from him and glanced at it, then took Neb's pen and put an X over the red wolf.

"Looks splendid," Cadryc handed the sheet back. "If it's dry enough, roll it up." He handed Neb a silver message tube, somewhat scratched and dented, but usable. "I don't have a proper seal, so a drop of wax will have to do. If we have any sealing wax, that is."

"We don't, Your Grace," Neb said.

"Ah. I was afraid of that. Well, the next time I go to Cengarn, you'll come with me, and I'll give you some coin to buy what we need. We've received the king's yearly bounty. The messengers rode in not long before you turned up." Cadryc stood up and yelled across the hall to Gerran, who was eating with the warband. "Gerro, I need a couple of men to take a letter to Cengarn."

Over the next few days, life in the dun centered around two things: waiting for the gwerbret's answer and storing the taxes. Grain had to be milled into flour or parched for winter porridge and the brewing of ale; hogs, rabbits, and chickens needed to be sorted out and housed until their eventual slaughtering. Cheeses and butter to be kept cool, fruit dried, beef smoked or pickled—the early taxes provided the dun's food supply for more than half a year. Lady Galla and Lady Branna put on old shabby dresses and worked alongside the cook and servants. Raised in a town, and a large one at that, Neb had never quite realized that outside of the rich provinces in the heart of Deverry, the noble-born were in their own way farm folk, much closer to the life of the land than craftsmen were.

During the day Neb saw Branna often as she went about her work and he, his. At times they had the chance to say a few words together, but at meals and in the evening, they sat at opposite sides of the hall, she with the noble-born, he with the servants. He would nurse a scant tankard of ale and watch her, sitting demurely beside her aunt at the honor table while Salamander earned his keep. So that the entire great hall could see and hear him, the gerthddyn stood on a table, telling tales punctuated with songs and juggling, performing little tricks such as pulling scarves out of thin air or plucking eggs from the hair of a passing servant. At times, when her aunt was engrossed in Salamander's performance, Neb would catch Branna looking across the great hall to watch him, not the gerthddyn. Yet when the tales ended, the two ladies and their maidservants would retire to the women's hall upstairs, closed to all men but the tieryn and the aged chamberlain.

One evening, as Neb was going upstairs, he met Branna face-to-face at a turning of the spiral staircase. She was carrying a candle lantern, and at the sight of him she stopped, smiling. Neb suddenly found that he couldn't remember her name—worse yet, he wanted to call her by some other name, but he couldn't remember that one either. Fortunately he could address her by her title alone.

"Good evening, my lady," he said.

"Good evening, Goodman Neb." She paused, as if waiting for him to speak, then continued. "I'm going out to the cookhouse. We're dyeing some thread, and we need a bit of salt for a mordant."

"Where's your maidservant?"

"Off somewhere. By the time I find her, I can fetch it myself." She hesitated, then smiled and stepped down past him. "I'd best be on my way."

Neb smiled and bowed, then stood and watched her go, until it dawned on him that he might have asked her if he could escort her. Running after her now would only make him look a fool. He hurried up to his chamber and threw open the shutter at the window. By leaning out at a dangerous angle he could just see the cookhouse and Branna, walking across the ward with her lantern held high. The candle's dim glow wrapped her round like a cloak of gold, or so he saw it. In a few moments she came back out with the lantern in one hand and a bowl in the other. Neb waited till she'd gone inside and he could see her no longer before he left the window.

That night he had another dream about the young woman called the most beautiful lass in all Deverry. *Once again she was sitting in the rough, smoky great hall, and once again he heard a male voice speaking though he could see no one but the lass. This time the voice said, "You should have recognized her. You should have seen her for what she was."*

Neb woke to find himself cold-sick and shaking. He lay in bed and listened to his heart pounding while he wondered if he had caught some fever, maybe the same one that had killed his mother. He felt cold, but the palms of his hands were sweaty, and he was gasping for breath. It took him some time to realize that rather than being ill, he was terrified. The dream and the voice lingered in his mind like an evil omen.

Beside him Clae slept in motionless peace. Neb slipped out of bed and walked to the window. Beyond it the Snowy Road of stars hung close and bright in the cloudless sky. The most beautiful lass in all Deverry. *Who was she? Why do I think I know her?* At last the strangest thought of all came to him: *why am I so sure she's dead?* He could answer none of those questions, and soon he was tired enough to go back to bed and fall straight asleep.

In the morning, as he was going down the staircase for breakfast, he saw Branna walking across the great hall. The words sounded in his mind again: *you should have recognized her.* The fear returned, one quick stab of it, like an icicle to the heart, then passed, leaving him bewildered.

Gerran finished his breakfast porridge quickly, his mind full of his duties for the day. As he was heading out the door of the great hall, he met Lady Branna coming in. Technically, thanks to his fostering, she was his cousin. She'd been a frequent visitor to Cadryc's old dun and demesne back to the east of this new rhan, but then she'd only been a shabby little child in the care of a servant. He'd hardly noticed her. The sight of her now, a young woman, bright and attractive, surprised him every time he saw her. When he started to bow, she laughed at him.

"What?" she said, grinning. "Am I such a fine lady now? Honestly, Gerro, after all these years!"

"A very fine lady indeed," he said. "And a lovely one."

Branna blushed profoundly and hurried past him, heading for the staircase. Gerran glanced back to see Lady Galla standing halfway up the stairs and watching with a small smile. Rather than blush himself, he went outside to the safety of his men's company. But as he jogged out to the stables, he was thinking of the truth of his remark. Little Branna had grown into a lovely lass indeed.

"Well, you know, dear," Lady Galla said. "For a lass in your position, Gerran wouldn't be a bad match. He's our foster son, after all, and your Uncle Cadryc favors him highly."

"So I've noticed, my lady."

"What do you think of him?"

Branna ran her needle into the cloth and looked at Galla. They were sitting and sewing up in the women's hall, a half-round room with a polished wood floor, partially covered with a pair of thread-bare Bardek carpets, and walls of dressed stone, hung here and there with faded tapestries. The morning light streamed in through the window and fell across the pale linen, stretched in a wooden frame, that eventually would become the first panel of her bed hangings.

"Gerran's very handsome," Branna said at last. "And his heart's closed up as tight as a miser's money box."

"That's true. He's had a hard life, losing his mother and father that way."

"You know, there's one thing I've never understood. His mother—why did she drown herself? Did she love her man as much as all that?"

"She did, but truly, I think she would have survived her grief if it weren't for one thing. The night before the warband left, she told me, she and her man had fought about somewhat—I forget what, some little thing—and when the warband rode out, she was still ever so angry. She never got the chance to tell him that she forgave him and end the quarrel. And that's what tipped the balance."

"I see. That's awfully sad."

"It was, and so I felt that the least I could do was care for her little son, but you know, it was odd about Gerran. He was so aware of being different, no matter how welcome I tried to make him feel."

"Different? You mean because he's not noble-born?"

"Exactly. You know your uncle well enough to know that a man's skill with a sword means more than rank to him, and certainly Mirryn's always treated Gerro like a brother." Galla paused for a small sigh. "It's a pity that you and Mirryn are bloodkin. Though I suppose no one would frown at a cousin marriage out here on the border."

"I'd frown on it. I mean, I hope I'm not being rude, but I know him so well that I'd feel like I was marrying my brother. We even look a fair bit alike."

"Not rude at all, dear. I'll admit that I'd have qualms myself about marrying my cousin."

"Besides, I wouldn't make a good wife for a man of his rank."

Galla hesitated—weighing words, Branna assumed.

"Well, I wouldn't," Branna went on. "I'd hate to have to entertain emissaries from the gwerbret and suchlike." She paused for a smile. "My dearest aunt, everyone knows I'm a bit strange. I'm moody and I have a nasty tongue. Isn't that what they all say?"

"Well, plain speaking isn't a good thing in the wife of a high-ranking lord, that's true."

Branna smiled and picked up her needle again. "What about in the wife of a captain?"

"You'd need to be courteous in the ordinary sort of way to get along with the other servitors' wives, but other than that, it wouldn't matter so much."

"I see. Well, I'll think about it."

And what if I were the wife of a scribe? Branna kept that thought to herself. Like most Deverry girls, she'd always hoped that someday she'd find a good husband, but given the situation in her father's dun, she'd never dared hope that she'd have two solid prospects. *Neb has a good position here,* she thought—*and I'll wager he'll live a fair bit longer than Gerro, too.*

Beyond that practical advantage of being the wife of a scribe, not a warrior, Branna had other reasons for favoring Neb. For as long as she'd known him, Gerran had kept his thoughts to himself so resolutely that he rarely spoke unless spoken to. The way he'd volunteered his opinion of her looks, earlier that day, had taken her utterly by surprise. She didn't fancy long evenings of silence when she would wonder if her husband were brooding over some deep secret or merely half-asleep. On the other hand, she'd noticed that Neb always had a cheerful word for everyone he met and could be positively chatty when he had a moment to spare. The way he cared for his young brother impressed her as well. He would doubtless take a real interest in any children he might father, whereas for Gerran, children would always be women's work.

Her gnome certainly favored Neb. Whenever she met the young scribe, the gnome would materialize, grin at Neb, and clap its bony little hands. Neb would glance around to make sure that no one else could see, then smile back at the little creature. Yet oddly enough, Branna could never quite bring herself to speak to Neb about the Wildfolk. They were always in danger of being overheard, but even more, she was afraid of where such a conversation might lead them—not that she could understand her fear.

Alone, up in her chamber, she could talk openly to the gnome, who did his best to answer her with gestures. Any mention of Gerran brought a sour face and a surly shake of the head. One evening, tired from her day's work, she took a candle and went up to bed early. As she sat in the window, combing her hair, the gnome appeared to perch on her dower chest.

"Do you think I should finish the shirt in there to fit Neb?" Branna said.

It nodded a yes.

"It's so odd about his name. I mean, that it's so, well, familiar. He really is like that ancient sorcerer, isn't he? He's got the same blue eyes and everything."

The gnome clutched its head with both hands and mugged disgust.

"It's absolutely impossible that he's the same person. My folk don't grow younger with time, you know. Besides, how can there be real dweomer? It's just somewhat from old tales, like the ones Salamander tells."

The gnome pointed at itself, then at her face.

"Well, truly, I do see you, and so does Neb, and other people say the Wildfolk aren't real, but—" She let her voice trail away. *But what?* she asked herself. The gnome crossed its arms over its chest and smirked.

In the morning, as she was coming down for breakfast, she noticed Salamander, standing near the foot of the staircase and idly looking over the great hall. He glanced up, saw her, and bowed.

"Good morrow, gerthddyn," Branna said. "Did you sleep well?"

"I did, truly. And you?"

"I did, my thanks. I've been enjoying the tales you tell. So many of them seem to have dweomer in them."

"There's naught like a good marvel to catch your audience's attention."

"True spoken. You've traveled all over the kingdom, haven't you?"

"I have."

"I don't suppose that you've ever come across—oh well, never mind. I don't mean to be stupid."

Branna started to turn away, but Salamander caught her by the elbow.

"Real dweomer, you mean?" He was grinning at her.

She pulled her arm free of his lax grasp and hurried away. *You dolt!* she told herself. *You've really made a fool of yourself this time!* At the honor hearth she risked a glance back, but Salamander had found a place at a table and was devoting himself to his breakfast. At the honor table Mirryn sat alone, slumped in his chair.

"Good morning!" Branna sat down opposite him and smiled.

Mirryn never looked up from his profound study of the table's edge. His hair, usually a thick smooth brown, looked matted and spiky, as if he'd been running his hands through it out of sheer nerves, and his puffy eyes made Branna wonder if he'd stayed awake all night. A serving lass brought a basket of warm bread and a crock of butter, then trotted off again.

"What is it, Mirro?" Branna said. "You look troubled about somewhat."

"Do I?" He ducked his head to avoid looking at her and reached for the basket.

"You do. What—"

"I shouldn't be surprised, I suppose, to hear that you don't want to marry a coward like me."

"What?" Branna laid both hands on the table and leaned forward. "What are you talking about?"

"My lady mother mentioned that you didn't want to marry me, and why else, but everyone knows I'm a wretched coward who never rides to war."

"Oh, don't be stupid! That's not it at all."

"You don't need to be kind—"

"Do hold your tongue and listen! I told her that it would be like marrying my brother. You can't possibly want to marry me, anyway."

"Well, I don't, truly." At last he looked at her. "It would be like marrying my sister."

She burst out laughing, and in a moment he joined her.

"And you're not a coward," Branna said at last. "Everyone knows that Uncle won't let you go to war. It's not your choice."

"How do you know that they think such?"

"Because I heard a lot of people talking about it when I was still back with Da. Da and his friends think Uncle Cadryc's daft when it comes to you."

Mirryn thought this over while he cut a chunk of bread in half with his table dagger. He handed her one of the pieces.

"Truly?" he said. "You're not just trying to soothe my feelings?"

"Not in the least! It's quite true. Butter, please?"

Mirryn slid the crock across to her and thought some more. "My thanks," he said finally. "That gladdens my heart to hear."

Branna was about to tell him more, but Cadryc himself was striding over to the table, with Aunt Galla trotting after. Branna rose, curtsied to them both, then sat down again when Galla took her place. For the rest of the meal they chatted about trivial things.

Later that day Salamander sought Branna out. To get a moment's peace from the busy, dusty ward she had climbed up the catwalk ladders to the top of the dun wall. By leaning between two crenels she could look out on a long green view, striped here and there with the west-flowing streams that would eventually join the Melyn. She was thinking of very little when she saw, out of the corner of her eye, something gleaming. She turned to look, and farther down the catwalk stood the figure of the old man in his ragged clothes, holding out a glowing opal. Branna caught her breath with a gasp, and he disappeared.

Am I seeing things? she wondered. *Or is he one of the Wildfolk?* Although the figure reminded her of the man named Nevyn that she'd seen in her dreams, he looked somewhat different. She had never had such a dream as that one, when the opal had glowed like a candle flame, nor about any such gem. The old man seemed to be promising to give her something mysterious but beautiful, a rare gift indeed, if only she would come closer and speak to him. But what if it were a trap, and the gem the bait? Standing in the summer sun, she shivered and clasped her hands together to keep them warm. *Don't be a dolt!* she told herself. *Why would anyone want to trap you?*

A pleasant voice hailed her from below. Salamander came climbing up the rickety wood ladder to join her on the wall. She started to make some mundane greeting, then stopped, shocked into silence. Wildfolk swarmed around him—crystalline sylphs, winged sprites, pale warty gnomes.

"Good morrow," Salamander said. "Is somewhat the matter?"

"Not at all, not at all. My apologies. You took me by surprise, is all."

"Then I should apologize to you. I just thought I'd keep you company, if that's acceptable."

"It is, but I'd best get back to my duties. My aunt will be looking for me."

"Perhaps later, then?"

"Perhaps." She hesitated, but the gerthddyn was certainly amusing, and good-looking as well. "I might have a moment later."

She swung herself onto the catwalk, then climbed down the ladder a little faster than was strictly safe. She could only wonder why she'd found it so frightening, that the Wildfolk followed Salamander around. It seemed to her that the world had turned suddenly strange. *From the moment I met Neb,* she thought. *That's when it all started.* She felt that she should know what Neb's arrival in her life meant, that she was looking at the back of a tapestry and seeing a tangle of color and thread hiding the true pattern. If she could only turn the cloth over and see the front, she would know the answer. If.

As Branna walked across the ward, she saw two dusty horsemen riding in. When they dismounted, she saw that their shields carried the sun blazon of Cengarn. *Messengers,* she thought. With a cold feeling around her heart, she hurried into the great hall. Behind her came a small mob of servants and riders, as anxious to hear the news as she was.

Nearly a fortnight after the tieryn had sent his letter, messengers from the gwerbret had finally arrived with the answer. Neb followed them in, hurried across the great hall, and knelt on one knee beside the tieryn's chair at the head of the honor table. A messenger knelt on the other side and proffered the silver tube. Cadryc took it, glanced at the seal, and handed it to Neb.

"Read it as loudly as you can," Cadryc said. "We might as well all hear the news at once."

Neb got up and turned toward the crowd in the great hall. "To his grace, Tieryn Cadryc of the Red Wolf, I send greetings. I have no intention of appealing to the high king for aid in the matter you put before me. You were appointed to guard the border. The high king was not." Neb glanced the tieryn's way. "It's signed—"

"We know who sent the cursed thing!" Cadryc had gone red in the face. He took a deep breath and paused to look over the great hall, crammed with every rider and servant in the dun, or so it seemed. Lord Mirryn worked his way through the mob and reached his father's side. At the sight of him the tieryn smiled and turned calm.

"Well, the gwerbret may not want to appeal to the king," Cadryc said, "but I see naught wrong with my appealing to the gwerbret. I'll take fifteen men for an honor escort. As soon as the taxes and suchlike are all taken care of, I'll ride to Cengarn."

"Father?" Lord Mirryn laid a hand on his father's arm. "I want to go with you."

"What? And leave the dun unguarded?" Cadryc said. "There's Horsekin prowling around, lad, and—"

"They've never raided this far east."

"We'll not argue about it in front of the whole great hall." Cadryc's voice turned into a growl.

Mirryn tossed his head, started to snarl, then smoothed his expression into bland indifference. "As you wish, Father," he said. "But I'd like a word alone with you later, if I may."

"Fair enough. Neb, you'll be coming with us. I'll tell Gerran to pick you out a horse."

"My thanks, Your Grace." Neb bowed to him. "May I have your leave to go? The chamberlain's waiting for me out in the ward. More taxes have arrived."

"You may. In fact, I'll come out with you."

Gerran had seen the messengers ride in, but by the time he reached the great hall, it was too full for him to squeeze his way inside. The news reached him, anyway, in the form of outraged chatter as the hall emptied. Servant and rider alike blustered and swore, that the gwerbret would treat their lord so rudely. Cadryc himself emerged only a few moments later.

"Did you hear what that blasted letter said?" Cadryc asked him.

"I did, Your Grace."

The tieryn took a deep breath and calmed himself. "Once I see all the taxes safely in, we'll ride to Cengarn. In the meantime, pick out a palfrey for the scribe and see if he knows how to ride it."

"Well and good, Your Grace," Gerran said. "The sooner we lay our case before the gwerbret, the happier I'll be."

They strolled together through the ward, which at the moment looked more like a market fair. Farmers stood beside wagonloads of winter wheat or chased after small droves of hogs and flocks of chickens while the frantic chamberlain ran back and forth. Two men dressed in the ragged clothes of shepherds were just coming through the gates, pushing a handcart piled high with shorn fleeces that looked a fair bit cleaner than they did. Off to one side Neb stood on a little island of calm and jotted down tallies on scraps of fraying parchment.

"The scribe seems to know what he's doing," Gerran said.

"He does, doesn't he? He's a confident lad for his age. I'd been a bit worried about old Veddyn, to tell you the truth. He forgets things." Cadryc suddenly stepped away and waved to someone across the ward. "Ah. There's Goodman Gwervyl. I'd best go speak to him personally. He's a decent man with a bow, and he's offered to train more archers."

Gerran found a place to wait out of the way. Serving lasses hurried by, their arms full of empty baskets, heading for a wagon down by the gates. When he saw Lady Branna following them, Gerran stepped forward and bowed to her. She waved, gave him a brittle little smile, and trotted on past. *Not a very encouraging sign,* he thought. She probably saw him as nothing but a common-born lout, or worse yet, as bloodkin of a sort, thanks to his fostering. Either opinion would keep him at a distance. He wished he had a better idea of how to court a lass. Fortunately, the tieryn returned and broke into his gloom-laden thoughts.

"I'm not sure what to say to the wretched gwerbret," Cadryc said. "Any ideas?"

"None, my lord."

"We'll have to think about it on the ride to Cengarn. I'll have to be careful about how I put things. For now, work with the pages, will you? You'll have to be firm with young Ynedd. His mother spoiled the lad, and he snivels all the time."

"Well and good. I'll see what I can do."

Like all great lords, Cadryc had noble pages in his household, sons of his vassals sent to him for their training in warfare and courtesy. At ten summers Coryn was a decent enough lad, but Ynedd, a skinny little boy, all big blue eyes and blond curls, had never been away from his mother before. Gerran refused to let pity soften the lad's training; someday Ynedd's life would depend on how well he could fight.

They went round the back of the broch to practice away from the wagons and the livestock. Gerran let Coryn rest in the shade of the wall while he showed Ynedd the proper grip for the hilt.

"We'll have to work on your wrists," Gerran said. "All right, lay it down on the ground, then pick it up again."

Glancing sideways at him, Ynedd did as he was told. Gerran had him pick it up and lay it down five times in a row, each time correcting his grip. Finally Ynedd flung the sword down.

"I don't want to do this anymore," he announced.

"Too bad." Gerran caught the lad's gaze with his own. "Do it anyway."

Ynedd crossed his arms over his chest and glared. Gerran slapped him across the face.

"You can't do that to me!" Ynedd's voice rose to a squeal. "You're just a commoner."

"But he can." Coryn got up and trotted over. "He's the captain, and you've got to obey him. You truly truly do."

Ynedd's eyes filled with tears, but he picked up the sword. After a dozen times or so, Gerran saw that his little hand shook on the heavy hilt and told him that he could stop.

"There," Gerran said. "You've done somewhat you didn't think you could do."

Ynedd shrugged and glared at the cobblestones. Gerran sent the lads off to the stables to get their ponies for a riding lesson. As he started after them, he noticed Clae, standing and watching some paces away.

"Am I doing somewhat wrong?" Clae said.

"Not unless you're supposed to be working," Gerran said.

"I'm not. I just wanted to see. I wish I could learn to fight."

"Oh, do you now? Why?"

"So I could grow up to be a rider and kill Horsekin."

Something flat and cold in the lad's voice caught Gerran's attention, making him remember what had brought the lad to the dun. He knelt on one knee so he could look him in the face.

"That's an honorable enough thing," Gerran said. "How old are you? Do you know?"

"Eight, sir. My da always kept count. Could I ever be a rider? I'm only a scribe's son."

"So? Riders aren't noble-born. But here, training is hard work. I wager you'd tire of it soon enough."

"I wouldn't. When I got tired, I'd just think of my uncle, and I'd hate them all over again, and I wouldn't be tired anymore."

Gerran had never seen such cold rage in a child's eyes.

"I keep dreaming about our village," Clae went on. "The Horsekin come, and I try to stop them, and they laugh at me. I hate that dream."

"I'll wager you do. Have you told Neb about it?"

"I haven't. He'd only tell me I shouldn't be dwelling on what we can't change. You know what hurts the worst? When we were up by the waterfall watching them, I knew I couldn't do anything to stop them. Naught!" His soft voice cracked. "I never want to feel that way again."

Gerran considered him, a healthy child and big for his age, but it was the hatred that impressed Gerran the most. A desire for glory made most Deverry men want to be warriors, but it took harshness, that bitter streak in mind and soul, for a man to become a successful one.

"Tell you what," Gerran said. "If your brother agrees, I'll take you on, but I'll warn you, it's hard work, and even a wooden sword will hurt if you get hit with it. Fair?"

"Fair." Clae grinned at him. "Will the tieryn let me?"

"No doubt, if I ask him, but the question is whether your brother will let you. He's the head of your clan now. You ask him and tell him to come talk to me this afternoon."

While he gave his noble charges their riding lesson, Gerran occasionally found himself thinking about Clae, who reminded him of himself as a child. He could remember his own burning rage that the Horsekin had killed his father. The hatred still existed, though transmuted to something cold after all these years, as clean as a new sword blade. The gods of war had given Clae just such a splendid gift.

When they returned to the dun, Gerran found Neb waiting for him. The scribe came with him to the stables and held the horse's bridle while Gerran unsaddled him.

"I take it Clae spoke with you," Gerran said.

"He did," Neb said. "You know, he's the only bloodkin I have left in the world, and it aches my heart to see him wanting to join a warband."

"I can understand that."

"But I can't stand in his way either. From what everyone in the dun tells me, he'll have the best swordsman in all Deverry to learn from."

"Indeed?" Gerran felt himself blush at the compliment. "They exaggerate by a fair bit."

"We'll see." Neb smiled, more than a little ruefully. "But if you'll take Clae on, I'll agree. His wyrd isn't mine, and there's naught I can do about that."

"True spoken. But he'll have to serve a sort of apprenticeship. If he doesn't have the raw gifts he needs to make a swordsman, I'll turn him back over to you."

"Fair enough. I—" Neb stopped in midsentence and stared at something over Gerran's shoulder.

When Gerran turned, he saw Branna, walking across the ward at some distance. From the look in Neb's eyes Gerran suddenly realized that the scribe was besotted with the lass. With the realization came a baffling thought: deep in his soul Gerran knew that Neb had the better claim on her. Yet the thought of stepping back for the scribe—this skinny weakling—why he even knew how to read! *I'll not give up as easily as that,* Gerran told himself. *We'll just see who wins her.*

Without a word aloud Gerran turned to follow her. Neb did the same, but they both stopped when they saw Salamander coming to meet her. The gerthddyn bowed to her with such courtly grace that she smiled and allowed him to take her arm as they strolled away.

"Curse his very soul!" Gerran whispered.

"It's not his soul that troubles me," Neb said.

In sullen brotherhood they turned and strode back to the ward, out of sight of Branna and the good-looking gerthddyn both.

Behind the broch, at a pleasant distance from the pigsty and the dung heap, the cook had planted a kitchen garden. Slender beds of herbs separated each plot of cabbages, turnips, and the like. In their aromatic midst stood a little bench, where Salamander led Branna for their talk.

"Tell me somewhat," Salamander said. "What do you think of young Neb? And of Gerran for that matter."

"Everyone seems to be asking me that these days," Branna said. "Are you trying to marry me off, too?"

"Do I look like a village matchmaker?"

"Truly, you don't. So why did you ask me about Neb and Gerran?"

"They both seem besotted with you. That's all."

"They are, aren't they?" Branna sounded deeply surprised. "How very odd."

"Now here! Not so odd for a pretty lass like you."

"But very odd for a lass who has no dowry to speak of."

"You don't value yourself highly, do you, my lady?"

"How could I? My stepmother never let a chance go by to remind me how lowly I was. She used to suggest that I become a priestess, since obviously I'd never make a good marriage."

"A nasty sort, was she? A veritable shrew, virago, termagant, and so on and so forth."

"All of that, good sir, and more. Do you know what it's like to have your kin begrudge the food you eat?"

"I do, oddly enough," Salamander said. "But I didn't have to suffer it as long. How did you manage to keep from going mad?"

"What? And let her claim a victory?"

They shared a laugh.

"But your question's worthy of an answer," Branna went on. "At first, I wasn't truly alone. When I was small, there were the servants' children in my father's dun to play with—not my precious stepbrothers, of course, who weren't allowed to talk to someone so far beneath them."

"It's a pity your stepmother didn't get carried off by Horsekin. They would have understood each other very well."

Branna grinned at him, then went on. "I did have Aunt Galla to look out for my interests, too." The grin disappeared. "Until her husband was offered this demesne, and they moved out here."

"So our good tieryn's not held this dun for very long?"

"He hasn't. He and Galla used to live about twenty miles east of here, not far from my father's dun, which is farther east still. But when the king established this demesne, the gwerbret assigned it to Cadryc. I saw Aunt Galla but rarely after that, and the servants' children had all been set to working by then."

"But you survived."

"I did. I learned how to be alone, you see. I made up little tales to ease my heart, like, about some other time and some other place in Deverry." She looked away with a sigh. A long strand of hair had pulled free of the clasp and hung beside her cheek. With an irritated wave of her hand she flipped it back, but when it fell forward again, she ignored it.

"What sort of tales?" Salamander said. "I find myself most curious, if you'd care to tell me."

"Oh, well, they were stupid things, I suppose." Branna suddenly blushed. "I'm sorry I mentioned them."

"Don't be. Please, they can't be very stupid if you told them. You strike me as a levelheaded lass."

"I do? Most people call me strange."

"Most people are half-blind no matter how good their eyes. But I *am* a gerthddyn, you know. Hearing about someone else's tales always interests me."

Another sigh, another glance away—for a moment she perched so uneasily on the edge of the bench that he feared she'd get up and bolt; then she settled back.

"I made up this other then, this other when, you see, another world, really, though it was much like Deverry. And in it, this world—" She paused for a moment.

Salamander gave her an encouraging smile.

"Well, I used to pretend that I was a mighty sorcerer. I traveled all over the kingdom, and to Bardek, and to marvelous islands far far away. I could call down a strange blue fire to light my way, and once, when I was trapped in a burning building, I commanded the wind to save me."

"Sounds splendid, indeed."

"In one tale, I could even turn myself into a bird and fly."

"And this bird, it was a falcon, wasn't it?"

Branna slewed around on the bench and stared at him while the color drained from her face. "How do you know that?" she was whispering. "Or are sorcerous powers a common delusion among lonely females?"

"Not at all. Most lonely lasses dream about meeting a prince who loves them madly."

She laughed with a toss of her head, and in that gesture he could see the hard common sense that once had been hers, in that other when, that other where. "True enough," she said. "But how did you know about my falcon?"

"My mysterious bardic powers, of course. Ah, I see you don't believe me."

"You're not a bard. If you were, maybe I'd believe you, but you're a gerthddyn. How did you know?"

"Ah, therein lies an enigma, most recondite, obscure, and elusive." Salamander paused. He could hear voices coming toward them. "And it's one you absolutely must solve for yourself." He stood up with a wave in the direction of the voices. "Here comes our good tieryn and his son, so, alas, I must leave you."

Branna jumped up and grabbed him by the shirt with both hands. "Tell me, you chattering elf!" She let him go and stepped back, blushing furiously. "A thousand apologies! I don't know what made me do that. I mean, you're not even an elf. It was wretchedly rude of me. Please forgive me!"

"You're forgiven, and here's one last bit of advice. Be careful around Gerran. He might carry the falcon mark, but I doubt me if he'll ever turn into a bird and fly."

"I figured that out on my own, good sir."

"Good sir, is it?" Salamander grinned at her, and in a moment she smiled in return.

Arguing in quiet voices, Cadryc and Mirryn rounded the corner and bore down upon them. When Salamander jumped back out of the way, the two lords finally realized that they had an audience.

"Apologies," Cadryc snapped. "Branna, my dear, I didn't see you."

"No harm done, Uncle." Branna rose and curtsied. "I'll just be going inside."

The three men paused and watched her trot off, holding her skirts up to keep them free of the dirty ground.

"I'd best be going, too," Salamander said. "My lords?"

They nodded their permission. Salamander hurried away, but he ducked behind the cook's little gardening shed to eavesdrop.

"I'll not argue one word more," Cadryc was saying. "We're leaving on the morrow, and you're not, and that's that."

"But—"

"I said not one word more!"

In a few moments Mirryn stormed past Salamander without seeing him. Cadryc followed more slowly, shaking his head. Salamander stepped out and bowed to him.

"Your Grace?" Salamander said. "Forgive me if I presume, but
one day your son is going to have to try his wings."

Cadryc tossed his head like a startled horse and glowered at him.
Salamander bowed again, then smiled in what he hoped was an in-
gratiating manner.

"Ah, well," Cadryc said at last. "You're right enough, gerthddyn. It's just—" He paused, chewing on the corners of his mustache. "It's just—well, you're a gerthddyn. You must hear plenty of
strange tales, eh?"

"More than a few, truly, my lord."

"Imph." Cadryc hesitated for a few moments more, then
shrugged. "Well, there was a prophecy, you see. I've never told
Mirryn or my wife about it, because to tell you the honest truth, I'm
cursed ashamed of believing it."

"A prophecy? From a priest?"

"A priest of a sort, I suppose you'd call him. It was what? about
ten summers ago now. The Horsekin were raiding up north, and the
old gwerbret summoned his allies. This was the raid where he was
killed, come to think of it. Anyway. We managed to find their stinking ugly camp, and we fell on them by surprise and slaughtered the
guards and their reserves. We freed the human captives, some of
the gwerbret's farm folk, and then some others who'd been
Horsekin slaves." Cadryc paused, looking away as if getting his
memories in order. "Now, among the human men was this one
scabby fellow, dressed all in rags, and his feet were all swollen and
crusted with calluses, just like he'd never worn shoes in his life.
Turned out he hadn't, actually. But all the folk who'd been born
slaves treated him like he was a king. The gwerbret's farm folk told
us that he was a priest of their cursed foreign goddess."

"Alshandra again?" Salamander said. "Huntress of Souls?"

"The same one, truly. Like that gold arrow we found in the
burned village."

"Indeed. Do go on. This is most fascinating, engrossing, mesmerizing, and the like."

"All of that, eh? Well, now, this priest fellow refused to eat. Said he'd starve himself to death rather than put up with being our prisoner. A lot of gall, if you ask me, since his cursed Horsekin had been taking our folk prisoner! We thought about killing him, of course, but it's risky, killing priests. What if their god decides to take a little vengeance, eh?"

"Quite right. You can't be too careful."

"So anyway, we lords got together and talked about forcing him to eat. But I spoke up and said let him do what he wanted, if he was so blasted keen on dying. I could see the indignity of it, being tied up and having gruel poured down your throat or suchlike, and so the other lords agreed. And the scabby fellow thanked me, if you can imagine it! Thanked me for letting him starve to death! In return, says he, I'll give you a prophecy. Keep your son safe till his nineteenth summer begins. Do that and he'll live a fair long time. Let him fight before that, and he'll die young." Cadryc looked down at the ground and shrugged again. "No doubt you think me a fool for believing the filthy bastard."

"I don't," Salamander said. "I can see where a prophecy like that would chill a father's heart. What happened to the priest?"

"He starved, just like he wanted. Took him a long time, but he went happily enough at the end."

"Do you remember his name, by any chance?"

"I don't, though I can still see his face clear as clear in my mind."

"And how old is Mirryn?"

"Eighteen summers now." Cadryc looked up. "I'm ashamed to admit it, but I've been keeping track. Every Beltane I put a mark on my saddle peak, just a little nick in the leather."

"You know, I can't say why, but I have this feeling that you're right to keep him out of the fighting."

"Do you now? Then my thanks. I just can't bring myself to ignore it, and ye gods, his nineteenth summer will start next year anyway. He's the only son I have."

The thing that Salamander couldn't admit to the tieryn was that he'd received an omen of his own. When he was listening to Cadryc describe the prophecy, he felt an icy cold ripple down his back, a warning from the dweomer that indeed, it had been a true speaking. *Too bad that wretched priest died,* he thought. *He must have had dweomer, and I would have loved to have asked him a few questions.*

"What about those rescued farm women?" Salamander said. "Are any of them still with us?"

"As far as I know. They were all young women then. Why?"

"Because I love a good tale. Indeed, my very living depends upon my having a store of good tales. 'Lasses captured by Horsekin but saved in the nick of time!' That should extract a few coins from those who lead safe but dull lives."

"You could be right about that, indeed. Well, my thanks for listening, gerthddyn, but I'll ask you not to spread my part of the tale around."

"Don't worry, Your Grace, I'd never presume. I have a son of my own, you see, and I can sympathize."

That son was very much on Salamander's mind when he contacted Dallandra again, late that evening when he could be alone to scry her out. First he told her what he'd gleaned about the situation in the dun, including Branna's tales.

"Well," Dallandra thought to him. "I'd say that she's ready to remember, and doubtless Neb is, too, with her there in the same dun, but you can't force such things upon people. If they're not ready to ask on their own, their minds will shy away like frightened horses, and then they might never come to the point of asking."

"Yes, that's very true. May I drop portentous hints?"

"Knowing you, you probably won't be able to stop yourself. Just make them hard to understand, will you?"

"Fear not. I shall do just that. Mystery, mazelike and mindfooling, shall be my mode."

Dallandra set her lips together and glared at him.

"One thing I wanted to ask you," Salamander said hurriedly. "Have you seen my Zan recently?"

"No. When the winter camps broke up, he went with your father's alar. They'll be at the summer festival, though, and I'll have news for you then."

"Good, and thank you. Soon, I hope, I'm going to Cengarn with the tieryn and his men. I'll take my leave of them there and start traveling around, plying the inhabitants with questions as I go. I have hopes of catching up with Rhodry as well as gleaning information about the Horsekin."

"Good. Just be very careful, will you? And stay in contact with me. I'll talk to Dar, but I can't imagine why he wouldn't lead the alar north. At some point we can meet up."

"A most excellent plan, Oh princess of powers perilous! And fear not, I shan't be silent. Being silent goes against my nature."

The summer festival took place during the days surrounding the longest day of the year. Prince Dar's scribe, Meranaldar, told Dallandra that in ancient times, when the great observatory at Rinbaladelan still stood, the festival had begun at noon on the longest day, but out in the grass no one bothered to measure time so precisely. Some alarli rode in early, others late, and no one stayed long before they were forced to ride out to find better pasture for their stock. By custom, however, the prince's alar always arrived first. By counting days, Meranaldar did his best to keep track of the sun's position in the sky in order to determine what he called the "real" start of the festival. At times he would thrust a wooden pole into the ground and study its shadow at noon—why, Dallandra didn't know.

They held the festival at the Lake of the Leaping Trout, the northernmost of the chain that Deverry folk call Peddroloc, the four lakes, all of which lay in steep valleys. To the north of Leaping Trout the land flattened, but rather than grass, trees grew there, an orchard of pines, pruned and planted in straight rows for fuel.

The People cremated their dead. Whenever a person died, his

kin took the seasoned wood waiting in one of the stone sheds near the lakeshore. After the cremation ritual, a tree was cut to replace the firewood, and a new tree planted in its stead. Thus the summer festival, held in the shadow of the death ground, tended to be a solemn affair, a time to remember those who had died in recent years, an appropriate sentiment since the longest day marked the turning of the year, when summer itself would begin to fade and die.

"There's something I've been wondering about," Dallandra said to Meranaldar. "The way the trees are cut and planted. Is that an old custom?"

"Ancient," the scribe said. "It goes back to the Seven Cities, most certainly. It sprang from a very odd belief, that every person lives multiple lives. Nothing but superstition, of course, but a persistent one."

"Indeed?" Dallandra managed to suppress her sudden urge to laugh. "I suppose then that the planting of the new tree was symbolic."

"Yes, of the person's supposed new life. That's what the priests of the Star Goddesses taught, at any rate. A number of texts survive. A bad lot, those priests, or so history tells us. Some survived the Great Burning, but they were thrown overboard somewhere in the journey across the Southern Sea."

"They were? By the Dark Sun herself! I never knew that."

"You didn't?" Meranaldar frowned in thought. "Oh, yes, of course. It was Princess Carra whom I told, and I don't remember you being there at the time. The refugees ran dangerously short of water, you see, and the priests claimed a greater share. They based their reasoning, if one can call it that, on doctrine. Since they'd been born into the religious elite, they claimed, then in a previous life they'd done something to accrue great merit, and thus they deserved more of everything in this life."

"What a pernicious idea! I'll wager there was a corollary, too, that the common people deserved whatever ill luck came their way."

"Exactly. The reasoning had ceased to be compelling, with Rinbaladelan in ruins behind them and so many people dead. The soldiers on the ship tossed the priests overboard, where they could have all the water they wanted." Meranaldar paused for a smile. "That very evening it rained, and the barrels they'd brought along for drinking water were filled to overflowing. The soldiers took this as a sign of the gods' approval. Thus are new doctrines born."

They shared a laugh as they walked on. Dallandra had often wondered why the dweomermasters insisted that their belief in multiple lives be kept secret. She was beginning to understand.

They were walking together in the forest, following one of the cool, shaded lanes between the trees. When he'd first come to the Westlands, Meranaldar had been a thin man, hollow-chested and stoop-shouldered, but forty years of riding with the royal alar had strengthened him. Now, no one would ever have confused him with a warrior, not with his slender arms and soft hands, but he stood straight and moved with the graceful ease of someone who knows his own strength.

"Tomorrow the first alarli should arrive," Dallandra said. "I'll be interested to see how many new babies we have, if any."

"There will be some," Meranaldar said. "At the Day of Remembrance, I noticed that a good many women were pregnant. What we need to do is tally up the number of our changelings."

"That's true. We were up to forty-seven of them this spring. I'm particularly wondering about Carra's new granddaughter."

"Indeed. So far, the changelings seem to have very kindly spread themselves around, one to a family. It's a good thing, since they can be such a burden."

"Yes. The gods must be taking a hand."

Meranaldar smiled, a bit too indulgently in her opinion. He could be condescending, the scribe, but she was too grateful for the knowledge he'd brought with him to hold it against him. Besides, she knew better than he did that it wasn't the gods who were lending their aid, but a once-human man: Aderyn.

Whenever she attended the birth of a wild child or held a newborn in her arms, she could feel Aderyn's presence—naught so perceptible as a ghost, but rather a touch of mind on mind, a sense that he was reaching out to her across the planes. To fulfill his wyrd, Aderyn in his last life should have helped her heal the Guardians and the flock of half-formed souls that followed them. He'd shirked that duty. Now, while he still existed in the state that ordinary mortals call death, he was carrying it out as best he could, guiding their souls to birth and physical life.

The first alar to appear at the festival brought with it the oldest wild child, Zandro, Salamander's grown son, who lived with Salamander's father, Devaberiel Silverhand, the most famous bard in the Westlands. The other men in their alar set up the bard's tent next to the prince's, a sign of rank as well as a convenience. Dallandra strolled over to greet them. Devaberiel seemed thinner than the last time she'd seen him, and his moonbeam-pale hair had turned completely white. His eyes, the dark blue of the night sky in moonlight, still snapped with life and good humor, and his face, though finely drawn, showed none of the folds and gouges of old age that signaled, among the People, approaching death.

His grandson couldn't have looked more different. Short and stocky, Zandro had pale brown skin and brown hair that he wore in a mop of curls. His eyes had changed color since childhood; they were now a deep sunset orange, not quite as red as blood. When he saw Dalla, he turned his head to look at her sideways and grinned, revealing his mouthful of sharply pointed teeth.

"Dalla," he said.

It was the first time Dalla had ever heard Zandro say anyone's name, and Devaberiel smiled as proudly as if his grandson had just rattled off "The Burning of the Vale of Roses" or some other equally long and complex poem.

"Yes," Dallandra said, "I'm Dalla. You're Zandro."

Zandro flicked his eyes his grandfather's way, then giggled and trotted off, heading for the pack of children and dogs playing on the lakeshore.

"He's got a long way to go yet," Devaberiel said, "but we make progress."

"You certainly do. I'll admit to being surprised."

"Valandario's been helping me, actually." Dev glanced around. "I don't see her. She's probably setting up her tent."

"I'd best go greet her."

Dallandra picked her way through the growing encampment. She had so many people to greet that she made slow progress, but at last she reached the edge of the camp. For the festival, she'd had some of the men position her tent away from the crowd, where she could find some quiet for her workings. As she'd expected, Valandario had done the same, picking a spot near but not too near to Dallandra's own.

Val's tent, so plain and gray on the outside, inside gleamed with color—elaborately woven panels and embroidered tent bags, mostly blue and green, touched here and there with gold, hung on the walls, while red, silver, and purple Bardek carpets and cushions lay strewn over the floor cloth. Sunlight from outside glowed through the walls. Entering the tent made Dalla think of walking into a giant jewelry box. Valandario herself sat on a red-and-gold carpet with jewels and gemstones spread out in front of her. She'd strewn them onto a scrying cloth, patched from Bardek silks. Some squares and triangles were plain, others embroidered with symbols, and here and there larger embroideries overlapped two squares. What they all meant only Valandario knew. She had derived this scrying system herself over a hundred years of hard work.

"Am I disturbing you?" Dallandra said.

"Not at all," Val said. "In fact, I'm glad you're here. I've done this reading twice today, and I can't seem to interpret it."

Dallandra sat down on the opposite side of the scrying cloth. Light came in through the smoke hole in the roof, caught Val's golden hair, and made it gleam like the silks. She held up delicate hands, clasped over a fresh handful of semiprecious stones. She whispered an invocation of the Lords of Aethyr, then scattered the gems over the cloth. Amethysts, citrines, lapis beads, dark jades, and fire opals—they lay glittering on the patches of silk among the rarer jewels. Here and there, as ominous as wolves lurking around a flock of sheep, sat tear-shaped drops of obsidian.

"I don't see any pattern at all," Dallandra said.

"Neither do I." Valandario looked up with a brief smile. "That's the problem."

"Which makes me assume that there's trouble coming our way."

"I'm afraid I have to agree. How many gems have fallen on their own colors? Only four out of twenty, and the black have dropped on the gold squares. I don't like this." Val shook her head. "I don't like it at all." She began gathering up the stones and shoving them into leather pouches. "I've spent too much time poring over it, and it still baffles me. The first spread was even more chaotic. Two stones rolled right off the cloth."

"That sounds ominous."

"Something is happening—no, something is trying to happen, some large event is struggling to be born, and it doesn't bode well." She frowned as she pulled pouch strings tight. "That's all I can say."

"It matches the omen-dreams I've been having."

"Then there's nothing we can do but wait."

"Wait and be cautious. I was wondering, do you think you could join your alar to the prince's? I'd feel better knowing that another dweomermaster rode on guard."

"I don't see why not. Dev always enjoys exchanging lore with the prince's scribe, and I'd be glad of the chance do some more reading in your books."

"Good. If we keep traveling fast, there won't be a problem finding enough food and water for both herds."

"And it seems to me that fast is the way we should be traveling, for a lot of reasons." Val patted the pouch of stones with one hand. "I'll tell you what. We'll leave a day before you and then camp where there's plenty of grass. Once you catch up, we'll head straight north. I'd best tell Dev now, so he doesn't plan an extra performance."

They went to look for Devaberiel and found him a little ways from camp, where he was standing and practicing his latest declamation with only the grass for an audience.

"Clinging like lice on the backs of hoofed death—" Dev broke off in midsentence, then grinned at the two women. "Not, of course, that I was speaking of you."

"I assumed that," Valandario said. "I just wanted to tell you that I've changed our plans. We'll be leaving the festival a little early, then joining the prince's alar."

"All right." Dev shrugged, smiling. "Whatever you two think best."

Dallandra left them discussing details and walked back to camp.

Over the next several days, some of the earlier arrivals rode out, taking their stock to better pasture. New alarli rode in to take their places, and one of them brought a changeling infant with them. The bewildered father, Londrojezry, escorted Dallandra out to the horse herd to see the child before he'd even unpacked his travois. On top of a pile of tied-down blankets, the baby lay in a cradle of leather stretched over a wooden frame, and his purple eyes showed nothing but suspicion.

"He hates to be touched," Lon said. "He screams if you try to pick him up."

"How has your wife been feeding him?" Dalla said. "He doesn't look malnourished."

"She has to express her milk into a bowl. First she dipped it up with a bit of cloth and gave him that to suck. Now, and my thanks to the Star Goddesses, he'll take it from a spoon. But it's still exhausting her, it takes so long."

"He was born when?"

"Six moons ago."

"Try feeding him something other than milk. Deverry oats cooked to a fine paste, and broths."

"My thanks, Wise One." For a moment Lon stood looking down at the cradle with tear-filled eyes. "I wanted a son so badly." Then he stooped, picking up the cradle. "I'll tell my wife about the food."

Dallandra watched him hurry away. She'd seen this type of changeling before, and she knew that nothing but more grief lay ahead for him and his father both. They became utterly withdrawn as they aged, this kind of child. Some wandered away from their alarli and were never seen again; others drifted along at the edge of their parents' camps, accepting food or the occasional piece of clothing but nothing more, never speaking, never reaching out.

And yet, as she walked back to camp, she found herself wrestling with a strange feeling: envy. Not envy of having a changeling, certainly, but—of what? Lon's wife loved that child so much she was draining her own life to keep him alive, and he'd never repay her with anything but grief. But would the grief truly matter to her? *To love someone that much. Is that what I envy?* Dallandra wondered at herself. It seemed a sick sort of thing, that kind of love.

Later that evening, Dalla stood just beyond a circle of firelight and watched Lon feeding his son a broth of oats boiled with milk. The wife, Allanaseradario, hunkered nearby and watched as the child slurped up the food. Now and then she would wipe its sticky chin with a bit of rag. Dalla felt all her familiar disgust with the mess and raw crudity of caring for infants. *I made my choice,* she thought. *I took the dweomer willingly.* Yet the envy came back, squeezing her heart, it seemed, as she stood in the shadows, looking into the circle of firelight. Finally she turned away with a toss of her head only to realize that Calonderiel was standing nearby, watching her in turn. She waited for him to speak, but he merely walked away, shoving his hands into his pockets and striding off.

The time was wrong to think of grievous things. The festival proceeded with songs and declamations, feasts and dancing, powerful enough to draw most of the changelings into a web of laughter and good music. For an afternoon here, an evening there, Dallandra could even forget the danger gathering in the west. But the threat never quite left her, and others feared as well. Carra in particular began to worry about her younger daughter, Perra, riding with her husband's alar.

"They really should have been here by now," Carra remarked one morning. "Dalla, don't you think so?"

"Perhaps, but the festival only began three days ago."

"I suppose," Carra said, "but you never know these days. Things happen. If the Horsekin start raiding . . . " She let her voice trail away.

"That's true enough," Dallandra said. "I'll scry."

Dalla walked down to the lakeshore and stared at the rippled water while she thought about Perra. The image built up fast: Perra was kneeling in the grass and lashing a blanket-wrapped bundle to a travois while her husband led over the horse chosen to pull it. *Thanks be to the Star Goddesses!* Dallandra thought. *I wonder how I would have told Carra if they'd come to harm?* Carra loved her children extravagantly, just like Londrojezry and his wife. *And I?* The question nagged at Dalla all day.

One worry solved itself when Perra and her alar rode in before nightfall. Dallandra was relieved to see that the new grandchild, some four months old, showed every sign of being an ordinary baby. In fact, she looked completely elvish, with furled ears and cat-slit purple eyes, just as if her grandmother's human nature had never tainted her blood.

"I'm glad, too," Carra told Dallandra. "She won't get teased about her ears the way poor Perra was. Children can be so awfully cruel."

"Well," Dalla said, "they do cruel things, but they do them out of ignorance. They don't know how much pain they're causing."

"I suppose. At least Rori's learned to fight back. The last time someone teased him, he knocked him down with one good punch."

"He seems to have something in common with the man you named him for."

They shared a laugh at Rhodry Maelwaedd's expense.

"It's so odd, Dalla," Carra went on. "Here you never wanted children of your own, but you've ended up the honorary aunt of so many. Every mother who has a changeling in her care turns to you for advice."

"You're right, aren't you? It goes to show, that you never know what your wyrd is going to bring you. But I did have a child once, a son—I must have told you that story."

"You did, yes. I'm sorry, I'd just forgotten him."

I tend to do that myself, Dallandra thought. *Poor little Loddlaen!* Aloud, she said, "Well, it was all a very long time ago now."

Carra let the subject drop.

And of course, there were more worries than those about children for the alarli to discuss. When she told the men in Perra's alar about Salamander's fears of a Horsekin incursion, they had information for her, a few scraps only, but better than nothing. She contacted Salamander that very evening. In the vision she could dimly see a stone wall behind him and a faint silver light.

"Where are you?" Dallandra thought to him. "I'm at the festival, and I've heard something about the Horsekin."

"Up on the catwalks of our good tieryn's wall. I came up to watch the moon rise, actually, though I had thoughts of contacting you once it had. Tell me what you've learned, oh mistress of magicks mysterious. I hang upon your every thought."

"Well, it's rather short on hard fact. One of the alarli here told me about an escaped Horsekin slave. They helped her get back to her people in Deverry, late last autumn, that was. As far as they can remember, she'd escaped from somewhere not all that far from the Westlands, up north and west somewhere. Either she didn't know, or they didn't remember just how far she'd traveled after she got away."

"Of course. But alas, alack, and welladay anyway."

"Now, they did ask her what Horsekin were doing, traveling so far south of their own country. She said she'd been brought along to cook for a group of important officials, whatever that may mean, traveling with a large armed escort. They were looking for something, she said, a good place to build something. She didn't know what. They wouldn't have told the likes of her any details."

"My worst fear begins to materialize before me, but you have my thanks."

"*Your* worst fear? It ranks high among mine, and Cal's, too."

"No doubt." His image turned thoughtful. "Have you seen Zandro yet?"

"Yes, indeed I have, and here's some good news. He can call some people by name now. He knows his own, and mine, and of course your father's and a few of your father's friends."

"Splendid!"

"And he's become quite protective of the little changelings. He and Elessi lead the little ones like a pack of wolves. They run through the camp together and laugh at everything. Zan's not hit anyone or pulled hair or any such nasty trick, not since we've been here."

"Wonderful! That gives me some hope he'll find happiness of a sort."

"Me, too." Dalla felt suddenly weary. "When I worked so hard at getting those souls born, I didn't stop to think of what they'd be like in their very first incarnation. Poor little spirits! They should have taken flesh when the world was new."

"Indeed. In time they'll grow full minds."

"So we can hope. I honestly don't know how many lives it will take them. But Zan at least has become very nicely behaved. Dev has the most amazing patience."

"Now. He certainly never showed any with me."

"Well, he was much younger then. He didn't know how to treat a small child."

"I suppose he did the best he could, given that my mother didn't want me."

Dalla could feel the bitterness in his thoughts—still, after nearly two hundred years. "She didn't have much choice," she said. "The fault lies in the way Deverry men treat their women, or so your father told me."

"Perhaps. I don't truly remember her, anyway, except that she was pink and soft and warm, and her name was Morri."

"That wasn't your mother. That was your nursemaid. Dev did

tell me that much, but you know, it's odd, he truly didn't want to tell me more."

In the image of his face she could see confusion, and his thoughts swirled round like autumn leaves, picked up and blown in circles by the wind, until, like leaves the wind has dropped, his mind steadied again. "Well, it hardly matters now," Salamander thought to her. "But sometime when we have a moment to spare for talking about things long past, I'd like to hear the story."

"Your father would most likely tell you more than he'd tell me." Salamander's image looked profoundly sad.

"But we could always ask him for the tale together," Dallandra said hurriedly. "I'm surprised you've not heard it already."

"So am I. Continually, perennially, and eternally surprised, every time the subject comes up between me and the esteemed progenitor." His face-image displayed a forced smile. "You would doubtless be even more surprised at the speed with which he can leap away from the subject, like a cat when someone empties a bucket of water nearby." His image smiled in unconvincing dismissal. "But it matters naught. Tomorrow we leave for Cengarn. I'll keep you informed of what happens there."

Abruptly Salamander broke the link. She'd touched on an old, deep wound, Dallandra realized, and one that, in time, she would have to help him heal.

I'm surprised you've not heard it already. After he broke the scrying-link, Salamander realized that his right hand had clenched into a fist and that he was tempted to throw a hard punch into the stones of the tieryn's wall. A gaggle of gnomes materialized at his feet and raised little paws, as if signaling caution.

"Yes, smashing flesh into stone means one thing only," Salamander said in Elvish. "The stone wins."

With the Wildfolk trailing after, he climbed down from the wall and headed for the broch. Thinking about his childhood always filled him with melancholy, and he was considering drowning the feeling with some good dark ale. He reached the door of the great hall just as Branna was coming out of it, a candle lantern in her hand. The light coming through the pierced tin dappled her face in a pattern like stars.

"Good evening to you, my lady," Salamander said. "Have you come out to enjoy the night air?"

"I have, truly," Branna said. "It gets stuffy up in my chamber."

"Hum, I find myself wondering if perhaps Neb's chamber grows just as stuffy. Could it be that he's out here as well, just by coincidence of course, out in the herb garden, say?"

"And would it be any of your affair if he was?"

"None, of course. But if I were you, I'd make sure Gerran didn't know what you were up to."

"Gerran is drinking with his men. They won't stop till they're all staggering."

"Love can make a man as drunk as ale does."

"True spoken, but when he's drunk on ale, he can't lift his sword."

"Nor can he lift much else. I trust Neb is the sober sort?"

"Oh!" Branna caught her breath and blushed. "Do hold your tongue, you chattering elf!"

"Now I wonder," Salamander said, grinning, "where you got that turn of phrase. That I chatter is a point beyond disputing, but someone else used to call me that, and I think me we both knew her well."

Branna stared at him for a long moment, then turned in a swirl of dresses and rushed across the ward, heading for the herb garden. Salamander stepped inside the great hall and saw Gerran and his men clustered around a table, wagering furiously on some game or other. Salamander considered joining them, then climbed the staircase instead. Behind him more Wildfolk materialized to follow in a silvery, translucent parade.

In his little chamber Salamander sat on the wide windowsill and looked out over the nighttime dun. Here and there points of light gleamed in a window or bobbed along, a lantern held in someone's hand. He could distantly hear, like the murmur of a river, the sounds from the great hall. A dog barked out by the stables, then fell silent.

"This could turn nasty," he remarked to the Wildfolk. "Neb, Branna, and Gerran, I mean."

The Wildfolk all nodded their agreement.

"But yet I have hope. From everything Dalla's told me, Cullyn well and truly broke that particular chain of wyrd in the last life he shared with Branna. If Gerran remembers—not that he'll know he's remembering, of course—but if he does remember, deep in his mind somewhere, then mayhap the outcome will be a fair one. And if the outcome is foul, then we'll know that he doesn't remember Cullyn of Cerrmor's wisdom."

The Wildfolk stared at him and solemnly scratched their heads, miming confusion.

"I could have put that more clearly, truly," Salamander said. "Mayhap it's time for me to get some sleep."

The Wildfolk all nodded vigorously, then one at a time, disappeared. Yawning, he took off all his clothes but his loin-wrap and lay down on the mattress. He considered a blanket, but the summer night was still hot. Wrapped in its warmth, he fell asleep.

Salamander woke to the sound of furious words outside his chamber and the pink light of a cloudy dawn beyond his window. He sat up and listened till he could place the voices: Gerran and Mirryn, arguing over Cadryc's predictable orders to his son and heir.

"You've got to rein that temper in," Gerran was saying. "You cannot challenge your own father to an honor duel, and you know it."

"It's all very well for you to talk, Gerro." Mirryn's voice shook with rage. "No one's going to think you're a coward. Now get your hands off me! I want to go back and tell Father—"

"You're not going to tell him one word more."

A pause, a long pause that brought Salamander to his feet, ready to intervene if things turned nasty. He took a few barefoot steps toward the door.

"Oh, very well," Mirryn said at last. "You're right, aren't you? My apologies."

"I knew you'd see reason eventually." Gerran sounded vastly relieved that his foreknowledge had proved true. "There's naught cowardly or womanish about keeping fort guard, not when the valley's crawling with Horsekin raiders."

No more words, and their footsteps moved away. *I'd best get dressed,* Salamander told himself. *Today's the day we ride to Cengarn.* When he went to the window and looked down, he could see the groom and the pages leading out horses for the men of the warband to saddle. Tieryn Cadryc was striding around the ward, giving orders and organizing the line of march.

Salamander was just finishing a hasty breakfast in the great hall when Lady Branna came downstairs. He started to rise to go meet her, but instead she came over to speak to him.

"Midda told me that you're going to Cengarn with my uncle," Branna said.

"I am." Salamander laid his spoon down in his empty porridge bowl. "I'm like a gleaner, always scavenging bits of other men's lives to bake into the bread of my tales."

"Oh, I like that fancy way of putting it! What sort of bits will you be looking for?"

"Tales of the Horsekin raiders, for one, and then information about the dragons. You know about the dragons, surely?"

"I've heard about them. The farmers on my father's lands were always afraid that they'd take their cows or their lambs."

"It's a justified fear, no doubt." Salamander glanced out the door, but the warband was still readying itself to ride. "Did you ever see them?"

"I think I saw the silver wyrm once, but it was just at twilight, and it was hard to tell." Branna's expression turned sour. "My dearest stepmother told me I'd seen naught but an owl flying high.

She made fun of me for days over it, too, but truly, I'd know an owl if I should see one."

"I'm sure you would." Salamander found himself thinking of Aderyn and suppressed a laugh with difficulty.

He was about to say more when Neb came hurrying downstairs, a bedroll slung over one shoulder. Branna smiled at the sight of him and left to join him without another word to Salamander. Together, talking softly, they went outside. Salamander followed, but he went to the stables, where he found Clae saddling his gray riding horse. His packhorse stood nearby, already loaded with his gear. Someone had made the boy a better shirt by cutting down an old one and resewing it to fit. On its yokes were faded blazons, the tieryn's Red Wolf.

"My thanks," Salamander said.

"Most welcome." Clae grinned at him. "You saved our lives and got us here, and I'm truly grateful, and so I thought I should tend your horses at least."

"A very courtly gesture, indeed. Well, lad, I may not see you for a while now, but I'll hope things work out well for you."

"And I'll do the same for you."

Salamander mounted, took the lead rope for the packhorse when Clae tossed it up to him, and headed out. He caught up with the rest of the riders just as they were clattering out of the gates. Neb was riding just behind the tieryn. *I should get the chance to talk with him on this ride,* Salamander thought, *and make some of those portentous hints Dalla agreed to.* The thought of finally being able to lord it over Nevyn, after all the times that the old man had reproached, rebuked, and generally reviled him, was so cheering that he broke into song as the troop headed for the north-running road.

The gwerbret's city of Cengarn lay two days' ride to the northeast of Cadryc's dun, at a spot where the tableland turned into hills on its rise toward the northern mountains. It was a strange sort of place, Cengarn, situated on three hills, surrounded on three sides by stone walls. On the fourth side, the western, a smooth-faced cliff provided a better fortification than any that hands might build. Even the approach to the southern gates was steep enough that the warband had to dismount and lead their horses up a winding path.

Inside the walls, however, the town sported as much greenery as it did stone. Among the thatched round houses, set along curving streets, grew trees and gardens—practical vegetables, mostly, but here and there they passed patches of flowers, blooming around cottage doors. In the middle of town, on the crest of a roundish hill, lay the grassy commons. Judging from the number of people and wagons clustered upon it, the town was setting up for a market fair. As they walked their horses round the hill, Gerran spotted a pair of wooden doors built right into the hillside—a dwarven inn, run by and for merchants from the Roof of the World. Gerran knew the town and the dun well. He and Lord Mirryn had been pages together in the household of Gwerbret Daen, the now-dead father of the current gwerbret.

On the highest hill, perched above the sheer western cliff, stood the dun of the gwerbrets of Cengarn. Behind yet another wall the towers of a multiple broch complex loomed. The guards at the great iron-bound gates recognized Cadryc immediately and bowed, ushering him in to the crowded ward, which held the usual jumble of stables, storage sheds, pigsties, and the like. Pages and grooms came running across the ward to greet the tieryn and take the horses from him and his men. A councilor hurried out to lead him into the great hall.

While the tieryn was presenting himself to the gwerbret, Gerran made arrangements with the gwerbret's captain for sheltering his men. Almost absentmindedly, he included the gerthddyn. The escort received bunks together at one end of the best barracks, up above the stables but near the broch complex. In the warmth of a summer afternoon, the stables below stank, and the stink rose through the rough wood floor.

"By your leave, Captain," Salamander said in a strangled sort of voice. "I think I'll find myself shelter in an inn."

"Oh, you get used to the smell after a while."

"A long while in my case." Salamander dropped his voice to a whisper. "Besides, I want to ask around about the silver wyrm. Some of the farmers might have seen him fly, and maybe they'll have some ideas about where he might lair."

"Ah." Gerran glanced around and saw that members of the warband stood close enough to hear. He decided to spare them Salamander's crazed belief that the dragon was his long-lost brother. "Well, suit yourself, gerthddyn."

"My thanks. Although—" Salamander hesitated. "I wouldn't mind eavesdropping on our Cadryc's conversation with the gwerbret."

"Well, then, leave your gear on my bunk, and let's go."

Gwerbret Ridvar had inherited a splendid great hall, with room for enough tables and benches to seat his warband of a hundred men and nearly as many visitors. Neatly twined rushes covered the floor, and the pale tan stone of the walls sported carvings of various animals between each pair of windows. At the honor hearth, an enormous stone dragon embraced the fireplace, hind legs on one side, front legs and head on the other, with its back and folded wings forming the mantel. Years of smoky fires had darkened the carving. In those same years assorted maidservants had made desultory attempts at cleaning it, with the result that the most deeply carved lines were black, but the raised portions a dirty sort of gray. This contrast gave the sculpture so much depth that in dim light, the dragon seemed to stir and stretch as if it were waking from a long sleep. Five polished wood tables, all of them surrounded with chairs instead of benches, stood before it.

"The gwerbret must be a wealthy man," Salamander remarked.

"He is," Gerran said. "A lot of trade comes through here." He paused, looking around the riders' tables, which stood in profusion across the hall from the dragon hearth. "Let's sit up front. I want to keep an eye on our lord."

Gerran pointed Salamander to a battered plank table, then turned back to collect his men and get them seated. As he was doing so, one of the gwerbret's sisters, Lady Solla, came hurrying to greet him. She was a slender woman, with dark brown hair caught back in a gold clasp, and wide hazel eyes that seemed to dance with life and good cheer. Most men found her beautiful; so did Gerran, but abstractly, thinking her not half so interesting as Branna.

"Good morrow, Gerro," she said. "Have your men been looked after?"

"We have, my lady. We've been given a decent barracks to sleep in, certainly. It's kind of you to ask."

"Oh, it's part of my duties here, truly. But why haven't you been given a chamber in the broch?"

"It's not my place, my lady. I'm as common-born as the rest of them."

Solla winced, then smiled in a vague sort of way. "Well," she said at last, "let's get your men fed." She turned away and signaled to one of the servant lasses. "Bread and ale for the tieryn's men. And tell Cook about our visitors."

Gerran joined Salamander, who had managed to acquire a pair of full tankards ahead of everyone else. He handed one to Gerran.

"That's a lovely lass you were speaking with," Salamander said. "She seems much taken with you."

"Horseshit! What would she see in a common-born man like me?"

Salamander seemed to be about to say more, but with a small sigh he turned away and looked across the great hall. From their bench they had a clear view of Cadryc, seated at the gwerbret's right hand. Across the table were two other men, silent as Cadryc talked urgently to his overlord, who sat at the head of the table in a half-round carved chair. Dark-haired and slender like his sister, Ridvar of Cengarn had just turned fourteen that spring, but he held himself straight and proudly, and every gesture he made was measured and firm.

"Ye gods!" Salamander whispered. "He's but a lad."

"He is, but never let it slip that you think him one. He had an elder brother, but he died of a fever a few years after the Horsekin slew their father."

"Leaving a child in charge of the rhan."

"These things happen. See those two men at the gwerbret's left?" Gerran pointed as he spoke. "The graybeard sitting across from Cadryc is the chief councillor, Lord Oth. The young dark-haired one in the next chair down is the gwerbret's equerry, Lord Blethry."

A painfully thin man, Oth had sparse gray hair, a neatly trimmed gray beard, and an abundant gray mustache that seemed to be trying to make up for the lack of hair elsewhere. Blethry was stocky and not particularly tall, though he wasn't particularly short either. His narrow eyes, set under full dark brows, and wide mouth spoke of some High Mountain blood in his clan.

"They're an interesting pair," Salamander said. "Different as chalk and cheese."

"They're both loyal men. That's what counts."

"True spoken, of course."

"Where's our scribe?" Gerran turned in his chair and addressed his men. "I don't want him lost."

"He hared off to the marketplace, Captain," Daumyr said. "Looking for ink and suchlike."

"Well and good, then. Let's hope he doesn't get into any trouble."

"I'll go look for him later if you'd like," Salamander said. "But I think we'd best stay here for the nonce."

Gerran turned his attention back to the honor table. Even from his distance he could see that Cadryc was fighting to keep his temper. The tieryn leaned forward, left hand balled into a fist, the other clutching the table edge as if he were afraid he'd float to his feet and hit someone.

"I don't like the look of that," Gerran said. "But I can't just go and impose upon the noble-born."

In a few moments a page solved the problem by coming to fetch him. Salamander tagged along uninvited, walking a few paces behind. Gerran decided that sending him back to the table would make bad manners into an incident and ignored him. When Gerran knelt by Cadryc's side, the gwerbret acknowledged him with a small nod.

"I've been telling his grace here about this last lot of brigands," Cadryc said. "He thinks sending more riders to Lord Samyc should be adequate. Do you agree, Captain?"

"Forgive me, my lord, but I don't, and besides, Samyc can't feed any more men."

Gerran looked only at Cadryc while he spoke, but the gwerbret leaned forward.

"You can speak up, Captain," Ridvar said. "I intend to maintain the men for Samyc out of my own pocket, and it won't be some token force. Twenty-five good men and coin to maintain them."

"Well, truly, Your Grace," Gerran picked his words carefully. "That would be more than enough to handle ordinary bandits and the like. But these are Horsekin."

Ridvar sipped mead from a silver goblet and made no answer.

"Twenty-five men won't be enough." Cadryc's voice snapped with barely-concealed frustration. "We need an army."

"It would be most inconvenient for me to ask the high king for an army."

Gerran wondered why he'd ever hoped for anything different. The king's aid brought obligations with it. Even so, given the situation, which threatened the survival of his rhan, the gwerbret's stubbornness did surprise him. Ridvar took another measured sip of mead.

"If Lord Samyc has the extra men," Ridvar said, "they can patrol his borders. Then the villagers will have plenty of warning if there's another raid, and they can get to safety."

"Leaving their farms and livestock and crops for the cursed raiders." Cadryc leaned forward. "If the Horsekin steal or burn the crops and the cows, who's going to feed us all?"

"Even if we have an army, there's no guarantee we can catch the raiders. We don't even know where they come from, do we?"

"Then maybe it's time we blasted well found out."

"Tieryn Cadryc, you forget yourself." Ridvar tossed his head, his eyes flaring temper.

Red-faced with rage, Cadryc stared him full in the face. Councillor Oth leaned forward, and Lord Blethry half-rose from his chair, ready to intervene. Gerran sighed, seeing the matter turn to the question of who could be more stubborn. He risked laying a warning hand on Cadryc's arm. Cadryc recovered himself and made a half-bow to the gwerbret.

"So I do," Cadryc said. "My apologies."

"Granted. My thanks for your advice, Captain."

Lord Blethry sat back down with a small sigh of relief.

"Your Grace?" Salamander stepped forward, bowed, and knelt at the gwerbret's side. "May I have your leave to speak to this point?"

Startled, Ridvar slewed around in his chair to look at the gerthddyn, who smiled blandly up at him.

"I'm a traveling man, Your Grace," Salamander said. "I hear all sorts of strange rumors and tidbits of news. Has Your Grace ever wondered why the Horsekin would ride so far for so few slaves and so little booty? I've gathered a few pieces of information that point to their having an armed camp or the like off to the west, one that they'd rather we didn't find. If that's true, it's no wonder that they want to make sure no one decides to farm out their way."

Councillor Oth caught his breath in a little gasp.

"Indeed," Ridvar said. He turned in his chair to give the gerthddyn his full attention. "Do you have any proof of this?"

"Not yet, Your Grace."

"I'm not about to ask the high king for an army on the strength of a gerthddyn's word."

"Fair enough, Your Grace. I did hear it from the Westfolk."

Ridvar hesitated, visibly annoyed. Everyone knew that the Westfolk never lied and only rarely exaggerated. "That gives it more weight." Ridvar sounded annoyed as well. "But it's still hearsay."

"True, Your Grace, but what if I bring you better proof than that?"

Ridvar crossed his arms over his chest and looked the gerthddyn over for a long cold moment. Councillor Oth leaned forward and murmured a few words in Ridvar's ear, but the lad never acknowledged them.

"Your Grace, there's an old saying." Apparently Cadryc could stand the silence no longer. "When the shepherds go missing, the wolves shit wool."

The lad set his lips together and considered the tieryn with narrow eyes. The hall had fallen utterly silent as everyone, warrior and servant alike, strained to hear. Finally Ridvar allowed himself a small smile.

"The point's well taken," Ridvar said. "I'll make you a bargain. If anyone, even our gerthddyn here, can bring me proof that the Horsekin have a permanent camp or suchlike out to the west, then I'll petition the high king."

"And do I have your word on that?" Cadryc said. "Your Grace?"

"You do." The gwerbret's eyes narrowed again, and he hesitated, but only briefly. "I'll swear it to you."

"You have my thanks, Your Grace. My heartfelt thanks."

Salamander seemed inclined to speak up again, but Gerran laid a hand on his shoulder and silenced him. He and the gerthddyn rose, bowed to the noble-born, then went back to the riders' side of the hall. As they regained their seats, Gerran glanced back to the table of honor, where Ridvar had leaned over to talk with his chamberlain and equerry while Cadryc glowered into his goblet.

"I don't understand," Gerran said softly. "Why is the gwerbret being so cursed stubborn, I wonder?"

"I wonder that myself." Salamander paused for a mouthful of ale. "My worst fear is that Ridvar doesn't want any more settlers down on the Great West Road. What if the king decides that the area needed a gwerbretrhyn of its own?"

"I hadn't thought of that."

"Let's hope Ridvar's thoughts are more honorable than mine." Salamander finished his ale in one long swallow. "But gwerbretion rarely cherish the idea of rivals on their borders." He wiped his mouth on his sleeve, then stood up. "I'll just be fetching my gear. I'll keep an eye out for young Neb, too, when I'm down in town."

Salamander was spared the task of searching for the tieryn's scribe. He was leading his horse and packhorse out of the gates when he saw Neb, carrying a laden basket over one arm, puffing up the hill toward him. Beside him skipped the fat yellow gnome. In a shirt that was too big for him, with his skinny lad's face glistening with sweat, Neb looked utterly unprepossessing. Yet Salamander knew that locked deep in his soul were latent dweomer powers so great that they bordered on the frightening.

"Ah, there you are," Salamander said. "I need to say farewell, lad. I'll be staying in Cengarn when you go back home with the warband."

"Then may you fare well indeed," Neb said. "I need to thank you yet once again. Clae and I owe you our lives."

"Well, it's a strange thing, this question of lives and gratitude." Neb stared at him.

"I mean," Salamander said, "who knows whether you found me by luck or by wyrd? Sometimes the most random-seeming acts have hidden causes."

"Er, I suppose so."

"Consider the river Melyn, a broad and fast-flowing waterway, isn't it? Yet its source must be some tiny spring or rivulet hidden from our eyes deep in the primeval forest. Wyrd may have such a secret font."

"Well, true spoken, but—" Neb paused briefly. "But why are you rattling on about this?"

"You really don't remember, do you?"

"Remember what?"

"Ah, that's the question, isn't it? While I'm gone, you might ponder, reflect, contemplate, even meditate upon it."

Neb's mouth curled in a twist of anger. Salamander laughed and with a wave of his hand, clucked to his horses and led them away. He had to admit that he was enjoying this small bit of revenge upon

Nevyn. *And yet,* Salamander reminded himself, *Nevyn was right, wasn't he? So was Jill, but you wouldn't listen to either of them.* The memories of his long years of madness rose up strong and made him shudder.

Neb stood staring after the gerthddyn as Salamander led his horse and packhorse down the steep road into town. *Now what was all that about?* Neb asked himself. *Utter drivel, most like.* During their ride north, Salamander had made other cryptic remarks centering around wyrd and memory. None of them had made any more sense than this set. And yet the gerthddyn's talk had touched something in his mind—he could recognize an odd sort of truth in it even though he couldn't quite understand what that truth might be. He did have the distinct feeling that this truth was somehow linked to his dreams about the most beautiful lass in all Deverry, though he couldn't say where this feeling came from. *Ponder it,* Salamander had said. *Meditate upon it.* Neb decided that he'd best do just that.

The gatekeeper recognized him and let him into the keep without any challenge. As he was crossing the ward, the yellow gnome appeared and pointed at the sky with a skinny little hand. Neb looked up and saw only a solitary raven, circling far above the ward. With servants nearby, Neb decided that he'd best not try to speak to the gnome. *It can't be the raven that's troubling him,* Neb thought. There were always plenty of birds overhead all summer long. A spirit, perhaps, that only the gnome could see might have been hovering in the air, but there was nothing that Neb could do about it if so.

Since he'd been spending the tieryn's money, Neb went looking for Cadryc. In his basket he had big chunks of dry ink, a proper grinding stone, a packet of sealing wax, and other such scribal treasures, all of which had cost plenty, out here on the border. He found the tieryn in the great hall, sitting alone at the honor table and nursing a goblet of mead. Neb bowed and started to kneel, but Cadryc waved him up.

"I take it you found what you needed," the tieryn said.

"I did, Your Grace." Neb set the basket on the table. "If you'd like to see—"

"No need, lad. I trust you to know your craft."

"My thanks, Your Grace." Neb bowed to him. "I'll put the purchases with my blankets and suchlike out in the barracks. Er, if I may ask, did the gwerbret—"

"He did not." Cadryc pitched his voice low. "Infuriating young cub! Here, I daren't say more. He and his councillor will be back down in a moment, no doubt. They're off discussing the matter twixt themselves."

Neb started to speak, but his voice choked on utterly unexpected tears. Cadryc laid a hand on his shoulder.

"Thinking about your kin, are you? Well, lad, I've not given up hope of avenging them yet. Gerran can tell you what happened—" Cadryc glanced around, "—in private, like."

A page told Neb that the tieryn's men had gone to their quarters. When Neb joined them there, most were sound asleep on their bunks or kneeling on the floor dicing for coppers. Gerran himself was sitting in the only chair in the room with his feet up on the nearest bunk. He waved vaguely in Neb's direction.

"Back, are you?" Gerran said.

"I am. Here, his grace told me to ask you about this afternoon."

"Not much to tell. Gwerbret Ridvar has no intention of going to the king."

"Did he say why?"

"He didn't. He did come up with another plan, but it won't work. Then we had a surprise of sorts. The gerthddyn thinks he might know why the Horsekin are raiding, to keep us from finding a fortress or suchlike further west."

"That makes sense."

"It does. I just wish the gwerbret could see it."

"Me, too. Well, the noble-born are supposed to be stubborn, after all, and Ridvar's so young."

"True spoken. Another thing, too—his family inherited the rhan through a female line, so they've always been touchy."

"I heard that they were related to the gwerbretion of Dun Trebyc."

"Just so. Mirro and I learned the clan's history backwards and forwards when we were pages here. Back when the Horsekin sieged the town, the gwerbret was named Cadmar. Both his sons died long before he did, but one of his daughters had a son. So the son—that was Gwerbret Tanry—inherited. His son was Daen, who was the father of our Ridvar. But Ridvar only inherited the rhan because his elder brother died of a fever."

"Ah." Neb repeated this important information to himself several times to ensure he remembered it. "My thanks. I can see how that might still irk our young lord."

"Truly." Gerran paused to swing his feet off the bunk and sit up straight. "I wonder how long we'll stay here. Not very, I'd wager."

The captain would have won that wager had anyone taken him up on it. The next morning, immediately after breakfast, the tieryn told his men to pack up and ready their horses.

"We're going home," Cadryc said. "I see no reason to stay here one cursed day longer. I'll just go pay my courtesies to the gwerbret, and we'll be off. Let's hope that blasted gerthddyn can come up with somewhat to change his grace's mind."

Gerran's mouth twisted, as if he thought the hope a waste of effort. Yet Neb found himself remembering the odd things Salamander had said to him and the way he could drop his daft and silly ways the way another man would drop a cloak.

"Well, I don't know, Your Grace," Neb said, "but I suspect that there's more to our gerthddyn than we might think."

"Then I'll hope you're right." Cadryc smiled briefly. "Now let's get moving, lads."

Packing up his purchases to travel unbroken took Neb a fair bit of time. When he hurried outside, he found a page holding the reins of his horse, and out in the ward the tieryn and his men were already assembled. Neb thanked the page and started to lead the horse over to the others, but Lady Solla hurried up and stopped him.

"Goodman Neb," she said. "May I ask you a favor?"

"Certainly, my lady." Neb bowed again. "I'd be honored."

"Could you give this to Lady Galla?" Solla handed him a message tube, sealed at both ends.

"Nothing would be easier, and I'd be glad to." Neb tucked the tube inside his shirt and settled it against his belt to keep it there.

"I do hope she's well? It seems like such a lonely life, out there on the border."

"She's doing well, indeed. And she has company now, her niece, Lady Branna."

"Oh, how nice for her." But Lady Solla's voice had turned flat, and she bit her lower lip. "I've not seen Branna for many years now. She was such a pretty child. No doubt she's grown into a great beauty."

"Not precisely, my lady. Now, I happen to think she's the most beautiful lass in all Deverry, but most men would call her pretty or handsome."

"Ah, I see." Solla smiled again. "And does Branna favor you, perhaps?"

Neb suddenly realized that he'd been indiscreet, perhaps dangerously so. "I'm but a scribe in her uncle's dun," Neb said. "I assure you I'm always mindful of that."

"Oh, come now, there's no need to despair! After all, she's a lass with no dowry, no position to speak of. If she decides that her rank matters naught, well, then, it won't matter, will it?" Solla lowered her voice. "Should I see her again, I'll speak well of you to her."

"Would you?" Neb could feel himself grin and hastily sobered his expression. "My thanks, my lady, my great thanks."

As the warband was mounting up, Neb noticed the lady standing in the doorway and watching them. From the direction of her glance, he could tell that it was Gerran who drew her interest. *Oho!* he thought. *No wonder she was so kind to me. She thinks Branna is her rival. And of course, in a way she's quite right.* Neb urged his horse up next to the captain's.

"Do you see Lady Solla over there?" he said. "She's certainly a lovely lass."

"I suppose." Gerran scowled at him. "What—"

"I think she favors you highly. You're a lucky man, Captain."

"Ye gods! You're as bad as that babbling gerthddyn!"

But Gerran did look the lady's way and make her a half-bow from the saddle, a gesture that made her smile and acknowledge the captain with a ladylike wave. In smug satisfaction, Neb clucked to his horse and rode back to his place, farther down the line of march.

Only later did he hear his own voice speaking in his memory, saying that to him Branna was "the most beautiful lass in all Deverry." A rush of feeling came with the memory: elation, triumph, and fear, all tangled together. He knew that he'd solved the riddle, that the dead lass of his dreams was indeed Branna, but how they could be the same person was a second riddle, and one that would take him a long time to solve.

After some searching, Salamander found an inn that catered to humans, not dwarves, or to be precise, he found a reasonably clean room above a tavern with a stable for his horses. Most merchants of the taller sort came with caravans and camped outside the town gates. Before he went out to work the market, he changed from his shabby riding clothes into a pair of new brigga of fine gray wool and a linen shirt, as stiff as canvas from the luxurious embroideries of flowers and interlacements on the sleeves and yokes. Inside the shirt, under the concealing embroideries, lay loops of thread and little pockets where he hid the various items for his sleight-of-hand tricks.

The rest of his gear he stowed in a corner, then stuck his head out of the door and called to the tavern owner's lad, a boy who was trying, with very limited success, to raise his first mustache.

"A bargain for you, lad." Salamander reached up into empty air and produced ten shiny copper coins, which he spread across his palm. "See these coins?"

"I do, sir." The lad's eyes had gone very wide.

"Good. Now, I desire to go out and walk around the market, but I also desire to find all of my possessions here when I get back. Do you think you can keep them safe?"

"I can, sir."

"Very well. Here's the bargain. If everything's safe, you get the coins. However, if anything's missing, I dock you one coin for each stolen good. Fair?"

"Very fair, sir." The lad crossed his arms over his chest and leaned back against the door. "I'll not have much work to do till later, so I can stay here."

Up on the commons hill, the market swarmed with farmers selling produce, craftsmen manning little wooden booths, townsfolk haggling with peddlers, horse-traders parading their stock back and forth. Salamander wandered through, studying everyone and everything, and planned his strategy. From Dallandra he knew a fair bit about the dragons already, but they provided an excellent way to open conversations. To ask right out about Horsekin might be dangerous at worst, if they should have a spy in Cengarn, or at the least, a good way to frighten off any potential informants.

Eventually Salamander found an empty ale barrel. He rolled it to a level spot, then turned it upside down and climbed on top of it. When a few people paused to watch him, he took a pair of silk scarves from his shirt. He flung them in the air, caught them, made them disappear up his sleeve and produced them again from his collar. A dozen fascinated children flocked around. After a few more scarf tricks, the crowd swelled to include adults.

"Good morrow, good citizens of Cengarn," Salamander said. "I am Salamander, a gerthddyn from Eldidd, come to amuse, distract, and delight you. Have you heard of Cadwallon, the mighty sorcerer who dwelt in the fabled halls of King Bran? Do you know that he once tamed a dragon with soft words alone?"

Most of those crowded around called out, "We don't!" When they all sat down on the ground, Salamander climbed down from the barrel. He proceeded to tell the tale for free while the crowd grew to a profitable size. At that point he made a great show of coughing and clearing his throat.

"Alas, good people, I am far too thirsty, parched veritably, to continue."

The crowd laughed, and some flung copper coins his way. As he collected them, a small boy trotted over with a tankard of ale.

"From my da," the boy said. "He'll want the tankard back."

"I'll make sure he gets it." Salamander took a long swallow. "And very good ale it is."

He finished the tale and the tankard together, punctuating the one with sips from the other. More coins came his way, which he answered with profound thanks; then he gave the empty tankard back to the boy.

"Well, lad," he said. "Did you enjoy the tale?"

"I did, sir. We've got dragons round here. Did you know that?"

"I'd heard it, truly. One black and one silver, is that right?"

"It is, but we don't see the silver one much. Just the black one." The boy sighed with a sad shake of his head. "She steals cows now and then. My da says there's naught to be done about it. Dragons are just like that."

Salamander sent the boy back to his father, then strolled through the market fair. Now that he'd made himself known as an entertainer—a rare and precious thing here on the edge of the kingdom—everyone was willing to strike up a conversation about the local dragons. While he learned little new, it did become clear that the silver dragon tended to shun human settlements, whether farm or town, while the black showed no fear of nor shyness around anyone or anything.

"A fair pest she can be," said a woman who was selling chunks of roast pork on sticks. "I'm just glad she scorns pig when she can get beef."

"She can't take too many of your animals," Salamander said. "Or she'd have eaten the town out of house and home by now."

"True-spoken, good sir. She must hunt venison, mostly, and other wild creatures. I suppose a good cow is a treat, like, to her.

The silver one must eat mostly deer, or maybe a nice fat bear now and again."

Salamander smiled, but his stomach twisted in disgust at the thought of his brother killing game and eating it raw. He's not really Rhodry any longer, he reminded himself. But still, the image appalled him, especially the thought of eating bears, laden with worms and other parasites. He went searching for more ale to wash the mental taste away.

Down near the town gates he found a temporary tavern, a round canvas roof on poles sheltering a cluster of ale barrels in the center. Men stood around, drinking from pottery stoups chained to the barrels, but one white-haired fellow was sitting on a three-legged stool and holding an unchained mug. Salamander stood everyone a tankard, a good investment, since he at last found the informant he'd been hoping for.

"Dragons, eh?" One of the drinkers pointed to the seated elder. "Now, if it's talk of dragons you want, our Mallo there's the man to ask."

When Mallo raised his mug in a friendly way, Salamander hunkered down in front of him.

"So you know a bit about dragons, do you?" Salamander said.

"I do, and more than a bit. I was captain of the town watch when the Horsekin sieged our town, and the black dragon was part of the relieving army. Arzosah, her name is."

"Were you now? Well, I've had a bit of luck, then. How big is she?"

"Big as a house, I'd say. Not so big as the gwerbret's broch tower, though there are some as will tell you so. But a good twenty-odd feet long, she were." Mallo paused to grin, revealing a few black stumps of teeth. "Oh, it were a sight, gerthddyn! There were them there filthy Horsekin, arrogant as all get out, riding their cursed big horses. Parading around the walls, they were, thousands of 'em, thinking they were going to storm our gates." Mallo leaned over and set his mug on the ground to free both hands. He crossed them, hooked his thumbs together, and waggled his spread fingers for wings. "Swoop! Down she comes, and that berserker silver dagger riding her. Oh, it were a sight and a half! The horses, they panicked and threw their blasted riders right off. I leaned against a merlon on the wall and laughed till I cursed near shat, I tell you. A beautiful sight, it were."

"I wish I'd been there to see it."

"Huh! You wouldn't have wanted to have been trapped there, gerthddyn." Mallo paused for a strengthening swig of ale. "Thought we were all doomed, we did, with them filthy dogs of Horsekin swarming round the walls, and their bitch of a goddess."

"I think I've heard of that goddess," Salamander said. "Alshandra's her name?"

"It is. Or was, I should say. Heh, no goddess at all, truly. Some sort of trick, is what she was." For a moment Mallo's expression clouded, as if he were remembering something puzzling. "Don't know how the filthy Horsekin did it, but some sort of trick." He shrugged the puzzle away. "Some of the folk farther out believed in her, though, and them two traitor lords did, too."

Dallandra had told Salamander about the two noble-born brothers who had worshiped Alshandra, but she'd never given him a clear idea of the geography around Cengarn. "These lords," Salamander said, "they held demesnes off to the west, did they?"

"North, not west, up in on the edge of the wild country. A good thirty mile, I'd say, if not a bit more."

"Near the foothills," a skinny red-haired fellow put in. "The ones that rise up to the Roof of the World."

"But not so far as all that," Mallo said. "Now, the river that runs hard by Cengarn? Follow it, and it'll take you there. Well, should you be a-wanting to go, of course."

A few more well-phrased questions on Salamander's part brought him to the captured priest of Alshandra. He'd died recently enough that all the men in the tavern knew the story.

"His name was Zaklof," the red-haired fellow said. "A miserable excuse for a man, if you ask me, but he died bravely enough. The gwerbret's men kept offering him food, more to tease him, like,

than to save him, but he turned it all down. My daughter was working in the kitchen up at the dun, and she saw it all."

"You know," Salamander said. "Zaklof's tale could be profitable
for a man like me. I've heard somewhat about it, but not enough,
truly. Did your daughter ever discuss this goddess of his? Or what
he believed about her, truly?"

"She did. She was impressed, like, that he'd hold so true." He
rolled his eyes. "Easily impressed, she was, but what do you expect
from a young lass, eh? She nattered on a good bit about his beliefs."

Another round of ale, and the fellow was glad enough to repeat
all he remembered on the subject. Some of the other men joined in
with bits and pieces of information about this new kind of religion,
though they all mocked it, and quite sincerely.

"Still," Salamander said at last, "it makes a good story. Now, the
Horsekin had taken some of our people prisoners, hadn't they?"

"They had," Mallo said. "Some lasses and children, but the
gwerbret's men rescued them."

"Ah, that sounds promising. Lasses in danger always add life to
a tale. Do they live in Cengarn?"

"Not that I know of. Farm women, they were, or so I heard." He
gestured at his stiff leg. "I wasn't riding with the rescue party."

"Now, one of them," the red-haired fellow joined in, "she married a man who farms north of here, Canna her name is. They hold
land in the old Mawrvelin demesne."

"I'd like to talk to her," Salamander said. "I need some details,
you see, to make the tale a good one."

"I don't remember her man's name." He frowned into his
tankard for a moment. "She was a pretty little thing back then. Red
hair down to her waist."

"Who holds those demesnes now, anyway?" Salamander said.
"The ones that used to belong to the traitor lords, I mean. It sounds
like there's another good story in that."

Mallo answered him this time. "The priests of Bel have the big
'un, the one that used to belong to that wormy dog of a Matyc. His

brother Tren's dun went to a cousin line. The current lord, now, let me think—Honelg, his name is."

"Honelg? That's a strange sort of name."

"He's a strange sort of man." Mallo shrugged elaborately. "But then, that whole clan's always been a bit strange, up there on the edge of nowhere like they are."

Salamander spent the rest of the day wandering around the market, stopping now and then to chat with local farmers. By late afternoon he'd pieced together a fairly good idea of the country to the north of town as well as the details of Zaklof's death, which had left a strong impression in everyone's mind. He bought market fare for his dinner, then went back to his room over the tavern. He paid the tavern lad—all of his possessions were safe and sound—then took his meal inside and barred the door.

Once he'd eaten, he had dweomerwork to do, and he didn't care to be interrupted. Since it was far too warm to light a fire, he sat in the window seat and looked out at the sunset sky. Wisps and streamers of clouds, caught in the scarlet light, made a serviceable scrying focus. He contacted Dallandra easily and told her what he'd learned at the market fair.

"So I'll travel north on the morrow," Salamander finished up. "There's a woman up there who was taken prisoner by the Horsekin some years ago. She may know useful things, such as where she was when the warband rescued her."

"That's true," Dallandra thought to him. "After you find her, what next?"

"It depends on what she tells me, but most likely I'll keep going north. At one point there was quite a colony of Alshandra worshipers up there, thanks to a certain Lord Matyc, who seems to have been a traitor. His demesne is now in the hands of the priests of Bel, so I'm not going to find a flourishing temple or the like, but again, someone might remember some useful thing."

"Matyc certainly was a traitor. Do you know why the priests have that land?"

"I don't, why?"

Dallandra's image appeared troubled. "Your brother killed Matyc in a trial by combat. The priests presided, and the demesne was their reward."

"I'd better watch what I say, then, about Rhodry and Alshandra both."

"You should be careful, no matter where you are. It's dangerous, scouting for Horsekin."

"I do realize that, oh princess of powers perilous. If I'm going to find them before the summer's out, I'll need to work fast, too. It's a pity that I have to ride or walk. If I could only fly—"

"It's too soon for that." In the cloud-vision her expression turned stern. "Your mind isn't fully stable yet."

"It never truly was, or so Nevyn always told me."

"Don't jest!" She shook her head in irritation. "Taking bird form's a tremendous strain. Do you want to go mad again? You didn't seem to much like it before."

"True enough, O Mistress of Magicks Mysterious. Don't worry. I'll follow your orders."

"I don't want you to follow what I say like orders. I want you to understand why I'm saying it."

"I do see. My apologies. I'm jesting, just as you said, and truly, I do know better."

In the morning, Salamander left Cengarn and followed the river north. Close to town lay free farms, that is, those owned by freemen who owed loyalty directly to the gwerbrets of Cengarn with no tax-taking lords in between. Their lands, nestled between rolling hills, stretched green with pastures and burgeoning crops. Everywhere he stopped, Salamander heard stories about the dragons. A great many farmers had lost cows to them, or so they claimed with varying amounts of hard evidence. One man did show Salamander a cowhide he'd tanned. It bore the long gashes made by huge claws.

"I keep it to remember the cursed thing by," the farmer said. "It's not often you lose a cow to a dragon, and I thank all the gods for that! Look here, all I found was this hunk of leather, licked clean inside, and the horns and hooves. Blasted dragon had eaten every-thing else."

"Was this the silver or the black?"

"The black. She carried the cow off in the twilight, so it was hard to see. The silver one would have stood out, like."

"No doubt. My sympathies."

"Oh, well, I was as angry as a boil-bum demon when it hap-pened, but then I think, well, at least the dragons keep the Horsekin off, and so maybe one cow's a cheap enough price."

"Do you really think the dragons are driving off the Horsekin?"

"Ain't any round here, are there?"

"True enough. My thanks for the information. I'd best get back on the road."

When Salamander decided that he was far enough away from Cengarn, he found the gold arrow he'd bought from Warryc and tucked it into a pocket in one of his saddlebags. It might come in handy, he decided, if any of Alshandra's followers still held true to their faith, up on the lands that Lord Matyc and his brother Lord Tren had once ruled.

On a muggy afternoon, under a sky black with storm clouds, Tieryn Cadryc led his men back to his dun. Branna was in the great hall with Lady Galla when they heard the clatter of hooves on the cobbles and the shouts of the pages and grooms as they ran out to greet the men. Branna had to stop herself from joining the general rush. She was surprised at how happy she felt merely from knowing she'd see Neb again. For decorum's sake she waited inside—but just inside, and by the door in the servants' and riders' half of the great hall.

Not long after she'd taken up her post, Neb came hurrying in, loaded up with a bedroll, a basket, and some lumpy parcels wrapped in his extra shirt. Branna glanced around and saw Clae nearby.

"Take those up for your brother," she said. "Well, if you can carry them all."

" 'Course I can!" Clae trotted over. "Here, Neb, hand them to me."

"I'll keep the basket," Neb said. "There are things in there that cost our tieryn a good many coppers. Just take the blankets—wait, don't tug!"

Branna solved the resulting confusion by grabbing the basket herself and letting Neb sort out the rest. Once a burdened Clae was heading for the staircase, she held out the basket. Smiling, Neb took it from her. For a brief moment their fingers touched. Mindful of her noble-born kin, standing not all that far away, Branna drew her hand back, but as they talked, exchanging ordinary pleasantries, she found that her hand kept reaching for his, almost of its own will, and that his definitely seemed to be seeking her fingers as well.

"Ah, well," Neb said at last, "there's your aunt coming. I'd best put the things I bought away, too. Oh, wait! I have a message for her from Lady Solla."

Neb fished in his shirt, took out the message tube, and handed it to Branna. "If you'll just give this to our lady?" He bowed and hurried upstairs, two steps at a time.

That evening, in the privacy of the women's hall, Branna read the message aloud for Lady Galla. Out of boredom as much as anything, Branna had badgered her father's scribe into teaching her how to read, an art that her aunt had never mastered.

"My dear Lady Galla," Branna began, "I send my greetings and my hopes that you are well. I have some news to give you, though for now I implore you to keep it shut up in your women's hall. My brother has started negotiations for a marriage. As of yet I'm not at liberty to tell you with whom, but as you can no doubt guess, she's the daughter of a man of high estate. I tell you this now because I'm sore troubled. Once my brother is married, his wife will be his chatelaine, and I fear me that I'll have only a grudged place here. If out of the kindness of your heart you might offer me a place with you as a servingwoman, I should be forever grateful. I do have a small legacy that I could contribute to my maintenance. I do hope you'll consider my plea, yours, Solla of Dun Cengarn."

"As if I'd ask a servingwoman to pay for her food!" Galla burst out. "The poor lass, she must be desperately afraid if she'd write such things."

"Just so," Branna said. "I rather know how she feels."

"Indeed. Well, she's certainly welcome here. On the morrow I'll send her my answer, that she's not to worry. We'll invite her for a visit, and then we can discuss the matter. Our scribe will doubtless lend you some ink and suchlike."

"It would be better if he wrote the whole thing. Reading's a fair bit easier than writing."

"Ah. I suppose it must be. I hope he can keep a secret."

"Oh, I'm sure he can. He's a man of excellent character. Well, or so it seems to me."

Galla suddenly smiled. "You seem quite taken with young Neb."

"Is it shameful of me?"

"Not in the least. He strikes me as the sort of man who becomes a gwerbret's councillor or suchlike one fine day."

Branna smiled in profound relief. With a little laugh Galla patted her arm. "In a way, my dear," Galla went on, "your father's nasty wife has done you a great favor. It's not many lasses who have the freedom you do when it comes to picking a husband."

"That's true, isn't it? I'd not thought of it that way before."

"Well, you see? It's a stingy flood that doesn't leave fish behind, as they always say. But I wouldn't be in a great hurry, either, to marry your scribe. You might wait to see what game the dogs rouse before you mark your hare. And besides, there's Gerran."

"True spoken. There certainly is Gerran."

Over the next few days Branna felt more like the hare than the hunter. It seemed that no matter where she walked in the dun, Gerran would suddenly appear at her side, attentive but no more talkative than he'd ever been. Aside from the usual greetings he would merely stare at her, silent but as tense as a strung bow. At first she tried to make conversation, and he'd usually manage to squeeze out a polite sentence or two before resorting to staring at her with an expression that might be considered devotion. She began to notice, too, that after a few strained moments of Gerran's silence Neb would suddenly come hurrying over to rescue her.

"They must both be keeping a lookout for me," Branna complained to Galla. "I can't go anywhere without one or the other just popping up out of nowhere like the Lord of Hell."

"Oh, come now, dear." Galla smiled at her. "It's very flattering."

"Of course, but what if they come to blows or suchlike? I doubt me if Neb could match Gerran."

"Now that's true." Galla's smile disappeared. "Neb is far too valuable a servitor to lose. I'll have a word with your uncle, and he'll have a word with Gerran. There's enough trouble with the wretched Horsekin. We don't need more inside the dun."

Lord Ynedd was screaming in rage while tears poured down his face and snot down his upper lip. He had set his skinny back against the dun wall and was flailing out with his fists. Clae and Coryn strolled back and forth in front of him and taunted, "Little lass! little lass! look at her pretty curls!" One or the other of the bigger boys would dance in, pull the lordling's hair, then dance out again to let the other have a turn.

"Here!" Neb yelled. "Stop it right now!"

The startled boys spun around just as he charged, slapping both of them, grabbing Clae by the shirt. "What would Mam say?" Neb growled. "To see you acting like this?"

Clae wilted. He slumped, stared at the ground, and made no answer. Coryn turned and raced off, disappearing among the storage sheds. Neb gave his brother one last shake and let him go. "Two against one," Neb said, "and both of you bigger."

"I'm sorry." Clae mumbled, looked at Ynedd, then mumbled a

little louder. "I'm sorry." With one last glance at his brother he took a few steps away. When Neb didn't respond, Clae turned and ran after Coryn.

Ynedd leaned against the wall and went on crying so hard that, Neb supposed, he might not even realize that his tormentors had fled. He knelt on one knee in front of the boy, then pulled an ink-stained rag out of his brigga pocket.

"Here, here," Neb said. "Come along, my lord. Wipe your face and blow your nose."

Gulping for breath, Ynedd took the rag and followed orders. "It's my hair," he stammered. "They keep mocking my hair."

"Indeed? Then perhaps we should cut it. I've got my pen knife with me, and I just sharpened it. Shall we have those curls off?"

Ynedd nodded and turned his back—and the offending curls—toward Neb. The pen knife's sharp but short blade could cut only one curl at a time, a process that must have cost the lordling a good many pulls and pains. Yet he never whimpered once as they came free and fell to the cobbles. With his hair short he looked a good bit older as well as more comfortable.

"There," Neb said at last. "That's better, a nice clean fit under a pot helm."

Ynedd reached up to feel the cut edges, then kicked a clump of curl with the toe of his boot. "My thanks, good scribe," he said. "Truly. You saved me."

"You're welcome," Neb said. "I'll take the cut-off hair and put it out for the birds. They'll use it in their nests."

With a smile for the thought, Ynedd trotted off in the opposite direction to the one the bigger boys had taken. Neb set his pen knife back in its little sheath, then picked up the curls. He straightened up and turned around to find Midda, Branna's servant, standing and watching him. At her feet lay a big bundle of dirty laundry, tied up in a sheet.

"That was nicely done, scribe," Midda said.

"Were you watching the whole thing?" Neb said.

"I heard our little lord shrieking and was coming to see what was wrong, but you got in before me and did such a splendid job that well, think I, no use in interrupting." She poked at the bundle with one foot. "I'd best be taking this out. The other women are already at the stream."

"Here, I'll carry it for you."

The stream ran across the long meadow out behind the dun's hill. The laundry party had set up in the shade of two willows. Servants knelt on the bank and rubbed soap into wet clothes or pounded out dirt with rocks. Already out on the grass lay a good many clean dresses and shirts, spread out to dry. Lady Branna was sitting with her back against one of the trees and singing to keep the lasses amused while they worked, though her song, an old folk ballad about the Civil Wars, seemed an odd choice, dealing as it did with treachery and murder. Midda called out to her, and Branna broke off the song in mid-verse.

"Here's the last of the shirts, my lady," Midda said. "The warband's filthy lot."

The servants all groaned aloud and put down their work for a moment's rest. Midda took the bundle from Neb and trotted forward to dump it onto the grassy bank of the stream. Branna got up, stretching her arms above her head and tossing back her long blonde hair. The sight of her standing by the stream—Neb suddenly found his breath gone, felt himself turn cold. For a maddened moment he wanted to rush forward and grab her, to haul her back from the brink to safety. *But she's not in any danger,* he told himself. *The blasted stream's no more than three feet deep!*

Fortunately no one had noticed his odd fit, as he labeled his reaction. The servant lasses were alternately giggling and groaning as they joked about the warband's stench. By the time Branna beckoned him over to chat, Neb had got control of himself again. He spread Lord Ynedd's curls across the grass, then joined her.

But the memory of his reaction stayed with him. All during that day and on into the evening he felt as if he were struggling to remember some important thing or event, yet he couldn't say what it was. Trying to recover it frightened him, not that the fear made him stop trying. Finally he realized that he was sure she'd drowned, even though that was impossible.

The fear clung to him until he went into the great hall for dinner. As he walked over to his usual table on the servants' side of the hall, he saw Branna, sitting at the honor table and chatting with her aunt. *There she is, you dolt!* he told himself, *and she's not drowned, has she now?* He'd just sat down when Gerran strolled over with a nod of greeting.

"A good evening to you, Captain," Neb said.

"Same to you," Gerran said. "My thanks for cutting Ynedd's hair, and for pulling our other lads off him."

"Most welcome. Seeing Clae acting the bully—I've not been that angry in a long time."

"So he told me." Gerran paused for a smile. "He said that when you get angry, 'it's like dragons.' But I've got a favor to ask you. Clae's doing well with his swordcraft, and he really should be sleeping out in the barracks with Coryn and Ynedd. A lad who's going to be a rider, he's got to get used to living in a warband."

"I see." Neb felt an odd coldness around his heart. "Well, he certainly may, if you think it best."

"I do. My thanks. I'll get him some blankets and the like. He might as well move over there today."

The captain strode off, heading outside. *Well, that's that,* Neb thought. *My brother's gone for a rider.* He had the distinct sensation that some mental door had slammed shut on his boyhood. He also knew, though he could find no words to express how, that meeting Branna had led him to another door somewhere deep in his very soul. What lay behind it, he couldn't quite see, yet he realized that soon, very soon, he would have to get up the courage to unlock the door and walk in to have a look.

Branna herself made the matter more urgent. At the end of the meal, she hurried over and sat down on the bench beside Neb. The very easiness of her gesture made his heart pound.

"I wanted to ask you somewhat," Branna said. "About the gerthddyn. Uncle tells me that you were the last person to speak to him in Cengarn, the last of our people, I mean."

"Most likely I was, truly," Neb said. "I was coming back to the gwerbret's dun just as he was leaving it."

"Did he say when he'd come back? Or, come to think of it, if he was coming back at all?"

"And just why do you want to know?" Neb heard a snarl crack his voice like a whip. He clasped a hand over his mouth as if he could stuff the words back in.

Branna laughed at him, then risked laying her fingers on his arm, just lightly and quickly. "You're jealous," she whispered.

"Am not!"

"Are, too!"

She continued smiling at him in such honest delight that he relented and returned the smile.

"Well, maybe I am," Neb said. "Salamander's a good-looking man."

"Huh! To some, maybe." She wrinkled her nose in mock disgust. "I just miss his tales of an evening, that's all. I wish my uncle had a bard, but he's never found one willing to move all the way out here."

"They were good tales, truly. All Salamander told me was that he was going to stay in Cengarn when the rest of us rode home."

"That's a pity, then. I did love it when he'd talk about dweomer. Did you?"

Her voice was just a little too casual, her words a little too careful. Neb abruptly realized that she was afraid of voicing some question.

"It was amusing," Neb said. "Overblown, but amusing. I doubt if anyone could really do the things he talked about."

"I suppose not." She looked away, suddenly sad. "Truly, I suppose not."

Before he could speak again, she got up and, with a little wave, hurried back to her side of the great hall, where her aunt was

waiting for her. Neb felt her disappointment like a blow. How
had he failed her? He knew that somehow or other, he had. *Just
like the night river,* he thought, *just like when she drowned.* He
found himself remembering Salamander's strange conversation
at the gates of Dun Cengarn. Lives and wyrd, gratitude and
wyrd—it still made no sense. With an irritable shrug he got up
and left the great hall.

Salamander was dimly aware that Neb and Branna were discussing him, thanks to his strong ties to both of them from former lives. That night he'd camped beside the road some fifteen miles
north of Cengarn. He sat watching the sunset while he ate the cooked
meat and bread he'd bought in town, then gathered some deadfall
wood from the forest fringe to build a fire. He'd been uneasy all day,
he realized, though he couldn't tell why, and he wanted the light.

While he watched the flames catch his kindling and spread to the
bits and pieces of branch, he opened the Sight and let the flames
guide the fragments of visions that came to him. He saw Rori, soaring high in the sky, dipping and swooping down as he apparently
hunted for game. He sensed Dallandra and Valandario rather than
saw them. The two dweomermasters were hovering on the edge of
the astral plane, working some sort of guarding ritual. When he
turned his mind to Neb and Branna, Salamander found them easily. Neb was talking with his brother in the great hall while Branna
sat with her aunt up in their women's retreat. *No danger there,* he
thought. *But there's some behind me.*

Salamander rose and turned in one smooth motion. A woman in
a tattered blue dress was standing at the edge of his camp, just beyond the circle of firelight. Or not quite a woman—when she
moved forward, he could see that her hair was as blue as the dress
and her skin, dead-white. She was floating a few inches off the
ground while she considered him with eyes that were luminous
pools of shadow.

"Uh, good evening," Salamander said in Elvish. "Should you really be here? In the physical world, I mean."

"Where's Jill?" Her voice sounded like a reed flute, thin, not truly alive.

"I'm sorry, but she's dead. Do you know what that means?"

"Yes, yes! Where's the new Jill?"

"Why do you want to know?"

The woman-spirit frowned, then called out, a high piercing wail like that of a banshee. As the cry faded, she disappeared. Salamander shuddered in a sudden cold sweat. Although he wanted to talk immediately with Dallandra about his visitor, she never answered his attempt to contact her. He could sense that she was still deeply immersed in her dweomerwork. He scrounged more firewood, then spent an uncomfortable couple of hours until at last he reached her.

"A most peculiar thing happened just now," Salamander said. "I just had a visitor from another plane of existence."

"Oh, did you?" Dallandra said. "Which one?"

"I've no idea, if you mean which plane. I certainly never summoned her or anything else, for that matter. She just walked into my camp."

"What was she like?"

"She looked like a woman at first glance, but then I realized she was floating a few inches off the ground. She had blue hair and dead-white skin."

"Was she wearing a torn dress, a blue one?"

"She most certainly was! But it was hard to tell if the dress shape lay over her body or was part of her body."

"I think I know what she might be. Did she speak to you?"

"Yes. She wanted to know where the 'new Jill' was, but I didn't tell her. There was something sinister or mayhap menacing about her. Perhaps I should call it—"

"Never mind! I take it she frightened you."

"I was not frightened."

"Imph. Anyway, if she's who I think she is, she can appear when she chooses, without being summoned. Stay on guard. She can be dangerous."

"You've met her before, I take it."

"Yes. I once helped the Lords of the Wildlands drive her into a trap. Do you remember when your brother first came to the Westlands? You went off to search for Devaberiel while he stayed with Aderyn."

"Ah. I think I know what you mean now. The sprite who was one of the Wildfolk, originally, and she fell in love with our Rhodry."

"It's much more complicated than that, but that's enough to get on with. She tried to make herself into a real woman to please him, and she nearly killed both of them before Jill and Aderyn caught her."

"Do you think she wants revenge on Jill?"

"I don't know. By rights, the little minx should be grateful. She was in a great deal of danger, wandering aimlessly in the physical world and afraid to go back to her own. But you never know with spirits. You might want to set wards around your camp tonight."

"Have no fear of that, O Princess of Powers Perilous! Pentagrams shall abound."

Even with the wards glowing all around him, Salamander had a restless night's sleep. He woke at every rustle of wind among the trees, but the white spirit never returned. Finally, with the first light, he gave up on sleeping as a bad job and left his blankets. Once he'd tended his horses, he got on his way north.

About midmorning Salamander rode up to a stone marker announcing that he was passing into the demesne of Mawrvelin, under the lordship of most holy Bel. Great Bel's priests apparently took their privileges as lords seriously. Toward noon Salamander rode past the temple, looming behind thick stone walls at the top of the big hill that had given the place its name. He could just make out the gates, shut tight, glinting with iron bands in the sunlight. Although the priestly lands looked just as well-watered and the soil just as rich as Cengarn's, he could see the difference between overlords at the first farm he came to. The farmer and his family wore ragged clothes, their roof needed fresh thatch, their plow horse displayed a good many ribs. The priests were appaently exacting their full measure of taxes if not more.

By asking around in a sad little village Salamander found Canna, the woman who'd been rescued from the Horsekin some years past. The fellow in Cengarn had described her as a "pretty little thing," but while she still had the long red hair he'd admired, she'd grown gaunt and stoop-shouldered. Deep wrinkles lined her face, but it was her hands that caught Salamander's attention. They were callused, scarred, and stained a yellowish brown, but he could tell that the bones beneath were thin and frail. Her wrists, too, were all bone and not much of that. As she stood in the farmyard to talk with Salamander, she held a baby on one hip. A toddler clung to her skirts, a little lass of perhaps six years leaned against her, and out in the fields beyond the house Salamander could see two older children, working with a man who, he could assume, was their father. When Salamander offered Canna a copper for her story, she snatched it, then hid it in a little pouch hanging round her neck.

"Well, now," she said, "all that about the Horsekin, it happened years ago now, and truly, I can't say I remember much. The terror—well, I do remember that. I was sure as sure, we all were, that we'd never see home again."

"A frightening thing, indeed," Salamander said. "I hope that none of you were harmed."

"We weren't, none of us women, I mean. They'd already killed our men." Her voice went flat with stale grief. "My da died that night, when they raided. But once they'd got us away, they treated us better than we'd feared. Gave us food, and no one touched us wrong, if you take my meaning." Canna narrowed her eyes in thought. "Well, there was two kinds of men there, the Horsekin men, and they gave us no trouble. Then there were some fellows who were human like you and me, good sir, fighting for the Horsekin if you can believe that. They wanted a bit of fun with us, but that old priest stopped them."

"Old priest? Zaklof?"

"Don't remember his name. I heard they let him starve to death later."

"Zaklof, then. So he kept you all from being raped?"

"He did, swearing at them and threatening them with somewhat or other. Couldn't understand a word of it, we couldn't, but the men did, and that's what mattered, wasn't it? He was saving us for the sake of some sort of goddess. Shandrala or somewhat like that."

"Alshandra. Did he tell you captives much about her?"

"Naught." She glanced at the baby, who was sucking dirty fingers. "Stop it!" She slapped his hand. "If I remember rightly, he was going to, but the gwerbret's men got there before he could start."

The baby whimpered and began pulling at the front of her torn gray dress.

"Now, I've got to feed my little one here," Canna said. "Can't remember much more anyway."

"Fair enough, then," Salamander said. "Just one more question, if I may. How far are Lord Honelg's lands?"

"Another day's ride. I've been told that there's a stone marker up, 'twixt his lands and the priests."

"What's his blazon, do you know?"

"He and his men ride by every once in a while. It's a blue circle with a black arrow across it, but not straight. Sort of tilted, like, pointing up."

"My thanks. Well, I'll be going on now and let you get back to your children."

As he rode away, Salamander was thinking about Honelg's blazon. *How very interesting! If that arrow means what I think it means, he's cursed bold, what with the temple lands right next to his.*

Yet, of course, Honelg had a perfectly legitimate reason to add an arrow to his clan's blazon. Eldidd lords had known about the power of longbows for many a year, but it had taken the Cengarn War, and the way that elven arrows skewered enemies, to catch the attention of the Deverry lords. Although they considered using a bow beneath them personally, the northern nobility all wanted archers among their freemen. A good many of them reduced the taxes of any farmer who could provide a longbow and the skill to use it in times of war. Once Salamander crossed into Honelg's demesne, he found young yew trees lining the road, some tall enough to supply a stout six feet of wood to a bowyer, all placed far enough apart to prevent them weaving their branches into a hedge. They must have been planted soon after the siege of Cengarn, Salamander figured. Like oak, yew grew in its own time and refused to be hurried.

He also saw a couple of farms where the cows and pigs looked well-fed, and the healthy-looking people he saw were decently dressed. When he stopped at their gates, they invited him inside and offered him a stoup of ale and a bit of food. Salamander played the affable gerthddyn, juggling and singing for the children, telling the adults tales based on the Cengarn War. Each time he mentioned Alshandra, calling her a false goddess, he watched his audience carefully, hoping for some betraying reaction. Finally, in the straggle of houses that formed the demesne's only village, his hunting brought game.

On a hot humid evening the villagers gathered around the stone well to listen to this unexpected delight, a performer from down in Deverry. Salamander put on his performance shirt and secreted scarves, eggs, and the other such things he needed inside its hidden pockets. As the twilight began to fade, someone lit a pair of torches, and the black smoke thinned the cloud of gnats and mosquitos that had joined the audience. Salamander perched on the stone wall at the well and described the lifting of the siege.

"But all this slaughter would have been in vain," Salamander said, "if the mighty magicians within the walls had not slain the false goddess, that demon, that illusion, Alshandra. How the Horsekin shrieked when she was slain—"

"That's not true!" It was a child's voice, from well back in the crowd. "She's not dead."

Everyone in the crowd gasped or swore, squirmed as they sat or turned to look back. At the edge of the pool of torchlight two figures, one short, one taller, shrank back into the darkness.

"Indeed?" Salamander said. "What's this? I don't understand."

No one spoke or moved. In the smoky light Salamander had trouble discerning their facial expressions, but they seemed to be terrified. Finally the local blacksmith stood up and stepped forward. Salamander had noticed earlier that he seemed to have some sort of authority in the village.

"He be just a little lad," Marth said. "Given to fancies, like."

"Ah, I see. Well, shall I finish the tale?"

"Please do."

Marth sat back down, and the crowd relaxed with sighs and murmurs, a soft sound like the wind in the yew trees that ringed the village in a living palisade.

That night Salamander camped outside the village in a fallow field. He could understand the villagers' fear. If the priests of Bel got wind of an alien worship, they would head straight for Cengarn and demand that the gwerbret root it out. No doubt Honelg lacked the men and the influence to protect them. But what, he wondered, of the lord himself?

Roughly an hour's ride on the morrow morning brought him to Lord Honelg's dun, unprepossessing except for its elaborate defenses. It perched upon a low but steep hill, wound round with a path that led, eventually, to the gates. Deep ditches ran alongside the path to keep any attackers upon it, easy prey for bowmen. At the top, a stone wall surrounded the dun, but it was rough work, not much better than the drystone walls surrounding farmers' fields, though the irregular rocks had been fitted with some care. In a few places Salamander saw mortar, holding the largest in place.

When Salamander rode up to the wooden gates, he found them open, though only by a few feet. A gatekeeper, wearing a hauberk and carrying a sword, stood between them. Salamander dismounted and put on his best shallow smile.

"And a good morrow to you, my good man," Salamander said. "I am a gerthddyn, ridden here from southern lands with a stock of tricks, tales, jests, and—"

"We know who you are," the fellow interrupted. "Marth sent a lad up to tell us you were on the way."

From the shadows on either side of the half-drawn gates two more armed men stepped out. Salamander kept smiling by force of will.

"Are you sure you've not mistaken me for someone else?" Salamander said. "I'm naught but a gerthddyn. I call myself Salamander, but my real name's Evan from Trev Hael."

The fellow's mouth twitched in something like scorn. He was a tall man, with black hair swept back en brosse and narrow dark eyes. He wore new-looking brigga, woven in a blue, black, and tan plaid, and under his hauberk his shirt appeared to be fine linen.

"Do I have the honor of addressing Lord Honelg himself?" Salamander said.

"You do, but I'm not sure how much of an honor you'll find it."

His voice, flat and hard at the same time, made Salamander's stomach clench. Salamander realized that he would have to risk everything on a bold gesture—because in one sense, he was risking nothing at all. Honelg would kill him in an instant should he think him a priestly spy or even just a busybody.

"A man named Zaklof told me you give a better welcome than this," Salamander said, "to the right sort of guest."

Honelg blinked several times, rapidly.

"I have a token to show you," Salamander went on. "It's in my saddlebags. May I bring it out?"

"You may."

Salamander's fingers shook, just slightly, as he unlaced the flap. *What if I lost the wretched thing on the road? Worse yet, what if he's been to Trev Hael and knows a gerthddyn never lived there?* The gold arrow, however, still lay in its pocket, and the lord, apparently, never went far from home. As soon as Salamander held up the arrow, Honelg nodded to his men, and sheathed his sword.

"My apologies for the scare," Honelg said. "Living so close to Bel's priests—we can't be too careful."

"Oh, fear not, I most assuredly understand. Haven't I been turned out by my own kin for my beliefs? Haven't I wandered the kingdom ever since Zaklof's death, desperate for more news of *her* yet afraid for my life?"

Honelg looked him over, his eyes narrow again. "Zaklof died a fair many years ago."

"So he did. Every summer, my trade takes me this way and that, traveling all over the west. Once a town's heard all your tales, they won't pay for them anymore, so it's taken me a while to return to the Northlands."

The lord's hand strayed to his sword hilt.

"I have—nay, I had—a wife and family," Salamander went on. "I couldn't just up and desert them. Not until our neighbors forced me to leave Trev Hael could I take up my search in earnest."

"Ah. *She'd* not have her worshipers abandon their little ones, that's certainly true. What did you do, start talking about *her?*"

"Not precisely. First of all, I had this arrow made when I was far from home, but one of our neighbors managed to get a look at it. That made them suspicious, and then just last year—" He paused for a dramatic shudder. "Maybe you've heard of the horrible disease that struck Trev Hael, a ghastly inflammation of the bowels, and it killed so many people? Well, my family was spared by some miracle. The neighbors ran to the meddling priests in the local temple. They were sure I'd worked witchcraft or suchlike to afflict the town, and I had to run for my life. My wife believed their lies and refused to come with me."

"I see." Yet the lord never moved, and his hand stayed on the sword hilt.

"I couldn't have come straight here," Salamander said. "It would have been too suspicious. I didn't want to lead anyone to your dun."

"You have my thanks for that." Honelg took his hand away from the sword. "Come in, gerthddyn. You can wear *her* arrow here safely enough."

With a smile of heartfelt relief, Salamander pinned the gold arrow to the collar of his shirt, then followed the lord inside the gates. The two men-at-arms sheathed their weapons, then began to shove the gates closed. A groom came running to take Salamander's horses. A young page appeared and bowed to Honelg and Salamander impartially.

"We have a guest, Matto," Honelg said. "Put his things in a chamber in the broch. Ask the chamberlain to help you."

"I will, Da." Matto ran off after the groom.

"My son, of course," Honelg said to Salamander. "I can't take pages in the usual way. Too dangerous."

Inside the walls stood a single flat-roofed stone tower, wider at the base than the top, and a clutter of wooden sheds. Off to one side Salamander caught a glimpse of a long narrow building, two stories high and made of wood, that seemed to house stables and warband alike. Over everything hung the rich, moist smell of livestock.

Honelg escorted Salamander into the great hall, a shabby dusty half-round of a room, housing a scatter of rough tables and rickety benches. They sat down together at the honor table, Salamander on a bench, the lord in the only chair. A servant brought them mead in pottery goblets, but despite these small signs of respect, the lord sat bolt upright in his chair and looked his guest over. Not once did Honelg smile. Salamander knew that if he made one blunder the lord would kill him.

"Tell me about Zaklof," Honelg said. "How did you come to know him?"

"I was in Cengarn plying my trade," Salamander said, "when the gwerbret's men returned with Zaklof. He'd made up his mind to die, but they were taunting him, waving food under his nose and trying to tempt him. He resisted them all, and with such calm." He put urgency into his voice. "I had to know how he could be so calm, facing death."

"It's a marvel, truly, how the Holy Ones can do that," Honelg said. "You said you spoke with him?"

"I did. There was a young woman working in the kitchen—her father lived in town—and she, too, was impressed with Zaklof. The gaol stood right out in the ward, you see, and so at night she went sneaking out to talk with him through the window in his cell. So I took to joining her."

"Ah." Honelg nodded, leaning back in his chair. "I wish I could have heard him myself."

"Toward the end he grew weak, but his voice stayed steady, telling us of Alshandra's power over death, and how he'd go join her soon. On the last day they brought him out of the cell to lie in the sun. It was his last wish, like. And I've never seen another man die like that, smiling, whispering a blessing upon his captors."

"I heard about that, truly." Honelg nodded again. "But here, I'm forgetting my courtesy. You must be hungry." He turned in his chair and beckoned a servant. "Bring bread and meat for our guest!"

Salamander let out his breath in a soft sigh of relief.

The servant had just set out the food when a woman, dressed in clean gray linen with a blue-and-black plaid kirtle at the waist, came down the spiral staircase and joined them. Honelg presented Salamander to her, then introduced her as his wife, Lady Adranna. To Salamander, she looked oddly familiar, a pretty woman if a bit short, plump and dark-haired, though her blue eyes were narrow as if with perpetual suspicion. He combed his memory, but he couldn't place her or where he might have seen her before. She sat down on the bench at her lord's right hand, across the table from Salamander.

"Evan saw Zaklof die," Honelg said.

"You did?" Adranna leaned forward. "Could you tell me about it? I don't mean to be rude, but—"

"Not rude at all," Salamander said hastily. "I should be honored."

Fortunately, he remembered a good many secondhand details, and this time through, he elaborated the story. Adranna listened, wide-eyed, her mouth slack, while Honelg nodded to himself at intervals, as if savoring the tale. Salamander began to feel more guilty than fearful, deceiving people who had entrusted their souls to a spirit he knew to be naught but an imposter.

Alshandra had possessed dweomer beyond the power of any human master of that craft. Although she'd used those powers coldly and deliberately to get herself worshiped, a goddess she wasn't, merely a strange spirit of the race known to the elves as Guardians. In the end she'd proved just as mortal as any elf or human, too, but her worshipers had refused to believe the truth, that she'd been defeated and slain. Salamander had never understood why, or why her legend continued to spread after her death. There was no doubting that it had grown in strength here in the Northlands. The lord and lady both sat as still as if they'd been ensorcelled by his story, until he finished with a small sob and a broken sigh.

"I heard that Zaklof's body smelled of roses," Adranna said, "not of rotting flesh at all."

"I wouldn't know, my lady," Salamander said, quite truthfully for a change. "After he died, they carried him away, and I wasn't close enough to tell."

Adranna plucked a handkerchief from her kirtle and wiped a tear from her cheek. "It's so sad," she murmured, "dying a captive."

"Ah, but we're all captives, prisoners in our flesh." Honelg turned to Salamander. "Zaklof visited us several times, you see. I remember him as a strong man, and so full of life, but we know he's now where we all want to be, free of this cursed rotten world at last, with *her* in our true home."

"Truly," Salamander said. "He crossed over into her kingdom on a bridge of prayers."

"It's a good thing you tell tales for your living," Honelg went on. "Can you stand to tell it again? Tonight we're having a very special guest." He shot a meaningful glance at his wife. "I think me she'll want to hear it. Zaklof died a true witness to our faith."

"I'm sure she will. And, Evan, you speak so beautifully."

"My thanks, my lady. You're very kind to say so."

At dinner that night, Salamander met the rest of the lord's family, his daughter Treniffa and his elderly mother, Lady Varigga. His son Matyc served everyone like a page, then sat down and joined in the meal. From their talk Salamander realized that even the lowliest servant in the dun believed in Alshandra and her false promises. Everlasting life in a glorious version of the Otherlands had its appeal, Salamander realized, but still he wondered why they would believe so fervently in things they'd never seen. The twenty men of Honelg's warband, eating on the other side of the hall, drank a toast to the goddess' name, marking themselves as believers as well.

So, apparently, were all the farmers and their families who sharecropped land in Honelg's demesne. Just as the meal was being cleared away, the farm folk began arriving, walking into the great hall in threes and fours, sitting down on the floor and chatting with each other so casually that Salamander realized they came here often. Among them he recognized Marth and a few other villagers.

"It's for the services." Apparently the aged Lady Varigga had noticed him studying the farmers. "You'll see. There's a great treat in store for you."

"Splendid, my lady. It's very kind of you to take me along."

"It's in *her* name. There's a place for every sort of person in *her* world." She paused to consider his dirty traveling shirt with no trace of a smile. "Even for the lowest."

Apparently those persons would be expected to stay in their places, too, but then, Varigga *was* noble-born, even if she and her equally noble son did live like foxes in a den, praying that the hounds would never run their way.

"It's time," Lord Honelg said. "Nearly dark out."

The lord stood up, and at his signal everyone in the great hall did the same. In a mannerly throng they strolled out of the dun and followed their lord across the twilit ward.

When he'd first arrived, Salamander had wondered why the lord's warband lived in a freestanding building instead of the usual barracks. Now he saw that a very different sort of structure took up that particular space. A shabby wooden door looked as if it would lead into a root cellar or suchlike, but in truth it led into a long, narrow chamber. The only fresh air came from chinks in the stonework, but fortunately, the masons had left plenty of those in their deceptively shoddy work.

Once inside, the only light came from a single candle, carried by Lady Adranna down to the opposite end of the room from the door. The lady, her mother-in-law, and the son and daughter sat down on a bench just at the foot of a wooden platform. Behind them sat the chamberlain and the equerry right next to the common-born cook and stablemen, and, on the next set of benches, the warband. The dun's servants and the farm people crowded together on the floor at the rear. Honelg closed the door, then stood in front of it and beckoned Salamander to do the same.

"We all have our places in the ritual." Honelg patted the hilt of his sword. "You and I will be the sentinels tonight."

"Very well, my lord," Salamander said. "Do you think we're in danger?"

"Not at the moment, but one day those cursed priests of Bel might find us, and so we need to stay ready for them."

As Salamander's eyes grew used to the dim light, he noticed a little door at the farther end of the long room. In a moment it opened, and a woman stepped onto the platform. She threw both arms into the air, tipped her head back, and called out a single word in a language he didn't recognize. Silver light bloomed between and around her hands like a skein of yarn. Salamander gasped aloud, which drew a smile from the lord. When Lady Adranna blew out the candle, the priestess tossed the bundle of light toward the ceiling, where it stuck, sending its silver glow over the crowd. By its light Salamander could see a wood altar, topped with a long slab of stone that was, oddly enough, cracked in half.

"There's our Holy One," Honelg whispered. "The priestess Rocca."

Despite the silvery glow, she stood far enough away that Salamander got only the most general impression of her—a slender woman, dark-haired and perhaps pretty, perhaps young, certainly vigorous.

"Did she ride in today?" Salamander whispered.

"She didn't," Honelg whispered in return. "She walks everywhere, all the way here from the Horsekin lands. She's got a regular circuit, like, of believers."

Salamander would have asked more, but Rocca was speaking. Her voice, low and pleasant, carried easily through the stuffy chamber, although she did speak with something of a rough accent. Her words sounded as if she were pronouncing them farther back in her mouth than most Deverry folk would, and her R's and Rh's were flat, not rolled. As he listened, Salamander realized from the way she used certain idioms that she hailed from the northwest, beyond Deverry and the Westfolk lands both.

"We be gathered here tonight in the shelter of our lord's dun," the priestess began, "to learn the truth. What be the questions we were about asking for our lives long?" She pointed at Honelg's mother.

Lady Varigga stood up. Considering her age, her voice was remarkably strong. "We wish to know what we were, where we came from, where we now are, who we are now, and where we are going."

"True-spoken. And the answers?"

"We are eternal spirits, we came from between the stars, we live in a prison, we are children of light still, and we are going to Alshandra's country."

"Also true-spoken."

Varigga sat back down.

"At the beginning of the world," Rocca continued, "Alshandra did make a green and lovely land, where pure water runs in crystal streams. Ripe fruit hangs heavy on every kind of tree, and when a fruit, it be plucked, a new one grows in its place. In her beautiful orchards the smell of ripening fruit wafts like perfume. And the flowers! I have seen in vision the banks of flowers, purple and pink and rose red, blossoming along the crystal streams. I do swear to you, my friends, that in her world all be color, and fragrance, and light." Rocca paused for effect. "But why, then, does this world lie shut away from us? Why lack we the power to travel there? Why did she, the goddess of all things good, hide it from us?"

Lady Adranna stood up and laid her right hand over her heart in an obviously rehearsed gesture. "She hid it not from us, but from the Dark Lord Vandar."

"True-spoken," Rocca said. "And what did the evil Vandar steal from her?"

"Her daughter, her only precious child."

"True-spoken. And why does Alshandra not appear to us? Once she walked among us, but she walks here no more."

"Because she searches for her lost daughter over all the world, wailing as she goes." Adranna paused briefly. "Why can she not find her daughter?"

This time the priestess gave the answer. "Because the Dark Lord has set evil guardians over the child and over the world."

Adranna sat down, and Varigga stood again.

"What minions did Vandar send?" Rocca asked her.

"His dragons of evil, spewing poison," Varigga said. "Huge they were, bent on destroying our goddess's creation."

"And did she slay them?"

"She did slay the mother and father of all dragons, but unknown to her their evil spawn still lived."

"True-spoken."

Varigga sat back down. Rocca leaned forward, staring into the crowd as if she wished to look each person there in the eye. "To this very day," she said at last, "the silver wyrm and the black dragon do roam and ravage. They do slay by night, they do poison by day, rabid, evil in the foulness of their hearts."

Ye gods! Salamander thought. *She means Rori and Arzosah.*

"The Dark Lord Vandar did set them at their post," Rocca went on. "By his orders they fall upon *her* people and destroy them. Until Vandar at last does die, they will have strength, but once the Dark Lord be slain, all his minions will sicken, fail, and pass utterly away."

Salamander was seized by the mad impulse to step forward and shout, "but Evandar's already dead" simply because doing so would have had such a splendid effect on the crowd. He managed to keep his urge toward drama under control, even when the assembled worshipers cheered in anticipated triumph.

"Soon, my well-loved friends," Rocca said, "soon that day will come on a wave like silver moonlight. But until that day does come, we have a task, a holy burden. What be that task?" She paused only briefly. "To witness unto her power over death. Indeed, it be upon us to witness even with our deaths, for what holier deed could we be about doing but to die with her name upon our lips?"

In unison the assembly shouted, "There be none!"

"True-spoken!" Rocca shouted as well. "Let us give thanks, let us pray."

Those sitting on benches fell to their knees, even the aged Lady Varigga; those sitting on the floor rose to theirs. Salamander followed Honelg's example and knelt as well. Apparently her followers believed that Alshandra took great delight in prayers. Rocca droned on and on, the crowd murmured responses, the room grew warmer and stuffier, until Salamander had to fight to stay awake. Since the prayerful kept their gaze on the floor, he could take comfort in knowing that no one would notice him yawning. In fact, he heard once or twice the distinct sound of a snore, hastily cut off, and knew that he was not alone.

At last the prayers, and the service, were over. Everyone left the hidden room and in silence trooped across the ward to gather in the great hall. Honelg's servants passed out chunks of bread, dipped in honey—whether as refreshment or as part of the ritual, Salamander didn't know. Everyone chatted pleasantly, until, a few at a time, the farm folk left the broch, slinking through the dark like cats. As they left, Rocca stood at the door and blessed each of them.

In the torchlight of the great hall Salamander finally got a clear look at her. Her long dark hair she wore in a sloppy twist at the nape of her neck, held there by two-pronged bone pins, but a good many short wisps had escaped, framing her face. Her eyes, too, were dark, and her features so delicate that she might have been lovely had she been reasonably clean.

As it was, dirt smeared along her cheekbones and matted her

hair; dirt ringed her neck and clotted under her torn fingernails. The tunic she wore over baggy brigga had once been linen-colored, but now appeared dark brown; it hung in stiff crusted folds. Her only adornment, if one could call it that, was a flat band of hammered steel curved around her right wrist. Her feet revealed how much she walked; they were huge, flat, and clublike from calluses and old scars. Salamander thought of Tieryn Cadryc, saying that Zaklof had never worn shoes in his life. Walking such long distances without them must have caused her constant pain, at least until the calluses had formed.

Rocca also reeked of sour sweat and general secretions. Salamander feigned a cough and raised his arm to shelter his nose with his sleeve, a gesture that Honelg caught. The lord elbowed him in the ribs and whispered. "They don't wash, the Holy Ones. It shows their contempt for the things of this world."

"I see," Salamander whispered as well. "But don't they get sores on their skin?"

"Horrible ones, truly. They call them Alshandra's jewels."

Once the last worshiper was out of the door, the priestess accepted a seat at the honor table. Lady Adranna moved down on the bench to allow Rocca to sit at the lord's right hand, across from Salamander, who was sitting at his left. Young Matto brought her a plate of dry bread and a goblet of plain water, bowed to her, then hurried away again. Rocca said a brief prayer over the food, then picked up a chunk of bread and gestured at Salamander.

"Now who be this?" Rocca said "A stranger, but he does wear the symbol of one who does follow our goddess."

"He does, Your Holiness," Honelg said. "His name is Evan, though he goes by Salamander, because he's a gerthddyn by trade."

"And he saw Zaklof die." Adranna leaned forward. "Do tell her, Evan."

For the third time that day Salamander told his borrowed tale. With such an attentive audience he could no longer resist embroidering every detail. He invented speeches for the guards and sermons for Zaklof. He worked himself up to scattered tears at the appropriate places and let his voice catch with awe at others. Even the warband turned on their benches and listened in dead silence, their mugs of ale forgotten, as Salamander described Zaklof's last hours in this world.

Salamander then turned to his own imaginary troubles, a tale of suspicious neighbors, of priests threatening to burn him alive, of a wife who reacted only with fury to his talk of Alshandra. This material held the great hall's attention equally well, until he at last truly understood that old turn of phrase about storytellers entrancing their audience. He might as well have turned them to stone for all the restlessness or skepticism they showed.

When at last he finished, he wiped tears from his face on one sleeve with a suitably rough and masculine gesture, then allowed his hand to drop into his lap as if he were exhausted. The women at the table, including the priestess, were staring at him moist-eyed.

"How much you did suffer," Rocca said softly, "so much will our goddess reward you."

"Never would I claim any reward, Your Holiness," Salamander said. "The only thing I long for is more knowledge of *her* and her ways."

"Well, that mayhap I could be giving to you, but there be a need on all of us to learn it slowly. Journeys, there be a need on them to proceed by single steps."

"Of course," Salamander said. "Is there novice lore, then?"

"There be such." Rocca paused for a sip of water. "The council of high priests mapped out our journey to *her* in safe steps."

"My heart burns to hear everything you deem me worthy of," Salamander said, "and naught more."

Rocca smiled and raised her goblet of water as if in salute.

"Unfortunately," Honelg broke in, "our Holy One can't stay here more than a single night. It's too dangerous. Besides, she has other souls in her care."

"Well, to tell the truth, like, at my leaving here, I'll be traveling straight back to our new dun, Zakh Gral. That be its name." Rocca turned in Honelg's direction. "We do build a shrine there, of course, and there be a need on me to be there for the consecration."

Salamander had to draw upon every bit of will that he possessed to keep his voice steady. "That's a pity," he said. "But perhaps, next time you come this way, would you tell me the lore then?"

"A better idea, and methinks our goddess did send it to me." Her eyes bright, she leaned forward. "Evan, truly, there be a need on you to come with me. You talk so well, you'd be a boon to the faith and the faithful. If the—well, the higher order of priests—if they do agree, it might even be allowed that you travel to the holiest of temples in our city off in the far west."

"Oh, I'd never be worthy of that." Salamander looked down at the floor and softened his voice to modesty. "My gifts are far too poor. But I'd love to see the shrine, a holy place dedicated to *her*."

"Then you shall!" Rocca smiled, suddenly merry. "It be a long way off, but while we go a-traveling, I may teach you the novice's lore, and you may teach me how to speak like you do."

"Your Holiness, you speak from the heart, and that makes your words far more moving than any a gerthddyn could say."

"How kind you be! But still, there be other wandering priests and priestesses, and as much as they do love our goddess, they do lack the words to make others see the truth and come to her. There be a need for such as you to help to us. Please—do come with me?"

"Do you truly think I'm worthy?"

"If I had not so thought, would I be inviting you?" She sounded on the edge of laughing. "Now, whether it be possible for you to someday see the temple in Taenalapan, I mayn't say. The deciding of that be for the holy council. But the shrine—certainly it does lie within my rights to take you there."

"If you command, then I can but obey."

Rocca smiled, Honelg and his womenfolk all smiled, and Salamander pledged them with his goblet of mead. Rocca got up, her smile disappearing into a yawn.

"I be fair tired," she remarked. "There be a need on me for sleep."

"Now, Your Holiness," Adranna said, "are you sure I can't give you a proper bed in the broch?"

"Very sure. Straw in the stables be good enough for me in this world. We shall all have so much better one fine day."

When she left, Salamander said his good nights as well and went upstairs to the spare little chamber he'd been given. Rocca's easy faith in his lies had made his guilt return in a breaking wave of shame. It receded, however, once he was safely alone and could do some hard thinking. He'd have wagered a fortune, had he had one, that Taenalapan, that city in the far west, must have once been called Tanbalapalim, an elven city destroyed by Horsekin over a thousand years before. The ancient lore stated that a vile plague had then conquered the conquerors, but Salamander knew that the ancient lore had already been proven wrong about one group of Horsekin, the civilized Gel da'Thae of Braemel. It could well be wrong a second time, as he remarked to Dallandra once he'd contacted her.

"That's certainly true." The thought-image of her face turned grave. "I don't know exactly where Tanbalapalim was, but I'll wager Meranaldar does."

"Dar's scribe? No doubt! He's a great man for lore, Meranaldar. Endlessly and perennially great."

"Now he can't help being a bit tedious."

"He could too help it if only he wanted to, but no matter, oh mistress of mighty magicks. What counts is this new dun that Rocca spoke of."

"Well, yes. I've been searching for that spirit you saw, by the way, the white womanlike creature. I've found no trace of her. She may have just been curious about Branna, not vengeful or the like."

"Let us hope so."

Salamander may have considered Meranaldar tedious, but he soon realized that he'd never known how tedious tedium could be. In the morning, when he and Rocca set off for the west, Salamander urged her to take his horse and ride, but she insisted on walking. She did at least allow him to tie her rough cloth sack, containing her few possessions, onto the packsaddle of the second horse. They left the dun and followed a leveled dirt road through farmland. Rocca strode along at Salamander's stirrup, talking all the while. Her harsh life, spent mostly out of doors, had given her a splendid pair of lungs.

"Numbers be the key," she began. "All the novice lore it does circle around numbers like ducks around a pond. The most important numbers be seven, thirteen, and fifty-two."

"Seven, thirteen, and fifty-two. Very well, I'll remember those," Salamander said. "You know, I could shift some of the packhorse's load so that we could both ride."

"I want not to ride." She sounded near laughter. "Our goddess did give me the power to walk where I will, and I'd ask for naught more. Now. We start with seven. There be fifty-two lists of seven sacred things each, and there be a need on you to remember them in the correct order. First, the planets."

Salamander allowed himself a brief surge of optimism. He knew the names of the seven planets already, and perhaps the rest of the lore would be equally easy to learn. Unfortunately, he'd forgotten that Alshandra's priests would never name any sacred thing in either Deverrian or Elvish.

"Azgarn and Rebisov be what we call the sun and the moon," Rocca said. "Then there be Jalmat, Ringonnin, Saddet, Fomthir, and Honexel. Repeat those back."

Salamander did manage to repeat that first lot, but as the morning wore on, and the lists kept coming, he felt his heart turn as heavy as sgarkan, one of the seven sacred metals, otherwise known as lead. He had hated the early teachings of the dweomer for just this same emphasis on memory, the lists of names, the formulae of rituals. Now he was starting over in yet another system, learning a vast bundle of minutiae, all of which would doubtless prove to be of crucial importance at some point, just as the dweomerlore had proved to be.

"Sooner or later," Rocca said cheerfully, "there'll be a need on you to learn the sacred language. That be where all these names do come from."

"No doubt," Salamander said. "It's the language of the Horsekin, isn't it?"

With a little gasp she stopped walking. He reined in his horse and turned in the saddle to look at her, watching him wide-eyed and frightened as she stood in the road.

"Rocca, everyone here in the north knows about the Horsekin," Salamander said. "Why do you keep trying to pretend they don't exist?"

"Well, I—" She let her voice trail away.

Salamander dismounted so they could talk face-to-face, but she refused to look at him, even when he walked up close to her.

"I've noticed a couple of times now how you nearly say some word and then shy away from it. That word's Horsekin, isn't it? Your Horsekin masters?"

"True enough. It does frighten people, Evan. They think the Horsekin be evil, horrible slavers who live to conquer the whole world."

"Aren't they?"

"Of course not!" She tossed her head and looked up at last. "They merely be wanting to spread the word of Alshandra and salvation. But Deverry folk understand this not, and they attack us."

"From what I've seen, I'd say that the attacks generally come from the Horsekin."

"Well, at times there be a need on us to protect ourselves by striking first." Rocca hesitated for a long moment. "Truly, once you meet the high priestess, then the understanding will come upon you, truly it will."

Salamander felt a ripple of dweomer cold run down his spine. No doubt he'd understand danger, though not a danger of the spirit, once he reached the new fort, but he'd expected nothing else. She took a step toward him and held out a hand.

"You will be coming with me, won't you?" Rocca said.

For a moment, with the dweomer cold all around him, he hesitated. She watched him silently. With her dirty face and rough clothes, she looked like a beggar child, utterly vulnerable.

"Of course I will," Salamander said. "I long to see Alshandra's shrine. Naught will keep me away from that."

Rocca smiled, and despite the dirt her face turned beautiful. Salamander soothed his guilt by pointing out that seeing the shrine meant seeing the dun that housed it, so that in a way, he wasn't truly lying to her.

By midafternoon they'd left the settled farmland behind. The road turned into a narrow track through sparse forest where slender pines grew among shrubby underbrush and long grass. Judging from the cut stumps and broken limbs, these trees had been supplying firewood to Honelg's people for some years. On such rough ground it became impossible for Rocca to walk next to him as he rode, and the horses had to pick their way on the uneven ground. With her long easy stride Rocca took the lead, though occasionally she would pause to let him catch up. Each time she'd ask him to repeat one of the lists—the wretched, revolting, vile, and despicable lists, as Salamander came to call them, though not, of course, aloud.

Toward sunset they reached a wild meadow, where he could tether out his horses and let them graze. Salamander made a bed of rocks, cleared the grass from around it, then stacked up scraps of deadfall wood that he scrounged from the forest edge. For kindling, he mounded up bark and dry leaves. After they'd eaten, and once it was growing dark, he struggled with flint and steel to light the tinder. In front of Rocca he didn't dare invoke the Wildfolk of Fire, though eventually they took pity on him and showered a few sparks onto the leaves. The bark caught, and with it the wood. Salamander sighed his relief, then sat down next to Rocca, who'd been watching all of this with a small smile.

"It truly does comfort the heart to have a bit of light at night," Rocca remarked.

"Don't you make yourself a fire when you travel?" Salamander said.

"I don't. Since there be with me no horse to feed or tend, I be accustomed to traveling till it be too dark to see, and by then I want naught but sleep."

"Ah."

She turned toward him and seemed about to speak—*more lists*, he thought.

"Somewhat I've been meaning to ask you," Salamander said hurriedly. "That iron bracelet you wear. Does it have a meaning?"

"I'd not call it a meaning, precisely. I do wear it to repel dweomer, were it to be used against me."

"Repel dweomer? Iron can't do that."

"The high priestess herself in Taenalapan did tell me of its power, and she'd not be lying, would she, now? There be a need upon anyone who goes east among Deverry folk to wear this blessed vambrace for the fending off of their nasty dweomer."

"Ah. You—I mean we—we see dweomer as evil, then."

"It be not a question of seeing. We ken its evil nature. Once there were among my people those who did work dweomer, and of the worst sort, too. They did boast of their power to turn themselves into animals and birds, so that they might creep or fly about and spy on people. Mazrakir, the Horsekin did call them. When the joyous light of Alshandra began to shine among us, most of these sorcerers did lay aside their foul ways and worship her, but there were some among us who were too puffed up with pride to surrender their evil powers."

"What happened to them?"

"A decree did go out, and they were slain. Their impious knowledge did vanish with them, so that none left among us now kens how to transform himself."

"Do the priests kill all magicians?"

"They do and with great dispatch, wherever they may find them."

Gods help me! Salamander thought.

"But what about the silver light?" he said aloud. "The kind you called down for the ceremony. That must have been dweomer."

"It be no such thing but a gift from the goddess. *She* be the one who did teach us how to draw down the light from her world."

"Well, but now that you know how, couldn't you teach someone else?"

"Speak not such foolish things! Without her blessing there
would be no light."

"So you pray and the light appears, is that right?"

"We do pray using the right words to beseech *her* and do prepare
our hands to receive it. There be somewhat of a trick to it."

"Ah, so you are causing the light—"

"Not by my own power, you dolt! It does come from *her*, the
power and the light both. I would die, truly, before I'd let filthy
dweomer stain my heart and soul."

A sudden rush of anger took him by surprise—how dare she
scorn the dweomer this way! She spoke with such exasperated certainty that he realized he'd never be able to change her mind.

"I understand now," he said, instead of trying, "my thanks."

It was late that night before Dallandra heard from Salamander.
He'd had to wait until Rocca had left the camp before he dared to
stare into the fire. Even if he appeared to be merely thinking, or so
Salamander told her, Rocca would have taken notice and asked him
why he seemed so preoccupied.

"She's my spiritual guide now," Salamander said. "I'm supposed
to tell her everything."

"Whatever for?" Dallandra said. "Alshandra seems to have
turned into an awfully nosy sort of goddess. But it is safe for you to
contact me now, isn't it?"

"Yes, Rocca had to go into the forest alone. We novices aren't allowed to watch the priestess praying her special prayers." He went
on to tell her of his day's traveling, but like the gerthddyn he was,
saved the most dramatic touch for the last. "This is all getting a bit
fraught. I just found out that they kill anyone who knows
dweomer."

"I'm not surprised," Dallandra said. "Most human priests are
jealous of the dweomer. Look at the Gel da'Thae, and how seri-

ously they take their religion. Horsekin believers are bound to be even more fervent about this new one."

"That's a good word for it, all right. Fervent, ardent, inflamed, and perhaps even rabid. And yet Rocca's such a happy soul, at root, always laughing and smiling."

"Of course she is. She thinks she has the remedy for every trouble in the world. Who wouldn't be happy, then?"

"A very good point, oh princess of powers perilous. Speaking of which, here she comes."

The link between them snapped as he broke it. Dallandra sat thinking for a moment, remembering a human woman named Raena, who some forty years past had made herself into a mortal enemy despite Dallandra's efforts to help her. *She was devoted to her goddess, too,* Dalla thought. *I wonder.* Rocca seemed far too happy to be that bitter, twisted soul reborn. Until she saw Rocca— if she ever did—she had no way of knowing. With a shrug she got up and went to find Calonderiel.

Mosquitos, gnats, and other night insects hovered around her in the humid air no matter how hard she swatted and swore at them. Summer in the Westlands had its difficulties. Now, with the festival over, the camp had dwindled to the prince's alar, a scatter of tents upon ground worn to bare dirt by the presence of so many feet. Some hundred yards away from hers stood Dar's gaudy tent. Beyond it, she could see to the meadows and the alar's horses, grazing the scant grass while some of the young men rode on guard.

Dallandra found Cal and his son, Maelaber, kneeling on the ground in front of the prince's tent and dicing in the elven way. Each had a handful of brightly colored wood chips in various shapes. In turn each shook his handful, then strewed it onto the tanned deerskin lying between them. Although Maelaber's mother had ostensibly been human, Lady Rhodda had had some elven blood in her veins, and Maelaber looked more like one of the West-folk than he did a Deverry man. His dark blue eyes appeared human if much larger than usual, but his ears curled in the elven manner.

From inside the tent came the sound of people talking in soft voices. Prince Daralanteriel himself sat nearby, watching the dice game by the light of a small fire. At Dallandra's approach the two players laid their dice down, and the prince acknowledged her with a wave of his hand. He was an exceptionally handsome man, Dar, even for one of the People, with his raven-dark hair and gray eyes, slit catlike to reveal lavender pupils.

"Come join us," Dar said.

Calonderiel swept up the dice and offered her the doeskin.

"Thank you." Dallandra sat down on the skin instead of the bare dirt. "I've got some bad news. Ebañy's heading straight into trouble."

"Why am I not surprised?" Calonderiel glanced at the prince. "It's a good thing we'll be riding north."

"And meeting up with Valandario's alar, too," Dar said. "Does Devaberiel know his son's stirring up trouble again?"

"Oh, yes. He says he's not in the least surprised," Dallandra said. "Where's your scribe, Dar? I've got a question for him."

"Inside, helping Carra get the children to sleep. They're suffering from the sudden end of too much excitement, if you ask me. He can tell some good tales when he sets his mind to it."

The fire was burning low, but even so, its heat on this humid evening was making them all uncomfortable.

"Mael, will you smother that?" Dallandra said.

He nodded his agreement and picked up a shovel from the ground. While he pounded the embers into oblivion, Dallandra raised her hand and called upon the Wildfolk of Aethyr. They clustered around her, and when she snapped her fingers, they produced a silver ball of light, as misty as a moon through clouds. She tossed it straight up, where the Folk of the Air caught and held it.

"That's better," Cal said. "But the smoke does keep some of these cursed gnats away."

"I'd rather have gnats than sweat," Dalla said. "We're almost out of wood anyway."

Not long after Meranaldar came out of the tent. Dar glanced his way and raised a questioning eyebrow.

"They're asleep, my prince," Meranaldar said. "Barely. The princess will stay with them until she's sure that Elessi won't wake." He bowed to the prince, then sat down next to Dallandra. "Did I hear that you have a question for me?"

"You did, yes. Where was Tanbalapalim? Do you know how it fared in the Great Burning?"

"It was the most northward of the Seven Cities, and thus the first to fall. The Mera went on a rampage, or so the old records said, smashing and burning the place. Later they tried to rebuild, but I don't know how successfully."

"They would have been wiped out, wouldn't they? By disease, I mean."

"I'd say so—eventually. Since the plague began in Rinbaladelan, down on the seacoast, it stands to reason that it would have reached Tanbalapalim last. Why?"

"Ebañy's been told that Horsekin are living there again."

Meranaldar stared at her in surprise, then turned thoughtful. "They must have moved back recently. Evandar told me on several occasions that the plague had wiped out the invaders in every city."

"He told me the same thing," Dallandra said. "Zatcheka and the Gel da'Thae have always assumed that they're the only group of Horsekin to live in a city. They did resettle Braemel, but then they built new towns south of it. How far south of Tanbalapalim is Braemel?"

"One book says a hundred and eighty miles, but another gives the distance as just over two hundred." Meranaldar frowned in thought. "I hate it when sources disagree, but we can be fairly certain that Tanbalapalim was indeed distant. It was a northern outpost, really, in the High Mountains."

"It's isolated, then." Dalla said. "And the Gel da'Thae don't travel too far from home unless they absolutely have to. They wouldn't have stumbled across the Horsekin there."

"Even if they had, what then?" Daralanteriel leaned forward to join the conversation. "If they've fortified one of the old cities, we won't be able to chase them out of it."

"I'm beginning to wonder if it's hopeless." Cal shook his head in frustration. "We can beat the Horsekin back and back, but in the end there's a lot more of them than there are of us. It's like trying to drain the sea with a bucket."

"Well, my dear banadar, we do have an available refuge," Meranaldar said. "The Southern Isles. The High Council has repeatedly invited his royal highness to take up residence among them, and of course that invitation extends to the prince's retinue."

"It would have to extend to every person in the Westlands," Dar said, "before I'd leave my people."

Meranaldar ducked his head and murmured an apology.

"Besides, go live in a stinking jungle?" With a jut of his jaw Cal interrupted. "I'd rather die defending the Westlands."

"I'd rather we all stayed alive in the Westlands," Dallandra said. "And I intend to find ways for us to do just that. Come on, Cal, we do have allies. The Deverry lords know that if we fall, the Horsekin will be camping on their border."

"That's true, and it means we can count on a good many reinforcements." Cal sounded suddenly cheerful. "They breed like rats, the Roundears."

"Here!" Maelaber rose to his knees. "You're talking about my mother's folk, you know."

"Be calm, lad!" Calonderiel was grinning at him. "If I'd thought ill of her, you wouldn't be here."

Mael opened his mouth to snarl, but Dallandra got in first. "Oh, do hold your tongue, Cal!" she said. "It's a wretched hot night, and squabbling will only make it feel worse."

"True enough." Cal turned to his sulky son. "Consider the circumstances. I meant 'breeding like rats' as a compliment."

Mael forced out a cold smile.

"Well, think!" Cal went on. "What's always been our curse, out here on the grass? Our numbers, that's what. Our women don't bear enough children. Not that I'm blaming them, but—"

"Oh, of course you are!" Dalla broke in. "I suppose it never occurred to you that you men might have something to do with the problem."

"What?" Calonderiel snapped. "Of course it has! You're so cursed touchy tonight—"

"Stop it!" Daralanteriel asserted his royal prerogative. "Stop it right now, both of you! It's the heat, and the wretched insects, and the ill news, everything all together, but fighting among ourselves isn't going to ease our troubles."

"No, it's not," Cal said. "Sorry."

"Quite so." Dallandra nodded the prince's way. "I apologize."

Daralanteriel smiled, but grimly. "Go on, dweomermaster," he said. "You were going to tell us?"

"About the children, yes. It's no one's fault. It's because of our long lives, Cal. No creature that lives a long time bears hordes of offspring, especially not those who hunt for meat, as we do. If they did, every tasty kind of animal would be wiped out. The dweomer calls this principle the balance of life against lives."

"Does it?" Cal paused, then shrugged. "You'd know better than I about that."

"Well, yes, I do." Dalla forced out a smile to soften the words. "You've heard the Deverry folktales, that we're immortal. It must look that way to them, but if we were, a woman would have a child once in a thousand years, if that."

"I'm cursed glad we're not immortal, then," Cal said, "and for other reasons as well. Ye gods, who would show the least bit of courage if cowards could live forever?"

"I'd not thought of it that way before," Meranaldar remarked. "To risk a death in battle if you were throwing away an immortal life? Why would you?"

"You'd be a fool to do it. It's one thing, when you get to be my age, and realize how little lies ahead, to go raging into battle. If you die, you die and only lose that little." Cal shrugged in dismissal. "As for our lack of children, and notice, please, Dalla, that I said *our*, I suppose when we all lived in those fine cities Meranaldar keeps talking about that it was a blessing of sorts, but out here it's a curse. The Roundears—er, the Deverry folk, I mean—have so many children they can't even feed all of them, and the Horsekin are much the same. So Deverry spreads from the east, and the Horsekin spread from the west, and here we are, squeezed and strangled in the middle."

"Or we would be," Daralanteriel said, "if it weren't for the alliances we have with Deverry men."

"True. They're on our side—for now."

"And they'll remain so," Dalla went on, "because they hate the Horsekin."

"Maybe so, maybe not." Cal thought for a moment. "I'd rather have my own kin at my side when things come to the arrows flying."

Maelaber, who had been silent through all of this, suddenly laughed, though it was more of a bark than a merry sound. "It's too bad," Mael said, "that we can't trade a few hundred years of life for more children."

"That's what we're doing, isn't it?" All at once Dallandra saw something that should have been obvious long before, or so she felt. "Every time one of has a child by a human man or gets a child on a human woman."

Cal swore, under his breath but at length. Everyone turned toward the prince, who shrugged, hands open and palms up.

"I suppose so," Dar said. "But I courted Carra for herself alone, and not for her—" He hesitated for a moment. "Childbearing."

The men all laughed, but Dallandra kept silent, struck by another thought. *Rhodry's wyrd is Eldidd's wyrd.* The prophecy, over a hundred years old, suddenly revealed a fresh meaning. It might well be Eldidd's wyrd—and the Westlands'—to give birth to a mixed race that would save a dying people.

"Well, Cal," Dar went on. "We'll find out soon enough just how steady our alliances are."

"And let's not forget that I have allies of my own." Dallandra rose, glancing around her. "I'd better warn Grallezar as soon as I wake in the morning. And Niffa, up in Cerr Cawnen. And speaking of waking, I think I'll go get some sleep."

Calonderiel scrambled to his feet. "I'll escort you back. We should have moved your tent in closer. I don't like the idea of you being alone out on the edge of things."

"It's hardly necessary," Dallandra said. "We'll all be leaving tomorrow, and I doubt very much that there are Horsekin assassins lurking out in the grass."

"So do I," Cal said. "But what about Horsekin sorcerers?"

Dallandra was about to repeat Ebañy's unpleasant news about the way the Horsekin treated sorcerers when it occurred to her that there was more than one faction of Horsekin. Some might have refused to give up their magic at the dictates of a priest.

"You have a point," she said, "but I'll be safe for one night. I'd feel a warning if one of their shape-changers was nearby."

"Good." Calonderiel glanced at the sky. "They're usually birds, aren't they?"

"All the ones I've ever seen took bird form, yes. So if you see an unusually large bird of some sort hovering around, tell me."

After thinking about mazrakir, as the Horsekin called their shape-changers, Dallandra was glad enough of Calonderiel's company as they walked through the dark, silent camp. A night wind picked up at last to cool the air and drive the worst of the insects away. Out beyond her tent the grass rippled and sighed at its touch, a green sea under starlight, stretching to the western horizon. And beyond the horizon, invisible at this distance, lay the foothills and high mountains of the far west, where once the People had lived in towns and farms, a settled folk, renowned for their learning and their literature.

"Having Meranaldar here has taught me a lot of things," Dallandra said, "but the biggest one is just how much we've lost."

"That's true," Cal said. "It would gripe my soul to lose the little bit we've got left. My curse upon them all, Horsekin and their false goddess both!"

"Well, the false goddess is long gone, at least. And she was the one who lied to them, you know, and set this whole ugly thing in motion. They aren't truly to blame for that."

Calonderiel snorted profoundly. "The Horsekin breed gods the way horseshit breeds flies," he said. "By the Dark Sun herself, if I could concoct another plague to wipe those hairy bastards off the face of the earth, I would."

"Don't ever say that! You can't know how evil a thought it is. Here, you met Zatcheka and her menfolk. The Horsekin aren't all savages."

"Oh, of course, of course. But it's the savages that are causing the trouble."

"Yes. Unfortunately. But if Zatcheka's tribe could leave their old ways behind and become Gel da'Thae, the rest of them can as well."

"And the moon might well turn purple, too."

"Oh, don't be so stubborn! There's nothing in their essential natures that keeps the Horsekin from changing their ways. They're not animals, like wolves or bears, driven to be what they are from within with no hope of learning better."

"So? Who's to teach them? I don't want them to do their learning over a pile of our corpses."

"Do you think I do?"

"No." Cal suddenly smiled. "The prince was right, you know. Our tempers have been rubbed raw by the news. Let me apologize again for snapping at you."

"And I'll apologize to you, too."

For a few moments they said nothing, lingering side by side in the soothing wind. Above them the River of Stars, where the elven gods sailed at their leisure in jeweled ships, flowed and glittered from horizon to horizon.

"Ah, well," Cal said at last. "I suppose I'd better be getting back."

She could hear his longing for her under the studied indifference of his voice. For a moment she was tempted to let him stay the night, just because she felt so lonely under the high arc of the stars, but that reason would have been profoundly unfair to him, or so it seemed to her.

"Yes," Dalla said, "you should. We'll all have to be up at dawn tomorrow."

"True enough." He raised one hand in a gesture somewhere between a wave farewell and a slap at the air. "Good night."

As Dallandra watched him stride away, she felt tempted to call him back. *You're just lonely,* she told herself. *Don't be a fool!* With a shake of her head, she went into her tent. Hot, stuffy air met her like an unwelcome embrace. She grabbed her blankets and took them outside to sleep in the grass.

Yet for a while she lay awake, watching the River of Stars and thinking of the Horsekin, moving inexorably east like another river. At least she could take comfort in knowing that help was on its way—not only military help, but that of the dweomer. She could depend upon Grallezar among the Gel da'Thae and Niffa in the Rhiddaer to guard their respective homelands. Beyond them, even, two of the greatest dweomermasters the world had ever known had been reborn, and now they were old enough to begin their training. *They'll learn fast,* Dallandra thought. *With them, it will be more like remembering.*

Or so, at least, she could hope.

With all the taxes received and stored, life in Cadryc's dun settled into a quiet routine, or it would have been quiet if Tieryn Cadryc hadn't been so jumpy. He snarled and snapped at everyone, servant and noble-born alike, then apologized, even to the servants. In between bouts of temper he paced around the ward, led the warband out for long aimless rides, or sat brooding in his chair in the great hall. The men picked up their lord's mood. Fights broke out over next to nothing beyond Gerran's ability to prevent them, though he broke them up fast enough. He'd get in between the fighters and start swinging the flat of his sword while he cursed them impartially.

The weather added its own measure of unease. The days were unusually hot, and every summer shower left the air so humid that it might as well have still been raining. In the damp afternoons insects swarmed around men and horses both. Cadryc took to drinking earlier in the day.

"It's the insult to his honor, I suppose," Branna said. "Uncle Cadryc, I mean. Somewhat's aching his heart."

"The insult does vex him," Galla said. "But he still has hope, you see, that the gwerbret will give in eventually. It's up to that gerthddyn now, he told me."

"Salamander? How could he possibly change the gwerbret's mind?"

"I don't know, dear, but Salamander said somewhat about finding a Horsekin fortress. If he does, it'll make a difference. Cadryc's not told me more than that. But hope can vex a man, too, just from the waiting to see if he's going to get what he's hoping for."

The two women were sewing up in their hall, their refuge against the general ill temper downstairs. They'd finished the first panel of Branna's bed hangings a few days earlier, and now the second lay stretched in the frame between them. With a bit of charcoal Branna had drawn bands of spirals separating rows of wolves, who faced each other in pairs, each one's tail laced with that of the wolf behind. All around the edge ran interlaced knots, mitered at the corners. The wolves would end up a rusty red, while the colors of the spirals and the knots would depend on what dyestuffs they could find.

"It's too bad the men don't have somewhat like this to keep them busy," Branna said. "I think I'd go mad if it weren't for our sewing."

"I've had that thought myself, dear, especially when we'd first moved out here, away from you and all my friends. The men do have their Carnoic and wooden wisdom games, but these days the gambling only seems to cause more trouble."

"Truly. They need somewhat soothing, like."

"Huh! No doubt they'd scorn anything quiet and peaceful." Galla turned thoughtful. "But you know, you've given me an idea. I'll suggest it to your uncle tonight."

At breakfast on the morrow, after everyone had eaten, Cadryc stood up and yelled for silence. Once he had it, he smiled broadly all round.

"What about this, lads?" Cadryc said. "We'll have a tournament to pass the time. I'll send a messenger to Lord Pedrys, to see if he cares to bring some of his best men to join in. Wooden blades and wicker shields, lads, and the winner gets a silver penny from the high king's bounty. Gerran and Mirryn will judge the combats, though I'm hoping they'll put on an exhibition, like, when the rest of the fights are over."

The men cheered him. Galla, sitting across from Branna at table, winked at her. All through the great hall, the talk picked up as the wagering got under way. Even though no one knew yet which fighters would face off with whom, apparently everyone already had their favorites.

"That was a splendid idea of yours, my dear," Cadryc said with a nod Galla's way. "Where's my scribe got to? I want to get Pedrys' invitation on its way."

"I'll fetch him, Uncle." Branna rose and curtsied. "I overheard him say that he'd be gathering feathers for pens."

"My thanks, child." Cadryc turned to Galla. "Do you think we should invite that blasted young cub of a gwerbret?"

"We should," Galla said. "And why not, since most likely he won't come."

Branna left them discussing the matter and hurried away, leaving by the back door of the hall. Out in the sun the day had already turned hot. As she made her way through the various sheds clustering in the ward, she could hear the geese honking and hissing. She found them at last in the kitchen garden, where they were snatching up snails and insects, pausing only to squabble among themselves. On the far side of the garden the goosegirl stood talking with Neb, who had already gathered two good handfuls of long feathers.

She was a pretty thing, dark-haired Palla, wearing only a single gray dress, torn at the neckline. She was alternately giggling and simpering as Neb told her some long involved tale. Branna walked a little closer, but before she could hear what they were saying, the geese saw her and gave the alarm. One old gander charged her, his head low, his clipped wings flapping. Branna stepped to one side and gave him a kick that sent him tumbling.

"You'd better tend your charges, lass," Branna snapped. "They're getting a bit above themselves."

Palla blushed scarlet. She mumbled something conciliatory, but the look in her eyes flashed pure anger. Branna glanced Neb's way, then walked off, heading toward the broch. In a few moments Neb caught up with her.

"Now who's jealous?" Neb said with a smug smile.

"Huh," Branna said. "I suppose you think I care about that flea-bitten lass. Talk with her all you want."

"I was just telling her the sort of feathers I need for my pens." Neb held them up. "It's the ones with a good stout shaft. The thin ones don't hold up well when you cut all the feathering off them." He grinned again. "You looked jealous to me."

"And what if I was?"

"Well, what indeed?"

"Oh, this is silly! Of course I was jealous. A bit. Just a little bit, mind. Well, actually, I wanted to slap her dirty face, and I was surprised I felt that way. I suppose you think it was stupid of me."

"I don't."

"Then my thanks."

"Most welcome, and don't trouble your heart about the lass." Neb hesitated for a long moment, then glanced away. "There's somewhat I've been wanting to ask you, and now's as good a time as any. Do you think you could ever stoop to marrying a common-born man? Just as a matter of general principle, like."

Branna wanted to blurt "I would if it was you." Instead, she reminded herself that she was supposed to show her good breeding, which most definitely did not include being forward with possible suitors.

"Oh, I've naught against the idea on principle," she said. "After all, it's not like I've got land in my dowry."

"That makes a difference, doesn't it?" Neb suddenly grinned, then wiped the grin away in what was most likely his own attempt at good manners.

"Quite a difference," Branna said. "My kin couldn't have any objections based on a demesne passing out of noble hands."

"Might they have other objections, do you think? Just as a matter of interest."

"My father was glad to get rid of me. Why would he object?"

"But your uncle?"

It was Branna's turn to hesitate. She was wondering if she should just tell Neb outright that Aunt Galla approved and would work her husband round to her point of view, but Neb took her silence wrong.

"I see I've gotten above myself." His voice turned stiff and cold. "My apologies for troubling—"

"Oh, don't be silly! You've not done anything of the sort. I was just wondering what Uncle Cadryc would say, is all."

Neb started to speak, but their eyes met, and all at once they both burst out laughing.

"You're being so formal," Branna said, "but your hands are full of goose feathers."

"So they are." Neb held the bundle out. "May I offer my lady a token of my esteem?"

"Why, my thanks, good scribe!" Branna plucked out a feather and held it up. "I shall cherish this in honor of you."

Neb started to laugh again, glanced over her shoulder, and abruptly fell silent. Branna turned and saw Gerran, standing some fifteen feet away, glaring at her with his arms crossed over his chest.

"Neb!" Gerran called out. "The tieryn needs you to write a message."

"He's right." Branna felt herself blushing. "I was supposed to tell you."

"Then I'd best go in," Neb said. "Will you accompany me?"

Gerran remained where he stood, scowling, between them and the broch.

"I won't," Branna said. "I need to talk with Midda."

She turned and strode away, then glanced back to see that Gerran and Neb were heading in the opposite direction. She shamelessly ran for the servants' quarters, but before she reached them, she hid the goose feather in her kirtle.

Midda and the other maidservants shared a long loft, spread with straw and scattered with mattresses and blankets. The younger lasses shared mattresses, two and three at a time, but Midda, the cook, and a few other privileged servants had a mattress apiece, and wicker screens to set off little areas they could call their own. At one end of the loft, near the only window, stood a wobbly plank table with benches on either side. At the moment shorn fleeces lay strewn on the table. Midda and three other women sat pulling them apart into fist-sized chunks with formidable bone combs. Before it could be spun, all this wool would need carding, using finer combs.

When Branna came in, the women started to rise, but she gestured at them to stay sitting. "Our lady wanted to know how you're coming along," Branna said.

"Not too badly," Midda said. She laid down her comb and stood up, stretching her back. "We've done a good half of them."

"Splendid! If you've got some ready for spinning, give it to me, and I'll get a start on that."

"I can give you a sackful, at least, my lady. I'll fetch it."

While Branna waited, the other women went on with their work. So many odd tufts of wool flecked their clothes that they looked as if they'd just come in from the snow. Fibers drifted lazily in the air, picked out by the sun coming through the window. Branna sneezed, thrice.

"I'll wait on the stairs," she called out.

In but a few moments Midda joined her in the cooler air outside. The maid handed over a pillow-sized sack, carefully packed to avoid tangling the fibers all over again.

"Ah, my poor lady!" Midda said. "I hate seeing you like this, having to spin like one of the servants."

"Oh, come now! It's not that bad. Even Aunt Galla takes a hand with the spinning now and again."

"Still, you deserve better." Midda set her lips tight—a sure sign that she was thinking of Branna's stepmother.

"Actually, Midda," Branna said, "I think I do, too. I'm just not sure what that may be. And speaking of better things, why aren't you all working outside, where it's cooler?"

"Because it keeps threatening rain. It's a fair job to haul everything out just to haul it back again."

"Oh, of course. I should have thought of that."

As she went back to the broch, Branna kept watch for Gerran, but since the men were planning their tourney, she managed to avoid him for the rest of the day. She did see Neb, however, as she was carrying a tin candle lantern up to her chamber after dinner. She'd just gained the second floor when Neb came down from his chamber on the floor above.

"We meet again, my lady," Neb said.

The words were utterly simple and ordinary, yet Branna felt as cold as if she were standing in a winter doorway. Neb took a step back, began to speak, then merely stared at her. All around them Wildfolk materialized, solemn gnomes clustering upon the floor, sylphs flickering in the dappled light from the lantern.

"There's somewhat we need to talk about." Branna pointed at the Wildfolk with her free hand.

"There is, truly. I don't know why we haven't."

"I was frightened. Were you?"

"Somewhat. I don't suppose it would be seemly for me to come to your chamber."

"It certainly wouldn't! We could go up to the roof."

Like most Deverry duns, the main tower had a flat roof, reachable from the top floor. Neb went up the ladder and through the trapdoor first. Branna handed him the candle lantern, then followed, scrambling up to find herself in the midst of pyramids of heavy stones, stored there in case of attack.

"Oh!" she said. "The air's so lovely and cool!"

After the heat of the day the night breeze felt like a caress. In the clear air the stars hung close and thick, as if the sky were a pierced lantern, and the stars' light shining through from the home of the gods. They picked their way through the heaps of stones to the edge of the roof, guarded by a waist-high crenellated wall. In its shelter Branna found a wooden chest, wrapped in oiled leather and no doubt containing bundles of arrows. She perched upon it, and Neb sat down on the roof facing her.

"Here," Neb said, "you'd best blow that candle out. Someone might think the broch's on fire or suchlike."

Branna opened the lantern's little door, blew out the candle, then put the lantern down beside her feet. Gnomes materialized to join them, and sylphs, glowing like moonlight, gathered in the air and gave them enough light to see each other. Branna's gray gnome climbed into her lap, squirmed like a child, then leaned against her whilst it sucked one of its bony fingers.

"Very well," Neb said. "We both see the Wildfolk, even though we've always been told that they don't exist. It must mean somewhat, somewhat beyond our seeing of them, that is. Do you think so, too?"

"I do," Branna said. "I keep feeling like there's a secret I know, or I should know, but I've forgotten it."

"I keep hearing riddles in my dreams, and they always seem to have you for an answer."

Once again Branna felt the peculiar cold, sheeting down her back. She shuddered with a toss of her head.

"Have you ever dreamed about me?" Neb leaned forward.

"Well, not precisely."

"What's that mean?"

"Oh, well, you see." Branna let her voice trail away. "It'll sound so foolish."

"Naught that you'd say could ever sound foolish to me."

He sounded, he looked so urgently sincere that for a moment Branna couldn't speak. Her heart was pounding, and she felt her face burning with a blush.

"My thanks," she said at last. "All my life, I've had such vivid dreams. They carried over from night to night, too. I'd go to the same places and talk with the same people. And one of them was an old man with your eyes, and his name's much like yours. Nevyn, it was."

"But that means 'no one.' " Neb started to laugh, then let his voice trail away.

"It means somewhat to you?"

"It does, but cursed if I know how or why."

By sylph light she could see him frowning; then he shrugged the problem away.

"Are your dreams like that?" Branna said. "Like tales, mine were, or even more like memories. I was so lonely, you see, and so I used to work them up like embroideries. I'd have a hazy little dream—that would be like the drawing on the cloth. Then when I'd wake up, I'd fill it in. Then the next night, the dream would be like the tale I'd made out of it, and go on from there."

"What sort of things did you dream of? Besides the old man, I mean."

"Oh, well, childish things, I suppose. Like dweomer. I could work dweomer in my dreams, and even turn myself into a bird and fly."

"I wish I had dreams like that. Most of mine are dull. That's why I can remember the ones with you in them. They stand out, like."

"What are—" She broke off, turning to listen, and Neb rose to his knees.

Down in the ward someone was calling for Neb—a high-pitched boy's voice.

"My brother," Neb said wearily. "Here, we'd best go down."

"I suppose so, but can we talk more some other time?"

"My lady, I'd like naught better."

They stood up, and Branna retrieved the lantern, its candle dead and cold. "I shouldn't have blown that out," she said. "It's going to take a bit of doing, getting down that rickety ladder in the dark."

Neb held out his hand and snapped his fingers. The candle wick glowed, then caught, leaping into golden light. Branna gasped aloud.

"How did you do that?" she said.

"Ye gods." Neb sounded terrified. "I don't know."

In the lantern's dappled light they stared at each other. Branna wanted to speak, to acknowledge and discuss what had happened, but she could see the raw fear in Neb's eyes.

"Neb!" It was Clae's voice again, yelling at the top of his lungs. "There you are! What are you doing on the roof?"

Neb trotted over to the edge and held the lantern up high. "Just getting a little air," he bellowed. "Oh, very well, I'll come down."

Neb helped Branna down the ladder from the roof, escorted her to her chamber, then took the lantern and hurried down the stone staircase to the great hall. He was wondering if Clae would tell everyone that he'd seen his brother with Lady Branna, but Clae was so full of his own news that it seemed he'd never noticed. He came running over the moment Neb stepped off the stairs.

"Guess what?" Clae was grinning, his eyes bright and wide. "It's about the tourney."

Neb could have cheerfully strangled him. "The tourney?" he snapped. "You brought me all the way down here for some news about the stupid tourney?"

Clae shrank back, the smile gone, and raised a hand as if he feared Neb would slap him.

"Well?" Neb snapped. "What is it?"

"I'm going to get to be in it, that's all. I suppose it doesn't seem like much to you."

His voice ached with so much hurt that Neb's anger turned to shame. "Oh, here, I'm sorry," Neb said. "It's the wretched hot weather. It's making me as nasty as a springtime bear."

Clae shrugged and looked down at the floor.

"Tell me more," Neb said. "Surely Gerran's not going to have you facing off with the warband."

"He's not." Clae looked up. "Coryn and I are going to get to fight. Coryn's been practicing for years, and I've only just started, but the captain says that I'm good enough already that we can fight in the tourney."

"Ye gods! Well, that's an honor, indeed." Neb thought of their father and of what he would have said. "You must be blasted proud. I know I am."

The grin returned like a blaze of sunlight. "I sort of am." Clae's voice trembled against this forced modesty. "The captain says I've got a cursed lot left to learn."

"Most likely, but I don't doubt that learn it you will."

When, at the end of the evening, Neb went to bed, he was hoping that he'd have another dream about Branna or the most beautiful lass in all Deverry. Perhaps his expectations made his dreams tease him, because he dreamed nothing he could remember in the morning but a few scraps of images, revolving around tallying up the dun's taxes, and a voice saying, "now they've all been paid." And yet, as he went down to breakfast, he found himself remembering the things Salamander had said in Cengarn, about gratitude and wyrd, and realized that they and the dream were—somehow— all of a piece.

Lady Branna was sitting near a window inside the great hall. Gerran, standing just outside in the bright morning light, could see her in silhouette as she leaned onto the table on one elbow to study the game board lying between her and Mirryn. *Carnoic, probably,* Gerran thought. *She plays well for a lass.*

"And just what are you staring at, Captain?" A woman's voice, and it came from behind him.

Gerran spun around to find a stout woman—a widow, judging by her black headscarf—standing nearby, glaring at him with her hands set on her hips.

"And just who are you?" Gerran said.

"Lady Branna's maidservant." Her dark eyes narrowed as she looked him over. "I've tended her from the time she was a tiny baby, and I shan't be letting any harm come to her, not from the likes of you, my fine lad, or anyone else in the wretched warband either."

"I'll not be doing her the least bit of harm, you old scold!"

The woman snorted. "I know how much honor you lads have around women. I warn you, I won't have my lady harmed even if I have to go to the tieryn himself to stop it."

With that she pushed past him and strode off. Gerran mouthed a few curses after her. It seemed that everyone was warning him off Branna these days. The little talk that Cadryc had given him, telling him in no uncertain terms not to cause trouble in the dun, still rankled Gerran's soul. *I'll wager Lady Galla put him up to it*—that thought wasn't much comfort. With a few more curses Gerran turned back to the window.

Much to his annoyance, he saw Neb, sitting down next to Branna as easily as if he had the right to be there. Gerran was hoping that Mirryn would send the presumptuous scribe away, but instead, Mirryn stood up, smiling, chatted for a moment or two, then walked away, leaving the game and Branna to Neb. Gerran jogged round the broch. He was planning on going inside to join them, but Mirryn met him in the doorway.

"We'd better exercise the warband's horses," Mirryn said. "Round up the lads, will you?"

Once the warband had left the dun, Mirryn decided that they should take a good long ride out in the open air, and Gerran could think of no reason that they shouldn't. By the time they returned, noon had come and gone, and Branna was keeping her aunt company in the women's hall.

Over the next few days, every time that Gerran saw Branna,

Neb was right beside her, except of course at meals, when she sat at the honor table and Neb sat with the other servitors. Gerran began to regret his own stubborn insistence on eating with the warband rather than taking a place with the family. He took to hanging around the broch in hopes of catching her alone, but if he saw her walking out to the garden and followed, there would be Neb, waiting for her. If he came into the great hall of an afternoon, she would be sitting with Neb and watching him write letters. At times in the evening she would disappear, and he could find her nowhere, not even the women's hall. At those times his suspicion that she and Neb had gone off somewhere together would turn him surly.

How could she prefer that milksop scribe to him? The question vexed Gerran more and more as it became more and more obvious that she did. He pinned his hopes on the tourney. Despite his attempts at modesty, he knew that he was the best swordsman in the western provinces. Other lasses had found his skill and flair impressive. No doubt Branna would, too.

Soon enough the answers to Tieryn Cadryc's invitations came back in the form of messengers from the duns of his vassals. Standing beside the table of honor, Neb read them out that evening. Lord Pedrys would be delighted to attend, but Lord Samyc's wife had just given birth, and he had just received the promised riders from the gwerbret; he felt he needed to stay home on both counts, particularly the latter, in case the Horsekin came raiding again.

The invitation had just missed Lord Ynedd's parents, who had left their dun to visit kin two days before the message arrived. At this news, little Ynedd burst into tears and ran out of the hall. The child had been desperately hoping to see his mother, Gerran knew, and coldhearted as it was, he was glad she wasn't coming. Ynedd would need to forget her coddling sooner rather than later. That left Lady Marigga, regent for her elder son, Coryn's brother. Since no one had expected her to come, no one was disappointed or slighted when she pleaded pressing duties.

"It's just as well that we won't have many guests," Lady Galla remarked at that point. "The harvest wasn't all it might have been, and I was rather worried about the food."

Two days after the messengers came home, Lord Pedrys, the riders of his warband, and his wife, Lady Omaena, arrived with their pages and servants and provided Gerran some relief from his brooding. Once they'd found places for Pedrys' warband in the barracks, Gerran and Pedrys' captain, Tidd, whose graying hair and mustache showed his age and experience in these matters, went down to the meadow behind the dun to mark out the contest ground. Their arms full of wooden pegs and ropes, Coryn, Ynedd, and Clae trailed after, chattering and laughing in excitement.

"I can remember being that young myself," Tidd remarked. "A tourney seemed like the best fun in the world then."

"It doesn't now?" Gerran said.

"Oh, here, Falcon. You know what we're practicing for." Tidd looked absently away. "Too many friends have ridden to the Otherlands for me to take much delight in tourneys."

"True-spoken." Gerran felt a sudden chill, as if a cloud had passed over the sun. "Well, the pages will learn that lesson one fine day, and probably too cursed soon."

Branna helped her aunt settle Lady Omaena and Lord Pedrys into their guest chamber, which sported the second-best bed and some fine tapestries. Pedrys glanced around the chamber, bowed to Galla, and hurried off to go drink with Tieryn Cadryc. Their personal servants carried up their bundles of clothes and the like while Omaena fussed until everything was stowed away to her liking. The lady then retreated with her fellow noblewomen to the women's hall, where she lowered herself into a cushioned chair with a sigh of relief.

"Are you tired, dear?" Galla said. "You seem a bit pale."

"No doubt I do." Omaena paused for a smile. "Soon I'll be having to wear my kirtle high, you see."

"Oh, how wonderful!" Branna said. "Your first child!"

Omaena, a limp little person despite her flaming red hair, smiled daintily. "I'm so pleased. Of course, we're both hoping that the goddess will bless us with a son."

"Of course." Branna managed to suppress the irritation, bordering on anger, that she felt every time she heard this conventional sentiment. "But a daughter later, I hope."

"Oh, so do I," Omaena said, "I should love to have a daughter after I've done my duty to my lord."

With a quick knock on the door, Midda came bustling in, leading a procession of servants with various refreshments, a flagon of Bardek wine, a pitcher of spring water, little cakes, and cheeses. After they left, Branna busied herself with organizing the food on a narrow table, then poured wine and water for the two ladies.

"Won't you have some, dear?" Galla said.

"Water's enough for me. Wine makes me feel so hot, and it's quite hot enough already."

In truth, Branna disliked the muddled feeling wine induced, but the excuse satisfied her aunt. Branna brought over her workbasket and mended various rips in one of Mirryn's shirts while the older women chatted about babies, their delivery and care, until, soon enough, the topic shifted to gossip.

"I had a rather sad letter from Solla of Cengarn," Galla said. "It's really time for her brother to marry, and she was wondering if she could have a place here as one of my servingwomen after he did. She seems convinced that she'll be unwelcome in his dun."

"Oh, please!" Omaena rolled her eyes. "She probably will be, but I'll wager that's not why she wrote to you."

"What?"

Omaena smirked, then helped herself to more watered wine before she continued. "It's your husband's captain," Omaena said. "The poor lass is absolutely besotted with Gerran, common-born or not."

"She is?" Branna could feel herself grinning. "How wonderful!"

Omaena turned in her chair and gave her a puzzled look while Galla stifled a laugh.

"It seemed to me," Omaena said, rather stiffly, "that the situation was more difficult than wonderful."

"Truly?" Branna arranged her best vacuous expression. "I was just thinking that true love's always so splendid."

"I suppose that at your age I would have thought the same," Omaena said. "May I have another of those little cakes, Galla dear? I seem to be so hungry these days."

Branna returned to her mending with a sense of deep relief. She had never wanted to break anyone's heart, much less Gerran's, whom she'd known and liked all her life. With a beauty like Solla to console him, his heart would doubtless remain in one piece. *I want to marry Neb,* she thought. *There! I've put it into words.*

The morning of the tourney dawned clear and hot. Servants carried benches and chairs for the ladies and Tieryn Cadryc down to the meadow behind the dun and set them up at the head of the marked contest ground. The men in the warbands sat on the ground along the sides, though well back from the ribands in case one of the fighters came crashing through. Thanks to Lord Veddyn's great age, his bench had a back, and Neb had brought a cushion for the chamberlain to sit upon.

When Neb sat down next to Veddyn, Branna made sure to get her chair placed beside his bench and on his side of it, too. Omaena sat next to her, but fortunately she was in the middle of an earnest conversation with Galla about, of course, babies. Neb grinned at Branna and slid over until they were but a few feet apart.

Branna had seen so many of these mock combats over the years that they profoundly bored her. They all followed the same pattern: the men of the warband would pair off, then fight, one pair at a time, with wooden sword and wicker shield till one combatant made three touches on the other. The winners of the first round formed new pairs and so on until only one pair was left for the final round. During this predictable course of action, the riders wagered furiously before each combat, then yelled and cheered their favorites on during them.

After the first round had run its course, Gerran brought out his pages and introduced them to the assembled warbands. While the men who were going to fight in the second round rested, the two older pages, Coryn and Clae, showed off what they'd been learning. The boys carried small wooden swords and cut down wicker shields, and each wore a little helm, again made of wicker, to protect their young heads.

The lads faced off, then began to spar, though they swung and banged on each other with a lot more enthusiasm than skill. The men in the warbands laughed and jeered, but always in the most friendly way possible. Branna noticed Neb watching with real interest and cheering his brother on. The two lads seemed evenly matched, and they also seemed ready to lunge and swing all afternoon. Gerran, however, decided when they'd had enough and stepped in between them.

"I declare the match a draw," Gerran said. "Well done, lads!"

When the warbands cheered them, they both blushed and ran off the field. Branna watched them for a moment as they pulled off their helms and piled them up with their swords and shields. Gerran strolled over to Neb.

"Your brother's doing well," Gerran said.

"Splendid!" Neb said. "I've not seen him this happy in some years. He never wanted to take up our father's craft. I'm not sure where Da would have found a prenticeship that would have suited him."

"Well, he's found one now." Gerran turned to Branna and bowed. "My lady, I hope you find the tourney to your liking."

Branna decided that this was one of those situations when lying was a necessity rather than a vice. "Of course, I certainly do," she said, but she was aware of Neb quirking one eyebrow and smiling as if to accuse her of the lie. Gerran shot the scribe a foul glance, then wandered away to confer with Pedrys' captain.

Once the second round of combats began, the careful ordering of rank broke down. Tieryn Cadryc and Lord Pedrys both deserted their chairs to pace the sidelines and yell, encouraging their own men and making wagers on one fighter or another. Money changed hands among the warbands, as well as insults, cheers, and friendly banter. Branna risked looking at Neb and was pleased to see elderly Lord Veddyn slumped against the back of his bench, sound asleep and snoring, in the midst of the general din and clamor. Neb winked at her.

"Branna?" Neb slid over to the end of the bench. "No one's looking our way."

"So they're not." Branna dropped her voice. "If I slip away, you could follow in a bit."

"To the roof, then?" he whispered.

"It'll be too hot with all this sun."

"The garden?"

She nodded her agreement, and he moved back next to Lord Veddyn.

Branna waited until the current combat came to an end. She got up, stretching, then went round behind Galla's chair. "Aunt Galla? I'm absolutely roasting in this sun. I'm going to go back to the broch for a little while and rest."

"Very well, dear," Galla said. "But you won't want to miss seeing Gerran and Mirryn spar. They really are quite good, both of them."

"If I don't fall asleep, I'll come back for that, then."

Before Galla could answer, Lady Omaena launched into another complicated question about babies. With smiles all round, Branna left. She walked sedately across the meadow until she could be sure that no one was watching her, then ran the rest of the way.

With the sun low in the sky, the little bench in the herb garden sat in shade from the wall, a welcome relief. Winded from her fast climb, Branna sank onto it and let out her breath in a long sigh. Her gray gnome materialized to sit beside her and dangle its spindly legs over the side.

"It's too hot," she said.

It nodded, then popped a finger into its mouth and began to suck on it. With almost everyone down at the tourney, the dun was abnormally quiet, except for the occasional cluck of a chicken or honk of a goose. Now and then the breeze brought her a snatch of conversation from the cook house, where the cook and the scullery maids were putting the last touches on the feast ahead.

While she waited, Branna thought over her last night's dream, one that grew in significance the more she contemplated it. *She was waiting for Nevyn in an underground chamber lit only by firelight. Around the top of the walls ran a strange frieze, a pattern made of circles and triangles, that stopped abruptly in the middle of one wall. She recognized the pattern, she knew she did, but she couldn't read it, no matter how hard she tried.* The sound of footsteps on the gravel path of the garden pulled her away from the dream, but when she looked up, she was half-expecting to see the old man rather than Neb.

"Wretchedly hot!" Neb sat down beside her and pulled at the open throat of his shirt. "I suppose we could go into the great hall. No one else is there."

"In just a little bit the serving lasses will be in and out," Branna said. "They need to ready everything for the feast."

"That's true. Well, at least there's a bit of shade here."

"There is, and I'm glad of it." Branna paused, then decided she'd best blurt out what she had to say. "I had another of those dreams last night, the ones about Nevyn. He could light a candle by snapping his fingers, too."

Neb slewed round on the bench and stared at her. He had gone so pale that she could see the blood pulsing in its vessels at his temples.

"Are you afraid?" she said.

"Somewhat. I had a dream, myself, although truly, it wasn't a dream in the usual way. I'd woken up and gone to the window for the air, and as I was sitting there, I thought that your name should be some other thing than Branna."

"Truly? What was it?"

"I don't remember." Neb smiled in a twisted sort of way. "In the dream, it seemed like you had several names, but I could remember none of them."

"How very odd! The old man only has the one name." She stopped, caught by a rise of images in her mind. "Well, perhaps there was one other."

"What?"

"I don't remember. Neb, all of this is so frightening!"

"Truly? Why?"

"I feel like there's another lass inside me. She's both me and not me, and she's struggling to—to—to be remembered, I suppose I mean. But if I do remember her, I shan't be who I am anymore. I'll be her." She paused, then took a deep breath. "Or even if I'm not truly her, I'll not be Branna, not the lass I am now, but sort of a mixture, like wine and water in the same goblet."

Neb considered, nodding a little.

"Do you think I'm daft?" Branna said.

"I don't. I feel somewhat the same, truly, but the man inside me—" He paused for a long moment. "I think I'd rather be him than me."

"Oh, here, there's naught wrong with you."

"My thanks, but that's not what I meant. It's so hard to put all this into words."

"That's certainly true."

Neb smiled, then went on. "Wait, I know! I feel like a man who's been ill for months and months, then begins to mend. He can remember being strong and doing all sorts of fine things, but now he can barely pull himself out of bed. There's part of me that knows somehow that once I was truly strong, but now—" He let his voice trail off. "Well, maybe that's not what I mean, either. I don't know, Branna. I can't make out the sense of all this, but it will make sense, I'm sure of it, if I could only learn one thing. There's somewhat, that one thing, that's going to make everything clear, if only I can find it."

"I think you should find it. I mean, you should be the one to find it, not me, since you want to be that other man."

"Probably so. After all, what am I now? A scribe for a border lord, that's all."

"That's good enough for me." She'd blurted it out before she could stop herself, and she felt her face burn with a blush.

"Truly?" Neb reached over and caught her hands in his, and he was smiling with such a pure joy that she felt her embarrassment ease. "Do you truly mean that?"

"I do. I truly do."

Neb pulled her close, then let go her hands and put his on either side of her face. "I love you," he said and kissed her.

Branna threw her arms around him and took another kiss. "I love you, too," she whispered. "That at least is one thing I do know."

"Then will you marry me?"

"Of course. I've been hoping you'd ask."

Neb laughed and let her go, then turned thoughtful. "What about your uncle?"

"I don't know, but I'll wager Aunt Galla can talk him around."

"If she approves."

"She's already called you a fine young man who'll doubtless end up as the councillor of some important lord someday."

"Well! That's promising, then!"

"Indeed. But I shan't be able to talk with her until after the guests leave."

"Ye gods! I hope I can stand to wait that long."

"It's only till tomorrow."

"An eternity, my love, of worrying, and all on account of the love I bear you."

"I do like it when you talk like that. But I like your kisses even better."

"Then far be it from me to deprive you of them. Although, you know, I think we'd best go somewhere else."

"That's true." Branna glanced around the garden. "Anyone could walk out and see us."

All at once they heard a shout, carried on the wind from some distance away, the sound of a good many men, yelling and laughing together.

"The tourney's over." Neb stood up and held out his hand.

"Curse it, everyone's going to come trooping right back to the dun."

"Just so." Branna rose and took his hand. "Is there somewhere more private we could go?"

"I do know an empty storeroom, but it reeks of onions."

"That won't do. If there are going to be tears in your eyes, I want them to spring from the depths of love."

"Quite so. Well, let me think."

Since Gerran and Mirryn usually put on an exhibition at tourneys, they had worked out a way of sparring without dishonoring either of them. Gerran always scored the first touch because it was expected of him by the onlookers. From there they sparred naturally, but they took care to score the third touch upon each other simultaneously, thus ending the match in a draw, not a humiliating defeat. The afternoon was so hot and sticky on this particular day that they made sure they scored the touches quickly. No one noticed their ruse.

"Well played, lads!" Cadryc said. "Both of you, but Gerran's a marvel and a half with that blade."

"He is," Mirryn said, grinning, "but then, we knew that even before I faced him."

Gerran ducked his head and looked away. He could feel that he was blushing, and he hated that as much as he loved hearing the praise.

"Let's go in," Cadryc said. "Have a goblet of mead all round. My wife's got the cook working on a roast hog, she tells me, and we'll give both Gerro and Mirro here a slice off the thigh."

Everyone within earshot cheered. As the crowd got up and started swirling around, ready to go uphill to the dun, Gerran looked for Branna. He was expecting to find her watching him, smiling, no doubt, in awe of his skill with a sword or perhaps the tieryn's praise. He saw Lady Galla, giving orders to the maidservants for the meal to come, but not Branna. Worse yet, he saw no sign of Neb, either.

"Captain?" Little Lord Ynedd came trotting up to him. "Are you looking for someone?"

"I am. You've not happened to see Lady Branna, have you?"

"Oh, she left and went back to the dun. Right after Clae and Coryn got to fight."

"I see."

Gerran glanced around. No one else seemed in a hurry to leave the tourney ground. The lords stood talking, the ladies still sat in their chairs, while the riders and servants milled around, discussing the fine points of this fight or that. With a muffled curse, Gerran took off for the dun at a jog. When he reached the ward, it stood empty and silent. He ran into the great hall in hopes of finding Branna there—no sign of her. For a moment Gerran stood by the honor table and swore; then he hailed a serving lass.

"Have you seen Lady Branna?"

"I have. She went off with the scribe some while ago."

Gerran felt as if he'd been kicked in the stomach. "How long ago?"

The lass shrugged.

"Before or after the last combats?" Gerran said.

"Oh, long before that, truly. I was walking back here to start my work and saw them in the garden."

Gerran muttered a few more foul things, then strode out of the hall. Yet, as he'd half-expected, when he reached the garden, Branna and Neb had already left. He stood on a graveled path and kicked aimlessly at a cabbage with the toe of his boot while he let the truth sink in: Branna hadn't stayed to see him spar. She hadn't cared enough about him to watch, not with her wretched scribe hanging around her. *Hopeless*, he thought. *Besides, if she'd want a man like that, what would I want with her, anyway? She's no fit wife for a fighting man.*

Gerran's newfound contempt lasted until he looked up, glancing around the ward, and saw the stables. *Hayloft.* The thought struck him like a blow, that Branna and Neb might well have taken refuge in one of the few places in the dun that offered privacy to a courting couple. He growled under his breath like a dog and strode off, heading for the stable.

The hayloft smelled of new-mown hay, and dust motes danced in the sunbeams that came through the tiny windows. Neb lounged on his back on a great drift of hay, while Branna sat demurely by his side.

"We really should go," Branna said. "Everyone will be back from the tourney by now. What if one of the riders goes back to the barracks for somewhat and hears us talking?"

"We can't have that, truly." Neb sat up and ran his fingers through his hair to get the straws out. "It's too hot up here anyway."

Neb went down the narrow ladder before her to steady it. When she reached the stable floor, Branna paused to look over her dress and pluck a few accusatory straws from the skirt.

"Are there any on my back?" She turned so he could see.

"Only a few." Neb's voice turned mournful. "It's not as if we were rolling around up there or suchlike."

"You're going to have to wait for that till we're formally betrothed." She turned back and found him grinning at her. "I like to think ahead, you see."

"And that gladdens my heart." Neb made her a bow. "Shall we go, my lady?"

They walked together out of the wide stable doors and stood blinking in the bright sun. Dimly, Branna could see a man striding toward them. "Someone's coming," she said. "Oh, by the gods, it's Gerran!"

"And he looks like he's been peeling Bardek citrons with his teeth," Neb said, "and washing them down with vinegar."

Branna giggled at the turn of phrase, and Gerran heard her. His face turned dark with fury as he strode up, his hand on his sword hilt, his red hair gleaming in the sunlight. Neb stepped smoothly in front of Branna.

"What's vexing you, Captain?" Neb said.

"You milksop little—" Gerran was struggling to get his words out. "What are you doing with Lady Branna?"

"Naught that concerns you."

"You—" Gerran stopped, and his face turned so pale that its dusting of freckles stood out like flecks of blood. He jerked his hand away from his sword hilt and stepped back. "Nah, nah, nah," Gerran said. "What am *I* doing? You've never fought with a sword in your life! Ye gods, I can't—I won't—ye gods!"

"Very well," Neb snarled. "Take the cursed thing off and we'll settle this with our fists."

Gerran looked him up and down, then laughed. For a moment Branna feared that Neb would charge him, sword or no, but instead Neb suddenly flung up both arms. Wildfolk rushed into manifestation. Sprites swarmed in the air, an army of gnomes clustered on the cobbles, an undine rose from the water in the horse trough and shook a wet fist in Gerran's direction.

"Laugh at this," Neb said, and calmly lowered his arms.

Before Branna could yell and stop them, the gnomes charged. Although Gerran couldn't see them, he obviously could feel them. He yelped, swatted, cursed, and yelped some more as the squad of gnomes leaped, pinching and flailing. The sprites rushed to the attack, swarming like summer flies around his face, pinching him and pulling his hair. With the press all around him, Gerran tried to step back and tripped over Neb's fat yellow gnome. He went sprawling onto his back and writhed, while Neb laughed and the gnomes pummeled.

"Neb!" Branna screamed. "All of you! That's enough! Stop it!"

"As my lady commands." Neb turned to her and bowed.

The chortling gnomes and sprites had already pulled back at her screamed order. When Neb waved his hands, they vanished, leaving a shaking, swearing Gerran lying on the cobbles.

"You've got a sword," Neb said. "I've got other weapons."

Gerran tried to speak and failed. Neb's smile was so smug that Branna felt like slapping him herself. Gerran got up, but warily, stepping back, glancing around as if he expected enemies to come from all directions.

"Well, Lady Branna," Neb said. "Truly you're a prize beyond price."

"A prize, is it? Is that supposed to be flattering?" Branna had the satisfaction of seeing his smug smile disappear.

"Uh, well, I—"

"Isn't it?" Gerran said, and his eyes had grown cold. "Lasses always—"

"I can't stand either of you!" Branna turned on him. "Do you think I'm a mare in heat? Eager to watch the studs fight over her?"

Both men stared openmouthed. With a last snarl Branna turned away, then ran across the ward. At the broch she ducked inside. In the great hall everyone had assembled for the feast, the riders on their side of the hall, her aunt and uncle and their vassals on the other. Laughter and talk rang out; the mead and ale were flowing. It was easy for her to sidle along the curved wall to the staircase, then run upstairs before anyone noticed her, though she was panting for breath by the time she reached her chamber. She slammed the door shut and barred it for good measure.

Her gray gnome materialized in midair, glanced around, then settled onto the bed.

"Ye gods!" Branna could hear her voice shaking in rage. "I hate them both, I swear it! I'll never marry anyone. I'd rather spend my life in a temple embroidering altar cloths for the Moon Goddess."

She strode over to the window and leaned out, twisting to see round the nearest shed. There was no sign of either Neb or Gerran. All at once she realized that she would have to face both of them at the feast.

"Maybe I'll just stay up here and pretend to be ill," Branna said to the gnome. "I'm not all that hungry anyway."

But there was a knock at the door, and Aunt Galla called out. "Branna dear, we're about to serve the food. Are you in there?"

Branna knew that lying to her aunt's face lay beyond her. "I am," she called back. "Just combing my hair, and then I'll be down."

As Branna hurried downstairs, she was praying that no one had seen the incident 'twixt Gerran and Neb. It finally occurred to her that her aunt and uncle wouldn't have believed the tale even if someone had seen and reported it. Their scribe, summon a small army of Wildfolk? And the Wildfolk, knock their captain to the ground? As she picked at her food, she kept glancing over to the servants' side of the great hall. Gerran did come in to eat with his men, but Neb never appeared.

With so many people and so much food packed into the great hall, the air turned stifling in the afternoon's heat. Branna nearly fell asleep during the long round of ritual toasts to the company. Just as the men were settling down to some serious drinking, she decided that she had to have fresh air or die. She excused herself and left, but just outside the door Gerran caught up with her.

"I want to apologize," he said. "I'm the one who started that little brawl, and it was dishonorable of me."

"Well, it was," Branna said. "But Neb was no better."

"True-spoken." Gerran hesitated for a moment. "What did he do? Did you see?"

Branna felt a brief flash of admiration: she'd not expected him to acknowledge his bizarre defeat. "I'm not really sure," she said. "It all happened so fast. I thought Neb pushed you, and then you tripped on a loose cobblestone."

"Truly, somewhat like that must have been it." Gerran shrugged, looked away, looked at the cobbles, glanced at her face, looked away again. "Uh," he said finally, "I was wondering if— were you going for a walk or suchlike?"

"I was, truly."

"I want—I mean, may I walk with you?"

"I'll have to attend upon my aunt in just a little bit. In fact, I probably should go back in—"

"You don't truly want my company, you mean. I know I'm just common-born—"

"Oh, do hold your tongue about your stupid rank! I don't care if you grew up in fosterage. You're still my cousin, aren't you? A member of my kin and clan."

"That's how you think of me, is it?"

Branna hesitated, but it was time for truth. "It is," she said finally. "You've always been like a brother to me, Gerro, an elder brother I look up to and honor."

He winced and turned half-away. She risked laying a hand on his arm. "I've heard the most wonderful gossip," she said. "There's a highborn lady in Cengarn who favors you mightily."

"Don't be stupid! What would Lady Solla want with the likes of me?"

"Hah! You've noticed her interest, have you?"

"I've noticed naught. I'd suggest, my lady, that you not listen to gossip." With that he pulled his arm away from her lax touch and strode off.

The gray gnome popped into manifestation, smiling and dancing back and forth in front of her. "You approve, do you?" Branna whispered. "Well, poor Gerro! Let's go find my aunt."

They found Lady Galla readily enough. She was going upstairs to the women's hall, and Branna joined her. They settled themselves by a window that let in the last of the summer daylight and picked up their sewing, hurrying to get a few more stitches done before dark.

"Where's Omaena?" Branna said.

"Taken to her bed," Galla said. "She tires easily these days, or so she says."

"I see. You know, I'm truly glad now that Solla is coming to stay with us."

"So am I. I gather you've told Gerro that he may as well stop courting you."

"Did you see us talking?"

"I didn't. But I saw him follow you out, then come right back glowering like a summer storm."

"Well, I did tell him it was hopeless. I just can't marry him. I may be a warrior's daughter, but I don't want to marry someone dark and grim. I had enough of that with Da."

"No doubt, dear. I really do understand."

"My thanks, then. But what about Solla? Will she be able to marry a man like Gerro? After all, she's a gwerbret's sister, and she's the chatelaine of his dun."

"She's chatelaine now, certainly. But Solla's right: Ridvar will have to marry and quite soon, and no doubt his wife won't want another woman giving her servants orders and suchlike. As for Gerro's lack of rank," Galla hesitated, frowning at her line of stitches, "well, that might present a problem. It would be to Ridvar's advantage if she married some highly placed lord, someone at court, say, or even our Mirryn." She looked up, still frowning. "Though, with Gerran captain here—well, she wouldn't do at all for Mirryn's wife."

"True-spoken. But Ridvar's got two other sisters. Isn't one of them already married to someone important?"

"She is, indeed." Galla smiled again. "The high king's equerry down in Dun Deverry. A very important man, truly. And if young Ridvar should ask the king for an army, no doubt she'll argue in her brother's favor. His younger sister's quite lovely, and in a few years she'll be able to make a good match, too."

"So Solla might have more choice than some?"

"Indeed, she might. After all, Gerran won't be in any position to ask for a dowry."

The light in the room was fading as the sun sank to the horizon outside. Branna folded her sewing and laid it in her work basket. "Shall I go fetch some fire from the great hall?"

"Please do, dear." Galla ran her needle into the cloth. "It's time to light the candles, and that's quite enough sewing."

In the great hall the men were still at their drinking, but Neb wasn't among them. Branna lit her lantern at the servants' hearth and carried it back upstairs. She saw no sign of Neb on the stairs or in the corridors, either. Now that she knew she'd not have to explain the peculiar fight to her aunt and uncle, her anger had faded, and she could think clearly again. *A scribe's son, but he can command the Wildfolk—do I truly know this man?* Yet deep in her soul she felt that she'd never known anyone better.

Eventually Lady Omaena rejoined Galla and Branna in the women's hall. Since her aunt now had company for the evening, Branna pleaded a headache and left them. As she was approaching the door to her chamber, her gray gnome appeared, grinning and dancing up and down.

"What is it?" Branna whispered.

The gnome turned and walked through the door. First he stuck a skinny little foot into the wood like a swimmer testing the temperature of a pond, then an arm, and finally, grinning at her all the while, he inserted the rest of himself into the wood and disappeared. Branna had seen him do tricks such as this before; she merely rolled her eyes and opened the door to find the room bathed in golden light. With a little gasp she shut the door and leaned back against it.

Neb was waiting for her, perched on the windowsill. The gnome trotted over to him and pointed a bony finger.

"You might as well blow that candle out," Neb said. "We shan't need it."

Branna set the darkened lantern down on the floor, then looked up, gazing at the ceiling, where a glowing ball of gold hung like a tiny sun. She should have been amazed, she knew, but the light seemed the most ordinary thing in the room. Its presence had turned the bed, the walls, her dower chest into strange and unexpected objects, so intensely foreign that for a moment she wondered if she'd gotten into the wrong chamber.

"The light," Branna whispered. "How did you do that?"

"I didn't. The Wildfolk did it when I asked them."

"You shouldn't be in here."

"I had to apologize. It was stupid of me, baiting Gerran like that."

He sounded so contrite that she condescended to look at him. He left the window and walked over, then knelt like a courtier. "Will you forgive me, Branna?"

"Oh, of course. I suppose I could pretend to be haughty and all that, but I can't say I want to bother."

At that Neb laughed and got up, dusting off the knees of his brigga. "You're right enough that I shouldn't be in here," he said. "I don't want to stain your honor. We'd best get rid of that light, too, before someone sees it from the ward."

"True-spoken." Branna ignored her heart, pounding in fear, and raised one hand. She had to know, she realized, what she might have the power to do. In the glow small sprites were swirling on translucent wings. "My thanks," she said and snapped her fingers.

The golden ball vanished. The candle she'd put out earlier bloomed into flame. When she picked it up from the floor, her hands were shaking so badly that it very nearly went out again.

"There is real dweomer in the world," Neb said, "and we both have the talent for it. It's time, my lady, that we both thought well on what that means."

"Apparently so." Branna crossed the room and set the lantern down on her dower chest. "I wish Salamander would come back. He said some truly odd things to me, and the more I think about them, the more important they seem."

"He did the same to me. I think me he knows cursed well what it means, and I'll wager he could answer a question or two for us as well."

"I hope so. Dweomer can't be just ordering the Wildfolk around. We must be able—I mean, there must be other things." She let her voice trail miserably away.

"There must, truly. You've dreamed of some of them, from what you told me."

She nodded, barely aware of his words, barely aware when he turned away and left. She heard the chamber door close, but the noise seemed to happen a long distance away. The gnome leaped onto the bed and sat cross-legged on the coverlet.

"Oh, very well," Branna snapped. "You were right."

It bobbed its head, grinned, and vanished. Branna shuddered like a wet dog. For a moment, or so she felt, someone else had looked out from her eyes, and that someone had never seen this chamber before. Someone else. But who?

All that evening, as he drank with the warband, Gerran kept an eye out for Neb, but the scribe never came into the great hall. One of the serving lasses told him, finally, that Neb had begged some dinner from the cook out in the kitchen hut. Gerran tried to convince himself that the scribe was afraid of him, but at root he was too honest a man to believe it. Neb had no reason to fear ordinary men, armed or not. *Dweomer?* Gerran wondered. Certainly he'd heard plenty of tales about dweomer, even though he tended to discount them. *Or maybe I'm just going daft.* The latter alternative seemed preferable. He solved the problem, finally, by drinking enough mead to wash away the memory of the clash.

On the morrow morning, Neb came whistling into the great hall as brightly as if nothing had happened. Gerran was lingering over a second bowl of porridge; the scribe spotted him and strode over to his table.

"Good morrow, Captain," Neb said. "It's a lovely morning."

"It is," Gerran said. "Seems like the heat's finally broken."

Neb smiled, nodded, and walked on, heading for the table he shared with Lord Veddyn and the head groom's family. Gerran had a brief thought of heaving the porridge bowl at his retreating head. Instead, he went on eating.

Near the noontide, Gerran saw Branna and Neb walking together toward the garden. He was tempted to rush after them and knock the scribe off his feet with one good punch, but the memory stopped him—an attack, a myriad of little fists, all pummeling him, while he could see not one assailant, not one thing at all. *Cursed if I'll be afraid of a milksop scribe!* was his first thought.

But it wasn't fear that was stopping him, he realized, more a sense that Neb had some sort of prior claim. The thought startled him. It seemed so foreign that he glanced around, half-expecting to find some other person nearby who'd spoken it aloud, but he saw no one. With a toss of his head, he decided that he'd been a fool to even find her interesting. After all, she was right about one thing: she might as well be bloodkin, considering how long they'd known each other.

"It's much cooler today," Branna said. "Especially up here."

"It is," Neb said, "thanks to all the gods!"

They had climbed the catwalk to the top of the dun wall in search of privacy, because the cook was busy in her garden and the grooms were mucking out the stables. Branna hauled herself up to perch between two merlons, while Neb contented himself with leaning against the cool stone wall.

"Do be careful," he said. "I keep being afraid you'll fall."

"Oh, heights don't bother me. They never have. I used to love to climb the walls of my father's dun, too." And in her dreams, Branna suddenly remembered, she could fly like a falcon, indeed, as a falcon.

"Is somewhat wrong?" Neb said.

"There's not. Why?"

"You went a bit pale."

"Did I? Oh, it's of no importance. I was just remembering a thing that Salamander told me once." Branna was afraid that Neb would ask more, but he apparently had a more pressing matter on his mind.

"Um, well, did you ask your aunt yet?" he said. "About our marriage, I mean."

"I've not had the chance. Omaena and Pedrys didn't leave till late in the morning, and my aunt's been going over accounts with Lord Veddyn, to see how much food and suchlike the tourney used up."

Neb looked as disappointed as a child when rain spoils a promised excursion. Branna turned slightly and gazed out over the long view, the green fields and tidy farmsteads, the sparkling little river. In one of the river's bends a herd of white cows had lined up to drink, looking like a drift of snow from her distance. She remembered, as she watched them, her dreams of swooping over the countryside on a pair of strong wings, and how the view had looked from high in the air.

"You still want to marry me, don't you?" Neb's voice turned urgent. "You're not too frightened, are you?"

"Frightened? Of course not!" Branna turned back to look at him. "Besides, whether I marry you or not, I'm going to have to make some kind of peace with the dweomer."

"You look frightened." Neb tilted his head to one side to study her face.

"Beast!" She nearly stuck out her tongue at him, then decided that the gesture lacked dignity. "Oh, very well, I'll admit it. Last night was frightening."

"I'm sorry. I shouldn't have asked the Wildfolk for that golden ball."

"Nah nah nah! That wasn't it. It's the other lass. The one that seems to live inside my mind. I was so aware of her last night, and I want to be me, not her."

"Oh." Neb considered this seriously for a moment. "Well, I feel that other man inside me, too, but—let me think, how to say this—but he seems to be me, or another me, or suchlike. I'm not frightened because I know he's part of me. What about that lass? Isn't she just part of you?"

"I suppose. But there's sort of a gap between us. Oh, that doesn't make any sense!"

"In a way it does. I just don't know enough to help you."

For a moment Branna came close to weeping. Why had she been so sure that Neb could help, that he would somehow solve the problem and banish her fear?

"Here, here," Neb said, and he held out his hand. "Come down, my love."

She nodded and jumped the little way down to the wooden catwalk. He caught her hand and drew her close, kissed her, brushed the tears away. In his arms she felt suddenly safe.

"Well, one of us will find the answer," she said. "If not, there's Salamander, and if not him, then maybe we'll find someone who knows." She looked up at him and smiled. "And I'll talk with my aunt as soon as ever I can."

"That will gladden my heart. I—" Neb abruptly paused and looked up. "That's odd."

"What?" Branna let go of him and looked up.

In the sky a single raven wheeled over the dun, a large bird, too large, really, for his kind. She shivered, watching it dip and circle in utter silence.

"It's the only one I've seen around here," Neb said. "I wonder if it's scared the others off?"

"I've seen this one before. When was—that's right. I saw it the first day I came here."

"Was it just circling like this?"

"It was."

Neb climbed to the top of the wall and knelt between two merlons. Suddenly the raven squawked in alarm. With the dip of a wing it turned and flew off fast, heading north.

"It knew we were watching it," Neb said. "I don't like this, not in the least."

"No more do I. Let's hope it's not an ill omen."

"True spoken." Neb smiled at her, a forced gesture as if he were trying to lighten the mood. "Especially not about our marriage."

"Especially not that. Let's go down to the great hall, shall we? I don't want to be up here, all of a sudden. I hope that beastly thing doesn't come back."

They climbed down, but as they walked across the ward, Branna kept glancing at the sky. All that day the image of the raven circling above the dun returned to her, as troubling as rumors of war.

As the summer afternoon stretched out long shadows, and the smell of cooking filled the ward, the warband and servitors, the servants and the noble-born all began to gather in the great hall. Neb took his usual place at Lord Veddyn's table, though the old man had yet to appear.

At the other end the head groom's wife was cutting up peaches

and handing out the pieces to her brood of five children. Long
streaks of sunlight, turned gold with dust, poured in through the
west-facing windows. At the honor table Branna and Lord Mirryn
were playing Carnoic while Tieryn Cadryc leaned back in his chair
and watched, a tankard of ale in his hand. The dun's dogs ambled
in to flop into the straw on the floor near the warband—the messi-
est eaters and the most likely to toss them a bone or two. Serving
lasses wandered around, handing out baskets of bread and tankards
of ale.

Neb sipped his ale and considered how the raven, flying so
silently over the dun, had ruined the peaceful ease of a summer's
day. Ravens, the largest of the carrion crows, were generally birds of
ill omen, but this particular bird seemed something more. Neb remembered bits of Salamander's fanciful tales, which often included
sorcerers who could turn themselves into birds. Neb could imagine
his mother heaping scorn on the very idea. She would have been
right, too, he decided, but the image of the raven kept hovering
around his mind as the bird itself had hovered over the dun.

Still, Neb refused to let it spoil his happiness. Branna had agreed
to marry him. Neb smiled out at nothing while he wondered what
it would be like to spend the rest of his life in this dun. Pleasant in
the spring and summer, no doubt, and cramped and vexing in the
winter, but bearable if Branna were his wife. *Where else could we
live?* he asked himself. *She'll not want to travel the roads as the wife
of a wandering letter-writer or suchlike.* Perhaps they could go back
to Trev Hael, where he might set up shop as his father had, a scribe
and dealer in parchments and inks. He decided that worrying about
this decision now was a waste of time. Everything depended on
winning approval for their marriage.

And that approval depended on Lady Galla. By the time she and
Lord Veddyn finally came in to take their usual places, the serving
lasses were beginning to bring platters of cold pork, left from yesterday's feast, and still more fresh-picked peaches to go with it.
Branna wouldn't be able to discuss the matter with her aunt at
table. The evening passed in a slow agony. First Lady Galla and

Branna lingered over their meal; then they retreated to the women's hall. Were they talking about him? Neb could only wait and see.

By the time that Branna came back down, Neb was half-asleep and alone at the table. Cadryc and Mirryn had retired upstairs, and most of the warband had left the great hall as well, including—thankfully—Gerran. As Branna walked downstairs, she looked so solemn that Neb feared the worst, but she sat down next to him, a gesture she'd not have made if her aunt was refusing to consider such a marriage.

"We've had quite the clan parley," Branna said, "out in the corridor in front of the women's hall."

"And?" Neb said.

"It's my father. The problem, I mean. Aunt Galla's all in favor of my marrying you, and Uncle Cadryc doesn't object. He was surprised, and so was Mirryn, that I wouldn't choose Gerran, but Uncle said, well, I'm not the one marrying the lad, so it's up to you." She paused, her eyes troubled. "But we'll have to ask Da, and the gods only know what he'll say."

"Here, if he didn't even want you in his dun, why would he object?"

"Oh, it's not me. It's the honor of thing. His daughter, marrying a commoner—he might start breathing fire and swearing at the very thought. We honestly don't know how he'll take it."

Neb groaned aloud. Branna reached over and patted his arm.

"Well, if worse comes to worst," she said, "we can run away together, and even if they catch us, I'll be dishonored and they'll have to let us marry."

"If he doesn't beat you—"

"Do you think the Wildfolk would let him?"

Neb grinned in slow satisfaction. "They wouldn't, and it would be a sight worth seeing if he tried. But what shall we do next? Write him a letter?"

"I don't know. Aunt Galla wants to think about it before we do anything. She knows him better than anyone, after all. She's his sister."

"Very well, then. I'll be guided by our lady's advice."

"I truly do think that's best." Branna frowned down at the table. "I wonder if there's going to be a war soon. I've been having the oddest sort of—well, they're not dreams, because I'm awake when they happen, but they're sort of pictures and the like, about our men fighting the Horsekin."

"Do we win?"

"They don't go that far." Branna looked up, her face pale. "You believe that I've seen omens, don't you?"

"I do. Why would I doubt you?"

Branna laid her hand at her throat and looked away for a long silence. Finally she said, "I wish Salamander would get back here! That's all. He'll either have news of the Horsekin or he won't, and he'll either know what's happening to us or he won't, and ye gods, I'm sick of waiting to find out."

Salamander himself was wishing that he were back in the tieryn's dun. Rocca had been leading him west by an improbably round-about route. Certain rock formations, she told him, were cursed and had to be avoided, just as certain ancient trees held evil spirits. A particular stream held water so heavily enchanted, or so she believed, that they followed it upstream for miles until it became narrow enough for them to jump across it. In the virgin forest, where bracken and shrubs grew thick between the trees, Salamander was forced to walk and lead his pair of horses along narrow trails.

"You know," he said one evening, "if we turned south, we could travel across grassland, and it would be faster."

"What? Never!" Rocca said. "This stretch of the journey, it be terrible dangerous enough as it is. The open land, it be worse."

"It is?" Salamander said. "Why?"

"Because of Vandar's spawn."

"Who?"

"The Lord of Evil, Vandar, did father children on beasts." Rocca glanced around and lowered her voice, as if she feared spies lurking in the wild forest around them. "They do look somewhat like men and Horsekin, but their eyes do give them away, all slit like cats and bestial. And their ears! It be a custom amongst them, that they do torture their children as babies, you see, to fill them with hate and bile. They do pull upon the child's ears and cut them with sharp knives. Betimes even do they touch them with hot irons." She shuddered dramatically. "Mayhap some knowledge of them has come your way. Men call them the Westfolk."

Salamander was so shocked that he could do nothing but gape at her.

"It be a horrible thing, bain't?" Rocca continued. "But fear not! The Children of Alshandra shall prevail in the end. It be our wyrd to kill every single one of the Spawn and make the plains clean and pure again. And then our people, they may graze their horses on the abundance of Alshandra's good grass."

"I see." Salamander managed to find his voice. "And what then? Once we have enough horses, are we going to conquer Deverry as well?"

"Nah, nah, nah, naught as horrid as that! With the Spawn destroyed, we shall live in peace on the grasslands, and we shall set about sending missionaries to Deverry. That be the dearest hope of every priest and priestess."

"What about your warleaders? Rakzanir, I think they're called. Do they want to live in peace?"

Rocca bit her lower lip and looked sharply away. "Well," she said after a moment, "it be true that they be a stubborn lot. Not always do they see eye to eye with our priestesses."

"I rather thought they wouldn't."

"But in the end, the holy council will win. Alshandra the Wise does help us, and she will melt their hearts and teach them mercy and mild ways. I do ken it in my heart, and so does Lakanza. She be the high priestess, Her Holiness Lakanza, and she be ever so old and wise. She prays every day that she may live to see the truth spreading among Deverry men. In my heart I ken that it be wyrd. Look at Honelg and his blessed kin and clan! Their faith be strong and pure, bain't? And you, too, for that matter—you did recognize the truth the moment you heard it."

"Well, so I did."

"We do call it waking up. Most people, Horsekin and Deverry folk alike, they do live their lives asleep. They do believe in their false gods and dream the years away. But Alshandra's truth be a silver horn, calling out the signal to wake and rise."

What Salamander desperately wanted at the moment was the signal that Rocca was going to lie down and sleep, but that night she seemed to be in a talkative mood. She insisted on drilling him on the lore lists, then talked some about her childhood, growing up a slave in a Horsekin tribe until Alshandra's religion brought her freedom.

"Anyone that the priests deem fit to serve *her* does gain their freedom, you see." Rocca paused for a yawn. "So I do count myself blessed."

"Indeed. What would your life have been like if you'd not been chosen?"

"Naught too horrible. My family did work, and they still do, at the growing of grain for the warhorses. Up on the high plains the summers be short and scant, so down among the valleys there be many a farm that owe the Horsekin dues and taxes. We did live, my kin and me, much like Deverry bondmen, only better, or so Honelg said once, after I did tell him about my early life. We held rights to keep a third of everything we did raise, while bondmen have to hand so much over to the lords that it be a wonder they don't starve."

"That's true." Salamander feigned a long yawn, which prompted her to yawn herself. "It's very sad, how the bondmen are treated."

"Now, I'd not lie to you. Some slaves do lead terrible lives, but the priests and priestesses, we be doing our best to change that. Some of the Horsekin leaders, they do begin to see the light, that all Children of Alshandra be worthy of respect."

"That's a noble cause, then." Salamander yawned again. "My apologies! For some reason I'm weary tonight."

"Me, too. I'll just be saying my prayers." Rocca got up, shaking her head as if she were trying to stay alert.

She trotted off, humming part of a hymn under her breath. Salamander fed their little fire with twigs and sticks until he could be sure she'd taken herself well away. Then he contacted Dallandra and told her what the Horsekin believed about Vandar's spawn. Her image, floating over the fire, stared at him for a long horrified moment.

"Well," Dalla said at last. "That's one up for Cal. He keeps insisting that the Horsekin are planning some evil thing, and they are."

"They see it as purging the world of a great evil, of course."

"Of course. Most people who work evil think of it as good in some way. That doesn't make it any better for those they hate."

"I'd never deny that."

"Ebañy, you're running a huge risk, a much larger risk than either of us realized when you started this journey. Hadn't you better just abandon this whole thing? You can ride away faster than she can follow on foot."

"I've had that thought." Salamander paused to glance into the forest, where Rocca still knelt at her prayers. "But it's more necessary than ever to know where this fort lies, isn't it?"

"True. But be careful. Be careful every single moment of the day."

"Fear not, I shall. And we can't be all that far from the thing by now."

In the northern stretch of the grasslands, at a place where a traveler coming up from the south would just begin to see the distant mountains of the Roof of the World, a huge outcrop of gray granite hunched like an animal. All around it tiny streams ran, fed by hidden springs. Dallandra and Valandario had decided to meet at this marker, and when Prince Daralanteriel led his alar up to Twenty Streams Rock, they found Val and her people waiting for them. Dalla left the work of setting up her tent to the others and immediately followed Valandario into hers. Val had arranged her piles of bright-colored cushions into seats on either side of her scrying cloth.

"I haven't told anyone about this yet," Dalla said. "I don't want panic. Ebañy's found out something terrifying."

"Does it have to do with that new religion you told me about?" Val said.

"Just that. The Horsekin think it's their sacred duty to wipe the People off the grasslands and the face of the world, just slaughter every last one of us."

Valandario went very still. Not even her eyelids flickered for a long long moment; then she let out her breath with a little sigh. She raised both hands and ran them through her hair, pushing it back from her face as if the stray golden wisps suddenly bothered her. Dallandra waited patiently.

"I see now," Val said at last. "Obsidian tumbling over lapis lazuli, fire over water—I see what that signified now. In yesterday's reading, I mean." She was silent again for some while. "Death along the water, of course." Another pause. "Yellow jewels, distance. Not necessarily our deaths, but death at some long distance."

"War, then?"

Val twisted around where she sat, dug into a small brass coffer, and brought out a pouch of embossed tan leather. She turned back, considered the scrying cloth for a moment, then poured jewels out upon it. A red ruby slid halfway across and came to rest on an embroidered spiral.

"War, yes," Val said. "With Deverry men." She touched a purple stone that lay nearby. "In the company of Deverry men, I mean, not against them."

"Soon?"

"Very. When Ebañy returns with proof of his warning." Val laid a slender forefinger on a piece of dark jade and moved it along a seam 'twixt two pieces of silk, one yellow, one red. "If he gets back."

Dallandra shuddered. "I was hoping we could get Ebañy out of this alive."

"So was I. Nothing I see here discourages me, but the Horsekin—"

They sat in silence for some while with the unfinished words hanging between them, a malediction upon those distant enemies. *Not distant enough*, Dalla thought. *Halfway across the world would be too close still.*

"You know," Val said at last. "I hope you didn't mind when I handed the job of curing Ebañy over to you. I feel guilty still, but I had no idea of what to do."

"No need for guilt. I offered, didn't I?"

"True. But I was afraid that I was failing my apprentice somehow."

"Not that he'd studied with you in—what?—a hundred and fifty years?"

"Something like that." Valandario was staring at her gems, sparkling on the silk before her. "I'm afraid I've gotten obsessed with my scrying. There are still so many problems, so many things to work out."

"You should take another apprentice, or no, a journeyman dweomerworker, to learn it, perfect or not. And I wonder— shouldn't you write it all down?"

"I suppose so, yes." Val looked up. "I doubt if I'll die soon, but these days, well, you never know, what with war in the west and all."

"I didn't mean to be morbid—"

"You weren't. Realistic, perhaps." Val sighed with a shake of her head. "Do you remember Nevyn? Aderyn's master in the dweomer?"

"Vividly, yes. I met him ever so long ago, but he was the kind of man who made an impression on people."

"Indeed." Val paused for a smile. "We discussed the ancient lore once, the lore of the Seven Cities, I mean, and how so much of it had been lost. They never wrote down the core of their teachings, you see. When Meranaldar first came to us, I had hopes. I thought that maybe the books of the innermost lore were safe in the Southern Isles. But they're not. There never were any. Meranaldar had read various things that made that clear. They simply didn't write down the biggest secrets."

"And that means the lore's gone forever."

"Perhaps. We might be able to rediscover it, if we're lucky, one day. But Nevyn told Aderyn something once, that the loss was the bitter price of secrecy. That phrase has stuck with me now for what is it? Almost two hundred years."

"The bitter price of secrecy." Dallandra nodded her agreement. "It's a very good phrase indeed. And now the Horsekin want to wipe out what lore we do have left."

"Yes. Well, it's on the knees of the gods, like the war itself. Let's assume that Ebañy's successful, that he finds this fortress or whatever it turns out to be. What, then? Do we ride to Cengarn and ask its child ruler for help?"

"Just that, but afterward, I'll be traveling south," Dallandra said. "I very much want to visit Tieryn Cadryc of the Red Wolf. Let me tell you why."

As the summer days slipped past, Neb found himself keeping an odd sort of watch over the dun. As children, he and the other boys in Trev Hael had played with slings and stones; Neb had had something of a reputation for his keen eye. He made himself a sling from some scrap leather he found in the stables and took to carrying it and a handful of pebbles in his brigga pockets in case the mysterious raven returned. It may have acted like a normal bird, but its size gave it away. When it had hovered over the dun, it had looked as large as a normal raven if that bird had been only some hundred yards up. But at that distance, Neb should have been able to see some details of its head and feathers, while this particular raven had only been a black shape against the sky.

Neb still had his doubts about it being some sort of sorcerer, but no matter what it was, he felt deep in his soul that something so unnatural meant naught but ill. Branna had her fear of that mysterious "other lass," and he had his suspicions of the raven. *Ye gods!* Neb thought. *What's happening to us?* The world seemed suddenly larger and stranger than they'd ever dreamed. He longed to bring the raven down, but as if it knew he watched, it stayed away.

Not long after the tourney, news of a second excitement arrived at Tieryn Cadryc's dun. Everyone was eating dinner in the great hall when Neb heard a horn calling outside, a cascade of three sour notes.

"The gatekeeper." Gerran rose from his chair at the warband's head table. "Pages! Go see what he wants."

Little Lord Ynedd ignored him, but Coryn and Clae both jumped up and ran outside. Across the hall by the honor hearth, Tieryn Cadryc got up and waited standing, staring at the door. In a few moments Clae and Coryn came rushing in from the ward, so eager to get to the tieryn's side that they tripped over a tan hound, who yelped and scuttled away. No one laughed; everyone fell silent to listen.

"Your Grace," Coryn said, panting a little, "Messengers from Cengarn."

Clae ushered in a pair of road-weary men, wearing dust-stained tabards embroidered with the blazing sun of Cengarn over their clothes. When the messengers knelt at the tieryn's side, one proffered a silver message tube. Neb got up and swung himself free of the bench.

"Scribe!" Cadryc called out.

"I'm on my way, Your Grace."

Neb trotted over to the honor table and took the silver tube, then pulled the letter free to scan it.

"I hope our gwerbret's seen reason about those raiders," Cadryc said.

"Alas, he hasn't, my lord," Neb said. "Not in this message, anyway. It's announcing his betrothal and coming marriage."

"Well, that's somewhat to the good. Read it out, lad."

The message was long, flowery, and full of courtesies, but the gist was simple. Gwerbret Ridvar had betrothed himself to Lady Drwmigga of Trev Hael. The gwerbret would be honored if Tieryn Cadryc and his people would come to the wedding.

"Oh, that's an excellent choice!" Galla said. "She's the daughter of Trev Hael's gwerbret, and her mother was the daughter of the gwerbret of Dun Trebyc."

"Old Drwmyc, you mean?" Cadryc said. "A good bloodline, then."

"Isn't she older than Ridvar, though?" Branna said.

"By a few years, but not too many." Galla considered for a moment. "I don't remember when she was born, but if she were too old, she'd have been married already."

"True spoken, with the alliances she brings," Cadryc said. "Neb, I'll need you to write some sort of fancy reply to his grace. Of course we'll all go. It gladdens my heart that our gwerbret's doing his duty to rhan and clan."

"Mine, too," Mirryn said. "Now let's hope he gets the lass with child, and quickly."

"Just that," Galla put in. "May the gods grant she's not barren! This *is* exciting, I must say! Branna, just think—mayhap we'll get to see our Adranna at the wedding."

"Well, now." Cadryc raised one hand. "Don't get your hopes up, my love. Ridvar won't be able to invite every lord in the rhan. His dun won't hold that many guests, and ye gods, can you imagine the grumbling if he asked some of them to quarter in the town? He'll have enough trouble housing all the tierynau as it is, to say naught of Drwmigga's clan."

Galla's face fell. "You're doubtless right." Her voice wavered slightly. "I do hope she's well."

"Well, how about this?" Cadryc said. "We won't be all that far from her husband's wretched dun. Mayhap we can ride north after the wedding and pay her a visit."

Galla and Branna both beamed at him. "We'll have Neb write her a letter," Cadryc said, "once we're in Cengarn, and it's a shorter ride for the messenger."

"My thanks," Galla said. "Now I can truly enjoy myself at this wedding."

"I suppose," Mirryn said, "I'll be left behind here."

"Someone has to hold fort guard, lad." Cadryc paused to smile at him. "Here, you're the one who'll be in the most danger this time. I'm entitled to an escort of twenty-five for the wedding, but I think I'll take fewer men than that, so I can leave you more. I wouldn't put it past the cursed Horsekin to try to siege the place while I'm gone."

Mirryn bit back angry words, took a sip of ale, and then managed a brief smile. "True enough," he said.

Still, they glared at each other, and the mood hung over the table like a swarm of angry bees. Branna leaned forward and changed the subject.

"Ridvar's betrothed—what's she like? I've never even seen her. Have you, Uncle?"

"I've not." Cadryc shrugged his shoulders. "Doesn't much matter. He can always blow the candle out."

The men all laughed, but Lady Galla and Branna exchanged a sour smile.

"She's a good-looking lass, actually, my lord," Neb said. "I used to see her, riding with her father through our town. Eldidd-dark hair and dark blue eyes, and she's slender though not dainty."

"Good." Cadryc turned to him. "I forgot you come from Trev Hael. Well, it gladdens my heart that the lad's marrying, but I'll admit I was hoping for news of that blasted gerthddyn. Call me daft if you want, but I just keep thinking he's on to some important thing that will help our gwerbret change his mind."

"Let's pray so," Mirryn said.

"You don't sound convinced, lad."

"I'm not." It was Mirryn's turn to shrug. "But he's the only hound in our pack that's picked up any scent at all. Might as well let him follow it down."

Salamander may have been on the trail of a metaphoric scent, but he was also hopelessly lost. If Rocca was following any sort of marked trail, he couldn't tell what it was or if they were on it. He needed to do more than just reach the Horsekin dun. He needed to be able to lead an army back to it. During the odd moments when he could contact Dallandra, he would describe whatever bit of the wilderness they had camped in, but he doubted if anyone was going to be able to tell one clearing among trees from another. Finally, after they'd gone straight west for some hours only to turn south to avoid the evil spirits in a particular ravine, he grew exasperated enough to ask her point blank if she were lost.

"Lost? Me?" Rocca laughed in her usual merry way. "Your eyes yet cannot find the marks along this trail, Evan, but truly, they be there, blazed by *her* as plain as Deverry cairns for those with eyes to see."

"Well, if you say so," Salamander said. "I know that I've only begun to learn *her* ways."

"There be ahead a stream we call the Galan Targ, the home border. Once we do cross that, our way will lie straight before us. All of Vandar's evil traps will lie behind us then. And it be not far. Fear not!"

Indeed, they reached the Galan Targ late that afternoon, a wide but shallow stream running over clean sand. On either bank someone had cleared away the underbrush, and big stones marked out the ford. Salamander offered to let Rocca ride on his horse for the crossing, but she refused.

"You do ride over, and then I'll be a-following after," she said. "There be a need on me to bless the waters as I pass through."

Salamander's horses crossed easily, as the water ran only a few feet deep. On the far bank he dismounted and waited, watching, as Rocca raised her arms into the air and intoned a short prayer. Perhaps the stream wasn't in the mood for a blessing, however, because as she stepped into it she slipped, falling to her knees. She got to her feet only to stumble again, falling headlong into the water. Her hair lost its bone pins, and the long strands spread out in the water around her head. Salamander started into the stream to help her, but she scrambled up, soaking wet but laughing, to wave him back.

"Stay dry!" she called out. "I did step on a sharp pebble or suchlike under the sand, but no harm done! Here, there be a need on me to find those hairpins, though. They be all I have." She knelt in the water and groped around the sand for a moment, then stood up, frowning. "They be gone, sure enough."

"I can whittle you some more," Salamander said.

"My thanks, then." Her smile returned in a blaze of good spirits.

She came splashing up on to the bank and shook herself like a dog, smiling all the while. Her thin linen shift, somewhat cleaner than before, clung to her body, and her wet hair, freed from the pins, draped over her breasts and hung nearly to her waist. Salamander turned away and concentrated on slacking his horse's bits so they could drink.

"We shall camp here tonight," Rocca said. "Safe at last, and your beasts will have good grass as well as sweet water."

Salamander busied himself with tending his horses as well as gathering firewood. He'd begun to think like a true neophyte, he realized, a change he'd not noticed until that moment. He was honestly ashamed of himself for looking lustfully upon a priestess, but there was no denying that he was. Her linen dress shrank as it dried, pulling tight across her breasts as she sat cross-legged by their fire, as unself-conscious as a child. She was concentrating on combing out her wet hair, a mass of snarls. Judging by its appearance she'd not washed or combed it in years.

"I could help you comb that out," he said. "Round the back, like, where you can't reach."

Rocca burst out laughing. "You be new to our ways, Evan. You know not what you did just say."

"My apologies, Your Holiness. Was it a wrong thing?"

"Not wrong, but unknowing. Among us a man will try to comb a woman's hair when he wishes to marry her. If she does allow him, then married they are."

"Ah, I see." Salamander had the loathsome feeling that he was blushing—his face burned with embarrassment.

Rocca cocked her head to one side and considered him for a moment. "There be a need on you to know that never shall I marry," she said at last, "nor shall I ever have aught to do with a man in matters of love."

Salamander made a strangled little noise that might pass for "of course not."

"It be a rule of our priestesses, that never shall we lie with a man for fear of getting a child," Rocca continued. "Why would we wish to bring more souls into Vandar's evil world? Would that not be cruel, to trap souls here for him to torment?"

"It would, Your Holiness. I'm truly truly sorry—"

"Oh, grovel not! Am I not a woman, too, and flattered?" Rocca paused to smile at him. "But I have no wish to leave *her* service."

"What would happen to a woman if she betrayed our goddess with a man?"

"Naught, but that she would have to take him in marriage, were he able to marry, or go back to her old life with her family were he not. *She* be a woman, too, and demands no punishment or the like. But a priestess the sinner would never be again."

"So a woman who'd been with a man could never become a priestess?"

"Nah nah nah, naught so harsh, just so long as she were no priestess at the time. No vow taken, no vow broken. She may forswear her love and take then the holy vows."

"You know, that seems a truly decent law. In Deverry things are harsher."

"I do hear that they bury any priestess alive who does break her vows."

"Oh, that's not true. They make her leave the Moon Temple, that's all. The man, though, they hang."

"That's a dreadful thing, to punish someone for a thing they can't help but do! What more can one expect from men, but—ah well, let me not ramble and say mean things. Let us pray together. I promise you, Alshandra will fill your heart with more joy and comfort than ever I could."

The threat of hours of prayer would be even better than hanging to prevent men from falling into sin, Salamander decided. Although he tried to pay strict attention to Rocca's words, he eventually fell asleep where he knelt, sagging over like a half-empty sack of grain. He woke to her gentle laughter and a boyish punch on his shoulder.

"My apologies," he stammered.

"None needed," Rocca said, smiling. "You be new to the faith and not yet tempered in your soul. Do go to sleep, Evan. Tomorrow we shall reach the holy shrine if naught impede us."

The Horsekin had chosen the location for their new dun well. Thanks to Rocca's roundabout path, Salamander could only guess at how many miles west of Cengarn they'd traveled—a good long way, he figured, at least a hundred—distant enough to make supplying an army difficult even if the high king should send one. Eventually, they came to a river that led them south into a part of the world he'd never seen before. First they left the hills behind, then the deep forests, until they traveled through scrubby, rocky grasslands, not quite flat and not quite hilly either. Off to the west Salamander saw dark smudges along the horizon—clouds, he thought at first, but when they never rolled in or away he realized that he was seeing the fabled mountains of the far west.

"Those mountains." He pointed them out to Rocca. "That's

where Taen—your city, I can't remember its name—but that's where it lies, isn't it?"

"It does lie in the mountains," Rocca said, "but you have a fine pair of eyes if you can see them from here."

"Oh, I've always been gifted that way."

Salamander could only be grateful that she lacked concrete information about Vandar's spawn. From now on, he reminded himself, he would have to be more careful.

The river cut its channel out of a reddish sandstone. As they followed a well-marked path along its western bank, the cut grew deeper and deeper, until finally it became a canyon. On their last night out, they camped at the top of a thirty-foot cliff while the river rushed by below. *And how,* he wondered, *are we going to get an army across without a bridge?*

"We'll reach Zakh Gral on the morrow," Rocca said.

"Good," Salamander said. "My heart longs to see our goddess' holy shrine."

On the morrow he caught his first glimpse. They had tramped along the canyon's western rim all morning when Rocca suddenly laughed and pointed straight ahead.

"There!" she said. "You can just see the fortress."

Salamander shaded his eyes with his hand and studied the view. For hundreds of yards around, the forest cover had been cleared down to the ground. In the midst of rock and weeds he could see a tower rising above walls.

"It be still made of wood," Rocca said. "Getting enough stone here from the quarries—they do lie in the foothills a fair bit west, you see, and it be far more difficult, fetching the blocks, than the builders did think at first."

Thank the real gods for that! Salamander thought. Aloud he said, "Well, it looks grand anyway, wooden or not. It's so big."

"It be so, truly. It will house hundreds of our folk when they do finish it."

As they drew closer Salamander got a better look. While the fort might well be grand when finished, at the moment it spread a scrappy sort of mess along the edge of the cliff, which fell away in a sheer drop to the river. Wooden walls, patched in places with blocks of stone, surrounded a wooden tower, some fifty feet high. Salamander noticed little windows at the top and assumed that it was some sort of watchmen's post. Over the walls he could see the roofs of scattered wood buildings and, here and there, parts of half-finished stone structures.

Even in this partial view the layout struck him as somehow familiar. As they drew near, he realized why. The Horsekin had modeled their fortress on the dun of their old enemies in Cengarn. He dismounted and led his horses while Rocca walked a little ahead. She was hurrying to the open gates, made of timber bound with iron bands and iron hinges. A wooden palisade of roughly-hewn logs surrounded a jumble of buildings also made of logs, some low and crude, others built more stoutly with more attention to windows and proper doors and the like.

Off to one side, however, lay an uneven circle of open ground, approximately a hundred yards across, and in its midst stood a small building made of polished and precisely cut stone. Slate tiles covered its peaked roof, and over the door he could see a carving of a bow and arrow. On either side of its door stood two young trees, protected by fences made of narrow boards.

"That must be the shrine." Salamander put excitement into his voice. "It's beautiful."

"The Inner Shrine it be, truly," Rocca said. "We did finish it first, as was right and proper for our goddess."

At the gate Horsekin guards, typical soldiers of their kind, armed with long spears as well as swords, stepped forward and blocked the view inside. They stood over six feet tall, and their huge manes of hair, braided here and there and decorated with little charms and talismans, emphasized their height. Their faces, bare arms, and hands sported solid masses of tattoos covering all but a few traces of their milk-white skin. Salamander noticed that some of the tattoos displayed their goddess' bow and arrow, along with stylized flames that might also have been a holy symbol. When they recognized

Rocca, they greeted her in their language, and she answered in the same, gesturing toward Salamander as if telling them who he was.

The guards ushered them both inside. One turned and called out in a booming voice. At this signal others came running—Horsekin and human men dressed in the same brown leather clothes as the guards, a handful of human women wearing tattered tunics and the iron band around one ankle that marked them as slaves. Mostly, however, Salamander saw Horsekin warriors, standing in little groups by what seemed to be a covered well, walking back and forth on the walls, sitting on the steps of a long wooden barracks. *There must be hundreds of them here already,* he thought.

A group of Horsekin and human women walked slowly and with great dignity to join Rocca and Salamander. The two humans and the pair of Horsekin all wore long doeskin dresses, heavily painted with symbols and abstract designs, that fell to their ankles but left their tattooed arms bare. While the Horsekin women had shaved their heads and wore little leather caps, the humans had kept their hair long.

"See you the elderly woman there?" Rocca pointed at a women with gray hair piled up high on top of her head. "That be Lakanza, the high priestess. Behind her come some of my sisters in the faith."

"I thought they must be holy women," Salamander said. "They walk with such gravity."

"They all be worthy of the faith. Well." Rocca's voice turned sour. "Except for one. But this be no time for that. Look you just beyond the shrine itself. See there that circle marked out with stones?"

"I do," Salamander said. "That flat boulder in the middle? Is that an altar?"

"It be the neophytes' holy altar indeed, and that be where we welcome those new to the faith. We do call it the Outer Shrine. Once they've dedicated themselves, then may they enter the Inner Shrine."

When the women joined them, Salamander noticed that the high priestess and the two Horsekin women greeted Rocca warmly, but the other human forced out a smile that was barely civil. Rocca in turn ignored her and spoke to the others in the Horsekin tongue. All of the women studied him as she spoke.

"Come now," Lakanza said at last. "There be a need on us to speak in language that our guest can understand." She glanced at one of the Horsekin women. "Dorag, take those horses to the grooms, then rejoin us among the holy stones. The rest of you, arrange yourself for prayer. It behooves us to bring out the relics of Raena the Holy Witness, she who were the first to give up her life as testimony to Alshandra's power over death."

Since Salamander had heard tales of Raena from Dallandra, he wasn't surprised to find her memory venerated among the Horsekin, though they doubtless would have been horrified to learn that she'd been a shape-changer. Lakanza hurried into the Inner Shrine, while in the Outer the others all knelt in front the massive gray boulder, chiseled and chipped flat. Carved in the center were the goddess' bow and arrow. Rocca gestured for him to kneel at the head of the crowd, and she knelt beside him. Fortunately for Salamander's knees, inside the circle grew thick, soft grass. He somehow just knew that a good long session of prayers lay ahead of him.

Lakanza returned, carrying a burnished copper tray. Placed as he was, Salamander had a good view of the altar. He studied the relics as the high priestess laid her tray and its burdens down: a miniature bow and arrow made of gold and copper, a wooden box with a lid inlaid with gold spirals, and a strange bone flute or whistle. It seemed to be made of two fingerbones glued together, but he could see that each bone was far too long to have belonged to either a human being or one of the Westfolk. Strangest of all, though, was the last relic, a black crystal in the shape of a truncated pyramid. Salamander knew immediately that he'd seen it before, but he couldn't remember where.

Lakanza raised her arms, said a few words in the Horsekin tongue, then began praying in Deverrian. Salamander risked a few glances around and noticed the other human priestess watching him. Her ancestors, immediate or otherwise, must have come from Eldidd, he realized. Though her eyes were an ordinary cornflower blue, they were strangely round, making him think of a bird's eyes, under arched brows. She wore her hair, shiny blue-black like a raven's wing, bound back with a twist of thin rope. Her painted leather dress hung straight to feet that were, like Rocca's, a mass of scar tissue and swellings.

When the prayers were over, and everyone had risen to their feet, this priestess went up to the altar, curtsied in front of it, and picked up the narrow wooden box. She stepped forward, bobbed her head to the high priestess, then turned to Rocca.

"This fellow," she said. "And for how long have you known him, Rocca, that you bring him here so boldly?"

"Long enough," Rocca snapped. "I do feel the sincerity of his heart."

"There be a need on me for a bit more evidence than that. I like not his pretty face, and I think me it did sway your judgment."

"Oh, hold your tongue, Sidro!" Rocca set her hands on her hips. "We all know you do try to humiliate me at every turn, and I say your words now be just one more case of it."

"There be reason to listen to my words." Sidro hefted the box. "This man stinks of danger."

"Hah! You do see mating everywhere, that be your trouble. It be no wonder that your lover did cast you off."

Sidro's face drained white, then turned red in rage. Lakanza raised both hands and stepped between them.

"Hush!" the priestess said. "Such nastiness among ourselves ill reflects upon our goddess!"

"You be right, Your Holiness," Rocca said. "Sidro, my sister in Alshandra, I did speak wrongly. I apologize."

Sidro said nothing until Lakanza tapped her on the shoulder. "I do accept your apology. But I do wonder if this convert would pass the test of the holy dagger. There be somewhat about him that speaks of Vandar's spawn to me."

"That be a foul thing for even you to say," Rocca said.

"Oh, does it be so?" Sidro gave her a smug smile. "If his heart be so pure, surely you'd not object to the ritual, would you? Since you do already think him fit for the worship, what harm could befall him?"

Caught, Rocca stared back and forth between Sidro and the high priestess. The two Horsekin priestesses stepped forward and began talking to Lakanza in their own language. Salamander could tell nothing of their feelings from their heavily tattooed faces, but apparently they were urging caution. Eventually Lakanza nodded her agreement and spoke in Deverrian.

"Very well," Lakanza said. "Bring the sacred dagger forward."

With a little smile Sidro opened the box. Salamander felt his heart freeze in his chest as Rocca's rival took out a silver dagger. He knew now what this test would entail, and his mind went racing down long chains of lies and ruses. Holding the dagger, Sidro returned the box to the altar. For a moment she paused, looking him over with a small smile that held no good humor, while she ran one finger down the flat of the silver blade. Finally she took it by the point, then stepped forward and thrust the hilt at Salamander.

"Take it," she growled. "Hold it if you dare. We'll see if the sacred wyvern bites you or not."

"Of course I dare." Salamander grinned at her. "I don't understand what you're talking about it. Is it hot or suchlike?"

"Just take it."

With a little shrug Salamander did just that. As soon as his fingers touched the dagger, blue flames exploded from the blade and leaped into the air. Salamander did his best to look dumbstruck— he yelped, flung the dagger down, and jumped back as Sidro howled in triumph. Rocca shrieked, then clasped both hands over her mouth.

"Vandar's spawn!" Sidro said. "I knew it."

"What?" Salamander stammered out the words. "I don't understand. What do you mean?"

"You lie!" Sidro said. "You may look like an ordinary man, but in your veins does run the blood of Vandar's spawn. I call and demand that he be executed as our laws require."

"Wait!" Rocca shoved herself in between them. "I've traveled with this man. There be no evil in him. I understand this not at all. Did you play some trick, Sidro? I'd not put it past you."

"You frothing bitch!" Sidro raised one hand.

"Stop it!" Lakanza moved in and took control. "Sidro, pick up the wyvern knife, and put it properly away. There be a need on us to purify it. Rocca, please, do now hold your tongue so that I may sort this out." She turned to Salamander. "By the testimony of this knife, either your father or your mother did come from the spawn. Be it that you dispute it?"

"Of course I do." Salamander glanced around as if deeply bewildered. "My mother was a farmwife down near Aberwyn. We lived with my grandfather. She told me that my father was a rider in a lord's warband. He was killed, and so we went back to her father's farm, and—"

"Stop!" Lakanza held up one tattooed hand. "Did you ever know this man, your father?"

"Not that I remember. He was killed when I was still in swaddling bands, or so my mother told me."

"Or so his mother did tell him." Rocca said. "Your Holiness, I do think that she did lie."

"It be possible. Vandar's spawn do seduce human women now and then, winning them over with sweet words and flattery."

"But—" Sidro was busying herself with putting the dagger away, perhaps to gain a little time. "He still be one of them."

"I care not!" Rocca turned on her. "How can you even think of slaughtering someone who means us no harm?"

"How can you be so sure that he does tell you the truth?" Sidro drew her thin lips into a greasy smile. "Evil be his birthright, evil does lie in his heart, no matter what sweet words he may say."

"It does not!" Salamander summoned all the righteous indignation he could. "What is this? I come here hoping and praying to learn more about our goddess. I leave behind my kin and clan, drawn by love of *her*. And now you call my mother a lying whore and tell me I belong to some evil race." He flung an accusing point Rocca's way. "What kind of trap is this? Did you have my death in mind all along? Sacrifices for *her* altar must be hard to come by if you have to lure unsuspecting victims."

"I did no such!" Tears welled in her eyes. "Evan, please, never ever think that!"

"I don't know what to think!" Salamander tipped his head back and raised both hands to the sky. "Alshandra, Alshandra, I swear it on your sacred name! Never did I mean offense to you and yours! Strike me down if I lie!"

Salamander heard a gasp from the surrounding priestesses and the rustle of clothing as they moved away from him, getting out of range in case Alshandra took him at his word. For a long moment he kept his gaze fixed on the sky, then slowly looked at Lakanza. The high priestess had clasped her hands together and raised them to her lips, but she regarded him steadily.

"I'll say more," Salamander continued. "If I am in truth Vandar's spawn, then I'd be better off dead than running any risk of somehow wounding you and yours and giving offense to *her*. Give the order, Your Holiness, and I'll—I'll—" He looked wildly around, then gestured at the watchtower. "I'll climb to the top of that tower and throw myself down naked upon the stones at its foot. I'll be a willing witness to *her* faith."

"Now here, be not so quick with your words," Lakanza said. "These be grave things you do say, just as the matter itself be most grave. I'll not be rushing you to your death, Evan. Mayhap there be a way to save you from it yet."

Salamander looked at Sidro, who glared narrow-eyed and furious in return.

"Your Holiness," Sidro hissed. "The knife—"

"I do ken it well," Lakanza interrupted. "The wyvern knife does never lie, and so, Evan, there must have been a lie on your mother's lips. No doubt she felt great shame for her intemperate act, and that very shame does clear her of such nasty charges as whore. Young lasses oft fall prey to handsome men, and they say that the Spawn have handsome faces to hide the foul souls within. As for your wyrd, there be a need on me to convene the council. A purification, perhaps, or some penance, a quest, a deprivation—some such thing to redeem your soul. I ken not *her* will. I shall call the council straightway. The leaders in this world, our razkanir—there be a need on me to consult with them as well as with my sisters in the faith."

"May I ask how long it'll be," Salamander said, "before I know my fate?"

"I have no wish to let you writhe in fear, but I ken not how long the council will argue the matter, though half the night be likely. If our law states and *her* will agrees that you must throw yourself down, you'll not die before sunset tomorrow. That be all that I can promise."

"And in the meantime, Your Holiness?" Sidro broke. "Is it that we leave this creature loose, roaming around our sacred home?"

"Call him not a creature!" Rocca said. "You be the beast here, Sidro the Sow, with your judgments so ready and sharp."

"Enough squabbling!" Lakanza raised both hands, then brought them sharply down. "Evan, since you did swear as to the manner of your death, should you face it, yondro tower room shall be your prison. There be a need on you to tarry there till the council does hand down its ruling. My heart aches for you, but in my soul I do believe that should you dash yourself upon the stones, *she* will stand ready to catch you on the other side of death."

Salamander bowed his head. "That's all I'd ever ask, Your Holiness. So be it, if the council wills."

"In the meantime, you shall have food and drink." Lakanza clapped her hands three times, and two armed Horsekin stepped forward from the crowd. "Do take him there and have things done as I have said."

The two guards grabbed Salamander's arms and twisted them behind him. He allowed himself one grunt of pain.

"Nah!" Lakanza snapped, then spoke quickly in the Horsekin tongue.

The guards released their hold. One laid a heavy hand on Salamander's shoulder.

"One last thing!" Rocca said, then caught her breath in a sob. "I pray you believe me, Evan, that I never meant you harm."

"I do believe you. Please, forgive me for accusing you. I was so confused, I just didn't know what to think. Forgive me?"

"Of course I do." Rocca managed a trembling smile. "Of course."

The guards turned him around and marched him away. As they walked toward the main building of the fort, they paused to grab his little table dagger from his belt and run rough hands over his clothes, searching apparently for weapons.

"You've found what cold steel I have," Salamander said.

The guards looked at each other, shrugged, and went on searching. Whether or not they spoke Deverrian he couldn't tell. They marched him into the main building of the fort, one huge room that still lacked a proper floor, then hauled him up the stairs of the wooden tower. At the top they opened a little door and shoved him through. A wood floor, an unglazed window, a small hearth set into one wall—other than that, the room stood utterly bare. One of the guards pointed to the window, said something in his own language, then laughed. It was not a pleasant laugh. Most likely the jest involved his being thrown through the window and down on the morrow. The guards slammed the door shut, and Salamander heard the rattle of metal chain.

A woman's voice, firm and commanding—Rocca, though he couldn't understand the words. The door opened again.

"I've brought you somewhat," she said. "To cheer your heart this night of waiting."

"My thanks, unworthy wretch that I am."

She handed him a miniature quiver holding four tiny arrows, each about three inches long, each dyed a different color. "This be a prayer token. The black arrow does stand for Vandar's world, sunk in its depravity. The red be the blood that will wash and redeem it, the white the purity of the cleansed world, and the gold—" Here Rocca paused for a smile, "The gold it does stand for the life we all will share in Alshandra's kingdom."

Salamander clutched it over his heart with what he hoped was a suitably pious expression. "You've given me great cheer indeed. Again I thank you."

Rocca's smile froze into something close to tears, and she turned quickly away. "I'd best be getting myself to the council."

Rocca hurried out, and the guards once more slammed the door. He could tell by the rattle of the chain and a thump of iron hitting wood that they had barred and tied it. He waited until their footsteps had gone down the stairs, then went to the window and looked out onto a straight drop far down. Below, gilded by the last of the afternoon light, lay cut blocks of granite, piled this way and that. A man who fell from the window would land on chiseled edges, not merely flat stone.

From his perch he could also see most of the fort spread out below and the land beyond as well. He spent some time carefully memorizing what he saw, noting details here and there, such as the postern gate and a half-finished course of stone running along the cliff top. Apparently, they planned an outer fortification that would enclose the entire citadel. Inside, he saw a number of water wells, and here and there deep pits lined with stone—food storage, perhaps? It seemed that the Horsekin were well aware that they might have to stand a long siege, but whom, he wondered, did they fear? Vandar's spawn, perhaps, or perhaps the Gel da'Thae or even another sect or tribe of Horsekin. *More's the pity,* he thought, *that you won't be staying long enough to find out.*

By then the sunset was turning the scattered clouds into streaks of flame against the sky. Salamander used them as a focus and contacted Dallandra. When he could see her face and the help and safety it represented, his thoughts ran away from him in a sudden spate of words and half-voiced feelings.

"Don't babble at me!" Dallandra said. "What's so wrong?"

"My apologies, and truly, it's babbling that got me into this, a bitter lesson I fear for one so enamored of his own voice as I am. I've reached the new Horsekin settlement, and as we feared, it's a fortress, all right, still a-building, but a dun nonetheless. It looks to me like it's been planned to stand long sieges, too. No wonder they didn't want any farmers claiming land out here."

"By the Black Sun herself!" Dalla's image briefly wavered. "Fearful, indeed! But at least you'll be able to describe it to Cal and the gwerbret, too, for that matter. I can't imagine that Ridvar will refuse to ask for the king's aid now."

"Nah, nah, nah, oh, mistress of mighty magicks! Not so fast. Rocca brought me here, and we were met by the high priestess herself. All seemed to be going well. Her holiness was downright welcoming in fact, but then something rather awkward happened. I seem to have aroused the jealousy of a fledgling priestess. She insisted on seeing if I could pass a test. They have a silver dagger. I don't know how or why they have it, but they do."

"Did it have a little wyvern on the blade?"

"Yes, actually. How—"

"I know whose it is. I saw it in an omen-dream, but never mind that now." In her image Dallandra's face seemed to have turned a dull fearful gray. "I take it they made you touch the thing, and it showed you up—"

"As Vandar's spawn. Exactly. Now, all is not yet lost. The head priestess here seems like a truly pious sort, and she's convened a council to decide my fate. I've managed to convince them I didn't know I had elven blood, you see. I spun an elaborate tale of being a bastard who'd never known his father."

"I never thought I'd say this, but I'm glad you're so good at lying."

"Thank you—I suppose. But in the end I managed to convince them to lock me up at the top of a high tower."

"Did you?" The color returned to Dalla's face. "Well, then, that gives me hope! But be careful, no matter what happens."

"Fear not! You're learning to appreciate mendacity, whilst I'm beginning to value caution, canniness, circumspection, and all its kin. However that may be, I shan't die before sunset tomorrow, no matter how the council votes."

"That will give you a little time, yes. Well, tell me, will you, as soon as you know the verdict? I'm going to go talk with Cal and the prince."

Once Dallandra broke off contact, Salamander sat down in a corner and watched the sunset sky first flame, then fade. He wondered how long the council would debate—not long, he'd wager. Since he was a stranger with only Rocca to argue in his favor, they'd doubtless decide quickly to kill him.

Just as the hazy twilight was giving way to night and the wheel of stars shone out, he heard footsteps on the stairs. He scrambled up, his heart pounding, and took a few steps toward the door. It opened to reveal an elderly human slave, carrying a basket over one arm, and two armed Horsekin guards, one holding a candle lantern.

"Food," the servant said. "And water."

He set the basket down, watching Salamander all the while, then backed out of the room as if he were afraid that the prisoner would spring upon him like a beast. The locks clanged shut again, and Salamander heard them all clattering down the stairs. He picked up the basket and peered in—half a loaf of fresh warm bread, a honeycomb in a twist of leaf, some slices of cold meat, and a leather bottle of water. When he took out the bread, he found beneath it a metal plate, heavily embossed. Running his fingers over it in the dark told him little about the design—some flowers, a circle of what was most likely writing.

"Decent of them," he muttered, "and their doom." He settled down to eat.

For much of the evening he slept, gathering strength. Toward midnight another visitor came up the stairs, this one treading so lightly that at first Salamander was unsure if someone were coming or not. Then a hand rattled the chain.

"Evan?" It was Rocca's voice, whispering, trembling in grief. "Evan, be you awake?"

"I am." He crossed to the door and spoke quietly. "I take it the council goes badly."

"It does, not that my heart be void of hope, but only Lakanza does seem to care about the justice of the thing. The others—I do think that Sidro, she did poison their minds or some such."

"They may just be afraid. I can't blame them."

"That be so noble of you!" Her voice caught, as if she choked back tears. "I did come to beg your forgiveness once again."

"And you have it, as you always shall. Here, if I didn't even realize that I'm tainted Vandar's spawn, how could you have known?"

"True-spoken." But she sounded no less miserable. "The council, they did end the debate for the night, but tomorrow they meet again after morning prayers."

"I see. Tell me somewhat, if it's safe for you to linger a moment. Sidro—you said she'd been cast off by a man?"

"Just that. Sidro were ill treated by a man she loved, left deserted and alone after her family did scorn her and force her to leave their home. She was with child, you see. Lakanza did offer her shelter at our old shrine. Sidro's child did die in her arms not two days after it were born. In penance she did vow to serve our goddess all her life."

"That's a sad thing, then." Salamander decided that one more lie on top of all the others wouldn't ruin his wyrd forever. "I'll pray that I may forgive her, too."

"She deserves far less than that, but it does speak well of you." Once again Rocca's voice sounded full of tears. "I'd best be gone."

Before he could say anything more, he heard her turn away, and her footsteps hurried down the stairs.

The morning, of course, would bring light, and Salamander needed darkness if he were to escape. He went to the window and looked up, using the stars as a focus, but try as he might, he couldn't reach Dallandra's mind. He did get a confused impression of her feelings, that she was mildly angry at something, a little frightened as well, but mostly methodical and intent upon some task. It occurred to him that most likely someone in camp had injured themselves in an accident, and as the alar's healer, she'd been called out of a sound sleep. He decided against waiting until he could talk with her. The sooner he escaped from Zakh Gral, the better.

First Salamander stripped off his clothing, then considered what he could carry—not much and still get clean away. He made a sack out of his brigga by tying the legs together. Into it he put the quiver of miniature arrows, a bit of building stone he found upon the floor, and the plate his dinner had arrived upon. His boots—he weighed them in his hand—heavy, but without them he wouldn't get far. He stuffed them in, then cinched the sack closed with his belt. He set it carefully on the corner of the windowsill.

And what would happen to Rocca when the guards found him gone? Would the razkanir blame her? If they did, she would die a very slow death at their hands. He had no doubt about that. How could he—he grinned at a sudden idea. Among the old ashes on the dead hearth, he found a lump of charcoal. The smooth wall of the chamber served him for parchment. Still grinning, he began to write in careful letters. (In the Deverry language his words rhymed, unlike those below.)

> "Death may threaten but never claim me
> For Alshandra claimed me for her own
> Long years ago. To Her now I cry aloud
> To save or slay me as she thinks best.
> What light do I see here my dark prison?"

At this point he dropped the formal rhyme and meter and scrawled his letters. "She comes! May I—" He broke the word off, then let the charcoal drop onto the floor.

"There," he muttered. "We'll see how that takes them! Or wait—they think dweomer light comes from the goddess." He raised both hands above his head and called upon the Wildfolk of Aethyr. In a shimmering silver mass they appeared, dodging this way and that. "Lords of Aethyr!" Salamander whispered. "I beg and beseech you! Fill this room with light long past my leaving of it."

The silver mass shattered. A hundred separate glitters of light rushed to the walls, to the ceiling, gathered and spread until the chamber filled with glow brighter than ten full moons.

"My thanks, most sincerely! O Great Lords of Aethyr, I beseech thee, let this light shine until dawn!"

From somewhere in his mind too deep for words a feeling rose— a tingling sensation all over his body, a raising of the hair on the back of his neck. The Lords had agreed.

The most difficult dweomer working of all lay ahead. Salamander went to the window and laid his hands on the sill beside the improvised sack. As he stared up at the stars, he felt power gather. Slowly he invoked more, felt it flow through him until his body became a mere channel, a thin shell, surrounding the power coursing through it. In his mind, he formulated the image of a black-and-white magpie, then sent the picture forward through his eyes until it seemed to perch on the windowsill between his hands. With a wrench of will, he transferred his consciousness over to the bird form until it seemed that he looked out of the small yellow eyes.

Now came the crux. He drew more and more of the life substance from the body standing behind his consciousness into the bird form until the magpie seemed solid and the man's body only an illusion. Since he'd not worked this spell in over forty years, he had to fight for concentration. One slip now meant death. He called on the holy names of the gods, called on Alshandra, too, in a moment of near-hysterical drollery, and kept on sucking more and more of the etheric substance into his new body. At last, as he uttered one last mighty Name, a sound like thunder burst behind his eyes, and the etheric substance dragged the physical with it. Salamander the man was gone from the chamber. A magpie—an abnormally huge magpie—perched on the windowsill.

With a caw of triumph, Salamander hopped onto the improvised sack and sank his claws into the cloth. He sprang into the air and flew, flapping in wide circles over the fort far below. On his last pass by the tower, he saw the window of his former prison still glowing with silver light. Out in the ward tiny figures of Horsekin scurried around, heading for the tower. Their frantic voices drifted up to him, but he could understand nothing of what they were shouting to one another.

There's nothing like a good miracle, Salamander thought, *to keep the holy-minded occupied.* Fighting the wind currents, he headed south.

Salamander had guessed right about Dallandra's distracted mood. Two of Cal's archers had been courting the same young woman, and eventually they'd come to blows. Dallandra had just fallen asleep in the grass near her tent when Calonderiel came running to wake her. She sat up and listened to his report in sullen annoyance.

"Why do you need me?" she said finally. "The bruises—"

"It's worse than bruises," Cal said. "One of them drew his knife."

Hurriedly, Dallandra got to her feet. "I need to get my tools from the tent," she said. "How bad is the cut?"

"More than one. The other drew his, too."

"Of course. Why did I ever think otherwise?"

While she was stitching up the worst of the slashes, Dalla was aware of Salamander trying to reach her, but with the blood still flowing down her patient's arm, she could spare the gerthddyn none of her concentration. After both love-sick warriors were stitched, dosed with herbs, and properly berated, Dallandra did try to contact Salamander, but this time it was his mind that refused to respond. She received a general impression of rushing wind and a view of night-dark trees that rose and fell in a steady rhythm. *By the Dark Sun!* she thought. *He must be flying.*

All she could do was wait for him to regain his proper body.

As the night wore on, Salamander found it harder and harder to stay in the air. His wings ached, and he took to gliding upon air currents whenever he could. His legs hurt as well; his talons in bird-form were at root his feet and toes, parts of the body that were normally spared such work as carrying heavy sacks. Still, he forced himself onward. He could think of two possible outcomes if the Horsekin caught him. In one, Rocca would prevail upon them to kill him quickly. In the other, the pains he was feeling at the moment would seem like pleasure compared to what they'd do to him.

Below him the scrubby tableland kept dropping down, until at last he saw only a roll of low hills and beyond, grassland. A river, silver in the gray dawn light, flowed steadily south between tree-lined banks. He circled an old, drooping willow, then flapped down through its curtain of fine twigs and leaves; he let the sack fall to the ground below and settled on a heavy branch to roost. He was greeted with a rattling call of rage from another magpie, who ducked his head low, spread his wings, and danced a threat close to the tree trunk.

"Aren't you the hospitable sort?" Salamander's voice came out as a croaking rasping parody of human speech.

The sound seemed to make the magpie notice just how large his sudden neighbor was. With a squawk of sheer terror, the real bird flew off screeching. Enough of Salamander's current nature was magpie for him to be tempted to go through the other's nest and steal whatever trinkets it had hidden there, but he put the temptation firmly out of his mind. That he'd even thought it signaled a dangerous exhaustion. With a flap of his aching wings, he settled to the ground next to the sack.

For some little while he rested among the rasping blades of marsh grass, but his wings trailed uselessly, and he needed feet more than claws. He reversed the dweomer, imaging his own body in his mind and sending the image out to apparent solidity in front of him. In spite of his ever-present fear of being trapped in bird-form, his real body built up fast, sucking the etheric substance back into it of its own will. Salamander heard a sudden click, a percussive hiss; then he was sitting dazed and naked on the hummock of grass, and there was nothing left of the magpie but claw marks in damp ground.

Just a few feet away the rising sun rippled and glinted in flecks like fire on the river. He dumped the contents of his sack, turned the sack back into brigga, and put them on before limping to the riverside on cramped feet. *Now for Rocca,* he thought. *I'll never forgive myself if she's come to harm.*

He knelt with a grunt of exhaustion. When he thought of Rocca, the vision built up on the sun-touched water. It seemed that he was hovering some twenty feet above the altar of the Outer Shrine. Rocca stood in front of it, her arms outstretched, her face glowing with such joy that he knew she believed in his artificial miracle. She was wearing his filthy, sweat-stained shirt around her shoulders like a cloak. On the ground Sidro knelt, her raven-dark head tossed back, her arms crossed over her chest. Behind her stood the Horsekin priestesses. Every now and then one of them gave Sidro a random sort of kick as Rocca continued her prayers.

Salamander focused the vision down until he could see Sidro more clearly. He was expecting her to be humiliated and terrified, but the look on her face and the trembling of her shoulders spoke of sheer cold rage. Watching her, Salamander felt oddly frightened. *Don't be stupid,* he told himself. *She's miles away, and she doesn't even have dweomer.* Yet suddenly he wasn't so sure of that. What had she seen that prompted her to call him Vander's spawn? Although anyone who knew the Westfolk well could have picked up traces of his mixed blood, still he looked far more human than elven. Yet Sidro had challenged him with perfect confidence. He broke the vision, half-fearing she would realize that he was watching her.

Besides, he needed to contact Dallandra. On the fiery surface of the water, Dalla's image built up quickly, wavered, then steadied.

"Where are you?" Dalla thought to him. "I've never felt your mind so exhausted! Where's your shirt?"

"In Zakh Gral, where it's become a holy relic," Salamander thought back. "So are my horses and all my gear, though I don't suppose those will end up on the altar. My manly chest, however, has escaped with me, although little black flies, alas, are trying to bite it even as we speak."

"Will you stop babbling like that?"

"I'll do my best. As you've doubtless guessed, I took bird-form and did get clean away, and I remembered to bring along some evidence that the place exists. Alas, I couldn't carry everything, which means I'm foodless as well as shirtless. And they kept my table dagger, blankets, horses—the lot. So here I am, alive but plunged into poverty and despair. I have no idea how far from you I am, but I doubt if I can fly again."

"I doubt if you should. Here, are you having those odd broken visions again?"

"Oh. I don't know. Here, let me see." He looked around and realized that the trees, the grass, even the cold gray rocks tumbled along the stream bank were refusing to hold steady. They pulsed around the edges, they seemed to glow from within—he shook his head hard. "Yes, the world is beating like a heart."

"I was afraid of that. I can feel the strains in your mind. One more difficult working, and your old madness could return."

"But madness begins to sound better than being eaten alive by gnats, flies, wild wolves, bears—"

"Ebañy, stop it! You're one of the People. You know how to survive in wild places. Besides, you won't have to walk the whole way south. I'm coming to fetch you."

Salamander felt a sudden burst of hope which, since he was exhausted, broke the vision beyond his power to call it back. He waded out to the shallows to drink the clean water there, then plastered his upper body with mud to keep off biting flies. By the time he finished, the pulsing world seemed to rotate around him; he barely had the strength to crawl back under the willow's lacy overhang before he fell asleep.

"Can you really reach Ebañy this way?" Valandario said. "When Evandar crossed the River of Life, didn't all the hidden roads close?"

"Some of the mother roads, yes," Dallandra said. "Those are the ones that led between different worlds. But the short paths, the ones between places inside our world, they still work. I think they existed long before Evandar came here. They're harder to find now, though."

"They must have drawn their life from the mother roads."

"They did, or, come to think of it, they must still do so. There has to be at least one mother road that's still open. Otherwise all the daughter roads would be gone."

"They might well disappear, someday. I just hope you can get back again."

"So do I." Dalla paused for a sharp laugh. "But I think the roads will last long enough for that. Ebañy's not all that far away. Five or six days' ride, I'd say."

"The fort's that close? By the Black Sun herself! Those Horsekin—bold as stoats and twice as stinky!"

"Well, Ebañy flew a good ways south before he came to earth. But if we're not back in two days, send Cal and his men north after us."

Dallandra borrowed a shirt for Salamander from his father, then put it and some food into a sack. She took Valandario along when she left the camp and headed for a nearby stream that ran through the tall grass out by the horse herd. Dallandra was looking for the subtle signs that mark the beginning of an etheric road. Since the combined auras of the horses and the men guarding them blurred the boundaries of the planes, she led Valandario along for a good mile before she finally found what she was looking for. The stream formed a pool at the bottom of a slight drop, and a tangle of hazel withes had sprung up around it. She could see the glimmer of etheric force marking a boundary.

"There!" Dallandra pointed. "On this side just before you reach the hazels. See it?"

"No," Valandario said, then sighed. "I just don't have your gifts."

"Well, I can't scry the future like you can."

"True. Now, be careful. I'll be watching for you both."

Dallandra stepped into the quivering lozenge of etheric force. For a brief moment elemental energy, an etheric outpouring from the running stream beyond, threatened to trap her. She felt it grab her with invisible hands, but in a quick slither she broke free and found herself standing on a low outcrop of rock, a peculiar rock as much blue as gray, that shimmered under her feet. She had found a road.

For a moment she paused to make a detailed image of Salamander in her mind. Since he had dweomer himself, the image came easily, showing him mud-encrusted and asleep under a willow tree. He seemed to be lying only a few yards away, but as she walked toward him the image receded, leading her onward. After what seemed a brief interval, the image held steady, then strengthened, turning three-dimensional as she stepped down off the etheric road onto the physical riverbank. In the sky sunset flamed. Traveling the roads meant stepping out of Time, which as usual had run far faster on the physical plane than on the network of astral roads.

Salamander woke with a start and sat up, stretching, grinning at her. "Ye gods!" he said. "You can't have flown all this way so fast."

"I didn't, no," Dalla said. "I took the secret paths, and we'll have to go back the same way. I brought some food."

"May the Star Goddesses bless you! I'm starved."

Yet, being Salamander, he washed in the river and put on the clean shirt before he ate.

Dallandra decided to wait for the moon to finish rising before they attempted the return journey. Moonrise sends waves of energy ahead of it, making etheric journeys even more dangerous than they normally are. While they sat by the dark-rushing water, Salamander told her about his travels in more detail, including the position of the fort. He scried, as well, and was able to report that the river by which they sat was indeed the same one that led eventually to Zakh Gral.

"That name, by the way," Dalla said, "means the red fort in their language."

"And red correlates to iron, strength, and manly virtue," Salamander said, "or so the novice lore I was learning has it."

"It's an odd name for that temple, then, isn't it? One that exists to spread the truth about a new goddess."

"Indeed. I suspect that Lakanza and her holy women are being cozened by the rakzanir on their so-called holy council. This business of Vandar's spawn—how convenient for men who desperately need pasture for their horses!"

"I had the same sour thought."

"And a slender excuse for killing looks fat to the Horsekin, just as it does to the Roundear lords." He paused, considering something. "Yet their peoples prosper, and ours dwindle. Why is that?"

"There's not enough of us for breeding stock. If the day comes when the Roundears and Horsekin stop dropping litters, they might become a lot more peaceful."

"Let us pray for that day, then. But you know, I had a thought, when I was riding west with Rocca."

"Just one?" Dalla grinned at him.

Salamander ignored the interruption. "And that was, we know that some refugees reached the Southern Isles. Could there be others who fled west? If so, they doubtless think themselves the only, lonely survivors, much as both we and the island refugees did."

"You know, that's a very interesting question."

"Some of the younger men might be tempted into going to find the answer, especially if we can get a sea captain from the islands interested in sailing west."

"You're quite right. Not this summer, though."

"Alas, not this summer. We have a rather large unpleasantness to deal with first."

"Unpleasantness. I like how you put that." Dallandra stood up, gazing off to the east, where the moon hung solidly above the dark horizon. "Well, let's get back. The sooner we get on the way to Cengarn the better, and the camp will be worrying about us."

"About you, anyway." Salamander scrambled up to join her. "Let me put the evidence I brought into that sack of yours. The gwerbret's going to have to admit that this plate, at least, isn't something you can buy in the marketplace."

"Let's hope so. Now—stick close to me. In fact, let me take your hand. This way of traveling can be tricky, so don't let your mind wander. Think of Valandario. She's waiting for us, and she'll be my focus. Build up an image of her."

"Very well, oh princess of powers perilous. I just hope my humble skills will be sufficient to—"

"Stop babbling and concentrate!"

Despite his fears, Dallandra found the road back easily enough, and he managed to walk it with her. After what seemed like a bare mile's journey, they stepped down from the shimmering blue rocks to find themselves in sight of the elven camp, just waking in the dawn of a new day. As they hurried toward the tents, the horse guards spotted them and shouted a greeting. Others came running from the camp, with Zandro in the lead. He rushed up to his father and threw his arms around him so forcefully that he nearly knocked Salamander over.

"Easy, lad!" Salamander said, smiling. "Your poor old Da's come up a bit lame."

Zandro bared his teeth in a smile and begin sniffing Salamander like a dog, his nose working, his eyes distant as he moved up his father's arm to his shoulder and hair.

"And what is all this?" Salamander said. "What do you smell there?"

Zandro considered the question for a moment. "Home," he said finally. It was the first time Zandro had ever answered a question with a clear meaningful word.

"Good lad!" Salamander said. "Do you mean I'm home now?"

Zandro shook his head. "Blue home," he said.

"He means the etheric, I think," Dallandra joined in. "Odd. I never thought of it having a scent before."

"No more did I," Salamander said. "But he's the one who'd know."

By then Dallandra felt too drained from the dweomerworking to worry about Zandro or anyone else, for that matter. She left Salamander to tell his tale to whomever wanted to hear it and went to her tent, where she flopped down on her blankets and fell asleep with barely a moment's thought.

Dallandra woke in midafternoon to find a council of war in progress. Three members of the alar had taken the children, both normal and changeling, away to play in a meadow out of earshot, but everyone else had gathered in front of Dar's tent. As she walked up, she noticed that Salamander was still speaking, but after a few more sentences he finished, nodded toward the prince, and sat down beside Devaberiel. Those assembled began talking among themselves, in whispers at first, then louder, until they sounded like the roar of a high tide on a graveled beach. Calonderiel got up and raised his arms for silence. After a brief flurry of talk, the assembly quieted to let the banadar speak.

"So now you all know what Ebañy told us earlier." Cal defined this "us" with a sweep of his arm, taking in Dar, Meranaldar, Devaberiel, and Maelaber. "Here's what we decided. I'll choose a squad of archers, and we'll take Dallandra with us, too, to guard the prince on his ride to Cengarn. Ebañy will come along, of course. As I understand it, some of the Deverry lords along the border will support us when we put this matter before the gwerbret. We're hoping he'll send messages to the high king."

"He's practically promised to do that," Salamander put in. "Tieryn Cadryc will make sure he holds to the promise."

"Good," Cal went on. "We've got to destroy that fort, no matter what it costs us. If our Deverry allies desert us, we'll have to call for a general muster of the People."

The assembly agreed, but with a long sigh of regret. Heads nodded yes, but no one cheered, no one leaped to their feet to shout their agreement. Here and there an individual wiped away tears from his or her eyes and whispered the names of friends or family killed in previous battles with Horsekin.

"The rest of you, the combined alarli, will head out to the usual grazing grounds," Calonderiel said. "But be very wary of riding too far west. Princess Carra will lead you, and Valandario will travel with her. Our dweomermasters can pass news back and forth, so we'll tell you what we learn when we learn it, if anything."

Again came the nods, the sighs of agreement. The assembly began to break up. Some of the People stood and immediately walked away; in twos and threes others lingered, talking among themselves or coming forward to speak with the prince or Calonderiel. By then Salamander had dark circles under his eyes; he let his father and his son lead him off to their tent. Dallandra waited until the crowd had completely dispersed, then joined Cal, Dar, and Meranaldar.

"I'll send off messengers to Cengarn tomorrow," Dar said. "They need to know that I'll be coming with my retinue."

"Retinue?" Cal wrinkled his nose, then turned his attention to Dallandra. "I'm assuming you're willing to come with us."

"Of course." Dalla sat down opposite him. "It's a sad enough errand."

"Yes, it is. You might have to convince young Ridvar about the dweomer. The cursed Roundears never want to believe in it."

"What?" Dar said. "It was dweomer that saved Cengarn in the Horsekin War. Everyone knows that story."

"They may know about it," Dallandra said, "but they don't want to know, and so they work at forgetting it."

"I don't understand why—"

"She's right." Cal interrupted the prince. "They don't want to hear about it, the Roundear lords. You want to know why? Because they take themselves and their petty little feuds so seriously, that's why. They think every wretched thing they do is of the greatest importance to the kingdom and the gods, and they like it that way. Tell them how big the world really is, all those other creatures and other planes and all of it, and they're forced to see how small and crude and miserable they are. Their king's the worst of the lot. Remember that if you ever meet him."

Meranaldar gasped and rose to a kneel, glancing back and forth between prince and banadar as if he expected a fight to break out. Calonderiel got to his feet and turned his attention to the scribe.

"Oh, stop snorting and rolling your eyes, you damp-arse bastard!" Cal said. "You're a bad influence, I swear it, always mincing around and bowing and swelling Dar's head for him with your 'my prince this' and 'my prince that.' "

"Oh, indeed?" Meranaldar rose to face him. "Well, there happen to be proper ways of doing things, not that you would know. The ancient ways of royalty are still valid."

"Oh, by the silver shit of the Star Gods! Ancient ways, my arse! Look at us, a pack of shepherds and horse wranglers!"

"And likely to remain so with churls and bumpkins like you in command."

Calonderiel took a step forward. Meranaldar took one backward.

"You know something?" Cal said. "If you don't hold your tongue, I'm going to beat some sense into you."

Meranaldar turned pale and sat back down. Dallandra thought of intervening, but there was justice in what Calonderiel was saying. Besides, she had to admit that Cal when angry displayed a pure kind of energy, a strong but fine-drawn maleness that she liked watching. The royal object of Cal's diatribe was watching the banadar with eyes that showed not the slightest emotion. Cal turned his head and stared right at the prince. For a moment the stalemate held; then Dar suddenly laughed.

"You're right," Dar said. "Not about beating my scribe, I mean, but about the rest of it. All of the rest of it—the things you said aloud, and the meaning just under your words."

"Good," Cal said. "I'm glad to hear it." He paused for effect, then bowed with an over-graceful sweep of his hand. "My prince."

Everyone burst out laughing, except Meranaldar, who did manage to force out a watery smile. He was close to tears, Dallandra suspected, and later, when they had a chance at a private word, Meranaldar admitted as much.

"I'm honestly afraid," the scribe said, "that one of these days the banadar is going to turn on me and slit my throat before anyone can stop him. If anyone even wants to stop him, that is."

"Oh, come now!" Dalla said. "He's not going to do that, and trust me, if he should lose his mind and try, a great many people will make sure he doesn't hurt you."

"That makes me feel a bit better." Meranaldar pulled an ink-stained rag from the waistband of his leggings and wiped cold sweat from his face. "I suppose. He must hate me."

"He doesn't hate you. He hates what you represent, the old ways, and the return of the refugees who believe in those ways. The Westlands are changing—we have to change if we're going to survive—and Cal loves the way things have been."

Meranaldar considered this for a long moment, then nodded his agreement. "Yes, I can see that," he said. "There are those back in the Southern Isles who hate the way things are changing, too. The high council used to rule a tidy little world where everyone knew their place and kept to it. Now anyone who can get passage on a ship can find themselves an entirely new place, here in the grasslands."

"I take it that not everyone's perfectly contented with life in the islands."

"I only wish." Meranaldar smiled briefly. "It's the young people, of course, who are discontented, and we do have some young people, though not enough. The volunteers who settled Mandra, for instance, and laid out its farms. You've noticed, I'm sure, how cheerful they are about all the hard work they do, keeping their town alive."

"Yes, I have. I was surprised, I'll admit it."

"So was I, but I understand them. In the islands we've devoted ourselves to honoring the past. You probably can't imagine how completely we live for the past."

"Young people would rather have a future."

"Precisely, which is why our banadar can't keep your future from arriving, one fine day. And you know, if we ever return to the ruins of the cities, everything will change again—no, that's too weak a word. Our lives will be utterly recast, Dalla, whether we're West-folk or Islanders. Both kinds of life will be transformed utterly, and none of us can tell how that will be, I'll wager, not even Valandario with her gem-dweomer."

"You're right, aren't you?" She felt suddenly cold, utterly exhausted. "I hate to say it, but you're right."

All that evening, Prince Daralanteriel held a council in front of his tent. Men from the alar came to ask questions or to listen to Calonderiel's plans for the coming war; after a short while, they pledged their support and left again. Princess Carra sat on the ground next to her husband and occasionally made a comment or explained a fine point of the various treaty ties between Cengarn and the Westfolk. Dallandra merely listened. As the most competent healer in camp, she would no doubt have to ride with the war party when the time came, and she was dreading the job—not the danger to herself, but the sights and stench of the wounds, the deaths, and the pain of those she considered her kin.

That night, when Calonderiel escorted her to her tent as usual, she succumbed to her dread enough to avoid being alone for as long as possible. She invited him to sit down in the soft grass and talk.

"You scared poor Meranaldar today," Dalla said. "He actually thought you were going to hit him."

"I had thoughts that way." Cal tossed his head in a defiant gesture. "He gripes my soul, with all his fancy talk about kings and the like. I—" He paused for a smile. "I suppose I'm just turning into a crabby old man."

"Oh, come now, you're not old."

"Of course I am, or getting that way. We were born under the same moon, Dalla, but while you were off with Evandar, I was still here in this world. I must be well over five hundred years old by now, even if you're practically still a girl."

"Hardly a girl! But you're right about the flow of Time."

He nodded, looking a little away, out to the grasslands where everything they'd known was changing, their old ways slipping away as fast as Time itself. Dalla felt such an odd tangle of emotion that at first she couldn't put a name to any of it. Sympathy for him, perhaps, and sorrow, a melancholy to match his—but among them, half-hidden by her love of solitude, lay something finer.

"Ah, well," Cal said at last. "I'd best be getting back."

"Must you?" Dalla said.

He turned his head sharply to look at her. Unsmiling, for she felt as solemn as a priestess, Dalla held out her hand. When he clasped it, the comfort of his warmth, the touch of another hand on hers, gave her such an intense pleasure that she couldn't speak. How lonely had she grown, she wondered, that a simple touch could move her so? When he leaned forward to kiss her, she slipped her arms around his neck with a sigh of profound relief.

Yet much later, when she woke in her tent to find him still asleep beside her, she wondered what she'd done. *There's going to be a war,* she thought. *You fool! Why do you always fall in love with men who are likely to get themselves killed?* She could wonder all she wanted, but it was too late to turn aside her feelings for him now.

The Westfolk camps usually woke right at dawn, and since the prince's alar had a long journey ahead of it, most of its members got up at the first sign of gray light in the east. Salamander woke a fair bit later to find everyone bustling around, cooking breakfast, loading horses, sorting out who would ride with Daralanteriel and who would stay under Princess Carra's command. The sun still touched the eastern horizon, but already a windless heat lay over the grasslands.

Salamander cadged some griddle bread and honey from his father, then stood to eat it while he contemplated poverty. His escape from Zakh Gral had left him his life but little else, not a horse, not a blanket, none of his usual traveling gear.

"I suppose," Devaberiel said, "you'll need a horse since you're going to Cengarn."

"I was thinking of asking the prince for one," Salamander said. "And a saddle and bridle."

"And some tether ropes and saddlebags and a blanket for you, and so on and so forth."

"That, too, alas."

"Well, fortunately I have enough to spare. Let's see. You've always liked that roan gelding. You can take him. And yesternight I sorted out some gear for you." Devaberiel waved one hand at a neat stack beside his tent.

Salamander nearly choked on the last remnant of bread. He'd been expecting a long lecture before he got so much as a rope halter out of his father. Devaberiel was grinning, well aware of the effect he was having.

"What did you think?" Dev went on. "That I was going to berate you after you risked your life to save us all?" The grin disappeared, replaced by mournful eyes and a hand to his brow. "I know I've been a terrible father to you, but not so bad as all that."

"Da, please, I don't want to listen to you berate either yourself or me." Salamander managed a smile. "Not first thing in the morning."

"Agreed. Besides, no doubt you'll be able to tell a few tales in the Cengarn market and end up burdened with more gear than before."

"I have hopes that way, truly, though my sleight-of-hand tricks will have to wait for a new performing shirt. A thousand thanks for the horse and everything else."

While he sorted out his new possessions, Salamander was thinking of Zakh Gral. He would have to tell his story to the gwerbret with the utmost care, he knew, both to convince Ridvar of what he'd seen and to protect Rocca. He wondered if she were really going to keep his shirt on the altar along with those other holy relics. Odd lot that they were, no doubt the shirt wouldn't look out of place among them. And if he convinced the gwerbret to attack Zakh Gral, what would happen to Rocca then? That he might be responsible for her death—the thought turned him sick and cold. *You'll think of something then,* he told himself. *You always do.*

Although her father's dun stood no more than twenty miles from Cengarn, Branna had never seen the city before. Tieryn Gwivyr was not the sort of man to take a daughter traveling with him, no matter how hard she begged to go. She'd had to be content with descriptions of the place from the servants who did accompany their lord when he paid his duty visits to the gwerbret. From those she'd built up a good many mental images of the city—not that she expected them to be accurate.

"It gladdens my heart," she remarked to Neb. "Finally I get to see what Cengarn really looks like."

Yet once the Red Wolf contingent rode up to Cengarn, perched so high on its cliffs, Branna was shocked to find that her imaginings did indeed match the reality. As they rode in the south gate, she kept looking around her, goggling like a peasant with her mouth half-open. Ahead rose the green market hill she'd seen in her mind; cut into the hillside stood the entrance to the dwarven inn, exactly as she'd imagined it. Near the gates to the dun itself stood the little hill with the spring on top, bubbling away so abundantly despite its location that everyone assumed it drew on magic as well as underground water. *I've been here before.* The thought intruded itself on her consciousness and would not go away, no matter how many times she told herself that such was impossible.

The great hall also looked exactly as she'd imagined it, though soot lay thick on the grand dragon sculpture embracing the honor hearth. Another baffling thought invaded her mind: *it must have been new when I saw it before.* The stairs and halls were so familiar that when servants led her and Galla up to their guest chambers, Branna could have told them the way had they asked her.

The tieryn and the noble-born in his party had been given chambers on the floor directly above the women's hall, a spacious, beautifully appointed room for Cadryc and Galla and a pleasant if small chamber for Branna. The faded bed hangings seemed familiar, as if perhaps she'd seen a scrap of the design in a peddler's pattern book.

"Have you seen that pattern of suns and dragons before?" Branna asked her maid. "Somewhere we visited, say."

"I've not," Midda said. "No one but the gwerbret's closest kin could use it, I should think. It's too much like his heraldry."

Branna sat on the window seat out of the way while Midda made up the bed with the sheets and blankets they'd brought with them. Out on the western border not even a gwerbret could afford to furnish every room in his dun.

"We're going to have an exciting time of it," Midda pronounced. "The cook's lass told me that a pack of Westfolk are coming."

"I'm not surprised," Branna said. "They're sort of vassals to His Grace—well, not vassals, I suppose. Allies."

"Their prince sent a message ahead of them. He won't have his wife with him, though. He probably left her behind in his tent or whatever it is they live in. A human woman she is, if you can imagine such a thing!"

"I can. The Westfolk men are awfully handsome."

"I don't want to see you flirting with any of them, mind."

"What? Right in front of Neb? Of course I wouldn't."

Midda snorted and scowled. Though she'd never said one word against him, Branna knew from her maid's dark looks that she considered Neb beneath her lady. Once she finished the bed, Midda trotted off to the servants' quarters to find a place to sleep and to catch up on the rest of the gwerbretal gossip. Branna went to the window and looked out on a view that seemed entirely too familiar.

A thin trickle of fear ran down her back, though she couldn't have told anyone why.

Neb had more standing than a maidservant, but he was still a common-born servitor, which meant he'd been given a bunk in the barracks along with the Red Wolf riders rather than a chamber in the complex of broch towers. As a peacemaking gesture, Gerran gave him the bunk directly under one of the two small windows, where the fresh air thinned the stink of sweat and horses. Neb thanked him in a way that told Gerran that the gesture had been accepted.

Once everyone was settled, Gerran led his men out, heading for the great hall and, hopefully, a tankard of ale. Neb walked alongside him. As they crossed the ward, they saw Lady Solla coming out of the cookhouse. She paused, waved, and smiled. Since Gerran believed she must be waving at someone behind him, he didn't respond, but the scribe nudged him with a sharp elbow.

"You could at least greet her," Neb said.

"How?"

"Smile, you dolt, and wave!"

Gerran followed orders. His reward was another smile from Solla, but just as he considered going over to speak to her, Lord Oth emerged from the cookhouse and began talking to her urgently. As they walked off together, Gerran caught a snatch of their conversation, "better slaughter another hog, then."

"This wedding seems to be running the poor lass ragged," Neb remarked.

Gerran grunted to show he'd heard.

"Ye gods, man!" Neb went on. "Surely you've noticed how lovely Lady Solla is."

"I've also noticed how much higher than mine her birth is."

"Oh, come along, Gerro! I'll wager you're the only person in Cengarn who cares about your rank."

"Huh! And I'll wager that her brother makes two of us. Besides, ye gods, I've better things to do with my time than stand around gossiping like a woman."

"Womanish, is it? Well, I say that only a fool would turn his back on a lovely lass like her. Especially since she's so well-disposed to you."

"How she feels isn't worth a pig's fart if her brother's ill-disposed. He can gain an alliance by marrying Solla to the right lord. Women like her marry to please their clan, not themselves."

Neb started to reply, then paused, his mouth half-open, his eyes narrow, as if something had startled him. Gerran caught his mood—he assumed, at least, that he'd been affected by Neb's mood. That old proverb, so common, suddenly seemed to hold a grave meaning, to resonate in the warm summer air like an omen of wyrd. Neb shrugged with a twitch like a fly-stung horse, and the moment passed.

"If Ridvar were so eager to gain an alliance," Neb continued, "he'd have made her a good match years ago. There's ill feeling between the pair of them. Why else does he treat her like a servant in her father's dun? I've no idea what caused it, but you can see it between them, and her with no one to lean on or to protect her."

"Truly?"

"Truly. Why else, or so Branna tells me," Neb went on, "would Solla appeal to our lady Galla to give her a place as a serving-woman? It doesn't sound to me like she's got some grand match in the offing."

"Huh. It doesn't to me either."

"Why, just the other day I saw her working in the dun garden, down on her knees like a servant."

"What? You mean the kitchen garden?"

"Well, nearly that bad. She's planted some roses, and she was tending them. But still, it's a sad thing to see such a lovely lass so unhappy!"

"It is, truly. Huh. Well, scribe, you know, I'll have to think about all of this."

Neb smiled, well-pleased and a bit sly. With a wave of his hand he hurried off, heading to the broch, which he entered by the door on the honor side. *He's bold as brass!* Gerran thought. Gerran followed more slowly, and he went in by the commoners' door. He still came face-to-face with Lady Solla, however, over by the servants' hearth, where she was giving a pair of kitchen lasses complicated orders about a barrel of dark ale.

As he watched, Gerran realized that first, her hazel eyes were indeed beautiful, and second, that they had dark smudges under them. Her flawless skin was more than a little pale. *She's been working too hard,* he thought, *and all for that ingrate's wedding.* When he bowed to her, she tucked a loose strand of hair back behind her ear before she spoke.

"Good morrow, Captain," Solla said.

"And a good morrow to you, my lady," Gerran said. "I've heard that you'll be riding back with us."

"I will, indeed. I'll be staying for some while." Solla pushed out a brave little smile.

"Only for a while?"

"Well, mayhap my brother might consider finding a marriage for me once he's less distracted." The smile wavered, but she managed to keep it. "I'm quite pleased that Galla's willing to shelter me in the meanwhile."

"I'm getting above myself, no doubt, but I'm pleased as well. Forgive me if I've offended you."

"Offended me?" The smile turned genuine. "Why would that offend me?"

She started to say more, then blushed. Gerran realized that no one had ever looked at him before with the intensity she was displaying, all wide eyes and soft smile, a gentle flattery that warmed his blood like mead. *Ye gods,* he thought. *That cursed scribe was right!*

"I've been told that I fret too much about my birth," Gerran went on. "It's far below yours."

"I've always seen you as Tieryn Cadryc's foster son. I don't mean to dishonor your real father's memory, but he matters not to me."

"No insult taken, I assure you."

She smiled again, and he was shocked to realize that suddenly he could think of things to say, as if she were an entirely different kind of female than any he'd ever encountered before.

"It's a pleasant afternoon," Gerran said. "I hear that there's a garden in this dun, and that you planted roses in it."

"So I did. Would you like to see them?"

"I would, my lady, if you'd not mind showing them to me."

"I should like to."

When she stood still rather than heading for the door, Gerran realized that there was something more that he was supposed to do at this point. Solla ended the awkward moment with another smile.

"You might hold out your arm like this." Solla crooked hers at the elbow.

"Oh. My thanks."

When he offered her his arm, she took it, and together they walked out into the ward.

Since her father had yet to arrive, Branna had an idle afternoon ahead of her and went to look for Neb. She found him seated at a table near the servants' hearth, writing on a scrap of parchment while some young lord, a man she didn't recognize, hovered nearby. Neb finished writing, sprinkled the note with sand, then shook it clean and handed it to the lordling, who gave him some coins in return.

"My thanks, my lord," Neb said.

The lordling hurried off. Neb jingled the coppers in his hand.

"Not bad for a few moments' work," Neb announced, then slipped the coppers into the pouch that hung inside his shirt. "Not a lot of people can write out here, or so it seems."

"Was that a love note?" Branna said.

"It wasn't, but a promise to pay off a gambling debt. Huh! Love's always on a lass's mind."

"As if it weren't on yours. I was thinking. Shall we ride out to see the sights?"

"Splendid idea! We can have a bit of a talk that way. For that matter, I've heard that the cliff's rather spectacular on the west side, so we've got a good excuse."

A page fetched their horses for them in return for one of Neb's coppers. They rode out from the south gate and then turned west, letting their palfreys amble slowly along in the warmth of the sunny day. All round the dun the summer grass stretched green and soft, a marked contrast to the dour gray stone of the town and the cliff both. Not far from the gate a narrow stream trickled out from under the walls.

"That must be from the well on top of the hill," Branna said.

"Probably," Neb said. "The townsfolk must dump their leavings in the run-off. It's more than a bit foul smelling." He turned in the saddle to point to the south. "Now, just down there it joins up with the bigger stream. Let's cross there at the ford. I don't want the horses splashing through this filth."

Branna let him lead the way. She could see a stream running roughly north to south, the ford glinting in the sun. *That ford*, she thought. *There's just somewhat about a ford, somewhat ominous.* As they rode up to it, she saw a line of white stones marking out the shallow water, pale against the sandy bottom. She caught her breath with a gasp. She knew this ford. She had seen this place at some important crux, some terrible point in—not in her life. She'd never been here before. How could it seem so familiar, so dreadful, and yet remind her of danger and security both at once? How could it give her a feeling that she was utterly helpless and yet utterly in command, both at once?

"Are you all right?" Neb said sharply.

"I'm not."

Branna twitched the reins to make her palfrey halt. When she leaned forward in her saddle to get a better look at the ford, she felt that she was looking out of someone else's eyes.

"It's that other lass," she whispered. "She died here."

"What? What do you mean?"

"I don't know. Oh, don't ask!"

Branna dismounted, dropped the horse's reins, then walked to the river's edge. She was aware of Neb doing the same, but the water captured her entire attention. It swarmed with Wildfolk, sleek silver undines rising up as thick as foam, holding out their little hands to her in welcome. Sprites appeared to hover around her and Neb. They bobbed and dipped in the air like flashes of light from a hundred silver mirrors. Neb caught his breath with an audible gasp.

"This place," he said, "it's brimming with dweomer."

"Overflowing its banks, I'd say. Remember that other lass, the one who seems to be inside my mind or suchlike? She died here. I don't know how I know, but I do, and if she's dead, she must be a ghost. She must be trying to possess me."

Neb threw one arm around her shoulders and pulled her close. "We don't know that," he said. "She may just have some sort of message or somewhat that's keeping her from her rest."

"They do say that's all that ghosts want, someone to ease a trouble for them." Branna did her best to sound brave, but she could hear her voice shake.

"And besides, she shan't harm you. I won't let her. Here, let's go back to the dun. She won't follow us there."

"But she will! I mean—earlier, I felt her there. It was like I was looking out of her eyes, not mine. I even felt taller, somehow, like my body had changed, too."

"I can't make sense out of this, and no more can you, from the sound of it."

"Of course I can't! If I could, I wouldn't be frightened."

"Well, true spoken. But here, let's go back to the dun. You can find your aunt and keep to her company. Now, either the ghost will shun a crowded place like that, in which case, you'll be safe, or else, she'll appear there, and others will see her. and then you'll know that, truly, she's a ghost."

"Well reasoned, indeed." Branna managed to smile. "No wonder my aunt thinks you'll be an asset to a lord's court."

"Let's hope she's right, so I'll be able to keep you in the luxury you deserve. Now let's get back, shall we?"

Branna shamelessly ran back to her horse. She was mounted and ready to ride before he even reached his, but she was afraid to ride away without him. He mounted up and urged his horse up next to hers.

"I've had an idea," Neb said. "There's a temple of Bel in town. I'll get you back, then walk down and consult with the priests."

"Of course!" Branna said. "They should know the local lore about ghosts."

"Just that. But it might be hard to sort out. After all, a lot of people died here during the Horsekin War."

"But none of the women. According to the tales I've heard, the siege didn't last that long."

"I heard that, too. Well, I'll see what the priests have to say."

"I'll come with you."

"I wouldn't, if I were you. They'll only make you wait outside the gates."

"True-spoken. I keep forgetting that I'm an unclean female thing in their eyes."

Once they'd ridden safely inside the gates of the gwerbret's dun, Branna began to feel more than a little foolish. Everything seemed too busy, too normal, for ghosts to be lurking about. Servants bustled around the crowded ward, carrying firewood and supplies to the cookhouse or lugging heaps of bedding and clothes into the dun. Pages trotted back and forth on errands. A pair of joking, laughing grooms took Neb and Branna's horses and led them off to join others tied up outside for want of room in the stables.

"I'll be back in a bit," Neb told her.

"My thanks," Branna said. "I'll be down in the great hall by then."

Up in her chamber, Branna found a pitcher of water and a basin waiting for her. She washed her face and hands, then changed her dusty riding clothes for a pair of blue dresses. To comb out her hair she sat on the windowsill and looked down into the ward. The sight of other people comforted her, as did the warm breeze and the gleaming sunlight. Ghosts seemed very far away. The gray gnome appeared and hopped up onto the broad stone sill to sit opposite her. When she told him about her reaction to the sight of the ford, he clutched his head in both hands and scowled at her.

"What's this? Are you saying I've not understood her?"

He nodded his head yes.

"Well, if she's not a ghost, then what is she?"

The gnome pointed at her.

"She can't be me. I'm me, and she's—well, she's her."

Once again it clutched its head, then with a last scowl disappeared.

There's no understanding them sometimes, Branna thought. *The Wildfolk!* She left the chamber and headed for the great hall. About halfway down the curving stone staircase, she hesitated, caught by her fears, until she spotted her aunt, standing by the hearth and greeting the various lords and ladies who came up to her. The sight of the one person in her childhood who'd always loved her gave her the courage to continue down the stairs and plunge into the crowd. Dodging people and dogs alike, she made her way to Galla and sat down beside her to wait for Neb to return.

The temple of Bel stood on the other side of Cengarn from the gwerbret's dun. As Neb made his way there, he saw a row of squat clay ovens outside a solid-looking round house with new thatch—the town's baker. He spent two of the coppers he'd earned by writing the lordling's promissory note to buy a big round loaf, made with clean white flour and still warm.

At the brass-bound gates of the temple complex a young priest leaned against the wall, yawning in the sun. He was a neophyte from the look of him, a skinny lad, his head shaved, and dressed only in a long tunic bound at the waist with a bit of rope. Had he been formally accepted into the god's service, a small golden sickle would have dangled from his belt, but as it was, the rope lacked any adornment. At the sight of Neb, he stood up straight and clapped his hands together.

"Are you bringing that as an offering for the god?" the lad said. From the way he was eyeing the loaf Neb could guess that the god wouldn't get more than a slice out of it.

"I am," Neb said, "and I need to ask one of the priests here a question. It's about a thing that happened in the past."

"Very well. Come in, and I'll carry that bread for you."

Neb handed over the loaf and followed him into the compound. In the middle of a cobbled ward stood the round temple, an imposing building made of solid oak and roofed with slate. The double doors, gleaming with bronze, stood half-open. The neophyte ducked inside with the loaf. Neb heard murmuring voices; then the lad reappeared.

"You're in luck," he said. "His Holiness Lallyn's awake, and he can see you now. I'll just take this bread off to the refectory."

It struck Neb as odd to mention the priest's being awake, but when he stepped into the cool shadows of the temple, he understood.

At first the big round room seemed empty, lit only by two shafts of sunlight from narrow windows at either side of the door. Once Neb's eyes adjusted to the gloom, he saw the statue of the god directly across from the entrance in the far curve of the wall. Some twenty feet high, Bel loomed in the shadows, the king of the world and lord of the sun, carved from the entire trunk of an oak that had been ancient, judging from its size, when it was honored by being cut down to serve the gods. Bel stood with his arms raised to shoulder-height and thrust at the observer in order to display the human heads, carved of a paler wood, dangling from his hands.

Nearby, in a three-legged half-round of a chair, sat a priest who seemed nearly as old as the tree. His wrinkled, frog-spotted skin stretched tight over his skull and his bony frame. Not only was he egg-bald, but he lacked eyelashes as well, and when he smiled, he revealed a single brown tooth off to one side of his mouth.

"Good morrow, lad." The priest's voice rasped and quavered. "Your name is?"

"Nerrobrantos, Your Holiness, scribe to Tieryn Cadryc of the Red Wolf."

"Ah. Come closer, lad. I can hardly hear you."

Neb hurried over and knelt before him.

"And what's this question you have?" the priest said.

"Well, Your Holiness, I've heard tales from the local farmers about the ford west of the dun."

"Ah." The elderly priest interrupted with a smile. "The haunted ford, most like."

"That was the tale, indeed, Your Holiness. Someone told me that at times the ghost of a lass appears. She seems to have a message for someone or some urgent task at hand. I was wondering if you knew who she might be."

"Now that's a new turn of the tale! I know of only one woman who died at the ford." The old priest paused to suck his tooth. "A great many men and Horsekin did, however, in the general rout. I remember it well, seeing the river run red with blood."

"It's a grim tale, then."

"It is." Lallyn nodded slowly. "Now, the woman who died wasn't a lass, but a white-haired female nearly as old as I am now. She was a witch, I suppose. How else could she have destroyed the demoness?"

"Demoness?"

"The one the Horsekin thought a goddess."

"Alshandra?"

"That was the foul thing's name, truly." Lallyn paused again, this time to look away with rheumy eyes. "The witch had a bond-woman's name. I've forgotten it. She and the demoness destroyed each other. Witches can call up demons, you know, but they always come to a bad end, the witches, that is. The demons too, I suppose. This one certainly did." He sighed, nodding to himself. "Just as well, too. Just as well." He let his chin rest upon his chest. In a few moments he'd fallen asleep.

Neb heard someone walk in behind him and turned to see the neophyte, no longer burdened with the loaf, gesturing at the door. The audience was at an end.

During his steep walk back up to the dun, Neb thought over the priest's answer. The priests of Bel would see all dweomer as evil witchcraft, he knew. Some witches were reputed to survive their deaths in one form or another, either as haunts or as magical birds who could speak to the living under certain circumstances. *Like that raven?* he wondered. Perhaps the bird wasn't an evil omen, but merely a ghost who wanted to tell Branna some secret or other. There was no doubt that his beloved had talent for dweomer. He had come to accept that fact, just as he had come to realize that he, too, was marked for a stranger craft than letter-writing.

If only I could find the room with the tapestries. In his mind Neb had the image of a suite of rooms in a tower. In the largest, fine Bardek tapestries decorated the stone walls. Between two of the hangings a shelf of seven books waited for him, seven priceless books that stood between a pair of bronze wyverns. But he'd lost the way. He'd forgotten how to reach his rooms. As he puffed up the last hill to the gates of the dun, it occurred to him that Branna somehow knew where those rooms were. All at once he saw it with a strange cold certainty. If he could solve the puzzle of this ghost or this "other lass" or whatever was haunting her mind, he would solve his own riddle as well.

By the time he returned to the dun, noble-born lords and their honor escorts thronged the great hall. Servants brought the men ale in tankards and the noble-born, mead in goblets. Talk and laughter boomed under the high ceiling and reverberated across tables set so close that the serving lasses could barely edge through. The womenfolk of higher rank had retreated upstairs, but after some searching Neb found Branna, waiting at the top of the curving staircase.

"There you are!" Branna said. "I was wondering where you'd got to."

"It all took a fair bit of time," Neb said. "I did speak with the high priest. He's immensely old. Why, he must be near seventy! His memory's not what it was either, but he did know somewhat about the siege of Cengarn. That's when a woman died at the ford, a witch woman, he called her. She somehow or other saved the city from the demoness Alshandra, destroyed her somehow, but it cost her own life."

"Calling her a witch strikes me as a nasty way of speaking, then."

"It struck me the same, truly, but what else can you expect from Bel's priests?"

"Naught, I suppose."

"She does seem to be the sort of woman who could come back as a haunt, doesn't she? And maybe have a message for someone?"

Instead of answering, Branna half-turned and looked away down the corridor, but Neb doubted if she was truly seeing the view of doors and the far stone wall. All at once she shuddered, then turned back with a brittle smile. "I've got to rush off to the women's hall. I should have been there ages ago, you see, to be presented to the gwerbret's betrothed."

Before Neb could say anything, she hurried off. About halfway down the corridor she opened a door and slipped into one of the few places in the entire dun where he was forbidden to go. *The idea of witchery scared her good and proper,* he thought. Later, he supposed, he'd be able to discuss it with her, once she'd had a chance to think it over.

The proper term for Lady Drwmigga, the gwerbret's new wife, was bovine, Branna decided. Oh, she was pretty enough, with her long dark hair and dark blue eyes, and she wore a beautiful overdress, a gift from the queen herself down in Deverry—blue Bardek silk embroidered about the neck and down the sleeves with floral garlands in the Westfolk style. As she half-reclined in a cushioned chair, her pale hands flaccid in her lap, she smiled at the ladies of the her new rhan as if everything pleased her impartially, whether it was a honeyed apricot or a fulsome compliment. When she spoke, her voice was low and even, and she tended to let her words trail away to a whisper rather than finishing them smartly off. *Gwerbret Ridvar's going to have some stupid sons,* Branna thought to herself, *but I'll wager she gives him a lot of them.*

The talk in the women's hall centered around gossip and children, drifting now and then to the price of Bardek silk and glass drinking vessels and other such luxuries. Branna did her best to pay attention, but she was wishing she'd brought a piece of embroidery from home to work upon during these duty stints in attendance upon the new lady of Dun Cengarn. Still, the boredom was preferable to letting her mind wander to the tale of the witch—or dweomerwoman—who had died at the ford.

Thinking about that woman made her feel as if the room had filled with a sudden icy mist. Yet try as she might to keep her mind on the present conversation, Neb's words kept creeping back. Release came at last in the person of a young maidservant, who slipped into the chamber with a curtsy for Drwmigga, then curtsied again to Branna.

"My lady," she said, "your father rode in a little while ago."

"My thanks for telling me!" Branna got up and curtsied to Drwmigga. "My lady, if you'll excuse me?"

"Of course." Drwmigga favored her with a good-natured smile. "Kin come before all else, I always say."

The great hall seemed a good bit quieter, and a little less crowded, than it had been earlier—the effects of the generous servings of ale, no doubt. Here and there at one of the tables on the commoners' side of the hall, a rider or manservant slept with his head pillowed on his arms. A pair of serving lasses wandered around, picking up tankards from the floor.

On the honor side, Tieryn Gwivyr stood near the doorway as he gave orders to his manservant. Gwivyr was a big man even for a Deverry lord, tall, barrel-chested, sporting a full mustache and a head of pale golden hair, dusted with silver. As Branna made her way down the stairs, she could feel her heart pounding in something like fear, but when she curtsied in front of him, Gwivyr smiled at her. With a flick of one hand he dismissed the servant.

"Good morrow, Father," Branna said. "I hope you had a pleasant journey."

"Pleasant enough." His dark voice suited his build. "You look well, lass."

"My thanks. I've been having a splendid time at Aunt Galla's."

"Good."

"Father, I've somewhat to ask you. I've met the man I want to marry, and he wants to marry me."

"You have, eh? And what does your uncle think of that?"

"He approves of him, and so does Aunt Galla. But, uh—well, uh—he's common-born."

"What?" Gwivyr wrinkled his nose. "Not a farmer or suchlike?"

"Not at all. He's Uncle Cadryc's scribe, and Aunt Galla says he has a great future ahead of him. She thinks he'll make a councillor at some great lord's court."

"Oh." Gwivyr turned a little away and looked across the hall. "Your stepmother's not down yet, I see. We might as well settle this now. About your scribe, if Cadryc approves, I don't see why I should argue. Marry to suit yourself, lass." He paused for a laugh. "He won't be demanding much of a dowry, will he now?"

"He's not so much as mentioned a dowry."

"Good. Let's see, when you left for Galla's, I gave you a riding horse and its tack, a cart horse and cart, and then you've got your dower chest. If he'll take that, by all means marry him."

"I'm sure that'll be quite enough."

"Good." Gwivyr paused to look at the staircase. "Here comes your stepmother, and I'd best go join her before she starts her cursed complaining again." With a last smile her way, he strode to the foot of the staircase, then greeted his wife with a bellow and a wave. The lady came down and hurried off without so much as a glance Branna's way.

Branna stood staring after them and wondered why she felt like weeping. Hadn't her father just given her the very boon she'd asked for? *But I wanted him to care*, she thought. *I truly did want him to care whom I married, even if he'd forbidden me.* She shook herself like a wet dog, wiped her damp eyes on her sleeve, then started back upstairs. Halfway up she met Galla, who was hurrying down to meet her.

"Well?" Galla blurted. "What did he say?"

"He agreed." Branna managed to force out a smile. "He said I could marry whom I liked. Well, provided Neb accepts the dowry. It's not much of one, just a couple of horses and a cart."

"I can't imagine he wouldn't, but if not, then Cadryc and I will give it a bit more weight. We've won the real battle. That gladdens my heart, it truly does! Does Neb know yet?"

"Not yet. I'm not sure where he's got to."

"Let's go down, and we can send a page to find him. I've had enough of the women's hall, if you have."

"Quite enough, my thanks!"

They walked on down and found an empty table near the dragon hearth, one equipped with proper chairs rather than backless benches.

"Now, let me think," Galla said once they'd seated themselves. "We can't announce your betrothal here and now, of course. It would be a terrible breach of courtesy. Naught should distract the guests from the gwerbret's marriage. But once we're home, we'll have a splendid feast and invite all our vassals. I am *so* pleased Gwivvo saw reason!" She paused for a wicked grin and a wink. "It's so unlike him."

At that Branna could laugh, and her disappointment at her father's reaction faded away.

"I don't know where Cadryc's got to either," Galla said. "But if we wait here, he'll doubtless turn up. Ah, there, however, is young Coryn. Page! Come here, lad!"

Coryn came trotting over, wiping his sticky face on the sleeve of his new shirt. Judging from the crumbs left on his chin he'd been eating honeycake, always in great supply at weddings.

"There you are," Galla said. "Do you know where Neb's got to? I want him to write a letter to our Adranna."

"I'll go look for him, my lady."

"Very good, and then once you've found Neb, find and fetch the tieryn, too."

With a bow, Coryn trotted off again.

"A letter?" Branna said. "Is there anyone in Honelg's dun who'll be able to read it?"

"Of course not," Galla said. "In that ghastly place? The letter's for the look of the thing, but I'll ask your uncle to send a pair of his riders to speak the actual message."

"You're worried about Adranna, aren't you?"

"I am. I never approved of that marriage, as you well know, not that your uncle or anyone else would listen to me, a mere mother though as noble-born as the rest of them." Galla paused, scowling. "Well, let us talk of more auspicious things. This should be a happy day, not a gloomy one."

Galla began pointing out the various noble lords in the hall and discussing their holdings. Now and then Branna thought of the witch's ghost, but whatever or whoever she was, that strange presence failed to reappear.

By the time that Coryn found Neb, who'd been discussing ink with the gwerbret's scribe in that worthy's chamber, most of the noble-born women had returned to the great hall. Their presence had finished quieting down the crowd of riders and inspired the servants to bring out baskets of bread and cold meats to go with the ale and mead. Near the dragon hearth, Branna was sitting with her aunt and uncle. When Neb knelt by the tieryn's side, Cadryc winked at him and smiled.

"Well, congratulations, lad," Cadryc said. "Our Branna's spoken to her father, and he approved your betrothal."

Before he could stop himself, Neb threw both hands into the air and cheered. Cadryc laughed and slapped him on the shoulder.

"I see the news doesn't vex your heart," Cadryc said. "Get up, Nephew, and take a seat next to your betrothed."

"My thanks, my lord and uncle." Neb rose, dusting the straw off his knees. "I'm honored and thrice honored, and a lucky man as well."

Branna was grinning at him. When he sat down on the bench next to her, she turned and kissed him on the cheek. He caught her hand and raised it to kiss it in return.

"I never thought I could be this happy in my life," Neb said, "not once, not for the beat of a heart, much less that I'd feel a joy like this."

"No more did I," Branna said, and her voice sounded thick with tears. "I'm so happy I could weep, and mayhap I will." With that the tears came, trickling down her cheeks while she smiled up at him.

With his free hand Neb found a scrap of rag in his pocket that he used for wiping pens and gave it to her. When she wiped her face, the ink left a smear across her cheeks.

"A fitting mark for the wife of a scribe," Lady Galla said, sniffling a little herself. "Oh, it gladdens my heart to see you both so happy!"

"Mine, too," Cadryc said, "oddly enough. Imph. A man never knows how these things will take him, eh?"

They all laughed. "My thanks, my lady," Neb said, "and my thanks to you, too, my lord."

"Now, we'll need to discuss the dowry," Cadryc went on. "Branna's father offers you her riding horse, a cart horse and cart, and of course all those things that women sew for their dower chests. I'll add a riding horse for you, and its tack."

"Your Grace, that's more than generous." Neb realized that he'd never given a single thought to a dowry. His mother doubtless would have haggled for more, but then, his mother wouldn't have been living on someone else's charity. "I'll take it gladly."

"Good lad!" Cadryc raised his goblet and saluted him. "I—" He paused, interrupted by the sound of silver horns, blaring in the ward.

"Now, who's that, I wonder?" Galla said. "Someone of high rank, judging by the noise his retinue's making."

High rank, indeed, as they found out when Clae came racing through the maze of tables and benches. Noble-born and servants alike scattered ahead of him. Dogs barked at his passing.

"Your Grace!" Clae blurted out. "It's a prince from down in Dun Deverry. Prince Voran his name is, and he's got ever so many riders and servants and carts with him."

"By the gods!" Cadryc shoved his chair back and rose to his feet. "Our gwerbret's being honored, indeed!"

"He is that," Neb said. "Voran's a younger son, but he's of the blood royal, sure enough."

Accompanied by Lord Oth, Gwerbret Ridvar went running out of the hall almost as fast as Clae had made his headlong dash into it. A dozen or so dogs followed him out, barking in excitement. As the news spread through the great hall, most of the gathered crowd followed Cadryc's example, getting to their feet, craning their necks for a glimpse of royalty. Over on the riders' side of the hall, some of the servants and pages climbed onto the tables for a better view.

"I can't see over everybody," Galla said with some irritation. "Neb, is Gerran in the great hall? He's our foster son, after all, and he should be introduced to the prince."

"I don't see him, my lady. He might be in the barracks. Shall I go find him?"

"Please, and my thanks."

As he made his way through the swirling mob to the back door, Neb felt as if he just might float free of the ground and sail through the heavens. *She's mine,* he thought. *She's truly mine at last! And after all these—*The thought stopped him cold. After all these what? *You only met her a few months ago,* he reminded himself. Still, he couldn't shake the feeling deep in his heart that he'd known her for a longer time than that, a far far longer time. Yet nothing, not even the strangeness of that feeling, could spoil his joy. Neb went whistling from the great hall.

Gerran had seen the prince's arrival, and he'd gone down to the stables to insure that the Red Wolf horses weren't slighted in the turmoil of arriving guests. Stout Lord Blethry, the gwerbret's equerry, was standing on a barrel by the watering trough and yelling orders. Grooms were rushing back and forth, trying to follow them and find room for the horses that the prince's warband had brought with them—nearly seventy in all, counting the mounts of various servitors and the cart horses. Gerran had no intention of allowing his own men's mounts to be tied up in the open on cobbled ground.

"Gerro, wait!" It was Neb's voice, barely audible in all the noise. "I've got a message for you."

Gerran turned to see Neb making his way through the mob of horses and men. Even though the scribe was slender and not particularly tall, and none of the men standing around knew who he was, they stepped back or drifted out of his path as if he'd been a great lord. Perhaps it was the confident way the scribe strode along, straight-backed, with his head held high.

"Our lady wants you in the great hall," Neb said.

"Oh, ye gods! Right this moment?"

"Soon. She wants to present you to the prince."

"By the black hairy arse of the Lord of Hell! Whatever for?"

"You're her foster son, aren't you?"

"I am, truly, but—"

"I know, I know, common-born. Give it a rest, Gerro! Everyone's sick as can be of you abasing yourself."

For a moment Gerran was tempted to slap him backhand across the mouth, but a gwerbret's ward wasn't a tavern, and brawling had no place in it. Neb stood waiting for an answer, smiling, his face a little flushed, as if he'd drunk too much, as well, and he shoved his hands in his brigga pockets with a jaunty sort of gesture.

"You look pleased about somewhat, scribe," Gerran said.

"I am, truly." But Neb let his smile fade. "You'll hear the news sooner or later, so I'd best tell you myself. As soon as we get back to our dun, Lady Branna and I will announce our betrothal."

Gerran considered his reaction while Neb waited unsmiling, his head cocked, as if daring him to object. Much to his surprise, Gerran realized that the prospect of their marriage irked him far less than the prospect of his warband's horses being turned out of the stables.

"My congratulations to you both," Gerran said. "I mean them sincerely."

"Well, my thanks, then! And what about yourself?" Neb said.

"If you're referring to Lady Solla," Gerran said, "I've got work to do at the moment. Tell Lady Galla that I'll join her presently, just as soon as I find out about our horses."

"I will, then. Here have you seen Clae? I truly should tell him about my betrothal."

"He's probably in the cookhouse. He told me that Solla—I mean Lady Solla—had asked him to help serve."

"*Lady* Solla, of course." Neb winked at him, then hurried off, heading for the cook house.

When the prince entered the main broch tower, the gwerbret escorted him up the stairs to a guest chamber. Right behind them came nearly everyone who'd been out in the ward, servants and noble-born both, swarming into the great hall; those that could find a seat sat, but most stood, waiting to catch a glimpse of the royal personage when he came back down. In the confusion Branna had hoped to escape the great hall and sneak away somewhere with Neb, who stood hovering behind her chair, ready to bolt. Aunt Galla, however, seemed to have suspected as much.

"I don't want you two running off now," Galla said. "It would be terribly rude with Prince Voran about to join the gwerbret's table."

"Oh, come now!" Branna said. "Neither of them are going to give a pig's—um—ear whether some border noblewoman like me is here to curtsy."

"Or about a scribe," Neb put in, "or so I'd think, my lady."

"Mayhap," Galla said, "but I do care about such things."

"Well and good, then, we'll stay." Branna patted her aunt's hand. "Besides, I've never seen a prince before."

"Well, they look much like other men." Galla was craning her neck and turning to peer around the great hall. "Now where is Gerran? I did so want—ah! There he is!"

Gerran was coming in the door on the riders' side of the hall. He managed to work his way through the crowd and join the tieryn's table just as the silver horns sounded again, this time from the foot of the stairs.

With a rustle of clothing like wind through winter trees everyone in the great hall rose, ready to bow, curtsy, or kneel. A page came first, carrying a small banner of the royal clan, a gold wyvern rampant on a cream ground. Behind him Prince Voran walked slowly, smiling pleasantly, one hand raised in greeting. He'd changed out of his road-dirty clothes into a clean pair of plaid brigga and a shirt of the finest white linen, embroidered with thick bands of red and black interlace down the sleeves and a pair of wyverns, couched in heavy gold cord, at the yokes. He was as tall as Branna's father but lean rather than stout, sporting a thick head of brown hair just touched with silver and a magnificent mustache of the same colors.

As the prince walked past each honor table, he would pause long enough to receive the bows and curtsies of those occupying it and to murmur a few words of acknowledgment. But at Tieryn Cadryc's table he stopped to greet Cadryc by name, giving Branna the chance to see that his eyes were gray and his face strikingly ordinary just as her aunt had warned. The mustaches couldn't quite hide a wide mouth with thin lips that made his smile tend toward the froglike. He had rather large ears, as well. Cadryc made a courteous remark or two with a calm that must have been hard-won, considering that a prince had singled him out, and introduced Gerran as his foster son. When the prince nodded his way, Gerran blushed scarlet.

Behind Voran stood Gwerbret Ridvar, his smile a bit fixed and grim, who nodded to the tieryn as well. When Voran led his little parade on past, Lord Oth peeled out of line and hunkered down between Galla and Cadryc. Everyone at the table regained their seats and leaned toward him to listen.

"The prince has been apprised of the possible danger from a Horsekin fort," Oth murmured, then raised his voice to a normal level. "Tieryn Cadryc, I hope you've been given decent accommodations."

"Splendid on all counts!" Cadryc pledged him with his goblet.

"Very nice, indeed," Galla said. "It's very kind of you to ask, and you with everything you've got to do."

"I'm beginning to see the end of this horse race, my lady." Oth stood up with a sharp little sigh. "Once the Prince of the Westfolk arrives, he'll be the last royal personage, but I have no idea of how large a retinue he's bringing with him. And Lady Drwmigga's father should arrive soon as well."

"I'm surprised he's not here already," Cadryc said.

"He's having to adjudicate a feud in malover. The situation could turn dangerous, or so the messenger told us, so he didn't dare put off the two lords involved any longer."

"Ye gods," Cadryc said. "That could take weeks."

"True spoken." Oth groaned under his breath. "But he made it clear we're to proceed whether he arrives or not. It's not like his son is the one marrying, after all. And, of course, if he does arrive, he'll be traveling with the escort fitting to his gwerbretal rank. That probably means every tieryn who's ever sworn fealty to the Eagle clan as well as an honor guard for each and the gwerbret's own riders. Ye gods, I hope we can squeeze everyone into the dun! We have a pair of pavilions for tourneys. I'm going to have to set those up in the meadow outside the walls for Cengarn's own riders. I hate to turn them out of their beds, but the guest lords might see the pavilions as slighting their men."

"Oh, well, here," Cadryc said. "I certainly wouldn't take it that way. Gerro, come to think of it, you could set up a rope pen of sorts, and put our horses out on the grass."

"Splendid idea, my lord," Gerran put in. "I don't want them tied standing on cobbles or hard dirt, but tethered on grass is a different matter."

Lord Oth smiled in profound relief.

"And the Westfolk will bring their own tents," Galla said. "They really do dislike sleeping inside proper walls. They can pitch them on the commons."

"Well, alas, not on the commons," Oth said. "Its use belongs to the townsfolk by right of royal charter, and his grace doesn't dare breach that. But at least they won't need chambers. They might prefer the meadow, come to think of it. Once Prince Daralanteriel gets himself here, we can have the great feast and the tourney, and that, thank every god in the sky, will be that."

Oth trotted off again to catch up with the prince and the gwerbret. Gerran left as well to tell the warband that they were moving camp, as he put it. Galla turned to Branna and winked.

"Now, if you and Neb would still like to go off somewhere," Galla said, "I'll forgive you."

"My thanks, my lady," Neb said. "My heart is as full of gratitude as ever a man's could be, that you'd smile on our betrothal."

"And my thanks, Aunt Galla," Branna said, "and you, too, Uncle Cadryc."

With the dun as crowded as a Beltane temple, the only private place that Neb and Branna could find was her bedchamber. Branna barred the door, then sat on the edge of the bed while Neb hovered near the window.

"Oh, do come sit." Branna patted the mattress beside her. "After all, we are betrothed."

Neb stared at her for a long moment, then smiled and sat down, facing her. Branna felt impossibly solemn, a little shy, now that the moment they'd both longed for had finally arrived. Neb took her hand in both of his and kissed her fingers.

"My heart's like a fountain," he said, "overflowing with love for you." He drew her close and bent his head to kiss her.

Out in the hall someone pushed on the door, then banged on it. "My lady?" It was Midda. "Are you in there?"

Neb muttered something foul under his breath.

"I am," Branna called back. "What is it?"

"I need to get that extra linen we brought along. Lady Solla needs to borrow it for some guests."

"I'll get it. Hang on a moment."

The sheets were neatly stacked on a rickety chair in the curve of the wall. Branna fetched them, then unbarred the door and opened it just wide enough to slip the sheets into Midda's hands. Midda was glowering at her.

"I suppose your wretched betrothed is in there with you," Midda said.

"You've heard about our betrothal?"

"News travels fast in a dun like this." Midda snorted profoundly. "Well, I'd hoped for better for you, but you never would listen to your elders."

"True enough." Branna paused for a smile. "I can't deny it."

Midda snorted and slammed the door. Branna replaced the bar and hurried back to join Neb on the edge of the bed.

"You were saying?" She grinned at him.

They shared a laugh; then he caught her by the shoulders. She slipped her arms around his waist and drew him close as he kissed her. They lay down together, sprawled across the bed. In her mind ran words like the best music in the world: *at last, at last we're together!*

"Gerran!" Lord Blethry hailed him. "Captain! Wait up!"

Gerran, who was on his way to the barracks, stopped

walking and turned to wait. The equerry dodged his way through a mob of horses and servants and reached him at last. His heavy squarish face was flushed from mead and exertion both.

"I want to thank you for agreeing to take your men down to the meadow," Blethry said. "The chamberlain's sent a squad of servants down with the largest pavilion. It's a wretchedly clumsy thing to set up, so there'll be a bit of a wait."

"There's no hurry, my lord," Gerran said. "I've got to collect my men and horses, and that'll take me a fair while, too."

"True-spoken. The pages you brought with you—how good are they around horses?"

"Coryn's a good rider, but Clae's just learning. Ynedd's too young and scrawny to control a warhorse."

"Can he lead a haltered horse? I don't have enough grooms to tend all these cursed mounts, even with the Red Wolf horses gone."

"Ah, I see. All three lads are good enough at raking hay and watering stock. Tell your head groom to come to me if there's any trouble with them."

"I shall, and my thanks."

By the time that the Red Wolf warband was settled in their improvised new quarters, down by the ford across the river, the afternoon was turning toward evening. Out in the meadows a breeze sprang up to blow the flies away, and the hobbled horses grazed peacefully among the long shadows of the trees. As the sun sank low, it gilded the dun, towering over them on its cliff.

"It's a long way to walk for dinner," Daumyr said. "But aside from that, this is a good bit better than being crammed into the barracks with everyone else."

"It is at that," Gerran said. "Have you finished digging that latrine?"

"I have, and well downstream. I've stowed the shovel in the pavilion."

"Good." Gerran hesitated, considering. "We'd best leave someone here to watch over the horses. You never know who might take a fancy to them."

Sorting out who would stand guard duty took a great deal of furious dicing among the men, but eventually they left two men on armed guard with the promise of having food brought to them by whatever servant Gerran could round up to run the errand. With their captain at their head, the rest of the warband strolled through the south gate and panted up the steep hill to the dun.

Despite the evening breeze beyond the walls, inside them the windless humid air draped itself over Gerran like a winter cloak. Men and horses stood so thick in the ward that pushing through them reminded Gerran of trying to walk through a flock of sheep. Inevitably the Red Wolf warband split up into twos and threes as they tried to follow their captain. Some of the men in his path tried to move out of Gerran's way at once. Others merely stared at him with eyes turned witless by the gwerbret's ale until one of their fellows said, "It's the Falcon. Move, lad! Haven't you seen him fight?" Then they'd step out of his way, and fast. Gerran thus reached the hall before the rest of his men.

On the top step of the doorway he turned and looked over the ward just as shouting erupted some twenty yards back toward the gates. The mob swirled and swelled as some men tried to get away from what appeared to be a fistfight. As man pushed against man, apologies met curses. Raised voices and clenched fists threatened to spread the trouble further. The horses nearest to the disturbance began pulling at their tethers and trying to rear; grooms began yelling as they worked their way through the clotted crowd. The inadvertent shoves and curses increased. The men hung at the edge of a cliff over chaos, Gerran realized. Drawing his sword would only make them drop. Fortunately a groom stood nearby, a heavy quirt dangling from his lax grasp. Gerran snatched it from him and plunged into the mob.

"It's the Falcon!" someone yelled. "Ware, lads!"

Men tried to part and let him through, but Gerran ended up brandishing the quirt and even using it on a few of the slower-moving lads before he finally got himself to the edge of the brawl. Perhaps half a dozen men were throwing punches, and three or four more were wrestling on the cobbles, all of them yelling insults and threats. By then, only a last few bystanders blocked his path.

"Move back!" Gerran held up the quirt. "Get away, all of you! Now!"

Those who could followed orders; those at the edge of the mob began to fall back as well; grooms grabbed whatever tether ropes they could reach and began leading horses away. Although the ward was quieting down, the original brawlers went on fighting in a moving tangle of men.

Gerran dodged into the melee and swung the quirt to good purpose, yelling "hold and stand!" the entire time. The Red Wolf men among the miscreants followed his orders straightaway, more afraid of him than of their temporary enemies. The other men, too, began to devote themselves to ducking under Gerran's blows rather than continuing to fight. A few lucky ones even managed to run out of range.

Behind them more shouting erupted, but of a very different sort. "It's His Grace! He's trying to get through. And ye gods, the prince is with him! Make way!"

The last of the brawl stopped cold. The rest of the watching mob found it could indeed move and quickly at that. The ward cleared remarkably easily as Gwerbret Ridvar elbowed his way to Gerran's side. Right behind him came Prince Voran. Ridvar crossed his arms over his chest, and stood scowling at the cowed brawlers. The ward grew oddly silent; even the remaining horses stopped their stamping and snorting.

"I'm cursed glad that this didn't happen on the morrow," Ridvar said, and his voice brimmed with fury ready to spill. "It's bad enough that one prince of the blood royal has had to see this! I'll remind you all that another's on his way here. If anyone dares break the peace in front of them again—" He let the thought sizzle unfinished on the humid air.

Apologies came as fast as summer rain. When Ridvar said nothing more, the men slunk away, heading to the barracks, the hall, the stables—anywhere out of the gwerbret's sight. Gerran started to kneel to the prince and gwerbret, but Voran stopped him with a wave of his hand.

"No need," the prince said. "Good job, Captain."

"My thanks, Your Highness. I'm honored you'd think so."

Voran smiled, Ridvar smiled; then they turned and strolled back to the great hall. Over by the dun gates a subdued Warryc crawled out from under a wagon and stood up, brushing horseshit and mud off his clothes. Gerran walked over to him.

"And what was all that?" Gerran said. "Were you in the middle of it?"

"I was not, Captain," Warryc said. "But one of the Stag clan riders, a burly fellow with a red beard, grabbed young Clae and smacked him in the face, and him three times the lad's size. He claimed the lad had dropped somewhat or other on his foot or suchlike. Cursed if we were going to let some stranger harm one of the Red Wolf pages."

"So you were in the middle of it."

"Not to say the middle." Warryc paused for a grin. "Out toward the edge, mayhap."

Gerran rolled his eyes, considered a reprimand, then merely shrugged. "Well," Gerran said, "I'm glad enough that someone defended the lad. Just don't let it happen again, will you? It would ache my heart to have one of my men flogged for causing trouble in a gwerbret's dun."

"It would ache a fair bit more of the fellow being flogged than his heart. Warning taken, Captain."

"Good. Don't forget it. Now, let's go in. I need to find a servant to take some food down to our lads. Better yet, help me find Clae. We'll send him down where that piss-proud bully can't find him."

"What's all that noise, I wonder?" Branna sat up on the bed. "It sounds like fighting in the ward."

Neb murmured a few incomprehensible words, then turned over and went back to sleep. Branna got out of bed, then picked her underdress up off the floor and put it on before she went to the window. When she looked out, she could see the brawl in progress, though the ward was darkening with evening shadows and far too crowded for her to identify the fighters. The sight below reminded her of a pot of oatmeal on a fire, pulsing and bubbling. Like a cooking spoon stirring the porridge, one man cleared his way through only to have the mob close behind him. His red hair made her wonder if it were Gerran, and sure enough, once the mob began to disperse, she recognized him. *He'll get the matter settled, then,* she thought. *No need to worry.*

She lay down again, hoping that Neb would wake up for still more lovemaking, but he slept stubbornly on. Soon enough she fell asleep herself, only to wake suddenly to a night-dark room.

Through the open window she could see the Snowy Road, bright against the sky, and hear the noise from the great hall like a river rushing over stones. She could smell dinner, as well. Her stomach growled and rumbled. She was about to get up when she realized that the chamber was full of Wildfolk. She could hear them rustling, see shapes like living shadows flitting back and forth in the air. She prodded Neb in the ribs.

"Wake up," she murmured. "Somewhat's going to happen."

"Imph." He sat up in bed, yawned, then glanced around him. "Ye gods, I've never seen so many Wildfolk!"

"No more I," Branna said. "We should make a dweomer light."

"No need. Look."

In the center of the chamber a point of silvery glow appeared and began to expand. It turned first into a gleaming sphere, then a cylinder. It hovered, glowing as brightly as twenty lanterns, then lengthened into a pillar of silver light that stretched nearly floor-to-ceiling. All of the Wildfolk skittered to the edges of the chamber and arranged themselves around the walls. Within the pillar the light seemed as solid as smoke, flowing and ebbing only to brighten again in long streamers.

Branna's gray gnome suddenly materialized on the bed between her and Neb. It did a little dance, laughing soundlessly and pointing at the shimmering pillar.

"Did you bring this?" Branna whispered.

The gnome nodded a yes and sat down, wrapping its skinny arms tight around its bony knees as it stared into the silver light. Inside the pillar two figures began to form. At first they were only the sort of misty shapes one sees in clouds or smoke; then they became solid and defined themselves into two vaguely human bodies. After some moments one form stepped out of the pillar and floated some inches above the floor.

Although still human in shape, she was far too slender to be an ordinary woman, and her skin, if one could call that tenuous membrane skin, was dead-white. Her hair, eyes, and lips shared the same shade of woad-blue, as did the suggestion of a tattered dress that she wore, but they glowed in a way that dyed cloth could never match. When she opened her mouth to speak, she revealed needle-sharp teeth.

"Jill." Her voice sounded with the hoarse rasp of ocean waves. It was one voice, yet echoed with many voices. "You saved me long years past, and now I've come to repay. Your little one brought me here because I have speech."

The gnome jumped up and clapped its hands. Branna tried to speak but could manage only a soft sigh. Neb caught his breath with a gasp and laid a hand on her arm.

"Don't you know me, Master of the Aethyr?" the spirit said to him.

The figure still half-seen inside the pillar pulsed with light and seemed to speak—perhaps it was a he. Branna sensed his speaking rather than heard him. The white spirit, however, nodded as if she understood.

"You don't remember," she said to Branna, then glanced at Neb. "Nor do you."

"Remember what?" Neb said.

"Who you are." The spirit raised her illusion of hands and pointed at each of them. "Remember who you are and who you were once." She turned to Branna. "There are no ghosts, only memories, in your dreams."

"You're saying that my dreams are true?" Branna whispered.

The spirit smiled, but her form was turning translucent. Her hair, her hands frayed into strands of silver light. "Remember!" she repeated. "You died at the ford. Don't you remember?"

The light in the pillar began to swirl, and the male form within swirled with it. The white spirit was nearly transparent, and her hands and hair were indistinguishable from the light. With a last smile she stepped back into the pillar and became only a drifting form seen through a glowing haze.

"Jill." Her last words seemed to ring through the chamber. "Remember."

The silver light was fading, the pillar shrinking. It seemed to turn inside itself; suddenly it disappeared, leaving the chamber wreathed in a faint glow. The Wildfolk swarmed into the middle of the room, then flew this way and that, soaring up high, dropping down, dashing this way and that, only to disappear themselves, winking out like the last coals of a fire. The gray gnome turned to Branna, bowed like a tiny lord, and vanished, taking the last of the silver light with him.

Neb rolled off the bed and, still naked, strode over to the chest in the curve of the wall. He picked up a candle lantern and lit it with a snap of his fingers. As the golden light brightened, Branna could see him grinning like a madman.

"That priest of Bel," he said, "the one I spoke with this afternoon—he said that the witch woman had a bondwoman's name. Jill certainly would fit that."

"It would, truly." Branna still found it hard to speak. "The name just means 'lass,' doesn't it?"

"Somewhat like that, I think."

Neb set the lantern down on the windowsill, then came back to the bed. He picked up his brigga from the floor and put them on.

"I still don't understand," Branna said. "How could I have died at the ford all those years ago and still be alive now?"

"It should be obvious." Neb was peering at the floor. Abruptly he stooped and came back up with his shirt. "There's only one thing it can mean."

"What? Don't tease me!"

"I'm not." He paused to pull the shirt over his head. "Remember what we discussed at the ford, all those old tales about how dweomerfolk can come back to life as birds and suchlike? Well, they must be able to come back as people, too, born in the usual way and all that."

"You're saying that I've lived another life before this one."

"Not precisely. I'm saying we both did." Neb sat down on the edge of the bed. "I feel like I've loved you forever, but we only met a few months ago. Don't you feel the same?"

For a moment Branna was tempted to lie out of an odd sort of fear, as if she stood on the edge of some high cliff and was about to leap off into a chasm that plunged down beyond her sight. Either she would find wings and soar, or she would fall to her death. For the briefest of moments, she remembered how it felt to fly. Seeing his face, shadowed in the flickering candlelight, made her remember another face, that of the old man who'd held out the glowing gem, a gift beyond price. *Your dreams are memories,* the white spirit had told her, *not ghosts.*

"I do," she said, "I do feel like I've loved you forever."

When he held out his hand, she clasped it in both of hers.

"We've found the way," Neb said, "the path to someplace grand. Or I should say, the spirit gave it to us. Seeing her, hearing her—I remembered. I'm still not sure exactly what I remember, mind, but I suddenly saw that I have things to remember. Don't you see that, too?"

"If you mean, that we've got another life to remember, then truly, I do see it."

"Exactly that. And that's the key. Now all I have to do is find the lock it fits in. You've got your lock—those dreams you told me about." He laughed softly under his breath. "Don't you see, my love? There's a treasure laid up for us somewhere. I know it in my very soul."

The eagerness in his voice, the joy, really, seemed to crackle around them both like the warmth of a fire, but still she felt fear like a sliver of ice in her heart.

"It's not going to be easy," she said. "It's going to be dangerous, remembering."

"Oh, no doubt." Neb shrugged the warning away. "I wish to every god that Salamander would get himself back here," he went on. "I've got a few questions for him, and he cursed well better have the answers."

"I wager he will. Some of the things he told me were—well—" Branna paused, trying to think of some grand word, but her stomach growled as loud as speech.

Neb's answered. They looked at each other and burst out laughing.

"Get dressed, my love," Neb said. "Let's go down to the great hall. I'm hungry enough to eat a wolf, pelt and all."

When he left the Westlands, Prince Daralanteriel took with him his scribe, his warleader, his dweomermaster, fifty archers for a royal escort, packhorses laden with supplies, extra mounts, and of course Salamander. The prince planned on traveling fast, but he'd sent Maelaber ahead with two archers for an escort and the extra horses that allowed them to travel even faster. The royal retinue wasn't far from Cengarn when the returning messengers met up with them. They had important news: the gwerbret was holding his wedding celebration.

"When we told him you were on your way, Ridvar just assumed that you'd received his invitation," Maelaber said. "He sent a herald with an escort, but they must have missed us."

"I hope they're not still wandering around the grasslands," Prince Daralanteriel said. "What did you think of Cengarn, by the way?"

"It's a splendid sort of place from the outside, but I didn't think much of it once we got through the gates. Ye gods, the stink! Maybe my father's right about my mother's folk."

"Only when it comes to cleanliness," Daralanteriel tried to sound stern, but he was grinning. "Let's not judge others too harshly."

"It's a good thing you sent off messengers." Salamander joined the conversation. "If we'd come blundering in without even realizing that the gwerbret's getting married—"

"Yes, it would have been awkward, to say the least." Daralanteriel finished the thought for him. "Well, fortunately we've brought along the perfect horse for a wedding present, that gold gelding I've been training. I can decorate his halter with wildflowers, and he'll look festive enough."

"A splendid gift, yes. Better than our gwerbret deserves."

"I'd better tend my horse," Maelaber said.

"Do that," Dar said. "Because on the morrow I'm sending you back to the grass with messages and orders to find that herald and his escort. They can't be allowed to wander around out there until they starve."

The prince's retinue found a good place to camp that afternoon, a grassy meadow next to a shallow stream. In the middle of this clearing stood a stone stele that marked the border 'twixt the Westlands and Arcodd province. The pillar bore inscriptions in both Deverrian and Elvish, not that many people in those days could have read either one. To compensate, on the east-facing side the stonecutters had carved the blazing sun device of the gwerbrets of Cengarn, while on the west, a rose under an arch of seven stars indicated Dar's princedom.

At sunset Salamander went down to the stream to scry for Rocca. Dallandra came along, and together they knelt by the water, tinged a flickering gold as it caught the last of the sunlight. He was about to focus his mind on the distant fortress when he became aware of an odd sensation, a prickling of hair on his neck, a cold stripe down his spine. He sat back on his heels and let the sensation gather.

"What's wrong?" Dallandra said. "You look startled."

"I most definitely am that, and discomfited as well. Someone's scrying *me* out, I think. It's like the touch of a clammy hand. As soon as I thought of the fort, it stroked me."

Dallandra got up and stood behind him. He could hear her murmur a brief invocation. The sensation of being watched vanished.

"Gone now," he said. "My thanks."

"Most welcome." She sat down next to him. "I think you'd best scry for the fort later. Maybe we can catch this person off-guard."

"I've suddenly discovered a well of patience in my heart."

"Who, though? None of those people should have dweomer, from what you told me."

"Quite so. Any Horsekin who did would have been slaughtered long ago. I suppose someone who was determined, someone with a strong gift for it, could hide it, if— Sidro."

"Is Sidro the one who's Rocca's enemy?"

"The very. There was something suspicious about her, the way she guessed my mixed blood, and the way she was so sure that the wyvern dagger would work its little miracle."

"I wish there was some way I could get a look at this woman."

"Why? She's not a pleasant sight."

"What is she? A crone?"

"Well, no. It's not that she's ugly, but there was something about her that creeped my flesh. Her eyes, and the way she cocked her head at times—it made me think of a lizard or perhaps, if I wanted to be kind, which I don't, a bird of some sort."

"Didn't you say she had glossy black hair?"

"Yes. Very Eldidd-looking, with the bluish highlights and all."

"Like a raven's feathers?" Dallandra thought for a moment. "The lore says that if a person's been a shape-changer in a former life, they may resemble their animal form when they're reborn."

"By the Dark Sun herself! You told me about that other priestess—Raena, isn't it?"

"That was her name, all right."

"She's now known as the Holy Witness Raena. The dagger and those other trinkets in the shrine were supposedly hers."

"I knew that she'd gotten her claws on the wyvern dagger, but I didn't realize she had the bone whistle, too." Dallandra thought for a long moment. "Well, Sidro might be Raena reborn, though then again, maybe not. Curse it all, I won't be able to tell until I get a good look at—" Dalla stopped speaking and raised a shaking hand to her suddenly pale face.

Salamander rose to his knees and leaned toward her, ready to catch her if she should fall into trance, but she waved him away.

"I'm all right now," Dalla said. "I just felt a frost omen."

"So I thought. Omen of what?"

"Danger, of course." She paused to take a deep breath before she went on. "That kind of cold is always a warning of something ghastly."

"We should raise a dweomer shield over the camp, then."

"You're right, but I'll do the working by myself. I don't want you putting any more strain on your mind." Dalla paused to look at the sky. "It's twilight now, so the astral tides will settle down soon."

Salamander went back to the camp. He saw that the prince, his scribe, and the banadar were sitting in front of the prince's tent. Some of the other men were still eating, though most had gone out to the meadow to bring the tethered horses in closer to the tents. They were hobbling them as well, just in case one of the dragons should fly over. The mere scent of wyrm would panic any herd, to say naught of the sight of them.

For a moment or two Salamander stood uncertainly in front of the tent he was sharing with Meranaldar and some of the archers. He needed to talk with Calonderiel about a delicate matter, a difficult proposition in the best of times, even though the banadar's affair with Dallandra had sweetened his general outlook on life. He decided to take the coward's way out and wait for Dallandra to join them.

The sky, in the west still a pale bluish gray, was turning as soft as velvet in the last of the twilight. Slowly it darkened; a scatter of stars came out on the eastern horizon, while to the west the last gold of sunset faded. Down on the earth, out beyond the horse herd, a flash of blue fire leaped up from the ground. It hovered in the air, then spread out, racing around the camp deosil to form a wall of blue flames. They grew taller, stronger, raced upward until they met at a center point high above the camp. At the cardinal points glowing gold sigils sprang into existence, the seals of the Elemental Kings, and another appeared directly above at the center point, the sigil of Aethyr. Dallandra had finished the astral shield.

Salamander realized that he'd opened his etheric sight without consciously choosing to do so, a very bad sign of that strain Dallandra had mentioned. He closed it down, then strolled over to meet her as she came back to camp. She strode along so purposefully that he could still see the gleaming sword of astral light in her warrior's hand, but when she smiled at him, that small illusion vanished.

"Let's sit down," she said. "I'm tired."

They joined the others in front of the prince's tent. Salamander sat down next to Meranaldar, while Dallandra took her place next to Calonderiel. For a brief while they all discussed the road ahead, but eventually Salamander steeled his nerve and caught Cal's attention.

"I've a favor to ask you, banadar," Salamander said. "When we lay our news before the gwerbret, I don't want you to mention Lord Honelg. The gwerbret and the priests between them will slaughter him and his men, and maybe even his womenfolk, for all I know."

"So?" Cal said. "That's what he deserves. He'd slaughter the lot of us if he could, wouldn't he?" He paused to spit into the small campfire. "Vandar's spawn!"

"That's true." Dallandra intervened, laying a hand on Cal's arm. "But if we betray him to the priests, won't his kin spread the word? Then the faithful will hate Vandar's spawn even more."

"Maybe," Cal said. "But I don't see how anyone could hate us more than they already do."

"Well, you might be right, but it would be good to have the chance to show them how wrong they are."

"You've got the best heart in the world." Cal sighed in mock admiration. "Unfortunately, they don't match you in that regard."

"Well, surely," Meranaldar joined in, "this sort of decision should be the prince's."

Cal turned his head and looked at the scribe—merely looked with eyes as cold and clear as ice on a winter stream. Meranaldar flinched.

"The banadar's quite capable of handling this matter on his own," Daralanteriel said. "As the old saying goes, too many fletchers crumple the feathers."

"Thank you, Dar." Cal turned to Salamander. "And what are you going to tell the gwerbret when he asks how you found the fortress? You just happened to meet a priestess on the road—that's not going to sound very convincing."

"Well, um, you're right." Salamander pulled a long face. "But I'll think of something."

"One of your lies, you mean."

"Honelg fed me at his table and treated me as an honored guest. I can't betray him."

"Yes, you can." Calonderiel crossed his arms over his chest and glared at him. "I respect the law of hospitality as much as anyone in the Westlands, but this is no ordinary time. Hasn't it occurred to you that our survival's at stake here?"

"Of course it has, but—"

"There isn't any 'but' about it. I know you're half a Roundear, but think, you chattering dimwit!"

Salamander flushed scarlet and laid a hand on his dagger's hilt. Dallandra rose to her knees.

"Enough!" she barked. "Cal, that Roundear remark was quite uncalled for! Tact has never been one of your gifts, has it?"

"Tact? What good is tact?" Calonderiel said. "I've tried that on people, and they still don't do what I want."

Prince Dar burst out laughing, and in a moment Salamander joined him, simply because the remark was so true to the banadar's nature. Calonderiel scowled impartially back and forth between them. Dallandra sat back down; she seemed to be suppressing a grin.

"By the Dark Sun herself," Salamander said when he'd caught his breath, "you are a marvel, banadar."

"I suppose I deserved that," Cal said with some asperity. "But listen. You've already betrayed Honelg, haven't you? You sat there at his table in his great hall and let the lies fall as thick as flakes of winter snow. So why are you having scruples now?"

Salamander's leftover laughter died. He opened his mouth for a retort, then realized that he had none. *It's not Honelg, it's Rocca,* he told himself. *She's the one you're trying to protect, but she won't be in his dun when the army arrives.*

"You're right, aren't you?" Salamander said. "I shall tell the gwerbret everything."

"Besides—" Cal stopped in midsentence. "Oh. You're agreeing with me."

"Yes, O Banadar Most Puissant. No more diatribes needed."

That night Salamander dreamed that Sidro was stalking him with the silver dagger in one hand and the obsidian pyramid in the other. He woke to a sense of profound relief that the dream had been only that. In the tent the other men were still asleep, and he gathered his clothes and boots and went outside to dress to avoid waking them. Dawn was just silvering the eastern sky. When he glanced around, he saw Dallandra, kneeling beside the stream and gazing into the water. He walked over and joined her.

"Scrying?" he said.

"Yes, actually." Dallandra sat back on her heels and turned to look at him. "I felt a presence last night, sniffing around the astral dome."

"Ah. I wondered about that. I did dream of dear little Sidro, but I suspect it was but an ordinary dream, dancing to the harp of a troubled heart."

"I hope you're right. Although—" She frowned down at the water again. "If it wasn't her, who was it?"

"That's an unpleasant question, but, alas, also pertinent, fitting, and germane."

"I have the awful feeling that we're going to find out soon enough."

"And we won't like the answer?"

"I'd bet high on it. Oh, well, let's go get some breakfast. I don't see any reason to renew the seals now. The tides are still turbulent, and we'll be leaving soon anyway."

It was just past noon when the prince's party came to Cengarn's river. Through the trees shading the banks, Salamander saw white stones out in shallow water to mark the ford. Dallandra urged her horse up beside Salamander's.

"This is where Jill died." Dalla pointed at the ford. "The river ran much deeper that year. There'd been more rain, I suppose. At any rate, the etheric veil destroyed her body of light—and Alshandra's, too, of course."

"I see." Salamander felt his throat tighten. He wiped away a scatter of tears on his shirt sleeve. "My apologies. Hearing the story always grieves me."

"Me, too, but I'm looking forward to meeting Branna. She won't be the same, of course, and I wonder if she'll remember me."

"Eventually she will."

"Yes, that's true. We became so close, working dweomer together, trying to save Cengarn. I suppose in a way we were like a couple of soldiers in a war. When she died—" Dallandra's voice faltered. "Well, it was hard on all of us there at the time."

With the prince in the lead, the Westfolk horses splashed across the ford. Once they were free of the trees on the far bank, Salamander could see the familiar cliffs of Cengarn, looming far above them. The meadow below the south gate held a surprise, however—a large canvas pavilion stood on the grass, and some thirty horses grazed at tether. Deverry men were standing or sitting on the grass near the pavilion. The prince called for the halt and rose in his stirrups to survey the situation. Dallandra shuddered; her face had gone a little pale.

"What's wrong?" Salamander said.

"Sorry." Dalla managed to smile. "I was just remembering the siege. The Horsekin had tents set up all around here."

"This one doubtless springs from an overflow of wedding guests," Salamander said. "A happier occasion all round."

"One should hope it's happier!" Daralanteriel reined his horse up next to Dallandra's. "Now, I wonder. Should we just set our tents up out here rather than dragging everything up to the dun?"

"I don't know." Dalla sounded doubtful. "I'm always so afraid of slighting the Deverry lords. They care so much about honor and courtesy. Maybe we should wait to be told."

With a shout of greeting, Gerran came striding over, his russet hair gleaming in the sunlight. He touched the prince's stirrup to acknowledge Dar's rank, then turned to Salamander.

"It gladdens my heart to see you alive," Gerran said. "We were beginning to wonder what had happened to you."

"A great many things, few of them good," Salamander said, grinning. "It's a very long tale, and I'd best not launch into it now."

"Fair enough."

"Let me introduce you," Salamander went on. "My prince, Daralanteriel, our banadar, Calonderiel, and our dweo—I mean, councillor Dallandra, this is Gerran, captain of Tieryn Cadryc's warband, otherwise known as the Falcon."

Gerran bowed to each as they were named. At Gerran's nickname, Calonderiel's eyebrows arched in surprise. The others acknowledged the captain with polite murmurs.

Gerran turned back to the prince. "Your Highness, the gwerbret's servitors were wondering if you'd prefer to set up your tents out here rather than in the dun. Me and my men would be honored to have you and yours among us. We could guard your horses along with our own, too."

"I would, and my thanks," Daralanteriel said. "Well, Dalla, there's our answer. We'll leave most of the men here to set up camp."

"And me and my men will be glad to help you," Gerran said.

Calonderiel urged his horse forward. "I'll stay behind for now to work things out with the captain here." He nodded to Gerran, then paused with that oddly surprised expression returning to his face. Gerran looked just as startled by something, or so it seemed to Salamander. "We've met before, haven't we, Captain?" Cal said at last.

"Not that I remember." But Gerran sounded profoundly uncertain. "Have you ridden our way before, sir?"

"Not to the Red Wolf dun, but I've visited Cengarn several times."

"Ah." Gerran smiled in sudden understanding. "My foster brother and I were pages here."

"That explains it, then."

Salamander glanced Dallandra's way and found her suppressing a smile. He was willing to wager high that Gerran was remembering Calonderiel from his previous life and not from his childhood at all.

"My thanks, Captain, for your offer of aid," Dalla said. "My prince, we'd best get up to the dun. Let's not forget the gwerbret's wedding present. And remember, everybody—speak Deverrian from now on."

When Daralanteriel led his much-reduced retinue into Cengarn's ward, servants ran to meet the man they knew as the Prince of the Westfolk, and pages raced off into the great hall to announce his arrival. Trailed by councillors and servants, Gwerbret Ridvar himself came out to greet the prince just as he and his escort were dismounting. Ridvar seemed to have grown an inch or so since Salamander had last seen him, or perhaps he merely seemed taller with newfound confidence; in new linen shirt with his clan's device at the yokes, with his dark hair bound round with a fillet of gold, he looked splendid, a true nobleman, as he strode over to bow to the prince.

"Welcome, Your Highness," Ridvar said, "to my humble dun."

"My thanks, Your Grace, though humble's not a word I'd use of Dun Cengarn." Smiling, Daralanteriel turned and gestured at the archer who was leading the golden gelding. "I've brought you a small token to congratulate you upon your wedding. I only wish it could be finer."

"Oh, he's glorious!" Ridvar forgot courtesy and rank both. He strode over to the gelding, who tossed his head in a ripple of silvery mane as if to greet him. "My thanks! A thousand thanks!"

Salamander glanced at Dallandra, mouthed a few words, then stepped into the crowd gathering around the elven party and slipped away. He was looking for Branna and Neb, but when he saw Lord Oth standing alone in the doorway of a side building, he hurried over.

"And a good morrow to you, gerthddyn," Oth said. "I don't suppose you have any news for me."

"About the Horsekin, my lord? I'm afraid I do, and it's the worst news in the world. I found the fortress they're building off to the west."

Oth swore under his breath.

"Indeed," Salamander went on. "I need your advice. When should I broach the topic? I don't want to spoil the festivities, you see, and—"

"The festivities may have to wait," Oth interrupted with a curt wave of his hand. "Do you have proof?"

"I do indeed, my lord. A plate with Horsekin writing, a bit of building stone, and an odd little packet of tokens dedicated to the false goddess Alshandra." Salamander pointed at Daralanteriel and the rest of the elven party. "The prince found it convincing."

"Good. I happen to believe you myself, mind. The gwerbret may or may not, but he knows that Daralanteriel and your cadvridoc would never lie to him." Oth paused, chewing on the ends of his mustaches. "How to break the news, I wonder . . . well, this will require some thought."

"I truly hate to spoil the wedding. His poor betrothed!"

"Huh! She's marrying Ridvar out of duty to her clan. I doubt if her happiness is at stake. Besides, she's the daughter of a gwerbret, and she understands the ways of these things." Again Oth paused, thinking. "Here, say naught until I bring you forward, but soonest will be best."

Eventually the gwerbret allowed a groom to lead his new horse away. Unfortunately, several lads, Clae among them, had just started to lead other horses out of the stables, and for a few moments men, Westfolk, mounts, and servants all milled around in a hopeless mob. Finally Ridvar took charge and began yelling orders. A path cleared between the guests and the great hall. Salamander caught Dallandra's attention and waved her over.

"Lord Oth says we should wait with our news till he summons us," Salamander said. "Could you tell the prince?"

"Certainly," Dalla said. "I'd like to meet Neb and Branna as soon as possible, remember."

"Of course. I'm just off to look for them."

Branna was sitting at a table in the great hall with Galla and Lady Solla when she saw Salamander, standing just inside the door, peering this way and that at the assembled guests. As well as the guests and the members of their various escorts, the great hall swarmed with servants, hurrying this way and that as they cleared the remnants of the noon meal away. Branna shoved back her chair and stood, waving to attract Salamander's attention. At last he saw her and hurried over, dodging around a manservant who was carrying an armload of table linens for the table of honor, the only table that had been graced with cloths.

"There you are!" Salamander said. "Good morrow, fair ladies." He bowed to Solla and Galla, then made an extravagant parody of a bow to Branna.

"And a good morrow to you, too, gerthddyn," Branna said. "It gladdens my heart to see you again."

"And mine to see you. Is Neb here somewhere?"

"My betrothed?" Branna said. "He just went up to *our* chamber for a moment."

"Well, my congratulations!" Salamander glanced at Galla. "I take it you approve of the marriage."

"Very much so," Galla said, "and more to the point, so did her father. Well, with you here, we shall have some pleasant tales of an evening, I hope."

"As pleasant as I can make them, my lady, though alas, alack, and welladay, I bring some very bad news."

"About the Horsekin?" Branna said.

Solla caught her breath with a little gasp. Two serving lasses who were walking past stopped, stepping forward as if to see if she needed their help, but she waved them on.

"Just that." Salamander's smile disappeared. "And about a certain noble lord who appears to be caught up in treacherous doings."

Behind him the manservant with the table linens paused in his work to listen. *You can hardly blame him for being curious,* Branna thought. Still, she caught Salamander's glance and made a slight movement of one hand to signal that someone was behind him. The manservant hurried off.

"But I fear me this isn't the place or the time to say more." Salamander picked up her hint. "I've consulted with Lord Oth."

"Splendid!" Galla said. "I suggest you follow his lead in this."

"Indeed," Solla put in. "He's the only person my brother will listen to."

"Then I shall put my trust in him, my ladies. Ah—here comes our Neb now." Salamander was looking past Branna. "Neb! Well met, indeed! Congratulations on your betrothal!"

On a tide of chatter Salamander swept Neb and Branna up and floated them away from the ladies at the table. The rest of the Westfolk were just coming in the door, escorted by the gwerbret himself. Branna, Neb, and Salamander stepped back out of the way and let the royal party pass on to the gwerbret's own table, where Prince Voran sat waiting to receive his equal in rank. Prince Daralanteriel looked much more like a prince should, Branna decided—amazingly handsome, easily the most beautiful man she'd ever seen, despite his long ears and strange violet eyes. *He looks familiar.* The thought came to her like a blast of winter wind, chilling her blood. *I know him.*

Lord Oth trailed behind the gwerbret; he gave Salamander a brief but pointed wave as they passed. Behind him walked an elven woman with long ash-blonde hair and gray eyes. When Salamander gestured her way, she left the gwerbret's little group and came over to join them.

"Excellent," Salamander said. "Branna, Neb, this is Dallandra, one of the prince's most trusted servitors."

Dallandra smiled pleasantly and murmured a "good morrow," but Branna felt that the elven woman's gray eyes were like a pair of daggers, cutting into her soul. *Servitor?* Branna thought. *I'd wager she serves him with dweomer.* Aloud, she said, "It gladdens my heart to meet you."

"My thanks, Lady Branna," Dallandra said. "And a good morrow to you, Goodman Neb."

Neb smiled and nodded to acknowledge the greeting. It was all perfectly ordinary, perfectly courteous, but Branna suddenly felt as if words were burning in her mouth, demanding to be spat out.

"Dallandra, I know you, don't I?" Branna said. "Or I should say, I did know you when—well, once. I mean, before."

"Ye gods!" Dallandra took a step back in sheer surprise. "You did, indeed."

"And you." Branna turned to Salamander. "I just didn't recognize you at first."

For a moment Salamander couldn't speak—*a rare enough thing on its own,* Branna thought. *Chattering elf? Of course, he's a half-breed!* She could also remember having been furious with him, so many long years before, though the reason why had vanished from her mind. Finally he cleared his throat, then glanced nervously at the crowd around them.

"I think we need to talk about such things at a greater length," Salamander said. "And where it's quieter, too."

"True spoken," Neb said. "The only private place I can think of is our chamber. It's a bit short on chairs, unfortunately."

To Branna, Neb's voice seemed to ring with new authority. *He remembers too,* she thought. *What's happening to us?* She felt as if she stood in some high place just before a storm, when the lightning gleams at a far distance, and the air crackles with alien energy, tempting and dangerous together. *I could learn to take that power for my own,* Branna thought. *And so could Neb.*

"The chamber will do," Dallandra said briskly. "I can barely hear myself think with all these people in here, anyway. I—Wait. Is that Lord Oth now? That gray-haired fellow on his way here."

It was indeed Oth, who hurried over to Salamander and laid a hand on his shoulder. "The gwerbret will grant you an audience right now," the chamberlain said. "And Prince Voran is also much interested in your news. I've sent a servant to ask Prince Dar-alanteriel to join us."

"Splendid!" Salamander said. "You'll forgive me, Lady Branna?"

"Of course."

"I have to go fetch my evidence." Salamander turned to Oth. "Shall I bring Prince Dar's cadvridoc back with me?"

"Please do. I wanted to include all of our border lords. They all have a stake in this, needless to say, but his grace refused. He wants a private hearing first, but of course, he can't say the princes nay."

Without another word Oth and Salamander hurried off. Dallandra watched Salamander until he left the great hall at a run, then turned back to Branna.

"We can talk later," Dallandra said. "I think we'd best stay here for the nonce."

"True-spoken," Neb said. "He's found that fort, hasn't he?"

"I'm afraid he has."

"Which means there's going to be a war."

"I don't see how we can avoid it." Dallandra turned, glancing around at the various tables. A good many people were staring at her.

Neb seemed to have noticed the onlookers. "Let's join Galla and Solla," he said. "I fear me I'm being rude to them."

"By all means," Branna said. "My apologies, Dallandra! You must be tired from your journey. I'm forgetting all my courtesy."

She paused for a smile. "Come have somewhat to drink and refresh yourself."

As they walked back to the table, Branna was thinking how glad she was that Neb was a scribe and not a fighting man. *I'm so glad I chose him over Gerran,* she thought. *But then, I did the choosing a very long time ago.*

Salamander had needed to hold the attention of many audiences in his life, but none quite so important as the group that assembled in Ridvar's chamber of justice for want of privacy in the great hall. Sunlight streamed into the room in long shafts from the arrow-slits of windows, leaving the rest of the half-circle of a room in shadows. Two menservants carried in chairs, then bowed to the gwerbret.

"Nothing more," Ridvar said. "Wait—one of you, stand outside the door and make sure that no one disturbs us."

"I will, Your Grace," a brown-haired fellow said.

The servants bowed themselves out and shut the heavy door firmly behind them. Gwerbret Ridvar took his usual carved chair behind a solid oak table. Behind him a banner of Cengarn hung from a ceiling beam; its cloth-of-gold sun sparkled in a shaft of real sunlight. Lord Blethry hurried forward and placed a chair at the gwerbret's left hand for Prince Voran; Prince Daralanteriel took the one to his right. Meranaldar and Neb sat on the floor nearby, each with a set of waxed tablets in his lap and a stylus at the ready for notes. Calonderiel, Oth, and Blethry leaned against the wall. Clutching his small sack of evidence, Salamander stood before the gwerbret and the princes.

"Very well, gerthddyn," Ridvar said. "Tell us your tale."

"I shall be honored to do so, Your Grace," Salamander said, "and in some detail, because the matter's truly grave. The Horsekin are building a dun off to the west of your lands, and it's going to be huge."

For a moment no one moved or spoke. Even though noises filtered in from the corridor outside—laughter as guests went by, the chatter of servants—the chamber seemed suddenly isolated, as if it

existed in a different world than the rest of the dun. Then Prince
Voran swore under his breath, and Ridvar nodded his way. "Indeed," Ridvar said. "Go on, gerthddyn. I take it you've brought us
proof."

"I have, Your Grace." Salamander reached into the sack and
pulled out the metal plate. "Note the writing on the rim, if you'd be
so kind." He set the plate down on the table in front of Ridvar and
pulled out the chunk of worked stone. "This came from the fortress
as well. You'll notice how different it is from the building stone
quarried around here."

Ridvar picked up the plate, glanced at it, then passed it to Voran.
In his sack Salamander still had the arrow token Rocca had given
him, but as he watched the lords passing round the plate and stone,
cursing softly at them, he felt suddenly reluctant to bring the token
out. He was already betraying Rocca; he hated the thought of defil-
ing her little parable of the holy arrows as well. Fortunately, the
noble-born found the plate and stone proof enough. When the
plate returned to him, Ridvar held it up.

"Horsekin work, no doubt about that." Ridvar set the plate
down again. "How did you find this dun?"

"By a bit of luck, Your Grace," Salamander said. "The gods must
favor you highly, because I found a traitor among your vassals as
well."

"Honelg!" Lord Blethry snapped out the name, then covered
embarrassment with a cough. "Well, er, I mean—"

"I see you've had your suspicions, my lord." Salamander allowed
himself a wry smile. "And you were quite right. Allow me to tell
you how I found him and the dun both."

Salamander had put some thought into the telling of his story.
He managed to touch the important points quickly while barely
mentioning Rocca at all. She became only "the priestess I followed to the fortress." The noble-born had little interest in
priestesses, anyway; they wanted to hear military details—the
fort's size and distance, an estimate of how big the garrison there
would be, how it might be provisioned, and the like. Since Sala-

mander could supply plenty of hard information, he also managed to gloss over his means of escape and the journey back to the Westfolk camp.

"Very well," the gwerbret said at last. "We're going to have to move quickly, before they turn more of their wooden walls into stone ones."

"Just so, and, worst thing of all, it's in a very defensible position, Your Grace," Salamander said. "It's on top of a cliff, overlooking a river gorge."

"On top of a cliff?" Ridvar paused for a grin. "We just happen to have an alliance with some people who can bring it right down again."

"But, Your Grace, do you truly think they'll join us?" Lord Oth said. "The Mountain Folk keep to themselves."

Calonderiel laughed, just a cold mutter under his breath, but everyone in the council turned to look at him.

"It's been forty years or so since this happened," Calonderiel said, "but a party of Horsekin once attacked some farming settlements that belonged to the Mountain Folk. They killed every man there, and in one of the most gruesome ways I've ever heard of. Forty years, good councillor, but I'd wager my bow and quiver that they still remember the names of every single dead man."

Salamander felt as if a cold wind had swept through the council along with the banadar's words. He shuddered beyond his control, but young Ridvar laughed as coldly as Calonderiel.

"You'd win that wager easily," the gwerbret said. "Very well." He gestured at Lord Blethry. "My Lord Equerry, get messengers on their way to Lin Serr. Better yet, go with them. We don't want the Mountain Folk to feel slighted because I've sent only common-born riders."

"Just so, Your Grace," Blethry said. "I'll do so gladly."

"And give my regards to your kin on your way there." Ridvar smiled, as if he'd just realized he'd been brusque with his servitor. "As for my vassals," he turned serious again, "we'll wait till we've heard from Dun Deverry to begin the muster."

"You can count on my archers, Your Grace," Calonderiel said. "I can easily raise five hundred of them."

"And swordsmen," Prince Daralanteriel put in. "Fewer of those, but all good men."

"You have my sincere thanks, Your Highness, and so do you, banadar," Ridvar said. "I also have hopes that my new wife's father will aid us."

"No doubt he will," Prince Voran said. "Ultimately this matter concerns every lord in the western provinces. I'll send messengers off to our king tomorrow. They have a fair bit farther to travel than yours will, so they'd best leave straightaway. I think I may safely say that his highness will lend his support. And of course, my men and I will accompany you when you ride west."

"That's most generous, my prince," Ridvar said, but his voice turned tense. "My humble thanks."

"More than generous, Your Grace," Oth broke in, "princely, indeed!" He turned toward Voran. "You have our deepest thanks, Your Highness."

Voran nodded and smiled with a wry twist of his mouth, as if he knew perfectly well how much Ridvar resented the offer. *He probably does know,* Salamander thought. *He doesn't miss much, I'll wager, froggy grin or not.*

Calonderiel stepped forward to rejoin the conversation. "I suggest that we deal with Honelg immediately. He's like a dagger aimed at your back."

Ridvar considered him but said nothing. Blethry cleared his throat. "I think he's right, Your Grace," the equerry said, "for what that's worth."

"I'll consider it," Ridvar said. "The man is my vassal." He put just a touch of stress on the "my." "If I remember Honelg's dun properly, we might need the Mountain Folk's help to breach his walls."

Calonderiel glanced at Salamander and gave him an encouraging nod.

"It's well fortified, all right," Salamander said. "The banadar has a point, Your Grace, because Honelg has a great many points on his side—iron ones, attached to arrows."

"And—" Cal hesitated, glancing at Daralanteriel, who shook his head ever so slightly. "As my lords decide, then."

"You have my thanks, banadar," Ridvar said. "As you do, too, gerthddyn. You risked your life to bring us the truth. I thank you from the bottom of my heart."

The gwerbret's thanks were apparently the only reward he considered Salamander deserved, but Councillor Oth thought otherwise. When Ridvar gave Salamander leave to go, Oth followed him out and pressed a small sack of coins into his hand.

"A token of our gratitude," Oth said, "and good silver, too. Please forgive my lord, gerthddyn. I fear me that he so hates being proved wrong that he's forgotten all his generosity."

"My thanks to you," Salamander said with a little bow. "As for your lord, it's a hard thing to rule men twice your age and more. I can understand his stubbornness."

"Good." Oth paused, his eyes suddenly wide. "Oh, ye gods! I just remembered—a few days ago Cadryc sent messengers off to Honelg's dun. I hope to every god that he hasn't had them killed."

"Would Honelg be that dishonorable?"

"I have no idea. Who knows what a madman will do?"

"True spoken, alas." Salamander was remembering Honelg standing between his gates, sword at the ready to cut him down if need be. "But, equally truly, he has no reason to kill them. Not yet, anyway. Although I just had an ugly thought. There must be other Alshandra worshippers in Cengarn. Do you think we should keep our news about Honelg quiet?"

"Ugly it may be, but a good thought nonetheless. It would doubtless be for the best. I'll speak to the gwerbret about it the first chance I get."

Despite Oth's fears, the Red Wolf messengers returned that very afternoon, some hours before the evening meal. The noble-born guests and as many of their captains and men who could crowd into the great hall had taken their places at the tables early, partly to honor the gwerbret's new wife but mostly to get a good start on the drinking to come. Salamander had talked himself into a seat at Tieryn Cadryc's table, where he had a good view of the gwerbret and the princes, seated together at the table of honor along with Lady Drwmigga, Calonderiel, and Dallandra, who had condescended to put on a blue linen dress—one of Branna's, judging from the fancy embroidered spirals down the sleeves.

Serving lasses were rushing around, filling tankards with ale and goblets with mead, when two dusty, road-stained men, one tall and beefy, the other skinny and short, appeared in the doorway. They stood hesitating, afraid to come forward, until Branna pointed them out to Tieryn Cadryc. He stood up and waved until he'd caught their attention.

"Oh, good!" Lady Galla said to Salamander. "Warryc and Daumyr have come back."

The messengers worked their way through the crowd and knelt in front of Cadryc. When Daumyr handed the tieryn a silver message tube, Neb shoved his chair back, ready to answer the tieryn's summons to read it.

"What?" Cadryc was examining the lump of wax at the end of the tube. "This is my seal."

"It is, Your Grace," Warryc said. "We couldn't deliver the letter to Lord Honelg. We only saw him from a distance, like. We got to his village, and everything seemed well and good there, but when we got to the dun, we found the gates shut against us."

"And?" Cadryc's voice went tense.

"Lord Honelg was up on the catwalk, Your Grace. So he leans over and shouts down that there's fever in his dun, a bad lot of it, and that we'd best get ourselves away before we catch it too."

Galla caught her breath with a gasp.

"My lady?" Daumyr said. "I'd not trouble your heart over it too badly. Honelg looked as fit as fit, and when we rode back to the village, we asked them why they'd not warned us about the fever."

"They hemmed and hawed," Warryc took over again. "But all they could say was that no one had told them. Could Honelg's people be that ill and no word get out? Wouldn't his servants all come from that village? I don't believe in that fever, Your Grace."

"And no more do I," Cadryc said. "You've done well, lads. Go get yourselves somewhat to eat and drink."

The two riders scrambled up, bowed, and trotted away to follow their lord's welcome order. When Salamander caught Neb's attention, the scribe merely shrugged to show puzzlement and slid his chair back into place. Galla turned to Cadryc and laid a hand on his arm.

"What is all this?" she said. "Why would Honelg lie?"

"I don't have the slightest idea, my love." Cadryc paused, frowning in thought. "I begin to think you were right about that marriage."

"Oh, do you?" Galla snapped. "It's a bit late now to see reason."

Salamander suddenly remembered Honelg's lady and the way she'd looked mysteriously familiar. *Oh, ye gods,* Salamander thought. *Adranna's their daughter!*

Apparently Gwerbret Ridvar had noticed the messengers' arrival and heard what they'd had to say. He stood up and strode over, with Oth following after. When they reached the table, Salamander heard Oth say, "but, Your Grace, not here!" Ridvar ignored him.

"My lady," Ridvar said. "I'm afraid I have some evil news for you."

The talk and chatter at the tables nearby suddenly died. Salamander could hear the various noble lords shushing their neighbors.

"Indeed, Your Grace?" Galla said.

"Indeed. I received word today that Lord Honelg has turned traitor."

Galla stared at him, her mouth slack with surprise. The shushing and resulting silence spread across the great hall. Everyone that Salamander could see was leaning toward the gwerbret and straining to hear.

"Your Grace!" Lord Oth kept his voice low. "I thought we'd agreed that silence—"

"You thought it best. I never agreed." Ridvar turned his head and favored Oth with a cold stare that made the councillor step back a pace. The movement, however, seemed to make Ridvar realize how insulting he'd just been. "And how can I call a council of war," Ridvar said, "without telling my lords the cause and occasion for it?" All at once he smiled. "Do you truly think we could have kept it secret in the middle of this mob?"

Oth relaxed and laughed, one sharp bark. "True spoken, Your Grace," he said. "There are servants swarming everywhere."

True spoken indeed, Salamander thought, *and I think me our Ridvar just might turn out well after all.*

"Um, Your Grace?" Cadryc sounded ready to burst from frustration. "Kept what secret? What has Honelg—"

"In a moment, my lord." Ridvar turned back to Lady Galla. "Don't distress yourself. No one will blame your daughter for the follies of her lord."

The eavesdroppers' silence reached the warbands. Those men who'd been drinking slammed stoups and tankards down on their tables and swiveled round on benches and chairs. For a long moment it seemed that no one even breathed. The gwerbret turned toward the crowd.

"Hear this!" Ridvar called out. "I declare Lord Honelg a traitor. He's a secret worshiper of the false goddess Alshandra, and he's cast in his lot with the Horsekin." Ridvar's voice shook with rage. "I'll have his head on a pike for this."

The crowd cheered, but briefly. The whispering started, a little flood of rage and fear spreading through the great hall.

"Gerthddyn!" Ridvar said. "Do you have any idea of why Honelg would turn to this false goddess?"

"I don't, Your Grace. I'm utterly baffled by it. Although—" Salamander found himself remembering the red-haired lass, swarmed by hungry children. "Although I can see why the farm folk up there would turn to a new goddess. The priests of Bel, the ones who rule that demesne near Honelg's? I've never seen such a greedy lot, half-starving their villagers the way they do."

"Indeed?" Ridvar said. "Well, since we'll be riding that way, I'll look into that as well. Calonderiel was right. We'd best deal with Honelg first." He turned back to the crowd and raised his voice. "My lords, I'm calling a council of war. We shall meet at sundown."

Galla shrieked, just once, then clamped her hand over her mouth as if to stifle another. She got up so fast that her chair went over with a clatter. She started to speak, then choked it back, turned, and ran for the staircase.

"My apologies, Tieryn Cadryc," Ridvar said. "I fear me I did a wretchedly bad job of telling your lady the tidings. By the by, the gerthddyn did find that Horsekin fort."

"Ye gods," Cadryc said. "Worse and worse."

"Your Grace?" Councillor Oth came forward and whispered a few words.

Ridvar wrinkled his nose at him, a sour gesture that reminded Salamander that despite his promise for the future, he was still a lad now. In a moment, though, he regained his dignity. "In fact, Tieryn Cadryc," Ridvar said, "I owe you an apology. I should have listened when you first came forward with your suspicions."

"None needed, Your Grace." Cadryc sounded exhausted. "I see no need to ever mention it again, eh?"

"Done, then." Ridvar favored him with a gracious nod. "And you have my thanks."

As soon as she heard Lady Galla scream, Branna leaped up from her seat, then followed her fleeing aunt up the winding staircase. She caught up with her in the corridor at the top, where Galla was leaning against the wall and shaking like the victim of a fever.

"Goddess help!" Branna said. "This is truly loathsome."

"It is that." Galla's voice shook as well. "My poor lass! The children!"

"The gwerbret's said he'll absolve her."

"If she lives through the siege. There's Honelg's poor mother, too. She's so frail."

"True-spoken. He might have thought of them before he went consorting with false gods."

Galla started to reply, then burst out sobbing. Branna threw her arms around her aunt and let her weep against her shoulder.

"Here, here," she murmured, "let's go to your chamber, away from all the noise and suchlike."

Galla allowed herself to be led to the chamber. She perched upon the edge of the bed while she tried to wipe her eyes with a sodden handkerchief. Branna poured some water from the jug on the little table into a cup and had her aunt drink a few sips. Galla stared fixedly at the far wall for some while, then handed the cup back to Branna.

"Well, there's naught left for us but to pray to the true goddess, is there?" Galla paused again, then breathed deeply and allowed herself a sigh. "And alas, I don't know what we're going to do now for your wedding. I'd wanted to give you a splendid feast, but the men will need the provisions for the war."

"My dearest aunt, don't vex yourself! We don't need to talk about that now."

"You may not, but I need to talk about somewhat besides our Adranna."

"Very well, then. I truly don't care about the ceremonies of the thing. I've got Neb, and that's all I wanted."

"How generous you are, dear! Unlike some menfolk we know." Galla looked at her soggy handkerchief and threw it viciously to the floor. "I think there might be a clean one of these in that wooden chest by the window."

Branna had just fetched the handkerchief when someone knocked on the door, and she heard Lady Solla's soft voice calling Galla's name. Branna hurried over and opened the door to find Solla and Dallandra, still in her borrowed dress, standing just behind her.

"How does our lady fare?" Solla said.

"Reasonably well, dear," Galla called out. "Do come in, and, how lovely, our guest is with you."

"I was worried," Dallandra said. "This whole thing is utterly ghastly."

Branna ushered them inside. Two chairs stood in the curve of the wall; she moved them near Galla. She herself sat on the broad stone windowsill. With Dallandra there, Branna's worst fears lifted, leaving her feeling like a nearly-lost child who at last sees her mother hurrying toward her in the crowded marketplace. Although she had no conscious memories of Dalla's dweomer, she knew that she was in the presence of a woman of great power.

"The men are having their council of war," Solla said. "My brother's taken all of his lords up to the chamber of justice, and most of the women have gone off to the women's hall with Drwmigga. I decided I didn't feel like sitting there. It's such a hot day, so airless."

"It is that," Galla said. "But it must be hard for you, too, being turned out of the hall that was yours until a few days ago."

"There's somewhat of that in it," Solla said with a rueful little smile. "Most of my things are packed, by the way, so I can leave with you when the time comes. Drwmigga has graciously offered me the loan of a horse cart to take them."

"Very gracious, indeed." Branna put venom into her voice. "No doubt she wants to be the only cow in the pasture. You can practically hear her moo in triumph."

"Branna! How awful of you!" But Solla smiled with a wicked light in her eyes. "Your Neb is sitting in at the council of war. He told me to tell you that he'll give us a report as soon as he can."

"Excellent," Galla said. "But I know what our menfolk are like. It's going to be a long evening, once they start. Branna, dear, I brought a set of wooden wisdom. Perhaps someone would like to have a game or two."

"I certainly would," Solla said, "and I'll send a page for some Bardek wine. We can have our dinner up here, too, if you'd like that."

As Branna got up to fetch the game box, she glanced Dallandra's way. The elven woman was smiling pleasantly, but her eyes seemed to be looking at some view a thousand miles away. All at once Branna felt the hair on the back of her neck rise. *She's scrying for danger,* Branna thought. *There's someone out there who wishes us harm.* Although she couldn't say how or why, she knew it as surely as she knew that fish have scales.

"The thing is," Salamander said, "Honelg's dun is going to be wretchedly hard to take. A handful of archers on the walls could hold off an army."

"Assuming they have enough arrows," Calonderiel said.

"He's a fearful man, Honelg, and for good reason. I suspect he has arrows by the bushel stowed here and there about the dun."

Calonderiel swore under his breath in a mix of Deverrian and Elvish. They were walking downhill through Cengarn. All around them the town lay asleep and dark except for the occasional line of candlelight from a shuttered window. Overhead, the drift of stars supplied just enough of a glow for their elven eyesight to find the way. Now and then a dog would bark as they passed. Otherwise silence wrapped the town.

When they reached the city wall, they found the main gates closed, but a yawning guard greeted them and held his lantern high to peer at their faces.

"You must be part of the Westfolk warband," he said.

"We are indeed," Calonderiel said. "Can you let us out?"

"I can. The gwerbret sent orders down to open the side gate for you whenever you wanted. Come round here."

Holding the lantern high, he took them past the little guard house to an oak plank door in the wall. It was bolted twice and barred as well. This side gate proved to be a mere slit between the stones.

"We're the last," Salamander said. "So you won't be bothered again."

"Ah, good." The guard nodded in satisfaction. "The prince and his escort came down a while ago. The lady with him—is that the princess?"

"She's not," Calonderiel said with something of a snarl in his voice. "She's my wife."

"Then you're a lucky man." The guard stepped back into the doorway, as if he feared a blow. "Good night, all of you."

"Wife?" Salamander said once they were out of earshot.

"It's the only Deverry word that fits at all," Cal said. "Or at least, the only one I could think of."

They went on down to the meadow below, where the dun's pavilion and the elven tents stood, ghostly in the pale light of the stars. In camp Dallandra, who had changed back to her tunic and leather leggings, and the prince were sitting by a small fire in front of the royal tent. Although most of the Westfolk archers and the men of the Red Wolf warband had turned in for the night, Gerran was still awake, sitting next to Dar.

When Salamander and Calonderiel joined the group by the fire, Salamander noticed that Cal not only sat down next to Dallandra, but clasped her hand as well. *I don't know why he's jealous*, Salamander thought. *He's the only man I know with the guts to court her, or at least, court her openly, unlike some that I could mention—and where is that little weasel, anyway?*

"Where's Meranaldar?" Salamander said aloud. "We've not left him behind, have we?"

"You didn't. I was transcribing my notes." The scribe came out of the tent, then sat down across from the prince.

"I've been telling the captain here about the council of war," Prince Daralanteriel said. "Well, as much as I could sort out of the general noise, anyway. By the gods of both our peoples! How do you Deverry men ever decide anything? I've never seen a council with so much shouting, arguing, cursing, and general confusion."

Gerran laughed and nodded his agreement.

"Fortunately," Daralanteriel went on, "Prince Voran finally saw fit to call an end to the wrangling."

"But by then, Your Highness," Gerran said, "he and the gwerbret knew what every lord in the chamber was thinking. If any of the noble-born are going to cause trouble, they know that, too."

"Good point," Daralanteriel said. "Your people seem held together by a web of alliances. They're so complicated that I can't say I understand them all. It looks fragile to an outsider."

"Spiderwebs don't look like much either, Your Highness, but when a fly blunders in, they hold up well enough."

"Um, what were they arguing about?" Salamander said. "I thought the gwerbret had already decided to march on Honelg."

"He had," Dar answered him. "The questions in dispute were with whom and how many of them. Day after tomorrow, he'll be taking half his own warband, our archers, the prince's men, and Cadryc's warband. The rest of the men will stay in Dun Cengarn on fortguard. The other lords will ride home and get their men and alliances ready for the march on Zakh Gral."

"Which is the real prize, of course," Calonderiel put in.

"Of course." Gerran turned to Salamander. "I've only seen Honelg's dun once, years ago, when I was but a lad. It stood on a good-sized hill, then, but it didn't sport much in the way of earthworks. His highness here told me that Honelg's fortified the gates."

"He's built a veritable maze." Salamander paused for a small groan. "There's a narrow path that twists back and forth through high earthworks. A murder alley, I'd call it, since he's got archers."

"We might have to invest the place and leave a force there, then," Calonderiel put in. "Some of the lords were arguing for that."

"You'll need every man you can get for Zakh Gral," Salamander said. "The place is teeming with Horsekin warriors."

Gerran swore under his breath.

"Let me make sure I understand." Dallandra leaned forward to interrupt. "We can't storm the gates, because Honelg's archers will be able to pick our men off. And our archers won't be able to get near enough to pick them off. Is that it?"

"It is and well put," Gerran said.

"Ah." Dallandra sat back. "I see."

The men waited for her to go on, but she merely smiled blandly at them.

"Well, Captain," Daralanteriel said at last, "we'd best get some sleep, I think. I wish we were marching out tomorrow."

"So do I, Your Highness." Gerran rose and bowed to him. "My thanks for telling me about the council."

Gerran strode off into the darkness in the direction of the Red Wolf pavilion. Calonderiel waited, listening until his footsteps had died away. Then he glanced at Dallandra and raised an eyebrow. "Out with it," he said in Elvish. "I can tell that you've got something in mind."

"Maybe I do, maybe I don't." Dallandra smiled at him, then stood up. "Ebañy, come with me, will you? We need to put a seal over the camp."

Before Calonderiel could object, she hurried off in the opposite direction from the one Gerran had taken. Salamander scrambled up and hurried after, catching up with her at the edge of the ford. Starlight danced on the surface of the placidly flowing river, mirroring the vast River of Stars above.

"This is the worst possible place to do an astral working," Salamander said. "And since I'm quite confident that you know it, I can but repeat the banadar's remark. You've got something in mind, don't you?"

"Yes," Dallandra said. "I'd already set the seals when we first came down from Cengarn. But I didn't want to make this suggestion where any of the men could hear because I'm not sure it'll work. I'm thinking of the dragons."

"Aha! They could just fly above Honelg's murderous gates and his archers both."

"If that will do any good." Dallandra turned and looked back to Cengarn's high walls, black and looming against the starry sky.

"Rhodry told me once that it was impossible to fight from drag-onback because you can't aim at anything."

"Well, that's discouraging."

"I thought I'd ask Arzosah herself. She's the one who'd know."

"Is she nearby, then?"

"I have no idea, but I can summon her. I know her true name." Dalla sighed sharply. "I only wish it were so easy to reach Rhodry."

"So do I. I've been scrying for him now and then, by the way. I can find him easily enough, but he must be off in the wilderness somewhere. I haven't seen one landmark I can recognize, just trees, rocks, meadows, so on and so forth."

"I couldn't recognize them either when I scryed for him. Well, if we summon Arzosah, maybe she can fetch him. Let's get this work-ing underway, shall we?"

"I stand ready to assist, O Mighty Mistress of Magicks."

"I don't want you to risk it. It's still too soon after your long flight. I do want you to stand between me and the camp and think up a good lie if anyone hears me and tries to join us."

"Anyone?" Salamander grinned at her. "You mean Cal."

"Him, too." Dalla returned the smile. "But Prince Dar has a touch of the ancient royal Sight, and for all I know, he has other dweomer talents as well and might feel drawn to come out here. I don't want to be interrupted."

"Very well. I shall be your faithful watchdog."

Salamander walked back to the midway point 'twixt camp and river and took up his post. The little fires between the tents and in front of the pavilion glowed red, burning down to coals. A light wind rustled the trees, and he could hear the river's murmur. In a moment Dalla's voice joined their music, calling out Arzosah's name. It was no ordinary shout, but an eerie vibration drawn from her very soul, or so it sounded, oddly metallic yet as resonant as a harp string as well. She repeated it three times, sending the name like an arrow flying across the etheric plane as well as through the physical air: Arzosah Sothy Lore-ez-o-haz.

As the last call died away, Salamander glanced back and saw her sink to her knees. He ran to the ford and flung himself down to kneel beside her. When he put his arm around her shoulder, she felt cold to the touch.

"I'm not ill or suchlike," Dallandra said. "I just need a bit of a rest."

"No doubt! You loosed those names with the power of a storm behind them."

"Well, I have no idea how far away she's lairing."

As they knelt beside the star-flecked water, Salamander found himself thinking of Rocca. The image of Zakh Gral built up before him, and he could see the altar of the Outer Shrine, glowing silver with dweomer light. Rocca knelt before the stone, her arms uplifted in prayer.

"Stop it!" Dallandra's voice cut into his vision.

Rocca and the stone vanished. Salamander felt as dazed as a drunken man abruptly revived by a bucket of cold water.

"Ye gods," he mumbled. "I hope I didn't put us in danger."

"No, but you put yourself in danger. Your aura's dancing about like a drop of water on a griddle stone."

"Well, I didn't mean to scry, I just—oh, wait. That's the problem, isn't it?"

"Exactly." Dallandra laid a hand on his shoulder. "Let's go back to camp. We both need sleep."

Salamander got up, then helped her rise. Together they began the walk back.

"I nearly forgot in all the excitement," Salamander said. "Did you get to have that talk with Neb and Branna?"

"I didn't, no," Dallandra said. "Neb stayed at the council till late, and Branna's aunt needed all her attention. The poor woman! Honelg's wife is her daughter."

"I knew I never should have mentioned Honelg, curse it all."

"No, no, you did the right thing. Honelg is dangerous. Galla told me a fair bit about him. He sounds loathsome."

"I'd agree with that judgment, yes."

"But in the morning, you and I will need to find a way to take

Neb and Branna some place where no one can overhear. They seem to have stumbled onto the truth. I'd like to know how."

T he noontime sun fell in a thin slit through the window in Branna's chamber and turned Dallandra's pale hair to a glowing silver, as shiny as a polished sword blade. As soon as the town gates had opened, Dallandra had come up to the dun, where she'd found Neb and Branna breakfasting in the great hall. The three of them had gone to Branna and Neb's chamber, the only place in the dun where they had enough privacy—and indeed, enough quiet—to discuss the dweomer and its secrets. They'd talked all morning, Branna realized, though the time had galloped by. Among other things, Dallandra had confirmed Neb's insight, that indeed, in another life they had both been masters of dweomerlore.

"There's one thing I truly don't understand," Branna said, then paused to choose careful words. "If we were those other people, why can't we remember more? I could remember a fair bit when I was asleep, of course, but Neb never had dreams such as I did. But I never—well—just remembered. When I was but a child, why didn't I have the feeling that Branna wasn't my real name—just for an example, like."

"I'll wager the answer leads to another question," Neb said, smiling a little. "So far everything else you've told us has."

Dallandra laughed, nodding her agreement. "I can give you a simple enough answer, but it won't tell you much. The part of your mind that does the remembering quite simply isn't reborn. Most of a person's mind dies when they die, unless they're a highly skilled dweomermaster. Even the masters lose a tremendous amount of knowledge and memories. Here's a way of thinking about it. Suppose you were setting off on a journey. And suppose you had two big sacks to carry things in, and you'd crammed them full of possessions. Then suppose the sacks were taken away, and you had only a single pocket to carry what you treasured most. You'd have to leave most of your things behind, wouldn't you?"

"I would, truly." Branna said.

"The memories that do remain," Dallandra went on, "are those forged from deep feelings or events that have touched your soul, such as a great love or a great hatred. Feelings don't necessarily bring words and images with them, though. That's why you can recognize someone without knowing why they're so important to you."

"Like I recognized Salamander," Branna said. "But, you know, I called him a chattering elf. I didn't have the slightest idea why I had. Now you tell me that Jill called him that all the time, but it doesn't sound like the sort of thing you'd remember from life to life."

"It doesn't, truly, but dweomermasters have highly trained minds. They remember more than people who've not spent years developing their memories."

"That makes sense," Neb put in. "But those dreams of hers! They were so detailed, and you've told us now that they were accurate."

"There's a reason for that, but I'm not sure if I can explain it. I doubt if either of you remember the meanings of the words that I need. Every craft has its own special words, whether it's smithing or carpentry or dweomercraft. Tell me, does the term 'astral plane' mean anything to either of you?"

Branna glanced at Neb, who shrugged his shoulders.

"Not to me," Branna said. "I don't even known what a plane is."

"Well, a plane is a craft term for a part of the world that most folk can't see—or sense in any other way either. There are a number of these planes, and the astral is one of them. Let's see, how can I put this? Part of the astral plane stores events the way writing stores words. The lore tells us that a record exists there of everything that's ever happened. These records are all horribly jumbled up, and sometimes they're unreliable, but they're there."

"Could I be seeing them when I'm asleep?" Branna said.

"You follow me quite well." Dallandra smiled at her. "Eventually you'll both learn to see these images when you're awake enough to use certain tools you'll also learn. That way you'll be able to tell true from false."

"It sounds like a true bard's visions of the past," Neb said. "I'm glad to hear it, too. I've been wondering why don't I remember things the way she does."

"I'm not sure." Dallandra raised her hands and turned them palms up. "I'm hoping to find the answer to that, though."

"I'd be grateful if you could," Neb said. "But, at least, from what you're saying, I can get my memories back from this astral thing if naught else."

"Just so." Dallandra paused to glance out the window. "Ye gods, the day is going fast! We have a good many more things to discuss, and it's going to take us a very long time indeed. I think we've talked enough for one day."

Neb was staring at the floor, frowning a little as if he were thinking things over. Branna realized that she was feeling more than a little disappointed. She'd somehow hoped that Dallandra could weave some sort of spell that would miraculously turn her and Neb into dweomermasters in a heartbeat, but now she knew better. There was so much lore, far more than anyone could learn in a short while, not even someone like her, who remembered bits and pieces of it. *Patience,* she told herself. *Patience means safety.*

"But can I ask one more question?" Branna said. "Is dweomer-lore the only kind of memory that someone can recover on her own?"

"Usually," Dallandra said, "but there are exceptions. Some kinds of knowledge shape a person's etheric double—I'll explain that term later—and that, in turn, shapes his body and skills."

"Like swordsmanship?" Branna said. "Gerran's always been a marvel and a half with a blade."

"You do piece things together, don't you?" Dallandra said, smiling. "That would appear to be one of those skills, truly."

Loud voices passed in the hallway beyond the chamber. Someone knocked on the door.

"My lady?" It was Midda, yelling over the general noise. "Are you in there?"

"I am." Branna got up and trotted over to the door. "Do you need me for somewhat?"

"I don't, but Lady Drwmigga's summoning the noble-born women. It's time for her to display her needlework from her wedding chest."

"I'll be right there." Branna turned back to the others. "Dallandra, did you want to come with me? It's a thing new brides always do on the feast day, and I truly can't get out of going."

"I would, actually." Dallandra got up, smoothing down her borrowed dresses. "I've never seen a Deverry wedding before."

"Most aren't this grand, but then, Ridvar's of very high rank."

Normally Branna enjoyed this particular part of a wedding celebration, but as they sat in the crowded women's hall, she found her mind wandering back to the dweomerlore. She felt as if the normal life of a grand dun was flowing past her like a river on its way to some destination that meant nothing to her. In years past she would have been daydreaming about an elegant wedding of her own, but no longer. If Drwmigga's life was going to flow like a smooth broad river, then her own would be more like a sea, with storms and half-hidden rocks and shoals where the waves broke in huge wings of white spray—dangers, yes, but it promised triumphs as well.

Once the womenfolk had exclaimed over Drwmigga's fine needlework, everyone but her serving women withdrew to let her dress for the wedding feast. A page had already taken the embroidered wedding shirt she'd made for her future husband to Gwerbret Ridvar. When Dallandra went off to find Salamander, Branna decided to walk around the ward. Always in the back of her mind was the coming battle for Lord Honelg's dun. Whenever she let herself think about Adranna, shut up with a madman for a husband, she felt cold and sick with worry. While the womenfolk carried out the pleasant rituals of the wedding, Ridvar, the two princes, Tieryn Cadryc, and their captains were planning the campaign.

Down by the dun gates she met Gerran, who seemed to be heading into town. He paused and greeted her with a friendly "good morrow."

"And the same to you," Branna said. "Where are you going?"

"Down to the camp in the meadows. His grace is sending off a message."

"To Mirryn, I'll wager."

"Right you are," Gerran said with a wry smile. "He's not going to like it much, but he needs to know we won't be back as soon as we'd planned."

"Does it tell him why?"

"It does, and he's going to be furious, being left out once again."

"Well, it's for his own good, I suppose. He'll be safer because of it."

"Oh, here, never tell him that!" Gerran said. "He feels dishonorable enough as it is."

"I'd never tell any fighting man that, fear not."

"Good." With a nod her way, Gerran turned and strode out the gates.

Branna watched him go, but she was thinking of Mirryn. All at once she knew that if he rode to this battle, he'd die and leave his father without an heir. *I'd best find Salamander or Dalla,* she thought. They could tell her the origin of her sudden certainty, or so she hoped.

Gerran sent two Red Wolf men off with the message, then returned to the dun to look for Calonderiel. Once they'd gotten the wedding out of the way—Gerran considered the festivities a delay and a nuisance—the warbands and servants could finish the preparations for the march north. Even though Ridvar was taking only half of his own men, what with the escorts brought by the two princes and the Red Wolf warband, the army would amount to nearly two hundred men against Honelg's handful of riders. If it weren't for the dun walls and the archers, the battle would have been a slaughter. But of course, Honelg did have archers, and good ones at that. Gerran wanted to know how many bowmen the Westfolk had with them, and how skilled they were, to counter this grim reality.

The banadar wasn't in the great hall. One of the pages had seen him walking in the general direction of the stables. Gerran was heading that way when he came upon Branna and Neb, talking together behind one of the storage sheds—or, more precisely, arguing. Although they kept their voices low, Neb had his arms crossed over his chest, and Branna was waving her hands in the air to emphasize some point she was making. As Gerran walked up, they both fell silent.

"What's all this?" Gerran said.

"A stupid idea," Neb said.

"Oh, hold your tongue!" Branna said. "Gerro, I want to ride north with the warband when you go. Someone has to be there to beg Honelg to let Adranna and the other women leave the sieged dun. I'll need to take care of Adranna and little Trenni once they're out, too. He wouldn't dare harm a supplicant kinswoman, not if he wants any of the gods to ever favor him again. Neb says that Dallandra will be there, but Honelg won't listen to her. She's one of the Westfolk, and Salamander told me that Alshandra's people hate them."

"True spoken," Neb said, "but—"

Branna ignored him and went on, "With Dalla there, it's not like I'll be the only woman in camp."

Neb shot her a dark look. "I'll wager you agree with me, Gerro," Neb said. "This is a scatterbrained scheme if I ever heard one!"

"I don't, and it's not," Gerran said. "Here, Neb, you're her betrothed, and you'll be riding with us. The tieryn needs a scribe to write out messages and the like. So she'll be safe enough, with you and me to look after her." He glanced at Branna. "I'll speak with your uncle, if you'd like."

"I would." Branna turned to him and grinned. "My thanks, Gerro. My most sincere and grand thanks."

"Welcome, I'm sure. Huh. I never did like Lord Honelg much. Neb, truly, I think it's best that—"

"Oh, very well!" Neb's tone of voice was more frost than graciousness. "As long as I'm riding with her, I suppose I can't object."

"You might have told me that," Branna snapped.

"You never gave me a chance," Neb said.

Branna set her hands on her hips, and for a long awkward moment the pair scowled each other. *Ye gods*, Gerran thought, *I'm cursed glad I'm not the one marrying her!* Aloud, he said, "Let's go broach this idea to our tieryn."

They found Cadryc and Galla as well up in their chamber. The lady was sitting in a chair by the window, and her husband was perched on the windowsill next to her. Judging from Galla's pale face and the damp handkerchief she was clutching, she'd been weeping, but she put on a brave smile.

"Aunt Galla?" Branna said. "Grant me a boon. I want to ride with the warband and plead with Honelg to let the women in the dun come out."

Galla's smile disappeared.

"Absolutely not!" Cadryc snapped. "Your aunt's distressed quite enough as it is, lass. I'm not letting you ride into danger."

"Well, Gerran thinks it's a good idea," Branna said.

"Truly, my lord," Gerran said. "Her betrothed will be along, and that Westfolk woman, too. We can keep her safe."

Galla's eyes filled with tears. She tried to dab them away, then crumpled the useless handkerchief and hurled it to the floor. Cadryc patted her shoulder.

"I shan't allow it, my dear," the tieryn said. "Don't trouble your heart."

"But, Uncle Cadryc!" Branna's voice rose to a wail. "What about Adranna?"

"The gwerbret's got a perfectly good herald. He can do the pleading."

"The herald's going to be all formal and reasonable. He can't put the heart into it that I can. After all, I'm her kinswoman."

"True enough, and that's why you're staying with your aunt." Cadryc glanced at Neb. "What do you think?"

Neb hesitated, glancing back and forth between Branna and the tieryn. Gerran found it in his heart to pity him. Finally Neb took a deep breath as if he were summoning courage. "I think," Neb said, "that she should stay here, my lord, and begging your pardon and all that, Gerran."

Branna opened her mouth to speak, but Cadryc crossed his arms over his chest and glared her into silence. "Your betrothed has bade you nay, and I've bade you nay," Cadryc said, "and that's the end of it."

Gerran considered arguing further, but he'd seen Cadryc in this mood before. "Well, our liege lord's spoken," he said to Branna. "But it was a generous thing for you to offer."

When she glanced Neb's way, Branna's expression hovered on the edge of rage. She was most likely thinking up some nasty remark, but Galla got up and walked over to take her hand.

"Please stay," Galla said. "I can't bear to lose both you and Adranna, and who knows what will happen in a siege?"

Branna let out her breath in a long sigh. "Oh, very well," she said. "Since *you* asked."

Once again Gerran found himself glad that she'd taken Neb instead of him. *A hellcat, sure enough,* he thought. *I'll wager our scribe's in for a long cold night!* He decided that he'd best leave the noble-born to sort things out in private.

"My lord?" Gerran said. "May I have your leave to go?"

"By all means." Cadryc managed a ghost of a smile. "There are times when a man needs to retreat, eh? Too bad I can't go with you."

As Gerran went downstairs, he was thinking that Branna could well be right about the herald, and the thought brought him an idea. He found Salamander sitting over on the riders' side of the hall, drinking ale and flirting with the prettiest of the serving lasses. Gerran unceremoniously sat down beside him and shot the lass a dark look.

"You've got work to do for the feast tonight," Gerran said. "Go do it."

With a scowl and a flounce she hurried off.

"Here!" Salamander said, grinning. "I was just beginning to scent victory."

"You can resume your campaign later. Listen, I've been thinking about Honelg. Prince Voran's trying to make Ridvar see reason and offer Honelg some kind of mercy or compromise for the sake of the women and children in the dun, but I doubt me that Ridvar will. The prince çan't outright order him to. He's not the high king, Voran, and never will be."

"True spoken, but it matters naught. Honelg will never surrender. I'll wager you coppers to horse apples that he's prepared to die for his false goddess."

"He's gone daft sure enough, then. When he dies, he'll be no loss to the rhan, but cursed if I want him to take his wife and daughter with him. We need someone to plead for the safety of the women in the dun. Branna wanted to, but her uncle's forbidden her to ride with the army."

"That's a pity. I certainly can't speak to Honelg, being as I've betrayed him, his hospitality, and his goddess all three."

"But you know a lot about Alshandra, don't you? How she's worshipped and all that. I want you to talk to the herald. His name's Indar. Maybe you can tell him how to convince Honelg that his goddess wants the women safe. Even the daft have reasons for the strange things they do, after all."

"Now, that is a most excellent suggestion, Gerro. I'll ask Oth for an introduction straightaway."

Later that afternoon Gerran saw Salamander and Indar, sitting together at a table in the great hall. Gray-haired Indar was a tall, wiry man who habitually sat slouched in chair or saddle. Now, however, he was leaning forward, elbows on the table, his long narrow face propped up in his long bony hands, listening intently as Salamander talked in his usual animated way. Every now and then Indar would nod, as if signaling the gerthddyn to keep talking. Gerran had no doubt that the herald's trained memory would store every scrap of Salamander's lore.

For most of the morning Neb managed to dodge being alone with Branna. He took written notes at the council of war, he found the gwerbret's scribe and discussed writing materials, he even helped the servants carry the noon meal down to the Red Wolf warband and the Westfolk camped below the dun. Every time he saw Branna during these errands, she would cross her arms over her chest and glare at him. Finally he realized that putting off the inevitable was only making things worse. Just before dinner he gave a serving lass a copper and asked her take a message to Lady Branna, who was in the women's hall attending upon the gwerbret's wife.

"My dearest love," the note ran, "I know you're angry, but it truly is for the best that you stay behind. I'll be in our chamber."

The serving lass trotted off with the note, and Neb went upstairs to wait. He sat on the wide windowsill in their bedchamber and looked down at the ward, where servants were sorting out supplies and loading carts in readiness for the march tomorrow. At the thought of the fighting ahead he felt a weary sort of fear—he himself would be safe, but he knew that he was going to see blood-soaked horrors. *Will it be worse than what I saw in Trev Hael?* he asked himself. He could remember the stench of the sickroom and his father's face, pale and gaunt, when Da had tried to speak. "Take care of your mother." That sentence had come out clear enough, but the next was lost in spasms and the choking sound of a man dying.

"I tried, Da," Neb whispered aloud. "Forgive me." Then he shook himself to drive the grief away. He had his answer. The death lying ahead of them all would be neither harder nor easier to see. It would be a different thing altogether.

The chamber door opened with a bang against the wall and Branna strode in, her face set and utterly expressionless. She slammed the door shut, then curtsied.

"And what does my lord and master husband want?" she said.

"Oh, for the sake of the gods!" Neb stood up to face her. "I said I was sorry, didn't I? If the tieryn had said you could go, I would have agreed, but he asked me—"

"Oh, so the men stick together when they're disposing of their women's lives?"

"Who said anything about your life? Except that I'm worried about you losing it."

"I wouldn't have been in any danger."

"You can't know that."

"I know it better than you. I'm a warrior's daughter. I've grown up with feuds and battles and raids, haven't I?"

"Oh, and I suppose I'm just a milksop scribe who doesn't understand such things."

"Well, you don't." She tossed her head like an angry horse. "But that's not what matters."

"What does, then?"

"That you'd order me around."

"All I did was tell the tieryn my opinion. He's the one who gave the orders."

For a long moment Branna hovered on the edge of rage. Neb could see it in her clenched fists, tight by her sides, and by her eyes, narrowed to slits. With the memories of his family strong in his mind, he suddenly realized what he needed to say.

"You're a warrior's daughter," he began, "but I'm the son of a man who depended on his wife to run his shop while he did the work of scribing. My mam—ah, gods, I wish you'd known her. She could read and write as well as he did, and keep accounts, and help with making the inks and suchlike he sold, and all the while she was keeping her household running. Our servants loved her, too, she was so fair-minded."

Branna started to speak, then said nothing, but her eyes looked less like an angry wolf's and more like her own.

"Everyone in town respected her," Neb said. "After Da died, she took over the shop. If it hadn't have been for that fever, she could have taken care of us all, on her own, like."

Branna's fists relaxed into hands.

"Don't you see, my love?" Neb went on. "I don't want a wife to breed sons or suchlike. I want a wife like my mam, strong and clever and—well, and all of that. You don't have a warrior for a husband. That's true-spoken. Is it a bad thing?"

"It's not, but mayhap the luckiest thing that's ever happened to me in my life." Branna's eyes filled with tears. "You're right, and I wish I'd known your mother, truly I do."

Neb strode over and flung his arms around her. She wept a brief scatter of tears into his shoulder.

"What's so wrong?" he whispered.

"I was thinking of your mother's death, that's all."

"But will you forgive me?"

"Oh, of course I will."

For a moment she fell silent, then looked up with one of her wicked grins. "We've got a while before the feast begins," she said. "I could hear the cook yelling at the kitchen lads about things not being ready."

"Indeed?" Neb answered her grin with one of his own. "Then let's go lie down for a little while."

The thought of another greasy meal in the crowded, smoky, and noisy great hall turned Dallandra's stomach, wedding feast or no. She found Calonderiel, told him where she was going, then left the dun. It took her some while to make her way through the town. The crowd that filled the streets stank of ale and cooking smoke and sweat. They had come out to discuss the gwerbret's marriage, and in pairs and families they were drifting uphill, ready to assemble in the ward of the dun to receive largesse and to cheer the gwerbret's new wife at the conclusion of the feast. Here and there she overheard someone praising the gwerbret for his generosity because he was going to distribute coins to mark the occasion.

Out through the gates at last—Dallandra sighed in profound relief as she gained the quiet of the open meadow, where the Red Wolf and Westfolk mounts grazed at tether in the long gold sunlight of late afternoon. Two of the Red Wolf riders and two of Calonderiel's archers were sitting on the grass in front of the pavilion and dicing to pass the time while they, supposedly at least, guarded the horses. When they saw her, they scrambled up and bowed with looks of profound guilt all round.

"It's all right," Dallandra said. "I doubt very much if anyone's going to try to steal any of them."

They grinned, bowed again, and sat back down to continue their game. Not long after, servants came down from the dun, dragging a small cart with them, laden with food from the wedding feast, a better distraction than any dice game could be. Dallandra took a chunk of bread and some of the omnipresent honeycake and ate alone, sitting in front of the prince's tent. The feasting was going to go on for hours, she supposed, giving her a welcome chance to be alone and think.

Yet just after she'd finished eating, Dallandra had a visitor. When she saw a woman leave the gates of the town, she stood up, assuming that someone had sent a servant with a note or message for her. Much to her surprise, it was Branna, waving cheerfully as she came trotting across the meadow.

"I couldn't stand the noise a moment longer," Branna said by way of greeting, "and Calonderiel told me that you were down here."

"I am, and it gladdens my heart to see you," Dallandra said. "Is Neb coming down, too?"

"Alas, he couldn't sneak away like I did. The tieryn has him writing some sort of fancy letter of congratulations to the gwerbret and his wife. My aunt will give it to them when we leave on the morrow."

"The Red Wolf's leaving so soon?"

"The army's riding out tomorrow. My uncle's sending us women home with an escort." Branna made a profoundly sour face. "I wanted to ride to Honelg's with the warbands, but Aunt Galla was truly upset about it, so I agreed not to."

"Your aunt's very fond of you, isn't she?"

"She is. You see, over the years she gave birth to four daughters and two sons. One son died when he was but a fortnight old. The other one's Mirryn. One daughter died of the choking fever when she was but a little lass, another grew up but died in childbirth, and the third married a lord who inherited a demesne down in Pyrdon, too far away for visits. Oh, and then there was the miscarriage Galla had, too. I think there was only the one, anyway, and I don't remember if it was a lass or a lad that she lost. But all of that trouble means that Adranna's the only daughter she's got left. When I was born, I filled a gap in her heart."

Branna spoke so calmly about Galla's domestic tragedies that Dallandra was taken aback. She had to remind herself just how common it was in Deverry for a woman to bear a good many children and then lose most of them.

"That's very sad," Dallandra said. "No wonder she's so concerned about Adranna."

"Truly." Branna paused, glancing around her as if she were looking for an escape route. She swallowed heavily before she spoke. "I had another one of those dreams last night, but I couldn't tell you about it in front of Neb." Her voice turned to a whisper. "Would it be tedious of me to ask you about it now?"

"Not at all. Here, let's sit down. I'll get some cushions from the tent."

Dallandra ducked into the tent, grabbed the first cushions she saw, and hurried out again, before Branna's nerve failed and she ran off. When they sat down, Branna drew her knees up to her chest and hugged them to her, as if she were trying to make herself as small as possible. For a long while Branna stayed silent, staring off into the distance. Dallandra had to force herself to be patient and let her speak first.

"Well," Branna said finally. "In the dream—wait! I'd best start admitting the truth. I remembered last night when I was asleep that before he died, Nevyn had lost much of his memory. He'd lived so long and seen so much that everything was jumbled together. At times he even had trouble remembering where we were or why we'd gone there. I was wondering if that might be why Neb doesn't remember things as vividly as I do."

"I'd say that it's entirely possible, even likely."

"But is there somewhat of Nevyn left in him?"

"There is, rather a lot of him, in fact. Neb stands like him, strides along like him, even at times says things that Nevyn always said. And then there's his dweomer talent. The Wildfolk always recognize it in someone, you know. They flock around him."

"True spoken. You Westfolk live so long, how do you keep your memories safe?"

"We have very different minds from Deverry folk, I suppose."

"It's like carrying things in sacks, then, like you told us." Branna smiled, but faintly. "Yours must be larger."

"Well, we also live simple lives, but truly, before the Horsekin came, we did live complex ones, in the lost cities, that is." Dallandra paused, struck by a sudden thought. "But they were very rigid lives, from what Meranaldar's told me. Very ritualized lives, truly—every day of the year had some meaning and some sort of religious rite that had to be performed. I wonder if that came about just because we live so long."

"How would that help remember things?"

"It would be like a skeleton, all those rituals, for us to hang the meat of our lives upon."

"Ah. I can see that, truly."

"And besides, we could read and write. Writing is really frozen memory, after all. Once you've written a thing down, you don't have to remember it perfectly."

"So it is! I'd not thought of it that way before."

Branna smiled, then let the smile fade and returned to staring off at the meadow. The sun had sunk low in the sky, and long shadows stretched across the grass and the grazing horses. In the east the twilight was beginning to velvet the sky.

"Branna?" Dallandra could stand the silence no longer. "Why are you so frightened?"

Branna hesitated, and for a moment it seemed that she might weep. She arranged an utterly insincere smile instead, a gesture that forcibly reminded Dallandra of her age, a bare fifteen summers, which by elven reckoning meant she was but a little child still.

"I want to be me," she said at last. "Jill was so strong, so powerful, that I feel like she's another woman entirely. She's living inside me or suchlike—I mean, I don't know how to say this well—but sometimes I feel her trying to take me over. Branna will be the dead one, then, and I don't want to die."

"No wonder you're frightened! You know, this is another reason why so few people remember anything of their past lives."

"It's truly terrifying." She was whispering. "Will I have to give myself up and turn into Jill again?"

"I intend to make sure you don't." Dallandra put all the calm reassurance she could summon into her voice. "You can have Jill's memories without being Jill. Think of them as tales you heard a bard tell, or for that matter, as dreams, just as they've come to you. There's valuable knowledge in them, but tales and dreams is all they are."

"But you'll help me?" Branna turned to her with a genuine smile. "I thought you'd—well, it seems truly silly now that I think of it."

"I doubt very much if it's silly, whatever it is."

Branna hesitated, but only briefly. "I thought you'd want me to turn back into Jill. I thought maybe I'd have to if I wanted to know what she used to know."

"Nah, nah, nah, never think that! Jill was a woman of great power, truly, but she had her faults and blind spots just as we all do. I suspect—and I hope—that she learned enough about them so you won't need to repeat them. You need to study dweomer as Branna, not as her."

"Thank the gods!" Branna began to say more, but tears welled and ran. She wiped them roughly away on the sleeve of her dress—a gesture that reminded Dallandra of Jill, not that she would have mentioned it.

"We'll work through this together," Dallandra said. "You and Neb both are going to have to come study with me and with another dweomermaster I know, Niffa of Cerr Cawnen. She's a human being like you, and a former apprentice of mine."

"Apprentice." Branna grinned at her. "I like that word. I've found my craft and the guild I belong to." The grin vanished. "But Aunt Galla will miss me."

"She'll have Lady Solla for company and, I hope, Adranna as well. We intend to do everything we can to get Adranna and her daughter safely out of that siege."

"My thanks. There's poor little Matto, too, but you may not be able to save him. I doubt me if Honelg will let him go, and I'm terrified that our gwerbret will have him killed even if he does leave the dun with the women."

"What? Whatever for?"

"So he doesn't grow up to swear vengeance. That's just the way things go out here on the border."

"But he's only—" Dallandra stopped herself from launching into a diatribe against Deverry ways. "That's very sad. I'll see what we can do to rescue him."

"A thousand thanks! I—" Branna broke off speaking and shuddered. "Dalla, someone's spying on us."

Dallandra felt the cold then as well, a thin line of ice drawn down her back. She got up and stood staring into the sky. Far above them in the gathering twilight a winged creature flew in lazy circles. For a moment she could hope that it was Arzosah, but it suddenly dipped into a turn and flew off with a flurry of wings. Since she was seeing it against a darkening sky, Dallandra could only make out a bird shape that may have been a raven—a very large raven.

"Mazrak," Dallandra whispered. "I'd wager high that you're no ordinary bird." She raised her voice to a normal tone. "Why is Salamander always off somewhere when I need him? I suspect he knows who that is. Here, hold a moment." When she concentrated on Ebañy, she could feel his mind, but it was so muddled with mead and food that she couldn't catch his attention. "How like him!"

Branna had been listening to all of this gape-mouthed.

"That raven's evil, isn't it?" she said. "It must be the same one that was spying on us at home, and now the beastly thing's followed us here."

"It was doing what? Tell me what you know about it!"

"Well, it looks like a raven, but it's far too big for that. It kept appearing over the dun, and it gave me a nasty cold feeling, truly, though I can't explain why."

"I know why. Do you know what a mazrak is?"

"I don't."

Dallandra sat back down. "Well, I think I'd best tell you, and right now."

"There's one thing I must say about these Deverry lords," Calonderiel said. "They set a good table."

"They do at that." Salamander belched profoundly. "Uh, sorry! Mayhap I shouldn't have had that last goblet of mead."

"And didn't I try to tell you just that? We'll be mustering at dawn for the ride north. No sleeping till noon for you, gerthddyn."

"Oh, ye gods, have pity on this poor fool!" Salamander looked up at the stars and raised his hands to implore them. "Let the dawn come later than usual!"

"The gods have better things to do. It's too bad about the tourney, though. They had to cancel it, of course, but I'd have liked to have seen that."

They were walking across Dun Cengarn's ward on their way out. Behind them the noise from the great hall still roared and murmured like a stormy sea. The feasting and the bard songs would go on for hours, no doubt, but Calonderiel, his mind on the coming war, had insisted they leave early. He'd already ordered the West-folk archers to go down to the camp ahead of them. Salamander had seen Gerran do the same with the Red Wolf men. Prince Dar-alanteriel, however, had found himself bound by protocol to re-main at the gwerbret's table until the proceedings were over. Meranaldar had volunteered to stay with his prince—to lick Dar's boots clean afterward, according to Calonderiel.

As they crossed the empty ward, their footsteps seemed to echo on the cobbles—their footsteps and someone else's, running after them.

"Salamander! Banadar! Wait!"

It was Clae, panting for breath when he caught up to them.

"What's all this?" Salamander said, smiling. "Now, don't tell me you can see in the dark. How did you know it was us?"

"I saw you leaving, and I followed as fast as I could. Can I come with you? I've got to talk to the captain. Neb told me to find you and see if you'd help me find him."

"He's down at the meadow camp. Come along, then."

They found Gerran sitting with Dallandra and, surprisingly enough, Branna at a campfire, burning for its light. With the Red Wolf men sharing the meadow, Dallandra wouldn't have dared to make a dweomerlight, no matter how warm the evening. Clae bowed to both women in turn, but it was a clumsy gesture, since he kept glancing Gerran's way as if for approval.

"Forgive me, my ladies," the lad said, "but somewhat's hap-pened, and I have to tell the captain."

"Then tell away," Dallandra said, smiling. "We don't bite."

Clae managed a smile, then bowed again, this time to Gerran. "Well, uh," he began, "a groom stole two horses and left the dun."

"If they were in the dun, they couldn't be our horses, lad," Ger-ran said. "You should be telling Lord Blethry this."

"Lord Blethry left this noontide to take some messages to some allies in the mountains. He won't be back for ever so long. And I didn't want to tell just anyone in case they believed in Alshandra."

"What? Why would that matter?"

"Because I think the thief's going to Lord Honelg to warn him."

Gerran swore and rose to his feet, as supple as a cat and twice as fast. "Why do you think that?"

"You know how we've all been helping tend the horses? Me and Coryn and the other lords' pages, and all the grooms, I mean."

"I do. Go on."

"So I heard things, the grooms talking and suchlike, and some of the other servants, too, when they'd come out to the stables to fetch a horse for some lord. And a couple of them worship Alshandra— well, maybe. They never come right out and say it, but then, they wouldn't, would they?"

"Cursed right, they wouldn't, not if they had half a wit between them, anyway." Gerran sounded more weary than angry. "Ah, by the black hairy arse of the Lord of Hell!"

"And so, this groom named Raldd, he took a pair of horses out of the dun to exercise them. I saw him go, and he had a couple of saddlebags and what looked like a rolled-up blanket tied to the saddle. And then he never came back. They were two of Prince Voran's horses, so they'd been put in proper stalls in the stables. That's how I know where they should have been. I kept looking for them, but it got dark, and they were never there. And so just now I looked all over the dun, and when I couldn't find him or the horses, I decided I'd best tell you."

"Good job, lad." Calonderiel nodded at Clae. "You have good eyes and the wits to match them."

"My thanks, sir," Clae said.

"The banadar's right." Gerran's mouth flickered in one of his rare smiles. "You've done truly well."

Even in the dim firelight Salamander could see Clae blush scarlet. He murmured a brief "my thanks" and stared at the ground.

"This is exactly what I was afraid of." Salamander said. "Everyone in the dun saw Zaklof die."

"Zaklof?" Gerran snapped. "Who's Zaklof?"

"A Horsekin prophet, preacher, and general proclaimer of Alshandra's cult," Salamander said. "He impressed Honelg most deeply. In fact, he's the reason Honelg developed his strange taste in goddesses. Apparently our lord of the Black Arrow wasn't the only person to wonder how Zaklof could face his death so calmly. From what I heard in town, Zaklof would preach to anyone who asked. He probably made a good many converts."

"I suppose he would have, curse him!" Dallandra said. "Captain, is there any way to stop this wretched Raldd before he gets to Honelg's dun?"

Gerran turned to Clae. "When did you see Raldd leave?"

"A long time before they served dinner." Clae thought hard for a moment. "The sun was about halfway to the horizon, halfway down from noon, I mean."

"Right when everyone was working the hardest and most frantically on the feast." Salamander joined in. "He chose well, our Raldd. Clae here is probably the only person who noticed he was leaving."

"The Lode Star's reached zenith," Calonderiel put in. "How far is Honelg's dun?"

"About thirty miles." Salamander paused to make a few quick calculations. "There's a decent road, too, at least for the first twenty, but part of it does run uphill."

"He's got two well-rested horses from the royal herd, the best horses in all Deverry," Gerran said. "No doubt he's willing to founder them."

"Which means he's at least twenty miles away by now," Salamander went on. "He'll be at Honelg's before dawn."

"You're saying we'll never catch him," Dallandra said.

"I am." Gerran shook his head in frustration. "We've got some sober men and good horses out here, but by the time we saddled up and set out, he'll have gained a little more distance on us. We'll have to circle the town, find the road, and follow it in the dark, when he doubtless knows the way."

"We could ride right into an ambuscade, too," Salamander muttered under his breath.

"This is a disaster," Calonderiel said. "Dalla, it means that by the time the gwerbret's army reaches Honelg's dun, it's going to be provisioned for a long siege. I'll wager he calls up the men of his loyal village, too."

"No doubt," Gerran said. "I would in his place."

Branna had been silently listening to all of this. She'd drawn her knees up and wrapped her arms around them, as if she were trying to make herself as small as possible. From the way her head rested upon them, Salamander could tell that she was half-asleep.

"Branna?" Salamander said. "Hadn't you better be going back to the dun? The town gates are closed, but if the banadar walked with you, no doubt they'll let you in."

"Oh, ye gods!" Branna was wide awake in an instant. "Neb's going to worry if I don't get back."

"True spoken." Calonderiel scrambled to his feet. "Here, my lady, allow me to escort you up to the dun. There's a candle lantern around here somewhere, I think. The rest of us should all get some sleep, anyway. We've got an early start on the morrow."

"Just so." Gerran turned to Clae. "Come along, lad."

"A moment more of your time, Captain." Dallandra stood up and joined them. "Will Tieryn Cadryc be sending his womenfolk back to his dun?"

"He will, truly."

"How many men can he spare for an escort?"

"Only a few, alas. It's not like we have the entire warband with us."

"That's what I was afraid of."

"Do you think they'll be in danger?"

"I do, though it's a hard thing to explain." Dalla glanced at Calonderiel and changed over to Elvish. "I want them to stay here in Cengarn, but I can't come right out and tell them I've had dweomer omens. Can you think of some rational reason?"

"Yes, and it might even be true." Calonderiel turned to Gerran and spoke in Deverrian. "The Wise One here is worried now that Honelg knows we're coming. What if he decided to send a fast-moving squad out to circle around our line of march and try to take the women as hostages? Branna and Galla would make splendid ones, to say naught of the gwerbret's own sister.''

Gerran muttered a few foul oaths under his breath. "I'll come back to the dun with you," he said. "Let's find the tieryn and suggest that the women stay here. I'm sure that Ridvar won't begrudge them his hospitality. Clae, you go back to the pavilion and get some sleep."

Until the others had all left and gotten well out of earshot, neither Dallandra nor Salamander spoke. From the tense way she stood staring into the darkness, he could tell that she had something in mind that she'd rather keep to the pair of them.

"Do you think you can scry without harming yourself?" Dallandra said at last. "Tell me honestly."

"Yes, it should be safe enough," Salamander said. "Scrying's always come to me easily, after all."

"That's true, yes. Have you ever seen this Raldd?"

"Not that I know of. He's probably traveling through dark forest by now anyway."

"Most likely. What about Sidro? Do you think she'd be somewhere near some light?"

"Maybe, maybe not. I can try."

They knelt beside the little campfire. Salamander fed in a few twigs and scraps of bark, then used the leap of flame as his focus. Thinking of Sidro made him remember how much he hated her, her and those sharp little eyes of hers that had nearly gotten him killed.

The image built up fast. He was seeing her by the light of a single oil lamp on a stone altar. The flickering glow reflected off the obsidian pyramid with sparks of dark fire, a glitter of blackness darting this way and that. Some of the sparks seemed to nestle gleaming in Sidro's raven-black hair.

"She's inside somewhere," Salamander began, "and I suspect it's the Inner Shrine. I can see her kneeling before an altar. Behind it is a painting of Alshandra, an oddly realistic picture from the little I can see of it, in the Bardekian style called 'perspective'. Sidro has her arms spread out, and she's mumbling in the Horsekin tongue."

"She's in Zakh Gral?" Dallandra was whispering in a soft monotone, lest she break his concentration. "You're sure of that?"

Salamander let the vision pull back. Under starlight the fortress spread out.

"Yes, very sure."

When he returned to Sidro, she was still on her knees and still wrapped in what appeared to be prayer. Since he'd never been inside the shrine, her surroundings faded off into mist as soon as he tried to look at any object more than a few feet from her.

"I can't tell if she's alone in there or not," Salamander said. "But on the altar there's a lamp, and it's exactly the same kind as they have in Bardek, little pottery things with a wick floating in oil."

"Bardek?" Dallandra's voice rang with urgency. "How very odd!"

"Yes, it is." Salamander broke the vision and sat back on his heels. "That's enough for now."

"Why? Do you think Sidro realized you were watching her?"

"No, but I know these people. They can pray for hours on end. There's not going to be a lot more to see."

"All right. Those things from Bardek, do you think they traded for them?"

"Not directly, if that's what you mean. In all the many many years I spent in Bardek, I never ran across anyone who knew that the Horsekin existed, much less traded with them."

"And it's not likely that Bardekian trade goods would get all the way north to Cerr Cawnen either."

"Even if some had, I doubt if any of the folk there would traffic with the Horsekin."

"That's true, yes. Now, the Bardekians, they have their own gods, too. Do men as well as women worship goddesses there?"

"Yes. Do you think that's important?"

"Yes. Alshandra seems to fill some sort of empty place among the Deverry gods, is why. We have our star goddesses, and of course, the Black Sun, but only Deverry women care about their goddess. Men need some contact with the sacred in female form, too."

"I have to agree with that. I doubt if Alshandra's caught on in Bardek at all, thanks to their bevy of goddesses. Although, you know, I wonder." Salamander paused, running over memories in his mind. "There's a place for her already there. Some Bardekians have a goddess with no name and no face. Sometimes she's depicted as a woman with a veil drawn across her face. At other times, her statues just have a sort of cylinder for a head. She's a death goddess. I think she protects the dead on their last journey, or maybe she punishes some of them. No one much likes to talk about her."

"That's usual when it comes to death gods. It would be easy for those Bardekians to see Alshandra as one of their own, then."

"Just so." Salamander started to get up, then sat back down abruptly. The world was shimmering around him. "I think I'm more tired than I realized."

"Here, I'll help you up. You need to sleep. First thing in the morning, I want you to have a look at Honelg's dun, provided you're not still exhausted."

"I shouldn't have any trouble with the scrying. It's the first thing in the morning part that troubles me."

"Well, we'll see how the muster goes, then. I'll wake you as late as I can."

Dallandra made sure that Salamander went straight to his blankets in the tent he shared with the archers of Dar's escort, then returned to her little fire to wait for Calonderiel. She'd been assuming, she realized, both that the mazrak she'd spotted earlier was Sidro, and that Sidro was indeed Raena reborn. That she might be the same soul as Raena was still possible, of course, but not even a dweomer raven could have flown all the way back to Zakh Gral in a single evening on the physical plane. In her day Raena had been able to travel the secret roads, but only because Alshandra had lent her the etheric and astral energies to do so. Without Alshandra, she would need long years of training to fly along those paths. Given her cult's denial of the dweomer, it was highly unlikely that she'd gotten it.

But if not Sidro, who was the mazrak? The thought of a Bardek lamp on a Horsekin altar and a Bardek-style painting behind it kept returning to Dallandra's mind. The best case would be that priestesses of the Bardekian nameless goddess had somehow linked up with the Alshandra worshipers, but considering the vast distances between the Bardekian islands and the Horsekin lands, it seemed highly improbable.

The other alternative disturbed her. Most Bardekians were highly civilized, cultured people, not the sort to become religious fanatics or to establish ties with the likes of the Horsekin, but as in all times and lands, some few became general riffraff, criminals, or worst of all, men who followed the corruptions and practiced the evils of the dark dweomer.

But why would a dark dweomerman—the dark guilds only allowed men to join—be consorting with Horsekin? Had some of the dark dweomer practioners fled the legal authorities in their homeland and come north to take refuge among the Horsekin tribes? If so, it was possible that her mysterious mazrak was one of them. But how had he managed to survive, when the Alshandra cult demanded death for anyone working dweomer?

"Too many questions," she said aloud. "There may be answers in Zakh Gral—if we can take the fort and get at them. If? We have to now. We absolutely have to."

Soon after, Calonderiel returned with the news that the prince and Meranaldar were still trying to think of some polite reason to leave the gwerbret's table.

"You know, I even feel sorry for our milksop scribe," Cal said, smiling. "He was nearly asleep and desperately trying to stay awake. It would be rude, after all, to start snoring at table, and the gods all know that being rude is his worst fear."

"You *are* mean sometimes!"

"I suppose so." He cocked his head to one side and studied her for a moment. "You look like you've got bad news to tell me."

"Mean you are, but also perceptive. I'm afraid I do. Branna and I spotted a mazrak this evening, circling above the camp. It can't be any of the priestesses from Zakh Gral. That means there's a rogue stallion hanging around this herd, and I don't know who he is."

For a moment Cal blinked at her; then he swore with some of the foulest oaths she'd ever heard him use.

"Well," she said when he'd done, "I felt somewhat the same."

"Only somewhat, or so I should hope. You must be sure of this, or you wouldn't tell me."

"Oh, yes. This mazrak is the real reason I didn't want Cadryc's womenfolk out on the road. Tell me, will they be staying in Cengarn?"

"Yes. The tieryn agreed with us instantly, and so did Lord Oth when we asked him." Cal paused for a long sigh that shaded into a growl. "At least one thing's gone our way. I suppose it was too much to hope that this campaign would be some nice clean military exercise and nothing more."

"Apparently it was. This whole situation positively reeks of dweomer, and I'm afraid that some of it might be the worst possible kind."

Much too early by Salamander's reckoning, Dallandra woke him. Except for the two of them, the archers' tent stood empty. Apparently he'd slept straight through all the noise of the other men rolling up their bedrolls and gathering their gear.

"They're waiting for you to get up," Dalla told him, "so they can strike the tent."

"Ah, um, urk." Salamander sat up. "I'll hurry, then."

He'd slept mostly dressed; he pulled on his boots and staggered outside to find the first pale gray of dawn a stripe on the eastern horizon. Muttering and complaining, he followed Dallandra down to the riverbank, where the water flowed glimmering from the silver day brightening in a cloudy sky. With such a ready focus, Salamander found the image of Honelg's dun easily. At first it seemed that he was watching it from a great height, as if he flew over it in bird-form. He could feel danger so urgently, however, that he found himself swooping down, focusing down, until he seemed to be standing inside the ward.

Four men were loading sacks and bedrolls onto a pair of pack mules, while servants held the reins of four riding horses at the gates. Lord Honelg stood nearby, watching the men. He was holding a long stick in one hand, an object that Salamander found puzzling until Honelg called one of the men over. Honelg began using the stick to draw a rough map in the muddy ground at his feet. He was talking all the while, but Salamander couldn't hear his words. He had no need, really, as the map made everything quite clear. Salamander broke the vision.

"Dalla, he's sending messengers to Zakh Gral."

"I was afraid of that." Dallandra had gone white about the mouth. "You're sure they're going to Zakh Gral?"

"And where else in the Westlands would they be going? Certainly not to consort with Vandar's spawn out on the grass."

"Well, yes. I just had a desperate moment of hope." She tried to smile and failed utterly. "Ebañy, if the Horsekin are warned—we may still be able to destroy their fortress, but how many of us are going to die doing it?"

For a moment Salamander could find nothing to say, just from the shock of seeing Dallandra frightened. "Now here," he said at last, "things aren't hopeless yet. It's a long ride to Zakh Gral from Honelg's dun. They'll have to cross the grasslands, and I'll wager that they have to stick to open country. When Rocca took me there, we went through forest, all right, but the route was so complex that the messengers would be lost in half a day if they tried to follow it. They'll have to head dead west through the grassland. And that gives us the time and chance to intercept them."

Some of the color returned to Dallandra's face. "We need to contact Valandario and Carra."

"Just that." Salamander paused for a yawn. "I wonder where the nearest alar is? Most alarli should still have their herds in the north grazing."

"Valandario will know. If you scry and tell her what you're seeing, they'll have some idea of where the messengers are."

"Better yet—if Val rides with them, I can guide them. I'll scry, then contact her and tell her what I've seen, and with a bit of luck, she can lead our men straight to the messengers."

"That might work, yes." Dallandra sounded doubtful. "But we daren't depend on luck."

"It would be far better if I were there with them. If I fly, I can reach Val's alar in a day."

"No! I absolutely forbid it. Ebañy, I do not want to spend another ten years putting the pieces of your mind back together." All at once Dallandra smiled. "Besides, we've got stronger wings than yours at our disposal, assuming they get here soon, anyway."

"Of course! The residue of all that mead must have fuddled my mind. Arzosah."

"Exactly. Here, let's walk a ways from the camp. I want to summon her again, just to make sure she knows it's urgent. And then we'd better tell Cal about this latest disaster."

"And the gwerbret, too, I suppose."

"No. Do you think a Deverry lord, particularly an arrogant child like Ridvar, would believe us?"

"Oh. Alas. No, he wouldn't."

"We'll have to make this strike without any help from the Roundears, and that's probably for the best. We can act more quickly on our own."

Branna sat sullenly on the edge of the rumpled bed. By candlelight she was watching Neb pack his scribe's tools into a saddlebag. He'd already rolled his few extra pieces of clothing up in his old set of blankets, lying ready by the door.

"I still wish I were going with you," she said.

"In a way, I wish you were, too." Neb looked up from his task. "My heart's going to ache every single moment we're parted."

Something of her bad mood lifted at seeing he shared it. "While you're gone, I'm going to finish your wedding shirt. Uncle Cadryc sent messengers back to the dun this morning, and I told them to get the pieces and bring them back. Some of the women servants know where they are."

"My thanks." Neb turned and smiled at her, but his eyes filled with tears. With a laugh he wiped them away on his sleeve. "I don't know why that moved me so, hearing you mention the shirt."

"I don't either, but I'm glad it did."

He sat down next to her on the bed, drew her into his arms, and kissed her. For a moment she clung to him, but from the ward below men's voices and the clop of hooves on cobbles drifted up to them.

"Ah, curse it all!" Neb said. "I wish I weren't leaving, but if I'm going to be the tieryn's servitor, I've got to follow his orders."

"It won't be for long, I'll wager. I mean, you won't be anyone's servitor in a little while. We've got to go study with Dalla."

"True spoken. I feel that I've treated your uncle's hospitality ill, though, taking you away and leaving him without a scribe."

"Solla can read and write. Why shouldn't she be his scribe? It's not like he sends lots of letters, anyway."

"Why not, indeed? That eases my heart a bit." Neb raised her hand to his lips and kissed the palm. "And at least now I know you'll be safe. I don't know why, but thinking of you and Galla out on the roads frightened me badly."

"Me, too. Dalla says it was a dweomer warning. You see, we can't get away from it."

"I don't even want to."

The noise in the ward grew louder. They could hear Ridvar yelling orders and men answering him.

"I'll walk with you down to the muster, my love," Branna said. "That way we won't be parted quite as long."

"Good." Neb grinned at her, then glanced out of the window.

His grin abruptly disappeared. "Better take your cloak. On top of everything else, it looks like it's going to rain."

The weather had held gloriously fair for the gwerbret's wedding celebration, but that night clouds had ridden in on a north wind, and by dawn a dark mass of them covered the sky. On the eastern horizon the sun made a brave stand, turning the storm's edge silver, but in the end, it fled in defeat.

"Cursed nuisance," Cadryc said. "We'll be riding wet by noon, lad."

"Most likely," Gerran said. "A bit of rotten luck, Your Grace."

In the meadow below Cengarn, the men of the Red Wolf and the Westfolk were waiting for the rest of the army to join them. The Red Wolf warband had already chosen up pairs and were organizing themselves and their horses into an untidy line of march. The Westfolk were still saddling up and sorting out weapons. Their longbows would travel on a pack animal, but each man carried a short hunting bow in a leather sling across his back. These they could shoot from horseback. Two of the archers stood off to one side, arguing with Calonderiel over some detail or other. Since they were speaking in Elvish, Gerran understood none of it.

Servants from the dun were taking down the pavilion. As Gerran watched, they pulled the guy ropes free of their pegs, and the canvas structure collapsed inward. It fell in white billows, and as they settled to the ground, Gerran saw Neb and Branna, who'd apparently been standing on the far side of the pavilion. They were enjoying a long and passionate farewell in each other's arms. Gerran felt a brief contempt—the scribe was obviously no honor-bound fighting man, if he'd make such a fuss about leaving his woman.

"I wonder where the blasted gwerbret and the rest of them are," Cadryc remarked. "I want to get everyone mounted up before the cursed rains come. Don't want to be riding on wet saddles, do we?"

"We don't, Your Grace."

"His men should have gotten their gear together last night.

Humph! The longer we sit here, the longer Honelg has to prepare for a siege."

"True spoken. But you know, Ridvar promised to have his dun and town searched for Alshandra's people. We don't need any more spies trotting off north with news. I'll wager he's setting the hunt in motion right now."

"I'd forgotten about that. And good thing it is, though a bit like setting dogs round the sheep fold after the wolves have been and gone. Which reminds me, I've got to thank Lady Dallandra." Cadryc made a sour face. "I feel like a fool, I tell you, for not seeing the danger to our womenfolk. Ah, well, mayhap I'll be in a position to do her a favor one day."

Gerran found Dallandra something of a puzzle, simply because the prince treated her with such deference. Some of the other West-folk referred to her as "wise one," as well. He wasn't sure if the term were some kind of official title or merely a compliment. In her doe-skin leggings and tunic, with her hair severely braided, she looked more like a lad to him than a lady, but as with all the Westfolk, with their smooth beauty he couldn't tell if she were young or aging.

Dallandra took the tieryn's thanks graciously indeed.

"It was truly Calonderiel who realized what might happen," she said. "I only had the strangest feeling about trouble coming."

"Well, you women have a way about you, eh?" Cadryc said. "In-tuition, I suppose you'd call it, seeing the things we men overlook. You have my thanks twice over."

Dallandra smiled in acknowledgment, then looked Gerran's way. Her steel-gray glance seemed to cut into his mind and probe his very soul. He found himself remembering all the rumors of dweomer that he'd heard over the years. Meeting her level gaze made him wonder if maybe they were true, after all. Certainly if anyone he'd ever met had dweomer, it would be this woman. *And Neb*, he thought, *the fight we had—if you could call it a fight. He and Dallandra spend a lot of time talking, don't they?*

His earlier contempt for the scribe vanished as he was forced to draw the inevitable conclusion: this war involved sorceries and dark powers. For a moment he felt like a man who steps off a ladder into a hay loft only to feel the floor giving way beneath him as long-rotted boards break at last. With a small smile Dallandra looked away, and the world steadied again under him.

Overhead, thunder rumbled. Gerran yelped like a kicked dog. He could feel his face burning with embarrassment. "My apologies," he said. "That startled me, for some cursed reason!"

"Me, too," Cadryc glared in the direction of the citadel, looming above them as darkly as any storm cloud. "I wish the gwerbret would get himself down here."

Gwerbret Ridvar, with Prince Voran riding beside him, did lead his men down before the rain broke. The army, however, had made a scant three miles from Cengarn when a hard downpour began, soaking everyone before they could even curse the stuff properly. At first it showed every sign of lasting all day and perhaps into the night, but not long after noon a wind sprang up from the west. Like a sheepdog it harried the clouds and pushed them toward the east. The rain turned to a drizzle, then dwindled to nothing. In a clear sky the sun hung low over the western horizon.

"Well, now, that's a bit of luck!" Cadryc said. "Storms usually last all day around here."

"So they do," Gerran said, but he suddenly wondered if it was luck or Dallandra who'd driven the storm away.

The message came back down the line of march that the gwerbret was going to call a halt as soon as he found a decent spot for their encampment. Cheers followed its progress from rider to rider.

"Let's hope it stays dry tomorrow," Cadryc said.

"True spoken, Your Grace," Gerran said. "We can't have gotten more than twelve miles from Cengarn. It's the cursed muddy roads—" He broke off when he realized that Cadryc wasn't listening.

The tieryn was riding with his head tipped back, staring up at the sky. When Gerran followed his lead, he saw something that looked like a bird circling high above them, a black bird of some sort, perhaps, but it was far too big for a raven.

"What in the name of every god is that?" Cadryc pointed. "Looks like the blasted thing is following us."

Up ahead the Westfolk archers had seen it, too. With a shout they began to free their bows from their leather slings. Calling out in Elvish, Dallandra turned her horse out of line and rode back level with the troop. Whatever she said made the men leave their bows on their backs. The bird dropped down closer in a lazy circle—no bird at all, not with those greenish-black scales glittering from the rain, not with those enormous but unfeathered wings.

"It's another blasted dragon!" Gerran said. "As if we didn't have enough trouble on our hands already."

Cadryc most likely would have agreed, but at that moment the horses got a noseful of the dragon's vinegarish scent. Even the best-trained warhorses began to buck and rear, neighing in terror, kicking out, until the entire army disintegrated into a mob. The dragon dipped one wing and turned, flapping fast away toward a stretch of open grass not far to the east. As it did so, Gerran could have sworn that it called out "My apologies!" in a deep rumble of a voice, but he had no time to consider the absurdity of such a thought until at last, with the dragon gone off, the horses began to calm themselves.

Dallandra dismounted, then turned her trembling horse over to Calonderiel and ran through wet grass to join the dragon, who had settled in a rough pasture downwind. Arzosah had grown a fair bit since the last time Dallandra had seen her. Not counting her polished black tail, now curved delicately around her immense haunches, she was nearly thirty feet long, with a massive head that shone a coppery sort of green in the sunlight. Arzosah greeted the dweomermaster with a rumble of good humor, then shook her enormous greenish-black wings dry and folded them along her plump green sides.

"A thousand apologies," Arzosah spoke in Elvish. "I didn't realize I was going to panic your horses. The last time I traveled with you Westfolk, they ignored me."

"That was Evandar's doing," Dallandra said. "He cast some sort of enchantment upon them, but unfortunately, I don't have the slightest idea of what it was."

"And of course he wouldn't bother to tell you, nasty clot of ectoplasm that he was. I should have known." The dragon snorted in disgust. "Well, be that as it may, here I am. I'd have answered your summons before this, but it took me a while to find you."

"I assumed it would, yes. How would you like to help us kill some Horsekin?"

"What a lovely idea for a summer's day!"

"Good. I wasn't truly afraid that you'd refuse."

"No need to worry! I swore a vow that I'd hate them forever, and they've done nothing recently to make me break it. Where are they?"

"They're building themselves a fortress off in the far west. I thought perhaps you'd seen it."

"No, and it's a pity. I would have enjoyed picking them off a few at a time."

"Well, it's not too late. They haven't finished building it yet. What you see here—" Dallandra paused to indicate the road full of warbands with a sweep of her arm, "—is just the beginning. We'll be mustering an army to go and destroy it."

"Splendid! Can I assume that any dead horses are mine?"

"Most assuredly."

"Then you don't even need to invoke my true name. What is it they say in Deverry? It would gladden my heart, that's it, and my stomach as well, to join you."

"Wonderful! I do thank you, but there are a couple of small matters we have to attend to first."

Arzosah heaved a gigantic sigh. "I should have known there'd be a price to pay. Small matters, are they? Doubtless some boring tasks vexing to dragons. They always are." She was looking past Dallandra. "I suspect one of them of arriving now."

Dallandra glanced back and saw Salamander, dismounted and trotting toward them. He waved a greeting with a swing of one arm and called out, "Arzosah, my dearest wyrm, oh, pinnacle of dragonhood!"

"What do you want me to do for you?" Arzosah rolled her massive eyes heavenward. "I know flattery when I hear it, elf."

Salamander grinned and bowed to her. "You're as perceptive as always, nay, not merely insightful, but perspicacious and sagacious as well."

Arzosah growled, but only softly.

"We need your help on two matters, actually," Dallandra said. "This warband you see here? It's on its way to deal with a traitorous lord who's gone over to the Horsekin. We can't spare the time for a siege if we're going to bring that fortress down, but he has enough archers to keep our men away from his dun walls."

"And I suppose you have the gall to expect me to do something about those archers. I don't fancy having arrows hissing around my head. If one hit me in the eye—"

"I hadn't thought of that," Dallandra said. "I most certainly don't want you injured."

"I don't see how we're going to take his dun with those archers in place." Salamander stepped forward. "And we can't afford to leave fighting men there to hold a long siege. We were hoping you could think of some maneuver to drive the archers off."

"I knew that a straightforward Horsekin-eating expedition sounded too good to be true." Arzosah paused for a snarl. "What's the second thing?"

"Lord Honelg is sending messengers to Zakh Gral," Salamander said. "They'll be two, maybe three days' ride to the west of his dun by the time we reach it. We'll never be able to catch up with them, but you, the very soul of speed, should be able stop them."

"A simple chore at last! How refreshing!" The dragon swung her head around to look at Dallandra. "I suppose you want me to carry this prattling gerthddyn on my poor aching back."

"Yes, I'm afraid so," Dallandra said. "I know it's a horrible imposition, but he's the only one who can scry for them. We could search the grasslands for days otherwise."

"And when we find them, what then? Do I get to eat them?"

"No, not the men." Dallandra put steel into her voice. "Absolutely not! No live horses, either, unless one's injured too badly to heal. However, once we take Lord Honelg's dun, I'm sure we'll find some cattle for you."

"Cattle? Ah, cattle!" Arzosah licked her lips. "I should consider myself well thanked, in that case. A hog would be nice as well."

"Two hogs, then, if we can find some. I've worked out a plan," Salamander said. "During today's ride, I've been in contact with another dweomermaster. Now that you're here, we can discuss things in some detail."

"And we'd better do just that before you leave," Dallandra put in. "Because it's very complicated." She shot Salamander a black glance. "Most likely too much so."

"I really wish that I'd never let Evandar find out my true name," Arzosah said. "It was stupid of me, stupid stupid stupid!"

"Be that as it may, you're stuck with us now." Salamander grinned at her. "The army's making camp. Dalla, why don't you tell this most marvelous, beauteous, and sagacious wyrm what we have in mind. I'll go over to the supply carts and get some rope. I'm not going to stay on her back without it, I think me."

Arzosah raised her head toward the sky and whined like a kicked dog. "Ropes! Fit only for a smelly old mule! What happened to my harness? I once had a fine leather harness with jewels upon it, not as many as I deserve, of course, but jewels nonetheless."

"It's in a chest somewhere in Dun Cengarn, I suppose," Dallandra said. "But there's no time to go back and fetch it now. Please, listen carefully to what we need to do. Oh, and one more thing, by your true name, Arzosah Sothy Lorezohaz, I enjoin you to obey Salamander as if he were me."

"You think of everything, don't you?" Arzosah muttered something else, but in Dragonish. Judging from her tone of voice, Dallandra was just as glad she didn't understand the words. "Oh, very well." Arzosah returned to Elvish. "I can but obey."

During the day's march north, Neb had been riding near the end of the column with the other servitors and the servants who were in charge of the baggage train. For them, the rain was a blessing—better to ride wet than to choke on the dust stirred up from a dry road by the warbands ahead of them. When the dragon appeared overhead, the gentle old palfrey Gerran had given him made a weak attempt to rear and buck like the other horses, then quieted down and merely trembled.

When the orders came back to dismount and prepare the night's camp, Neb followed them gladly. Although he was by no means a terrible rider, he certainly wasn't a good one either, and the dragon's proximity was keeping all the horses nervous. The baggage train turned into an orderly if confusing mob as the experienced servants hurried to their work, tending horses, unloading tents from wagons, and going through the provisions to ensure that any wet food got eaten that very night. Neb stood off to one side and watched, wondering what he was supposed to do. Fortunately, Salamander came jogging up to him.

"Give that horse to one of the servants to tend," the gerthddyn said. "Never forget that you're a highly educated scribe and thus too valuable for sweated labor. Besides, Dalla wants to talk to you."

"Very well," Neb said. "I take it she summoned that creature?"

"She did, but the creature's actually quite intelligent. You've got to treat her as if she were a great lady." Salamander paused, thinking. "Actually, you know, she *is* a great lady, merely of the scaly variety. I'll introduce you in a bit, but now I've got to find rather a lot of rope. Could you help me carry it over?"

"Gladly. I have to admit, this is all a cursed lot more interesting than sitting around the Red Wolf dun."

With a coil of rope each slung over their shoulders, Neb and Salamander left the camp. With distractions all around him, Neb hadn't quite absorbed the idea of "dragon," but as they jogged across the pasture to meet up with Dallandra, he could finally get a good look and see just how huge the creature was, as long as one of the stone tax barns near Trev Hael. When she raised her head to look his way, her scaly ears and spiky crest reached the inside height of a barn, too. Despite his best intentions, Neb found himself slow-ing to a walk and lingering behind the gerthddyn. Apparently she had noticed.

"I won't eat you," the dragon called out. "You're much too skinny." She made a rumbling sound that stopped Neb cold.

"That's her idea of a jest," Salamander said, "and when she rumbles like that, she's laughing."

"If you say so." Neb summoned as much courage as he could and walked on. "I've heard of dragons, but this is the first one I've ever seen."

"They stick to the border country, truly, and the wild places. Her name's Arzosah, by the by. I need your help to rig her up with a rope harness."

"Ye gods! You don't expect me to ride the beast, do you?"

"I don't. I'm the one who's going to do the riding. Dallandra will explain everything after we've gone, but speed is of the essence."

Neb's share of the harness work consisted mostly of holding pieces of rope taut while Salamander tied them together, following Dallandra's directions. Ropes went around the dragon's pale green belly like a cinch, then around her chest like a martingale, but she absolutely refused to allow anything resembling a crupper. Throughout the process she grumbled, moaned, and complained so much that Neb began to lose his fear of her. With the rope harness finished, Salamander tied on a bag of provisions and his bedroll.

"That should do," he said. "Is it comfortable enough, oh pinnacle of dragonhood?"

"Just barely." Arzosah paused to hiss softly to herself. "It will have to do."

"One thing quickly," Dallandra said. "I'd been hoping that the silver wyrm would come with you. Do you know where Rori is?"

Arzosah went very still, except for her tail, which thrashed back and forth, apparently of its own will, because when she turned her head to scowl at it, the thrashing stopped. "We'll discuss that later," the dragon said at last. "Once we've done this errand."

"Is somewhat wrong, then?" Dallandra said.

"We will discuss it later." Arzosah swung her head around to glare at the dweomermaster. "When I return."

Neb suddenly realized what Salamander had meant when he called the wyrm a great lady. Her tone of voice allowed no argument; she might have been a dowager queen rebuking a maidservant.

"Very well," Dallandra said. "You need to get on your way."

"And I need you to lower your head," Salamander said to the dragon. "So I can climb aboard."

"I am *not* a ship, gerthddyn," Arzosah snarled. "You may ride upon me, but I am still a dragon, and I'll ask you to remember that."

"My dearest wyrm, how could I ever forget it?" Salamander made her a bow. "Where shall I impose my ugly and unworthy self upon you?"

"Put one foot on my neck." She laid her head upon the ground. "Where it joins the shoulders. Then swing the other leg over. You can perch just behind my crest and cling to the last spike of it."

Salamander followed her instructions, and she slowly and carefully raised her head, allowing him to kneel on her back between her wings but well forward. He slid both feet under a cinch rope and clutched the tall spike of her crest with both hands.

"Now remember," Dallandra said. "You are to obey Salamander instantly and as thoroughly as you'd obey me."

"I know, I know. And I promise to keep him safe as well." Arzosah heaved herself to her feet. "Stand back, young scribe! I need a bit of room."

Neb darted away to stand beside Dallandra. He watched openmouthed as the dragon stretched out her wings, and out and out, a vast wingspan like the ceiling of a great hall. Arzosah bunched herself, her haunches quivered, and with one huge flap of wing she leaped into the air. Her wings beat into the wind with a sound like enormous drums as she gained height, circled once over the pasture, then headed off west, flying fast and steadily. For a long moment Neb could say nothing at all.

"Well, there they go," Dallandra said. "I suppose you'd like to know what all this is about."

"If you'd be so kind, truly," Neb said. "Ye gods, I feel—I'm astounded—I never thought I'd see such things!"

"I suggest you get used to it. You're going to be seeing a good many stranger ones, and quite soon now, too."

Apparently, most of the army shared his fearful bewilderment. As they walked back to the encampment, no one said a word to them. Most of the men they passed stared gape-mouthed and crossed their fingers in the sign of warding against witchcraft. Some others stepped back and rushed off to be busy elsewhere. A few of the braver ones did bow to Dallandra, and Gerran came to meet her.

"My lady." Gerran bowed as well. "Prince Daralanteriel tells me that you'd like our scribe to move over to your camp."

"If the tieryn agrees," Dallandra said.

"I asked him, and he does. He owes you for the safety of his womenfolk, he told me. We were just wondering why."

"Do you really need to ask?" Dallandra caught Gerran's gaze with her own. "Branna told me about the squabble between you and Neb."

"Oh." Gerran swallowed heavily, but his voice stayed perfectly calm. "I see."

"Good. Still, you can tell the tieryn that I'll need help when it comes to tending any wounded Westfolk after the battle. Our bodies heal differently from yours, and I want to start training Neb."

"I see," Gerran repeated. "Neb, I'll help you carry your gear over."

"My thanks," Neb said. "I didn't bring much with me, but I do have the horse and its gear, too."

The Westfolk had made their camp at a slight distance from the main clutter of tents, wagons, piles of horse gear, and the like. Neb would have a place in the tent shared by Calonderiel's archers. Neb and Gerran put Neb's gear inside at a vacant spot near the door. With a quick bow, Gerran left them, striding back to his own camp.

Dallandra sat Neb down inside her own tent, and there, in safe privacy, she explained why she'd summoned the dragon.

"Not a word of this to your lord or any of the lords," she finished up. "They need to surround the dun and ensure that Honelg won't be sending any more messengers. I don't want them rushing off to the Westlands."

"Very well, then," Neb said. "I take it Salamander can scry the messengers out because he's seen them before."

"True-spoken. Here! Did you just remember that?"

"I did. It's been interesting, the last few days. I've found bits and pieces of lore coming back to me at odd moments. I'm cursed glad, too. I want to be worthy of Branna, after all."

"I'm quite sure you already are." Dallandra gave him a smile. "Now, listen carefully. I think we're being spied upon by a particular kind of dweomerman, and perhaps one of Alshandra's priestesses can see us as well. I want you to stay on your guard. If you ever have the slightest sensation that might mean someone's trying to scry you out, tell me straightaway. I don't care how silly or small you think it is. Tell me anyway."

"I will. You needn't worry about that."

Salamander found that riding on dragonback was a much greater adventure than he'd anticipated, and most assuredly less comfortable. Like all children raised among the Westfolk, he had learned to stay on a horse so early that he couldn't remember not knowing how to ride. He'd been assuming, therefore, without really focusing on the assumption, that he could easily adjust to riding on Arzosah.

He was, of course, quite wrong. To an observer on the ground, she seemed to fly steadily and straight, but in fact the beating of her enormous leathery wings produced a rocking motion, a quick lift up and then a sink down. She stirred up quite a wind, too, forcing him to hunker down to find shelter behind the spiky scales of her crest. They'd traveled a good many miles before he learned how to roll with her motion. Still, his discomfort was a small price to pay for her speed. When he looked down, he saw the countryside moving far below as if it were a Bardek carpet, slowly unrolling itself across a floor. Well before sunset they spotted Lord Honelg's dun, a small dark wart on the green landscape far below.

"Turn west here," Salamander called out.

"Hang on!" Arzosah banked one wing and swung herself around, heading toward the lowering sun.

The maneuver left Salamander feeling sick, but he clung to the ropes and managed to stay secure. Not long after, they left the farmland north of Cengarn behind them, covering a distance that would have taken a horse half a day. Just as the sun was touching the horizon, they saw Twenty Streams Rock, an apparent pebble, gray against a blanket of green. Thin lines of blue water gleamed amidst the grass.

"Land there!" Salamander yelled.

Arzosah banked into a turn and circled down to land gently in the tall grass. Salamander slid down from her back and squelched a desire to throw himself down on solid ground and kiss the earth in greeting.

"Now what?" Arzosah said. "I don't suppose you'll take these wretched ropes off me."

"If I did, I'd never get them back on. I thought you'd like a rest and a chance for a drink. I've got to scry for our prey."

"Some water would be very nice, indeed."

Arzosah waddled over to the nearest stream and hunkered down to drink, lapping water like a dog with her long black tongue. Salamander was amazed at how clumsy she seemed on the ground. Her short legs bent outward at the knees, and while they supported her full weight, long graceful strides were beyond her. In flight, however, she moved like a dancer. *A true creature of air,* he thought to himself, *but still fiery withal.*

Salamander sat down and watched the bluish twilight play on the long grass. As the sunset wind picked up, the grass bowed and sighed as it moved. Against it, he formulated an image of Valandario, and she answered him immediately. He could see her standing out in the grass and looking up at the sky to the east, where a few stars were already shining like carelessly dropped gems.

"Where are you?" Salamander thought to her. "The dragon and I have reached Twenty Streams."

"We're not far, about half a day's ride to the west. Have you spotted those messengers yet? In the flesh, I mean."

"No, but we'll be flying again as soon as Arzosah's rested. I'm expecting them to light a campfire. After all, they don't know we know and all that. Once I spot them, I'll contact you again."

"Very good. I've got eight archers and two swordsmen with me. Do you think that will be enough? I don't understand matters of war, I'm afraid."

"More than enough, really."

"What about the prince and the others? Where are they?"

"Still crawling along north with the Roundear army. It will take them a while to reach Honelg's dun." Salamander paused to glance behind him. Beside the stream Arzosah was wiping her chin dry on a patch of grass. "Ah, the dragon's finished her drink, I see. We'd best get on our way."

Sure enough, a trace of twilight still gleamed in the west when Salamander spotted a pinprick of fire glowing among a tumble of boulders about five miles north of Twenty Streams. Rather than announce their presence to the messengers by flying directly over them, they made a wide circle around. As a gibbous moon rose in the east, Salamander's half-elven eyes could spot various landmarks, a stream with a tangle of hazel wands along it, and the boulders themselves.

"That's enough for tonight." Salamander had to yell at the top of his well-trained voice for the dragon to hear him. "Head straight south from here."

"Are we joining up with the other dweomermaster?" Arzosah's rumble carried quite well.

"Yes, we are."

"I'll look for another campfire, then. Hang on tight!"

Salamander wrapped his arms around the nearest spike of her crest. The dragon dropped one wing, banked into a steep turn, then righted herself and headed south.

They found Valandario's small encampment easily. A small herd of horses, watched over by a mounted guard, grazed at tether near a single large tent. A campfire burned in front of the tent, and Salamander could see the men of the squad, figures as small as dolls from the air, walking back and forth on various errands. Arzosah landed some distance away to avoid spooking the Westfolk horses. Salamander slid down from her back with a small silent prayer of gratitude to the solid earth. All that circling had left him more than a little queasy.

"I want to go hunt," Arzosah said. "I spotted some deer not far away."

"You certainly may," Salamander said, "but if you make a kill, bring it back here before you eat it. I don't want you falling asleep while you're off somewhere."

"How very clever of you to think of that! Oh, very well. I'll nest here after I eat. When do we leave again?"

"After the dawn."

"At least it should be warm and sunny tomorrow. I should be thankful for small boons, I suppose."

With a long rustle of her wings, the dragon dashed forward and took to the air. Salamander watched her fly for a moment. He was remembering scrying out his brother and seeing him in dragon form, stooping to kill a deer. The huge silvery mouth had closed around the fleeing doe's neck with a spurt of red, an omen of the raw feast to come. With a shake of his head Salamander banished the memory. He strode off, heading for the Westfolk camp, where Valandario stood waiting for him.

"All's well so far," Salamander called out.

"Splendid!" Valandario said. "Come have dinner. You're just in time."

"Good, good." Salamander realized that his stomach had a very different opinion than his mind about eating right away. "I'll just contact Dallandra first, I think. She might be worried."

"She probably is. So are we all, worried that is. Ebañy, I had an awful thought. You told me about that raven mazrak. Why can't he just fly off to Zakh Gral and warn them?"

"What would he tell them? That he found out we were attacking by using forbidden dweomer? And then flew all the way there in mazrak form? They'd kill him on the spot."

"Oh." Valandario allowed herself a soft, warm smile. "It's lovely when your enemy throws his best weapon away, isn't it? Well, you contact Dalla, and I'll finish getting dinner ready."

I n the middle of the noise and bustle of a camping army, Dallandra was kneeling by a small fire, feeding it twigs to keep it burning. Even as she reached for a larger stick of wood, she kept her gaze firmly on the flames, her body as taut and poised as a strung bow. Now and then her lips would move as if they were forming words. Neb watched, awestruck. She was speaking to someone through the fire. He was so certain that he knew what she was doing that when she finally broke her concentration, he knelt beside her.

"Did Salamander find the messengers?" Neb said.

"He did, and they've joined up with Valandario as well," Dallandra said, then sat back on her heels with a laugh. "You took me by surprise there. When did you remember?"

"Just now, watching you."

"That's truly interesting." Dalla cocked her head to one side and considered him for a moment. "You may remember a great deal more than we thought at first. You don't have the words for your memories, but you recognize dweomer when you actually see it worked."

"So I do!"

"That pleases you, doesn't it?"

"It does." Neb gave her a sheepish grin. "I've been so jealous of

Branna, you see, with her wonderful dreams, and I felt lower than a snake for envying her, too."

"Well, it's perfectly understandable, the jealousy, I mean. Don't berate yourself for it."

"My thanks, I shan't, then. Do you think I could try scrying in the fire? I've been wondering how Branna is—"

"Nah nah nah! Slowly, now! I know it must be horribly tempting, the idea of just plunging ahead, seeing what you remember and what you can do with those skills, but it could also be very dangerous."

"Dangerous? How?"

"In a number of ways. First, it comes down to the old adage about learning how to mount a horse before you can ride. Or, wait, here's a better example. When you learned to write, did your father just show you a page from a book and tell you to copy it?"

"He didn't. First he made me analyze each letter, how many strokes made it up and what kind of strokes they were. Then I filled lots of wax tablets with just the strokes, up and down, round and round, and the like. It was tedious, as you can well imagine, but I was glad I'd done it when it came time to form the letters themselves."

"Well, dweomer is much the same. You've got to learn all its tricks of the mind first, to say naught of the lore, details like the names of spirits and the various levels of existence. You have to know everything as well and instinctively as you know how to walk, so that you can do certain actions without having to concentrate upon them."

"I see. It's going to take years, isn't it?"

"It is, but you've got to be patient. Now, as for trying to scry right now, what if some enemy is watching us? What if they overheard you, as it were, instead of Branna? Do you know the seals and commands to banish their efforts?"

"I don't, truly." Neb felt a cold wave of disappointment. "Very well, I can see what you mean by dangers."

"Good, but here's another one. If you rush ahead without knowing what you're doing, you could go mad."

"What? How?"

"By opening yourself up to unseen things without knowing how
to seal them off again. When Salamander returns, I want you to ask
him about this. He's in position to know how badly things can go
wrong if you're not careful."

"Well and good then, I will. He should be back soon, shouldn't he?"

"I hope so, and if everything goes well on the morrow." Dallandra hesitated, glancing into the fire again. "Salamander always has
to do things in the most elaborate way possible. It's enough to drive
one daft!"

Despite Dallandra's fears, Salamander's plan was for him, at
least, remarkably direct. With the first light of dawn he
woke and dressed, then trotted out to the nearby meadow to join
Arzosah. She was crouching by the stream, lapping up water.
When she was done drinking, she dipped her entire head under the
water for a brief moment, then raised it to shake herself dry.

"There!" Arzosah said. "All nice and clean. I do hate having
dried blood on my face."

"It must be an unpleasant sensation," Salamander said. "I take it
you found prey last night."

"I did, thank you, and I feel much restored. I suppose you want
to set off immediately. I was hoping to warm my poor aching wings
by lying in the sun for a little while."

"Go right ahead. There's no use in making our strike until the
messengers have taken the hobbles off their horses." Salamander
glanced at the pale sky, brightening as the sun inched itself above
the horizon. "They'll be desperate to make all possible speed to
Zakh Gral, but they've got to let their mounts graze nonetheless."

"Let's hope they get nice and fat." Arzosah paused for a yawn, displaying teeth the length of sword blades. "The horses, I mean, not the men. I remember Dalla's orders."

"Good. I'm going back to camp to get some breakfast and consult with Valandario."

Over a scant meal of flatbread and spiced honey-water, Salamander went over the details with Valandario one last time. She and her squad would ride slowly north, waiting for his signal to dismount and continue on foot. Two of the men would stay back to control the horses in case they got a good whiff of Arzosah's sour scent.

"I just hope we all end up in the right place at the right time," Valandario remarked.

"I'll make sure you do," Salamander said. "Don't forget that I'll be able to see you from the air, too. It's surprising and a little wonderful, really, how far you can see from dragonback."

"I suppose it must be. I can't say that I have a burning desire to try it myself."

"It does take some getting used to. So. I'd better scry and see just what our quarry is up to."

Just as he'd expected, Salamander found the messengers still at their camp. Out in the sunny grass their horses still grazed with their forelegs hobbled. Now and then they'd take a few rabbity steps to reach fresh grass. The men were rolling up blankets and gathering their gear. Soon, no doubt, they'd saddle up and ride. He broke the vision.

"They're just where I left them last night," Salamander said.

"Good," Valandario said. "I've been meaning to ask you, what about the silver wyrm? Is he going to join the siege?"

"I don't know. He hadn't appeared by the time I left, and Arzosah refuses to discuss him."

"That bodes ill. It really is ghastly, you know, thinking of Rhodry's transformation."

"Yes, but never ever let Arzosah hear you say it." Salamander tried to smile and failed. He got to his feet and turned away, looking out to the north. He could see Arzosah's shiny black bulk lounging in the grass a fair many yards away. "Rori's nearby, I think. I've scried for him at odd moments over the past month or so, ever since I saw him in the flesh. He's always been in the wilderness, but now I've gotten a good look from on high at the countryside around here. I recognized a couple of the places I'd seen him in."

"If he does turn up, you'll try to help him, won't you?"

"Of course!" *If anyone can,* Salamander thought. *If it's possible to help him.* "Well, we'd best get on our way."

Salamander waited until Valandario and her armed squad had left the camp before he rejoined the dragon. Once he and Arzosah had taken flight, Salamander scried again, using her patterned scales as a focus. This time he found the messengers saddling their horses, freed from tethers and hobbles. He broke the vision, then leaned forward to yell to Arzosah.

"It's time to make our strike."

She dipped her head to show she'd heard him, then began climbing higher into the sky. Salamander grabbed her crest spike with both arms and held on as tightly as he could. He could feel his legs sliding under the restraining rope behind him. If he should lose his grip on the spike, he'd flop onto his belly and doubtless slide all the way free to fall helplessly to earth. At last she leveled out, flapped twice, then let herself glide on the wind.

Below, the land seemed to have shrunk to a tapestry in green, with the occasional stream or rock only an embellished detail. Yet among the threads of grass, tiny figures moved, men and horses.

"There they are!" Arzosah called out. "Shall I swoop?"

"Yes!" Salamander wrapped his arms around the spike again. "Now!"

Downward she shot straight for the little band of messengers. Salamander could see nothing but the back of her neck and head, but he could hear the sudden neighing of panicked horses and the yells and curses of the men. When he risked a glance to one side, he saw grass rushing upward to meet him. With a muttered oath he concentrated on looking at the back of Arzosah's head and nothing else.

Just as suddenly as she'd dropped she banked into a turn, then began flapping her wings to gain height.

"Two of the riders are off," Arzosah called out. "And the pack-horses have pulled free, too. They're galloping south."

"Good!" Salamander called back. "Let's make another pass."

For a moment, however, she steadied her flight. From that height he could see Valandario's squad far off to the south. When he focused his mind on his old master in the craft he felt her mind respond almost instantly.

"Now, Val!" he thought to her. "We're—oh, by the Black Sun—dropping again!"

He wondered if she could hear the scream that followed, torn out of him, it seemed, as Arzosah plunged down and down. Once again, he heard men yelling and horses neighing. Once again the grass rushed at him. Suddenly Arzosah laughed in a huge rumble and leveled her flight.

"The last two are on the ground," she called out. "Shall I drive them south?"

"Yes!" Salamander could barely find the breath to yell. "Toward the other Westfolk."

This time Arzosah descended more slowly. Salamander could sit up and look over her neck. Some fifty or sixty feet below—he was in no mood to worry about precise measurements—the four men were running south or trying to, shoving their way through the tall grass that hindered them. Once one of them tripped. The other three kept running, but the fallen man managed to get up and take off after them, following their path through the trampled grass. Arzosah soon overshot them; she rose straight up, then banked into a turn to circle round and come at them again.

"There's Val and the squad," Salamander called out. "I think we can leave the messengers to her."

"Very well," Arzosah yelled back. "But this has been great fun."

"What was? Scaring the messengers or me?"

"Both, of course."

"You promised to keep me safe."

"If I'd felt you slipping through the ropes, I'd have leveled off and caught you. Don't you trust me?"

When Salamander didn't answer, she rumbled with laughter, then went into a long smooth glide with outstretched wings. Salamander could see the four messengers throwing themselves down at the feet of Valandario and her archers in abject surrender.

"Head back east to the army," he yelled. "Val seems to have everything under control here."

Since her morning's amusement had left her tired, Arzosah flew more slowly on their return journey. They reached the army late in the afternoon, just as it was making the night's camp near Mawrvelin. From their height, the dun of Bel's priests looked like a handful of pebbles. The dragon flew over it, giving Salamander a glimpse of the round temple inside the walls, then circled back over a pasture dotted with white cattle. With one last flap of wing to pull free of the turn, she began a long smooth glide down on silent wings.

"There's the army by that stream," Arzosah called out. "Just below the temple hill."

"Good!" Salamander called back. "It looks like they've made splendid progress."

"Splendid? They can't have gone more than twelve miles!"

"For a spur-of-the-moment army like this, with those wretched supply carts and their wooden wheels, on a road that runs uphill—that's splendid progress."

Arzosah snorted in disgust, then concentrated on landing a decent distance from the army's nervous horses. She curled her wings and hovered for a brief moment, then gently lowered herself to the earth in a nearby fallow field. Salamander let out his breath in a long sigh. When she lowered her head, he slid off her neck to the beautifully solid ground.

"A thousand thanks, oh wyrm of great splendor," Salamander said.

"What lovely manners you have when you're not exploiting poor pitiful dragons!" Arzosah looked heavenward. "The gods know how I suffer, thanks to that wretched Evandar."

With a shout and a wave of greeting, Dallandra came running across the field. Salamander hurried over to meet her.

"All's well," Salamander said. "Val and her archers have four prisoners."

"Excellent!" Dallandra paused for a moment to catch her breath. "I must go thank Arzosah."

"And take these wretched ropes off!" Arzosah had apparently heard her. "I am not a smelly old mule."

"There's no doubt about that." Salamander called back. "I'm on my way to release you." He glanced at Dallandra. "Where's Neb?"

"Up at the temple with Ridvar and Voran. They took Cadryc and some of his men for an escort. The noble-born agree with you that the taxes the priests have set are far too high. Neb's acting as scribe for the meeting."

No one could have accused the head priest of Temple Mawrvelin of growing fat at the expense of his poverty-stricken villagers. Since the priest was wearing only a knee-length linen tunic and sandals, Neb could see the outlines of most of His Holiness Govvin's bones under his pale skin. His shaved head looked more like a skull with deep-set dark eyes than part of a living body, except that, unlike skulls, he never smiled. He sat as straight as an iron poker on a backless bench, his scrawny hands clasped in his lap, and stared directly at Prince Voran, sitting opposite in a rickety chair, for the entire meeting, except for a few brief moments when his eyes flicked Ridvar's way. The young gwerbret said very little, merely leaned against the wall with his arms crossed over his chest.

Neb, who sat on the floor near the gwerbret's feet, was profoundly relieved to be out of the priest's line of sight. They'd been taken by the gatekeeper to a little reception chamber in what had once been barracks and stables, the usual long wooden building built into the curve of the wall. Aside from the bench and the chair, it contained nothing, not a statue of Bel, not a tapestry on the wall, not even straw on the stone floor. As Voran talked, noting the pitiful condition of the farm families along the road, Neb wrote a few words on his pair of wax tablets for each point the prince made. He left space for the priest's answers between each, but in the end, he might have filled the tablet for all the need of that space he had.

"Let me see if I understand you," Govvin said finally. "You've spoken many fine words, but as far as I can tell, your message is simple. You're concerned for the villagers because you expect this temple to furnish military aid in time of war. I refuse to do any such thing, so you may lay your concerns aside. Naught that happens here is your affair, Prince Voran. The priests of Bel answer to a higher justice than your father's." He stood up, nodded to the prince, then turned and walked out of the chamber, leaving the door open behind him.

Voran rose and clasped his hands behind his back to stop their shaking. He was white around the mouth in sheer rage. "The gall," were the only words that he could force out.

"Indeed," Ridvar said. "We'd better go back to camp, Your Highness."

"So we had." The prince took a deep breath, then spoke normally. "We can talk more freely there."

Neb scrambled up and followed them as they strode out of the chamber. Out in the ward the young gatekeeper was waiting for them. The only sign of deference he gave was a brief bob of his head in Voran's general direction, and he said not one word while he showed them out of the dun. The two lords were just as silent as they walked down the hill to the road, where some of their own men were waiting—the priests had earlier refused entry to their escort. Tieryn Cadryc stepped forward and raised one eyebrow in a silent question.

"Worse than we expected," Ridvar said. "We'll hold council later this evening. My thanks for the loan of your scribe."

"Most welcome, Your Grace," Cadryc said. "By the by, that

dragon's come back. It's over by the Westfolk's camp." He glanced at Neb. "Or is it a he?"

"A she, Your Grace," Neb said. "Her name's Arzosah. Dallandra tells me that she's the same dragon who saved Cengarn from the Horsekin siege. Apparently they live a long time."

Cadryc blinked rapidly, then shook his head, as if he were making sure he was truly awake and hearing correctly.

"Well, then, Neb," Prince Voran said, "go tell her she should poach as many of the temple's cattle as she can eat. It would soothe my heart a bit, and I'd imagine the gwerbret's heart as well."

At that Ridvar managed a smile, but only a thin one. Neb bowed to the nobility all round, then jogged off to rejoin Dallandra. He could see her and Salamander standing near the dragon in a field on the far side of the Westfolk tents. He wasn't sure if the prince had been only making a jest about the temple cows, but he was angry enough himself to relay the order to Arzosah.

"What a regal heart Voran has!" Arzosah paused to rumble in laughter. "I think me I'll take him up on that."

"When we flew over the temple," Salamander put in, "I spotted a fine-looking herd of white cattle out in one of its fields."

"I smelled them," Arzosah said, "and my mouth watered. I take it that the prince was displeased because the priests were as stingy as always."

"Worse than stingy," Neb said. "I'd say they were threatening open rebellion."

"What happened?" Dallandra snapped. "I'm beginning to get a bad feeling about that temple."

"If you'd been inside with us, it would have been worse. Let me just look at my notes."

Quickly Neb gave them a summary of Voran's points. When he repeated the priest's response, Salamander swore under his breath, and Arzosah hissed like a thousand cats. Dallandra, however, listened quietly, her mouth set in a twist more thoughtful than angry.

"Voran wasn't asking the priests to stand ready for war themselves," Neb finished up. "Nor did he want them to furnish troops.

He merely wanted the villagers to have the strength to defend themselves if need be."

"They'd also need some reason to defend the temple lands," Salamander said. "If I lived under that temple's rule, I'd desert the moment I saw the least sign of danger."

"Me, too," Neb said. "I suppose the priests could be asked to help provision an army in time of war. Maybe that's what vexes their miserly hearts."

Dallandra took a few steps away, then stood staring up at the distant temple.

"Or is it more than that, Dalla?" Salamander spoke softly.

"It may be, it may not." Dallandra kept staring at the temple. "I don't see any astral seals over the place."

"Would they bother to raise seals?" Arzosah joined in. "They may not know there are dweomermasters among us."

"If they were studying dark dweomer, they'd know. Believe me, they'd know. They'd have sentinels of a certain kind posted. I've not seen any."

"Ah, but what if they're being clever?" Salamander said. "They may have withdrawn all their workings so we won't spot them."

Dallandra let out her breath in a puff of frustration.

"We can draw reasonable conclusions all night," Salamander went on, "but alas, alack, and welladay, we won't know if they're true or false."

"Just so," Dallandra said. "But I think me I'd best find out."

"Dalla, you're not going to try to go up there, are you?" Neb said. "The priests will never let you in."

"Oh, that's true enough." Dallandra glanced his way with a smile. "But I don't intend to ask their permission."

Although Neb couldn't put his insight—or memory—into words, he suddenly guessed what she was planning. "Dalla, are you sure it's safe? The feel of that place—there's somewhat gravely wrong up there. It's almost enough to make me believe in evil dweomer."

"You should believe in it, because it's real, sure enough." Dal-

landra said. "As to whether or not someone in that temple is working it, well, that's what I want to find out."

Dark dweomer? Neb shivered in revulsion. He desperately
wanted to believe that no such thing existed, but deep in his mind
he saw memories, mere bits and flickers of images barely formed,
but enough. It existed, then, the evil perversion of dweomer, and he
realized that he'd never really doubted it. Other memories struggled to rise, and this time, he could give them words. "The high
priest might well be walking that path," Neb said. "He was trying
to ensorcel Voran."

Salamander caught his breath in a gasp of surprise. Arzosah
swung her head around to look Neb's way.

"I take it he didn't succeed?" the dragon said.

"He didn't," Neb said, "but Govvin was staring at Voran the entire time, and trying to manipulate his—his—ye gods! I've forgotten the word."

"Aura." Salamander supplied it. "This Govvin must not be very
skilled."

"True spoken," Dallandra said. "But let's not rush to underesti-
mate a man who might be an enemy. Although—" Again she
paused to gaze at the temple. "He might merely know a few mental
tricks."

"And where would he have learned them?" Arzosah said.

"From someone who takes coin for his dweomer teaching." Dallandra turned away from her study of the distant temple and
glanced at Salamander, who nodded his agreement. "There are silver daggers of the soul as well as of the sword. The ones with the
swords are far more honorable, of course."

"Secrets like that don't come cheap," Salamander said. "It would
explain the miserliness, if the high priest were bartering his taxes
for tricks from one of the dark masters."

"That's true," Dallandra said. "If I'm wrong, and they're all
merely coldhearted misers, then getting in should be easy enough."

"And if they're not?" Salamander quirked an eyebrow.

"Then it will be difficult, of course." Dallandra laughed, a brittle little bark. "I need to plan this very carefully."

"I'll be flying over the temple later tonight on my way to those cows," Arzosah said. "I'm no match for you or for Salamander, but I do know a few bits and pieces of dweomer. I can take a look around, if you'd like. A scouting expedition, we may call it."

"I would like, and my thanks." Dallandra suddenly grinned. "And may you have luck on your cow hunt, too! Neb, Ebañy, we'd best go back to camp and get our own dinner. No doubt Cal is boiling over with curiosity, wondering what we're up to out here."

The sun was long gone, and the wheel of stars was marking the midpoint of the summer's night, when the entire army heard a concatenation of noise—a distant bellowing of cows, men yelling at the tops of their lungs, and the drumming of enormous wings, beating the sky. Neb pulled on his boots and hurried out of the tent along with all of the archers and Salamander. Most of the army woke, stumbling out of their blankets to stare at the sky. Up at the temple points of light bobbed along the walls—torches, most likely, in the hands of servants.

In the pale moonlight Neb could just make out a dragon shape, circling high above the priestly dun, then moving on to plunge down out of sight behind it. In but a few moments Arzosah rose again, but slowly. Her wings were beating so hard that the camp could hear them, at that distance rather like the sound a hummingbird makes, though up close it must have been deafening. Limp white shapes, barely visible, dangled from her claws.

"She got two!" Neb said with a laugh. "By the gods, she's strong!"

"Dragons are generally known for that," Salamander said. "I hope she's not going to eat them near the horses."

Arzosah had apparently kept the horses in mind. She flew well clear of the army's camp, landing beyond their sight somewhere off to the east. Shaking their heads, laughing or cursing in awe, the watching men slowly migrated back to their blankets and a few more precious hours of sleep, but the shouting up at the temple went on for some time.

With the morning light the high priest of Bel, flanked by four priests each carrying a quarterstaff, marched down from the temple and across the road to the camp. Two sentries hurried to meet him. Neb, who happened to be close by, stayed to watch as the priest demanded to speak with Prince Voran.

"His dragon has stolen some of our cattle," Govvin said with a snarl. "I demand repayment."

The sentries both bowed, and one darted off to fetch the prince. While he waited, Govvin stood with his feet spread a bit apart and his hands on his hips. Voran, with a chunk of bread and cheese in one hand, ambled slowly over to meet him. He smiled his froggy grin and bobbed his head Govvin's way to acknowledge him.

"What's so wrong, Your Holiness?" Voran said.

"That dragon!" Govvin shook a finger in the prince's direction. "It stole two of our best cows. The beast is obviously yours, and I expect you to pay for them."

"Mine?" Voran took a bite of his bread and chewed it thoughtfully for a long moment. "No man owns a dragon, Your Holiness. She's chosen to accompany us, is all, for some reason of her own."

Govvin's hands tightened into fists.

"Besides," Voran went on, swallowing hastily, "yesterday you told me, and I quote, 'naught that happens here is your affair, Prince Voran.' I believe I've got that right." He glanced Neb's way. "The scribe would know."

"You have, Your Highness," Neb said. "Word for word."

"It stuck in my mind, like." Voran waved his chunk of bread in the priest's direction. "So why are you bringing this matter to me?"

Govvin started to speak, stopped himself, turned red in the face with narrow-lipped fury, then turned on his heel and stalked off, followed by his guards. It took a great effort of will, but Neb managed to keep from laughing. Voran, however, did laugh, only a gruff masculine chuckle, but the head priest heard him.

Govvin turned around and glared. Voran fell silent, but the priest kept staring at him. Slowly, guards in tow, Govvin took a step toward the prince, then another, while Voran stared back as if he were naught but a carved statue. *The bastard's done it!* Neb thought. He flung up both hands, and Wildfolk appeared, swarming around him, a troop of spider-spindly gnomes and furious sprites, dancing in the air. The fat yellow gnome stood among them and shook a tiny fist at the priest.

"Go!" Neb whispered.

With a howl of rage like a distant winter wind, the Folk charged. Govvin suddenly screamed and swung around to face them as they mobbed him, a wave of angry fists and teeth. The priest swatted and writhed; his guards rushed forward; Voran woke from the spell with a toss of his head and a few choice curses. The prince's men rushed forward to his side as Voran barked orders.

"Get the chirurgeon!" the prince said. "His holiness is having a seizure."

Govvin's guards surrounded the priest and tried to shield him from the gawking onlookers, but Govvin swore and raged in a steady stream. Two of his guards dropped their staves and caught Govvin by the arms. Apparently they, too, thought that the priest had taken ill, judging from the soothing words they were chanting like a spell. "Just rest, please lie down, we're right here, Your Holiness, please lie down!"

"Enough," Neb said quietly.

The Wildfolk vanished, except for the fat yellow gnome, who came skipping back to Neb's side. Govvin let out one last whimper, then fainted into his guards' arms. Voran's chirurgeon came running with his apprentice, burdened with two bulging sacks, trotting after. Someone hurried up behind Neb and called his name—Salamander.

"Neb, come with me." There was a bark of command in the gerthddyn's normally pleasant voice. "Now, before that misbegotten miscreant wakes up."

"I want to see what happens," Neb said. "Why leave?"

"So he won't recognize you, you dolt!" Salamander laid a heavy hand on Neb's shoulder. "Dallandra wants to talk to you."

"Oh." Neb turned cold. "I see."

Neb let Salamander chivvy him along at a trot until they were well away from the priest and the crowd around him. They slowed to a walk, but a fast one, and found Dallandra waiting in front of her tent. The three of them ducked inside.

"He was ensorcelling the prince," Neb said. "I had to stop him."

"I know that," Dallandra said. "I was watching from a distance. I'm going to go have a look at Voran and see if his aura needs clearing. But I don't want the priest knowing who summoned the Wildfolk."

"Indeed," Salamander joined in. "I just hope he didn't notice Neb before they attacked."

"So do I," Neb said. "They were swarming around me, but it all happened so fast that I don't know if he saw or not."

Salamander groaned under his breath.

"You can't protect yourself yet," Dallandra said, "but I can handle his malice if he tries it on me. I'm going to lay a false trail."

Dallandra took a sack of medicinals with her so she could pretend that she was merely offering to help the chirurgeon, then summoned Wildfolk. Sylphs and sprites streamed after her like an icy cloud following a north wind as she strode through the camp. When she reached the side of the road, where the incident had happened, she found a small mob of men and Westfolk gathered in a rough circle. At an order from Prince Voran, the crowd parted to let her through.

In a clear area in their midst, His Holiness Govvin was sitting up, slumped against another priest, who knelt behind him to support his back. Blue and purple bruises pocked Govvin's face and arms. The chirurgeon and his apprentice were kneeling to either side. Voran, who was standing nearby, waved Dallandra over. The cloud of Wildfolk followed her.

"His holiness has refused our aid," Voran said. "His other men have gone back to the temple to fetch a litter."

"He probably needs to rest more than anything," Dallandra said. "And to eat more." She turned and spoke to the two priests. "Your Holiness, you really must have nourishing broths and gruels. See if you can manage a little breast of fowl, chopped fine, too."

"She's quite right," the chirurgeon said. "If you won't let me examine you, Your Holiness, you could at least take our Westfolk healer's advice."

Neither priest responded. Govvin's attendant glanced at her, then away, but he seemed indifferent rather than resentful. Govvin was so exhausted that Dalla could tell nothing from his aura, which had shrunk around him to a faint gray-green haze. He raised his head and gave her a look of such malice that she stepped back. There was no dweomer in it, just hatred, a pure cold hatred like a sword of ice. She could assume that he had seen the Wildfolk drifting around her and marked her as his attacker.

From the edge of the crowd someone called out, "The litter's here, Your Holiness." The mob parted and let four priests through. They carried a litter made of long poles with a blanket attached.

"No more to see here, lads!" the prince called out. "We need to get on the road."

Murmuring assent, the men began to drift away, heading back to their various encampments. Dallandra turned her Sight upon the prince. His aura glowed strongly and clearly, a faint yellow heavily streaked with red, a typical coloration for warrior lords. Apparently Neb had ended the priest's attempt at ensorcellment before Govvin had managed to sink his claws in deep. Govvin knew the techniques of ensorcellment, but he lacked power to put into his spell. She shut down the Sight, and as she started back to camp, Prince Voran fell in beside her.

"I wonder why the old man starves himself," Voran remarked.

"He may just have worms," Dallandra said. "But I'd guess that he fasts as part of a ritual. Prolonged fasting is supposed to give priests visions of their gods."

"Ah, I see. I didn't know that." He smiled again, but ruefully. "If

I'd known the old man had the falling sickness, I'd have minded my words a little more."

"Oh, I wouldn't blame yourself, Your Highness. You didn't know, and besides, I'd say he deserves whatever he gets."

"I'll admit to having similar thoughts. Very well, then, and my thanks."

With a pleasant wave, Voran strode off. *He's a strong man,* Dallandra thought, *and it's a blasted good thing, too!* Still, she decided that she'd best keep an eye on him from then on, just in case Govvin's attempt at dweomer wasn't as clumsy as it appeared.

The army had finished breaking camp and was assembling in the road when Arzosah finally returned. She swooped over the line of march, then settled into a nearby field. Dallandra and Salamander ran out to join her.

"My apologies for being late," Arzosah said. "I seem to have overslept. Perhaps I shouldn't have eaten both cows last night, but I did hate to waste any."

"I take it they were delicious?" Salamander said.

"They were indeed. Grain fed and nice and fat." The dragon licked her black lips.

"Grain fed?" Dallandra raised an eyebrow. "They eat well, those priests."

"Or else they sell the cows for coin," Salamander said, "but I'm not sure where the market would be. In big Deverry cities like Trev Hael, the wealthier merchants and guildsmen will pay more for better beef, but out here—" He shrugged his shoulders.

"They may barter them outright," Dallandra said. "There's a certain kind of man who eats his meat raw."

"That's true." Salamander winced with a little shiver. "But something else has just occurred to me, to wit, taxes for the central temple down in Dun Deverry. Have you ever seen it? They've gilded the walls in a pattern of tree branches and oak leaves. The statues of Bel may be wood underneath, but they, too, drip with gold and jewels. The priests? Ah, the priests! Their simple tunics and cloaks are patched together from scraps. It's just that the scraps are velvets and silks. The sickles they carry—"

"That's enough," Dallandra interrupted. "I see your point. Someone has to pay for all of that."

"Indeed. And, as usual in this world, the coin's extracted from the hides of those least able to afford it."

"Which reminds me," Arzosah said, "I took several turns over the temple on my way to the pasture. They're up to somewhat, all right. When I flew directly over, I could feel—" She paused, and the black tip of her tongue stuck out of her enormous mouth like a cat's while she thought the matter through. "I'm not sure what I felt, truly. It was a pulsing sensation, as if the etheric was beating like a heart. But I didn't see any etheric sigils, nor any traces of astral domes, naught so obvious."

"What about deformed Wildfolk?" Dallandra said.

"How can anyone possibly tell if Wildfolk are deformed?" Arzosah said. "They're always ugly."

"True, but the ones I'm thinking of usually have big fangs and claws, and they're black as charcoal or shiny like beetles. A few even look like they've been flayed."

"Ych!" Arzosah rolled her eyes in disgust. "I did see some small ugly things scuttling into the temple itself, but I just got a glimpse of them. They might have been dogs. I detest dogs. Too much noise and bone, too little meat."

"It's a puzzle, then," Dallandra said.

"An enigma, amazement, conundrum, and riddle indeed," Salamander said. "But I doubt me if we can linger here to solve it."

"True-spoken, alas," Dallandra said. "I'm more determined than ever to investigate that temple."

"What?" Salamander said. "If Govvin's marked you for his enemy, that's going to be dangerous."

"It may be, it may not. If Govvin's the only person with dweomer knowledge up there, it won't be."

"And if there's someone else, his teacher, perhaps?"

"Then it will be, but it needs doing anyway."

"Well, you can't do it right now. We've got to get back to the army, or they'll leave without us."

"I know that," Dallandra snapped. "Arzosah, if you'll just fly ahead? I wouldn't put it past Honelg to lay an ambuscade. He's most likely desperate enough to try."

"Now that is a good thought," Arzosah said. "He might also have sent a second batch of messengers, for all we know, in case the first lot ran into difficulties. I'll keep an eye out."

"A thousand thanks!" Dallandra said. "But tonight, when we camp, it would gladden my heart if you'd tell what's happened to the silver dragon."

"Would it?" Arzosah looked away. "I doubt that."

"Here, is he still alive?" Dallandra's voice was sharp with alarm.

"He is that," the dragon said. "I'll tell you more later. Perhaps."

"But—"

Arzosah began to turn around, moving with her usual slow waddle, but Salamander still had to jump back to avoid her tail as it swung after her. She put on a bit of speed, reached the open field, then spread her wings, bunched her muscles, and sprang into the air. No one spoke until she'd flown away out of sight, heading north in the direction of Honelg's dun.

"May her scales turn greasy and itch," Salamander muttered. "Dalla, the way she keeps putting you off—it's truly worrisome."

"It is, indeed." Dallandra said. "But she'll tell us what she wants to tell us and when she wants to, not a moment before."

Around noon Gwerbret Ridvar's army rode up to Honelg's village. Gerran wasn't in the least surprised to find it deserted except for a handful of old women and young children. Dressed mostly in faded black, the women stood around the village well, with the children clinging to their skirts, and watched the army file in. No one either cheered or jeered, they neither scowled nor smiled, merely watched with wary eyes. They had, no doubt, seen plenty of trouble in their lives and seemed utterly unsurprised to see more.

The army stopped in a swirl of dust and confusion out in the road, but Gwerbret Ridvar rode on toward the women. Prince Voran urged his horse forward and blocked his way.

"This could be some sort of trap," the prince said.

"It could, truly, Your Highness." Ridvar paused, looking the women over. "But I doubt it."

Ridvar stopped his horse a few feet from the crowd at the well. He leaned over his horse's neck to speak.

"None of you nor your homes will be harmed," he said. "Where are the others? Up in the dun for the siege?"

The women exchanged glances and kept silence.

"We'll find out soon enough. Did they leave you any food?"

A stoop-backed woman with gray hair and only a few teeth shuffled forward to answer. "They did, Your Grace, enough for the children."

"But not for the rest of you?" Ridvar turned in his saddle and beckoned to his captain. "When we make camp, send back supplies."

"Done, Your Grace." The captain raised a hand in salute.

The women sighed, moved a few steps here and there, and turned to look at one another, in a rustle of clothing like wind in dry branches.

"What about the younger women?" Prince Voran called out. "I swear to you that no man here will harm them. If any do, they'll answer to me."

The old women exchanged more glances. The crone speaking for them seemed to be studying the blazons on the prince's shirt and the various banners and pennants among the troops.

"Very well, Your Highness," she said at length. "We'll tell them they can come back to the village."

"Do that." The prince glanced at Ridvar. "Let's ride on. I take it that we're not far now from the traitor's dun."

"So the gerthddyn said." Ridvar turned in his saddle and with a sweep of his arm, sent his men forward.

With their goal so close, the princes and the gwerbret led their army at a trot and let the clumsy carts and servants follow as best they might. In but a little while they rounded a curve in the road and saw the dun, squat and ugly in the midst of its defenses and walls. *Like a scab on top of a pusboil,* Gerran thought. He could see that the gates were shut. Archers, half-concealed behind the crenels, lined the top of the wall.

With shouts and a wave of his arm, Ridvar disposed his men and his allies. The warbands spread out, some riding left, some right, and surrounded the hill, but they took care to stay out of arrow reach. Since his daughter's safety was at stake, Tieryn Cadryc and his men were given the position next to the gwerbret's own, where they had a good view of the gates. At Ridvar's call, Indar the herald rode up to his lord's side. He carried a staff wound with variously colored ribands, the mark of his office, and a silver horn. When he blew three long notes, a horn answered him from inside the dun.

"At least the bastard's willing to parley," Cadryc muttered to Gerran. "That's somewhat to the good."

"It is, Your Grace." Gerran rose in his stirrups for a better look. "They're not opening the gates, though. Oh, wait! They've got a side portal."

Carrying a beribboned staff of his own, a herald slipped through the narrow door and began walking down through the maze of walls and ditches. Indar handed his staff to the gwerbret, then dismounted and took the staff back.

"I'd best go to meet him, Your Grace," Indar said. "I've got the terms of surrender well up in my mind, not that it will matter, I suppose."

"Unfortunately, you're most likely right," Ridvar said. "Well, let's give him his chance to turn them down."

Indar trudged off, staff held high to ensure that the archers on the walls saw it. The elaborate earthworks seemed to swallow both heralds and hide them from sight. There was nothing for the army to do but wait and try to soothe their restless horses as the parley dragged on.

Finally, just as everyone's patience was running out, Indar returned. He bowed to prince and gwerbret both.

"Lord Honelg refuses our terms," Indar said. "He asks you to quit his lands. From what his herald told me, that's the only answer he'll give—quit his lands, and then he'll consider a true parley."

Ridvar turned red in the face and muttered a few foul oaths.

"I expected naught better, somehow," Voran said. "What about Honelg's womenfolk?"

"I pled for mercy upon them with all the feeling I could muster," Indar said. "I followed the gerthddyn's instructions, too, pointing out that womenfolk were especially treasured by his goddess, and that his little daughter represented a future hope for Alshandra's fame and glory, should she live to spread the tidings about her goddess. The herald listened most carefully. There were even tears in his eyes at one point. He said that he'd present my message to his lord with great care. So, there it stands." Indar shook his head with a sigh. "We can only hope that Honelg will listen."

If Honelg did listen to his herald, there was no sign of it that afternoon and evening. Salamander kept a watch at the edge of the Westfolk camp. With his normal sight, he could see that men on guard stood behind the crenellation at the top of the dun wall. Once a man who seemed to be Honelg himself appeared, walking restlessly round the battlements. Now and then Salamander would scry, but inside the walls he saw only things that he and the lords already knew.

As well as Honelg's riders, the men from the village were patrolling on the walls or sitting in the great hall. Salamander recognized Marth the blacksmith, giving orders to a contingent of younger men as they stowed bales and barrels of provisions inside the dun. Out in the stables he saw cows and hogs instead of horses; apparently Honelg had sent his riding mounts away to some safe pasture. But Salamander never saw the herald, nor any sign of a beribboned staff. The dun's women had shut themselves up in the women's hall. He saw Adranna weeping, and the aged Lady Varigga apparently comforting her, holding her hand and speaking gravely, but he could hear nothing of what she said.

As the long summer twilight deepened, Salamander gave up his futile watch and went to find Dallandra. The two princes and the gwerbret had agreed that the Westfolk archers were such an important weapon that they should pitch their tents well behind the lines of the besieging army. No one wanted to lose them to a unanticipated sally from the dun by a desperation squad. They'd found reasonably flat ground along a rivulet for the tents, but near an outcrop of rock from which sentries could see Honelg's dun. Between them and it stood the Red Wolf encampment, also set back, while Ridvar and Prince Voran had disposed their men in the actual siege line circling the dun's defenses.

Salamander wandered among the tents, asking the archers if they'd seen Dallandra, but none had. Finally, he met up with Calonderiel at the big campfire in the middle of the encampment.

"Where's Dalla?" Cal said. "Do you know?"

"I don't," Salamander said. "I was hoping you did."

Calonderiel made a growling sound under his breath. "One of the men tells me that she might have gone to the Roundear camp to talk with Voran and the other lords. I'm on my way to look for her."

"Good idea. And if I see her first, I'll tell her you're looking for her."

"Please do. I hate it when she just wanders off like this."

Eventually, when the twilight had faded into night, Dallandra returned to the elven camp with Calonderiel shooing her along in front of him as if he were a sheepdog and she the prize ewe. Salamander hurried to meet them.

"Ah, there you are!" he said. "I see that Cal found you."

"I was merely speaking with Ridvar and the princes." Dallandra shot Cal a poisonous sort of glance. "I gave them some ideas on how Lord Oth might root out the Alshandra worshippers back in Cengarn."

"I suppose it's necessary," Salamander said.

"Of course it is!" Cal joined in. "Do you want someone there to send a warning to Zakh Gral?"

"No, of course not. I doubt if anyone could, though. Most of them are probably servants, like Raldd the groom, or maybe some of the town's craftsmen and the like, no one with the horses or the knowledge to find Zakh Gral."

"Still, I refuse to take even the least bit of risk," Dallandra said. "If the gwerbret hangs a hundred traitors when he gets back, that'll be a terrible thing, of course, but I'll do what I can for them then."

"By the Black Sun herself! You've turned ruthless lately."

"Of course." Dallandra set exasperated hands on her hips. "Ebañy, don't you realize what's at stake here? Our very survival as a people out in the grasslands, that's what. If we fail, if the Horsekin take over the plains, then the only elven culture left will be in the islands, and the only Westfolk left will be the ones who manage to reach those islands as refugees."

For a moment Salamander couldn't find the words to speak. "I see it now," he said at last. "Somehow I hadn't wanted to see it so clearly."

"Oh, I don't blame you for that," Dallandra said. "Fortunately, Prince Voran and Ridvar both realize that if we fall, their western provinces will be next. They're planning on fighting the Horsekin with every weapon they have. Voran just assured me that his father—that's the high king himself—will see that the matter's urgent. And that's the only thing giving me hope."

"Hope?" Calonderiel said. "Of course, but it's also bringing obligations. Do you realize that, my darling? Prince Dar will be beholden to the Deverry high king from now on."

"So?" Dallandra said. "Better beholden than dead."

Cal laughed. "True," he said. "You're quite right."

"You know," Dallandra went on, "no doubt Dar could use your advice about handling our part of this siege. I have work to do in our tent. Ebañy, why don't you come with me?"

"Now just wait," Cal snapped. "What kind of work?"

"Dweomerwork. I wouldn't need privacy for anything else."

"Privacy, is it? With Ebañy right there?"

Dallandra merely stared at him for a long puzzled moment. Salamander, however, felt like running and hiding somewhere, anywhere, from the cold, suspicious look that Cal was giving him.

"Please," Salamander said feebly, "don't tell me you're jealous of me."

"Of course not!" Cal snarled and crossed his arms over his chest. "I just want to know what she wants with you."

"His dweomerlore, you idiot!" Dallandra laid a firm hand on Cal's shoulder. "I have to scry, and he knows what to do if something goes wrong."

"Oh." Cal considered this for a moment. "I tend to forget that you've got dweomer, Ebañy. You play the prattling fool so well." He turned on his heel and stalked off.

"I sincerely hope he gets over this fit, seizure, or spasm of unfortunate emotion," Salamander said, "or my life is going to be difficult. Difficult? Not that alone! It might even be shorter than the gods intended."

"He wouldn't dare harm you. He knows that we need every bit of dweomer we have if we're going to win these battles."

"How nice to be useful! But I'm grateful, mind." Salamander mugged relief and wiped his brow with an exaggerated wave of one hand. "On to the work ahead! I take it you want me to guard your body while you're off scouting."

"Just that. We've got to take a good look at that wretched temple."

On the way to her tent, Dallandra saw Neb, hailed him, and brought him along. He would have the important duty of sitting directly outside of the tent door and keeping out anyone who might want to enter, including Calonderiel.

"I'll gladly try," Neb said, "but I fear me that Cal won't listen to a word I say."

"Then stand up and block the door," Dallandra said. "If you need to, summon Wildfolk and threaten him. I love him dearly, but

I cannot be disturbed. Tell him that if he comes charging in, he could break my concentration and kill me."

"Is that true?" Neb sounded shocked.

"It is. Very true."

"Then don't worry." Neb laid his hand on the hilt of his table dagger. "No one will get past me."

"Good. Come on, Ebañy."

Once inside, Dallandra made a ball of light, then flung it to the center of the roof of her tent, where it stuck, glowing silver. Shadows danced around the circling walls. Salamander knelt on the floor cloth and stared at the flickering play of light.

"I see Govvin," he said after a moment. "Not much else, but I do see Govvin. He's lying on a pallet of straw on the floor of what appears to be a tiny chamber. There's a candle lantern burning on a table near the bed, if you'd call that miserable heap a bed. He's lying so still that I'd say our priest was asleep, but his eyes are open."

"He's not dead, is he?"

"No. I can see his bony ribs rising and falling."

"He might well be exhausted from this morning."

"Or in trance?" Salamander turned to her.

"Maybe. Let's find out."

Dallandra lay down on her blankets, and Salamander moved over to kneel at her head. She crossed her arms over her chest, then slowed her breathing to a steady rhythm. First, she summoned the mental image of a silver flame. She visualized it so clearly that it seemed to be glowing in front of her rather than in her mind. Slowly, she enlarged the flame until it became the height of a tall woman, glowing above her, fed by her own life-energy, streaming from her solar plexus like a silver cord. At that point the image had become her body of light.

Dallandra transferred her consciousness over to the body of light. She imagined herself looking out from a silver hood, as if the flame were a cloak she wore. She heard a strange hissing sound, a click. It seemed that she floated within the flame and looked down at her sleeping body, lying far below, and Salamander, encased in his pale gold aura. Behind her, the silver cord paid out like a fisher-man's line as she rose higher, swooped through the tent roof, and out into the open night.

Above the stars hung close, vast silver globes that echoed her body of light. The encampment far below blazed red and gold from the auras of the men inside it. On Honelg's dun walls a gleam of auras rose from the archers on guard. The stone, the rocky hill, all the dead things in both dun and camp looked black, so black in fact that they seemed more like shapes cut out of the very fabric of life than objects with an existence of their own. All around them the grass, trees, and other vegetation shone a dim reddish brown.

Dallandra swept away from the camp and headed back along the road to the fortress of Bel. When it came into view, looming on its squat hill, she paused to study it. Here on the etheric plane, its stones loomed black and dead, but the timber of the actual temple inside the walls displayed a faint reddish light, like the last gleam of a sunset, indicating that the temple's wood had been cut fairly recently. She saw no astral dome, no seals of blue light, nothing that would indicate the presence of dweomerworkers inside, whether they followed the light or cherished the darkness.

Cautiously, slowly, she drifted closer. She saw no one outside in the dun's ward, not that she worried about the usual kind of sentries, those whose consciousness lay on the physical plane alone. She was expecting an etheric challenge, should a dark master be dwelling there, but no inverted pentagrams shone to ward away the dweomer of light. She wove herself a shield of bluish etheric substance, just in case a dark master should suddenly appear, clothed in lurid images of evil instead of a body of light.

Closer, closer—no one rose up to threaten her, yet it seemed she could sense—something. Arzosah had told her that above the temple itself the etheric forces seemed to be beating like a heart. Dallandra had no idea of what such an image might mean; etheric forces in her experience swirled, flowed, or occasionally spurted up and twisted like waterspouts, but she'd never seen any throb. Yet, as she drifted over the dun walls, she could see, high above the temple, an area, roughly circular, where the silver blue etheric light brightened, then dimmed, in a fairly regular rhythm.

She paused again, turning to scan all around her for enemies. Again, nothing. She rose higher until she hung in her flame-shaped body just below the pulsing circle, which proved to be the mouth of a tunnel stretching into a bluish-black darkness. Within the tunnel swirled images, strange geometric shapes, human faces, little twisted stars, deformed creatures, flowers and leaves and tendrils, all floating through an indigo haze. Someone had opened a gate to the lower astral plane and left it there, a trap and a danger to any etheric creature, such as the Wildfolk, who might drift into it.

Dallandra moved away from the tunnel mouth, then rose higher until she could look at it from above. Hanging below her, it appeared as a long tube, wide at the mouth, dwindling down and disappearing into a haze at the far distant end. The tube's surface seemed velvet-soft or perhaps slightly furred, but utterly unnatural in any case. As she studied it, she realized that the far end of the construct was moving, twitching back and forth like the tailtip of an impatient cat. The motion would account for the pulses of etheric force.

But what was it? It was much too complex for a simple astral gate. Her first instinct was to retreat, to return to her body and consult with Salamander and Valandario, but the astral gate was a potentially fatal hazard to the weak creatures whose world it had invaded. Within her cloak of fire she raised the images of her hands and called upon the Light, the pure Light that shines behind all gods, the Light that the dark dweomer hates above all else. She dedicated the working with its name.

All around lay the raw power of the etheric plane. Dallandra sent her body of light spinning in a slow dance, gathering in the blue light the way a spindle gathers in the freshly spun thread. She used the magnetic force she collected to fashion a pentagram, and within the glowing silver points of the inner star of the pentagram she placed the sigils of the elements, Fire, Air, Water, Earth, and Aethyr. In the center she placed the holiest of names.

"In the name of the Light," she called out in a wave of thought. "I banish thee!"

With a thrust of will she sent it floating toward the gate. She was expecting the tunnel to simply vanish when the two collided. The pentagram sailed forward, touched the tunnel shape, and burst into black flame. The tunnel exploded.

Force, pure force that burned like acid surged and caught her. She felt her body of light rip and tear as a great wave flung her upward, tumbled her this way and that, threatened to throw her into the stars themselves, or so it seemed to her as she careened this way and that. Her useless shield fell away in tatters. All of her concentration, all of her will went into strengthening the silver cord that linked her to her body, so far below. If that broke, she would be dead beyond recovery. Wave after wave of power, a burning power, battered her. The silver cord was stretching thin. She had no choice but to retreat, to spin away, to follow the cord before it snapped and rush back to her body. The waves of force followed her, burning, tearing.

Someone was coming to meet her, another silver cloak of flame— Ebañy. From his own substance he was weaving a rope of light. He tossed it, she caught it, and she felt his energy flowing toward her, renewing her torn body of light. Together they spiraled down toward the Westfolk encampment. She could see the auras of men, glowing beneath them, and dots of fire between the tents—safety at last. She had just the energy left to look back and see the remains of the tunnel collapsing inward. As they fell, they dissolved back into the blue light. She had closed the gate.

Down and down—suddenly they were in the tent, hovering over their bodies. To her surprise she realized that her body was lying twisted on the opposite side of the tent from her blankets. Salamander's lay flopped on its back, arms outstretched. He drifted over it, then dropped. The flame that encased him shrank, dwindled, turned invisible. The body below sat up, its aura glowing gold, though a fair bit less brightly than it had been before.

Salamander got up, staggered over to her physical body, and dragged it back to the blankets. He laid her out like a corpse—

though the silver cord hung unbroken though dangerously thin—
in order to minimize her pain when she returned to her flesh. Dallandra slid down the cord, felt her consciousness slip free of the
body of light, then fell gratefully into the physical world. A click, a
rushy hiss, and she was back, aching in every muscle and tendon,
with Salamander leaning over her.

"My thanks," she whispered. "You saved my life."

He smiled, too exhausted to speak.

From outside she heard a voice—Cal's voice—yelling and
threatening Neb in two languages with vile things if he didn't step
aside at once. Dallandra staggered to her feet and managed to walk
to the tent door. She flung it aside to find Calonderiel grabbing
Neb by the throat.

"Stop it!" she said. "He's just following my orders."

"Thank every god in the sky!" Cal said and let Neb go. "You're
alive!"

Neb staggered back, rubbing his throat. With a shock Dallandra
realized that half the Westfolk camp was standing around gawking
and that the other half was running to see what the disturbance was.

"We were going to stop the banadar from killing him," one of
the archers said, pointing to Neb. "We'd just got here when you
came out."

"I see," Dallandra said. "My thanks. Why don't you all go away
again? There's nothing wrong anymore. Neb, bless you! Come in,
and Cal, you, too."

With Dallandra safe, Calonderiel turned apologetic. He insisted
on arranging the softest cushions for Neb to sit upon and poured
him mead in a silver goblet to ease the ache in the scribe's throat.
That done, he rummaged through tent bags until he found a slab of
honeycake, purloined from the gwerbret's wedding, which he divided between Salamander and Dallandra. She bit into it greedily.

"I'll fetch water," Calonderiel said.

Dallandra was too busy stuffing the cake into her mouth to answer. She and Salamander both needed to anchor their consciousness firmly to their bodies, and food was the best way to do so.

Neb sat sipping his mead and watching them with a stunned expression. No doubt his daydreams about mighty dweomer workings hadn't included raw hunger. Calonderiel returned with a waterskin and filled more goblets all round. When Dallandra held out her sticky hands, he squeezed the waterskin and washed them clean, but he handed the water to Salamander and let him clean his own hands.

"A thousand thanks, my love," Dallandra said in Deverrian. "You've been around dweomermasters for a very long time, haven't you?" She managed to smile. "Do you realize that Salamander saved my life?"

"I got that impression," Cal said. "I was walking up to the tent when I heard you scream, and Ebañy start cursing. Then Neb and I heard the sound of some heavy thing flopping like a caught fish on a riverbank."

"I somehow knew that the noise came from you." Neb's voice rasped and croaked. "So I told the banadar that your body was suffering some kind of repercussion from whatever you were doing out there."

"But he wouldn't let me by him." Calonderiel looked honestly contrite. "My apologies, Neb."

Neb smiled weakly and had another sip of mead.

"As for me, I couldn't hold you down," Salamander said, "so I went out after you."

"And a cursed good thing you did," Calonderiel muttered. "I was afraid Dalla would break her neck."

Dallandra drank another sip of water. She was wondering how much Calonderiel actually understood of what had just happened. Even more, she wondered if she wanted him to understand.

"Dalla, what was that construct?" Salamander went on. "I caught a glimpse of it before it collapsed. It didn't look like a normal astral gate to me."

"It wasn't," Dallandra said. "I'm not sure what it was, frankly. I've never seen anything like it before."

"Do you think Govvin made it?" Salamander said.

"I don't know for certain, but I doubt it very much."

Salamander turned slightly and began staring at one of the tent bags hanging on the wall, but his eyes moved as if they were following some living thing. His skin was far too pale, his hair plastered down with sweat. Dark blood was gathering under the skin below his eyes.

"What are you seeing?" Dallandra said.

"Govvin. He's up and walking through the ward. Some of the priests are following him." Salamander paused, his mouth slack, for a long moment. "Ah, they're leaving the dun now through the postern gate." Suddenly he laughed, a small exhausted sound. "He's setting a guard over the remaining cattle."

"If he's doing somewhat as mundane as that," Dallandra said. "He can't have the slightest idea of what just happened on the etheric above his wretched temple."

"Just so." Salamander paused for a yawn. "Which means he can't have made the thing. I doubt me if the man who did build it realized you were destroying it either, or he'd have come charging up to defend it."

"I don't understand," Neb broke in. "Do you mean this dark dweomerman's not in the temple?"

"I'm guessing he's not," Salamander said. "We don't know, unfortunately."

"True spoken," Dallandra said. "We'll have to keep a watch on that wretched temple, though. If he does come back, I want a good look at him. He must have been staying in the temple. Why else build above it? Let's hope he returns before the siege is over."

Calonderiel growled, a whisper of frustrated rage. "I don't want you putting yourself in danger like this again."

"I don't want you putting yourself in danger by riding to battle either, but will that stop you?"

Calonderiel opened his mouth and shut it again without speaking.

"Neb?" Dallandra turned to him. "The gwerbret's going to send messages back to Cengarn on the morrow. Write Branna and tell her to be on her guard every moment of every day."

"I will." Neb's voice seemed a little less raw. "You know, you told me that I shouldn't rush ahead with dweomer. I didn't want to be patient, but truly, now I see what you mean. I don't understand what happened to you, but one thing's clear. There's danger in working dweomer, more than I ever thought possible."

"True spoken," Dallandra said. "Tell her that, too. Thanks be to all the gods that she can read."

With Ridvar on campaign, overseeing the life of the dun fell to his lady. Each morning Drwmigga sat in Ridvar's chair at the head of the table of honor by the dragon hearth. Keeping her company there were Galla and her two serving women, Branna and Solla, as well, of course, as the four women Drwmigga had brought with her from her father's dun. Drwmigga would lean back in her chair and smile at everyone, her large eyes as placid as always, as the various servitors and servants came forward to listen to her orders of the day. She tended to agree with everyone and grant their requests with a minimum of discussion.

"I'm still learning the ways of the rhan," she remarked several times. "Dear Solla, you've been such a great help to me."

Solla would smile in return but say nothing. At first Branna thought that Drwmigga was pouring vinegar on Solla's wounds, but finally she realized that Drwmigga truly didn't understand her sister-in-law's situation. After that, Branna found herself more and more tempted to respond to Drwmigga's comments with a moo.

Five days after the army rode out, Ridvar's first messenger arrived. Branna, who was up in her chamber, heard a strange sound outside, an odd thwacking noise, as if someone were cleaning an enormous tapestry by beating it with an equally enormous stick. She went to her window and leaned out. Down below in the ward, a scattering of servants had stopped whatever tasks they were about. They stood still, heads tilted back, staring at the sky. All of a sudden a maidservant screamed aloud and went careening across the ward to duck into the great hall. The others stood as if frozen for a brief moment, then rushed after her. The dun dogs began howling, running this way and that across the ward before they too sought shelter inside.

Branna looked up to see a dragon circling the dun. In the bright light of afternoon her coppery-black scales gleamed with a greenish undertone as she dropped lower, aiming for the flat roof of the main broch. Without thought or hesitation Branna called out, "Arzosah! Arzosah Sothy Lorezohaz!"

"I am that," the dragon called back. "I'll just land."

Branna rushed out of her chamber and ran, panting a little, up the stairs to the trapdoor that led to the roof. She climbed up the ladder and emerged into sunlight to find the dragon settled, her huge wings neatly folded, her tail tucked round her haunches. Yet despite her comfortable posture, reminiscent of a hearthside cat, under her scales muscles bulged, and when she yawned, she displayed teeth as long as Branna's arms.

"I take it Dallandra told you my name," the dragon said. "So you must be Lady Branna."

"I am, indeed." Branna felt as if someone had just hit her sharply in the face. How had she known that name? Dalla had never mentioned that she knew a dragon, much less the beast's name. She fell back on ingrained courtesy. "It gladdens my heart to meet you. It's a great honor."

"My thanks, and the same to you, I'm sure. I've come with messages from the gwerbret. If you could just untie them for me?" Arzosah raised her head to reveal a leather pouch hanging from a strap around her neck. "I offered to bring them, just for somewhat to do. Sitting around and watching an army hold a siege turns out to be tedious in the extreme."

"I imagine it would be, truly. Here, let me just undo this buckle, and you'll be free of that strap."

"My thanks."

The strap had been pieced together out of a good many belts and bits of tack to make it long enough to go round the dragon's neck. Unbuckling it required ducking under Arzosah's head, which she obligingly raised high to give Branna room. Branna had the strap off and the pouch of message tubes safely in hand before she realized how dangerous the job might have been. She stepped back and glanced down at the ward to find it full of gawkers, fort guard, servants, and Aunt Galla, leaning heavily upon Lady Solla as if she'd nearly fainted.

"I'll be back tomorrow morning for the answers," Arzosah said. "Now listen carefully, because this is truly important. One of the letters is sealed with Prince Voran's wyvern. Lord Oth is to read that one first and silently. It will explain why."

"Well and good, then. I'll tell him."

"Good. Now, I'm off to hunt my supper. You'd best go back inside, though, before I leave. My wings tend to whip up a powerful gust of air."

"No doubt. May you have good fortune on the hunt!"

"What a polite child you are! I do like that in a hatchling."

For want of an answer, Branna curtsied, then wrapped the strap and pouch around her waist several times to leave her hands free for the climb down the ladder. Lord Oth and two men from the fort guard were waiting for her on the landing below. The men bowed to her in honest awe.

"Ye gods!" Oth murmured. "You've got ice in your veins, Lady Branna."

"I don't know what came over me," Branna said. "But she does seem courtly in her own way."

From above, wingbeats sounded, as huge as thunder. In a rush of air the dragon flew off, and as her shadow passed over the open trap, darkness fell for a moment. Oth wiped cold sweat off his face with his shirt sleeve, and one of the guards turned more than a little pale.

"Here are the messages, my lord." Branna unbuckled the strap and held them out.

Oth took them with shaking hands. As they went downstairs, the two guards preceded them, allowing Branna to repeat Arzosah's instructions concerning the letter with the wyvern seal in privacy.

"Very well." Oth seemed surprised. "Let's stop here on this landing."

Oth looked through the messages, found the correct silver tube, and broke the seal. He shook out the parchment within, and as he read, his surprise turned into a certain grim look about the eyes. "I see." Oth rolled up the message and shoved it back into the tube. "Let's go on down."

The great hall was mobbed. Everyone crowded inside to hear the news, servants, pages, fort guards, and noble-born ladies alike. Branna made her way through the whispering crowd to the table of honor, where the noble-born had gathered, and sat down next to her aunt, who turned to her, tried to speak, then gave it up with a shrug. *I'll be in for a talking-to later,* Branna thought, *on the subject of not consorting with dragons.* The thought made her giggle until Galla silenced her with a black look.

Lord Oth had paused a few steps up the main staircase and was still surveying the crowd. "Is Varn here?" he called out.

Varn, the captain of the fort guard, made his way through the murmuring crowd. When he started to kneel, Oth stopped him. "Come have a private word with me," Oth said.

Oth and the captain climbed halfway up the stone staircase to speak quietly between themselves while everyone in the hall watched and murmured speculations and rumors. Finally the captain hurried down again. He began rounding up some of his men and posting them here and there about the great hall. Oth followed more slowly.

"No doubt your hearts are all longing for news," Oth called out. "I shall therefore read the messages out loud."

He climbed onto a table and made a great show of opening the tubes and taking out the letters, then read them as loudly as he could. Although Branna wanted to hear the details as much as anyone, she realized that she was watching the crowd as carefully as she was listening. At first, she wasn't quite sure what she was looking for, but when Lord Oth reached the portion of the message that dealt with the dragons, she got her answer.

"As you must realize by now, since you are reading this message, the black dragon has been of great and estimable service to the princes and the gwerbret," Lord Oth read out. "We have hopes that her mate, the white dragon, will join us for the siege of this traitor to Great Bel."

Near the back door of the dun stood a little clot of servants: two lasses, a groom, and a kitchen lad. The lad abruptly covered his mouth with one grubby hand, as if stifling a curse or scream; one of the lasses turned pale; the groom took two steps backward as if he were going to ease himself out of the hall. Unfortunately for him, three fort guards blocked the way. The lad darted forward, only to be collared by another guard. Here and there in the crowd, more guards were laying heavy hands on some of the listeners. Noise erupted—people whispering, then talking louder to be heard, moving, turning, straining to see. The dogs began barking in reflected excitement.

"Clear the hall!" Oth called out. "Later, good folk, you'll understand. For now, all those free to leave, leave. Guards, bring the rest forward."

In a flood of talk the crowd began flowing though out the doors. One of the lasses, caught in a guard's strong grip, screamed. Oth clambered down from the table as the guards began hauling their captives forward.

"Um, Lord Oth?" Drwmigga said. "What, pray tell, is happening?"

"One of your husband's advisors came up with a clever way of rooting out traitors," Oth said. "The gerthddyn Salamander told us that the Alshandra cult thinks those two dragons are some sort of supernatural apparition, demons or suchlike, rather than ordinary wild animals. Silly, I know, but apparently they believe the dragons to be their bloodsworn enemies. So when I read the bit about them, some of our people here had a rather strange reaction. It's suspicious if naught else."

The people in question were being dragged forward by the guards. One by one they were forced to their knees in a line in front of the dragon hearth—some eleven culprits in all. One lass and the little kitchen lad were weeping, but the rest were putting on a good show of defiance, crossing their arms over their chests, scowling up at Oth, or merely watching him without a trace of feeling showing on their faces.

Lady Galla stood up from her chair and glanced Branna's way. "I feel rather ill," she said, "thinking about our Adranna, shut up with these people. I'm going to retire to my chamber."

"I'll come with you," Solla said. "If Lady Drwmigga will give us leave?"

"We'll all go to the women's hall." Drwmigga stood and collected her serving women with the wave of a pale hand. "I'm sure Lord Oth can handle this matter."

Branna was planning on going with them, but some thought or feeling caught at her mind. She was hard-pressed to put it into words, but she knew that she needed to hear what the prisoners had to say for themselves. She slid down a few inches in her chair and shrank into herself, or so she called it, a particular trick she'd developed as a child when she didn't want to be noticed.

Oth stood looking at the line of prisoners until the great hall had emptied behind him. Varn joined him and counted up the prisoners.

"This is the lot, my lord," Varn said. "As far as we can tell, anyway."

"Well and good, then," Oth said and turned back to the prisoners. "So! You're all suspected of worshipping the false goddess Alshandra. I want to—"

"Not a false goddess." The groom's voice rang clear with defiance. "She's the one true goddess, and I shan't deny *her* now."

"No more will I," cried a serving lass. "If you kill us, we'll go to *her* country, and there's naught you can do about that. We shall die as witnesses to her truth."

One by one they all joined in agreement, even the kitchen lad, though Branna noticed that his young voice wavered in terror. He was about Matto's age, she decided, and seeing his tears made her wonder if her nephew would live to see another summer. Oth listened, stared gape-mouthed, took a step back, and stared some more. The captain swore under his breath in amazement, and his men shook their heads in stunned disbelief.

"Don't you realize," Oth said at last, "that the gwerbret will have you hanged if you persist in this daft idea?"

"Let him," the groom said. "It matters naught to us."

The others murmured, agreeing, except for the kitchen lad, whose silent tears ran down his cheeks.

"He might be persuaded to mercy." Oth tried again. "But you must forswear this false goddess and—"

"Never!" the groom snarled.

"Well and good, then," Oth said with a shrug. "Guards, take them out to the gaol. His grace will hold malover on the matter when he returns."

"Wait!" Branna uncoiled herself from the chair. "I mean, please?"

Oth yelped, and the startled guards nearby did the same.

"My dear Lady Branna!" Oth laid his hand on his shirt as if soothing a startled heart. "I didn't see you there."

"My apologies, my lord. But that child, the kitchen lad—he's far too young to know what he's doing."

"That may be, but his grace will be the one who decides that when he returns."

"But should he wait in gaol with the others? It seems so harsh."

"I have my orders, my lady. Your taste for mercy becomes you, but there's naught I can do." Oth turned back to the guards. "Take them away."

From his grim tone of voice Branna decided that further argument would be futile. As the guards marched the prisoners away, the kitchen lad kept glancing back at her with tear-filled eyes. The adults in the group, however, began chanting a prayer, their heads held high, their voices strong. *And what about our Adranna?* she thought. *Will she be just as determined to die?*

For a moment she felt like weeping. She brushed the impulse away and hurried upstairs to join the other noblewomen in the women's hall. When Branna came in, she found them all sitting in a tight little group of chairs and cushions, as if the evening were cold instead of sweltering with summer heat.

"There you are, dear!" Galla said. "We were wondering where you'd gone."

"I stayed to listen to the prisoners." Branna glanced around, found an empty half-round chair, and sat down. "I think they must all have gone quite mad. None of them would renounce their false goddess."

"It's so terrible." Drwmigga was practically whispering. "Traitors in the dun! They might murder us all in our beds or suchlike."

"I doubt that, my lady," Branna said. "If there are some of them still free, they're going to want to flee for their lives. If they stay, they won't want to call attention to themselves or their fellow believers."

"I suppose so." Drwmigga sounded doubtful.

"I think our Branna may be right, my lady," Galla said. "But there's naught wrong with our keeping our wits about us at all times."

"There's never anything wrong with that, Aunt Galla." Branna smiled at her. "I—"

Someone knocked at the door. Branna went to open it and found Midda, looking slant-eyed this way and that down the corridor, visibly enjoying the feeling of intrigue. "Lord Oth would like to speak with you privately," she murmured. "He'll be in the gwerbret's chamber of justice."

"Honestly, Midda, you don't need to whisper like that!"

"Oh don't I now? Aren't there traitors in the dun? What if they murder us—"

"All in our beds?" Branna finished the thought for her. "I doubt if there are any more, and even if they were, they'll be running or hiding, not giving themselves away."

"Well, mayhap, mayhap not," Midda said darkly. "One never knows."

But I do know, Branna thought. *I just don't know how I know.*

"My thanks for the message," she said aloud. "I'll go meet him straightaway."

In the chamber of justice, Lord Oth was sitting behind the long table in a shaft of sunlight from a window above. The messenger pouch, various documents, and silver tubes lay spread out in front of him. Seeing him, she was struck by the strong feeling that she'd known him, too, back in some other life. The image that came to her was of a table in a cheap tavern, and a bald fat man pulling apart a roast chicken with his hands, an image so different from the slender and elegant Oth that she decided she must be mistaken. He stood up to bow to her.

"Ah, there you are, Lady Branna." Oth held out a message tube. "I've got a letter for you from your betrothed."

"My thanks!" Branna practically snatched it from his hand. "I was so hoping he'd send one."

"Well, there you are. Now, about that kitchen lad. I agree that he's very young, and the situation is very sad. Mercy becomes a noblewoman, certainly. But this is a matter for the gwerbret."

"And not for me to meddle in?"

"Precisely." Oth smiled, attempting to soften his words. "Now, you're very young, after all. I suggest you discuss this matter with your aunt and take advantage of her wiser years."

Branna found herself wishing that the dweomer really could turn people into frogs, just like in the old tales. Since it couldn't, she forced out a smile.

"You're in command of the dun," she said, "and so I'll do as you ask, of course. I wonder, though. If these Alshandra worshippers weren't allies of the Horsekin, would their belief really be evil?"

"Of course! Don't you see? They're atheists, when's all said and done. They claim that their wretched demoness is the only true god and the others are just illusions." Oth stopped pacing and turned to face her. "If we let them spread this ugly belief, the real gods might well turn against us. And then where would we be?"

"In grave danger, truly."

"Truly." Oth favored her with a smile. "Now. I'll be sending messages back to his grace on the morrow. Did you want to include a note for Neb?"

It was her reward for saying what he wanted her to, Branna supposed. For a moment she considered telling him just that, but in the end, with the force of law and command behind him, he'd win any sparring match.

"I do," Branna said, "and my thanks. I'll ask Lady Solla to help me write it. I've got lots to tell him."

Yet, after she'd read Neb's letter with its warnings and its talk of dark dweomer, Branna realized that she could never tell him the things that truly mattered, her remembering Arzosah's name, her strange feeling that she'd known Oth as well, and all her insights into the dweomer of these things. Solla would have to hear them in order to write them down, and Prince Daralanteriel's scribe could possibly read them by mistake. She ended up dictating a short note, telling Neb that she was well, that she was taking his letter to heart, and that she had interesting things to tell him when he returned. She finished by telling him how much she loved and missed him.

"It would gladden my heart to learn to write, Solla," Branna said when they had finished the message. "Do you think you could teach me?"

"Gladly," Solla said. "It will give us somewhat to do to make the waiting easier."

"Are you worried about Gerran?"

"Of course." Solla blushed scarlet. "I suppose it's foolish of me to care so much about a man who has so little interest in me."

"Oh, Gerran keeps his heart locked up, but that doesn't mean he hasn't got one. You just wait, this winter, when we're all in the dun together. I'll wager he speaks up then. He's not blind, you know."

Solla smiled, then let the smile fade. "If he lives," she said. "Branna, I'm so frightened."

"It's in the laps of the gods now." Branna caught Solla's hand and squeezed it. "And we've got powerful allies on our side."

"That's certainly true." Solla gave a nervous little laugh before she went on. "Branna, that dragon! You could have been killed."

"Why would she have harmed me? She was carrying messages from the princes and the gwerbret. She can speak. She's not some maggot-crazed wild bear or suchlike."

Solla started to answer, then fell silent and began to tremble. With little clucks and comforting words, the other women in the hall came hurrying over.

"Here, here," Galla said. "You poor child! Today's been wretchedly strange for all of us. I think me you're exhausted. I know I am."

"Me, too," Branna said. "I can go find a servant to make us some mulled wine, if you'd like that, Solla."

Solla nodded and managed a feeble smile.

"Truly," Drwmigga said. "I've never known a day like this one in all my eighteen years. Ye gods! Traitors in the dun, and they're nasty rebellious servants at that, and then a dragon of all things! Do let's have some wine."

"A splendid idea," Galla said. "And Branna my dear one, you really shouldn't go consorting with dragons. This one may act tame, but you never know with wild animals, when they'll turn on you."

That's exactly the talking-to I knew I'd get, Branna thought to herself. Aloud, she said, "You're doubtless right, Aunt Galla. My apologies."

As she was leaving the women's hall, it occurred to her to wonder just how she could have been so calm around Arzosah. And why had she known the dragon's name? For a moment she felt dizzy, and rather than slip and fall, she paused halfway down the stairs to the great hall until her head cleared. *I wish Dalla and Salamander were here,* she thought. But most of all, she wished she

could run to Neb and feel his arms around her, a solid comfort in a
world that had turned alien and grim.

rzosah returned to the army late on the following day with
the message pouch around her neck and another white cow
from the temple of Bel clutched in her claws. Dallandra was ex-
plaining the properties of her healing herbs to Neb when they saw
the dragon flapping slowly along, weighed down by her dead prey
as she headed for a nearby field.

"I can tell you more about comfrey root later," Dallandra said.
"Let's go fetch those messages."

Salamander joined them as they made their way through the
crowded Westfolk camp and left it for the meadows beyond. Arzosah had found a nesting place a safe distance away from the
army's horses. A clump of big granite boulders rose from uneven
ground like the knuckles of a fist pushing through a leather glove.
Water trickled from a spring in their midst to a flat and sunny pasture where the dragon could warm herself. When Dallandra and
the two men arrived, Arzosah was lounging on the grass and considering a pit beside the cool water of the stream. The dirt crusting
her claws made it clear that she'd dug it herself. Apparently, the
dead cow lay in the pit on its back because all Dallandra could see
was its legs, pitifully akimbo.

"I prefer to eat at night," Arzosah remarked, "and the stream
will keep it fresh. It's quite hot up in the rocks."

"A good idea, truly," Salamander said. "Uh, what's that smell?
Do you have another cow decaying somewhere?"

"I don't. I've been licking the hides clean and saving them for
our scribe here. They won't make the best parchment, but I'll
wager you can write on them once they're tanned or treated or
whatever your people do to them."

"I certainly can," Neb said. "My humble thanks! I truly do appreciate it."

"We'll bring a servant down to fetch them later," Salamander put in. "I'm surprised you know about such things, oh, pinnacle of dragonhood."

"I've seen books and the like before," Arzosah said. "I am not some sort of savage." She swung her head around to speak to Dallandra. "I assume you've come for the messages. Or the answers to them, I should say."

"We have indeed," Dallandra said. "Ebañy, if you'll just unbuckle that strap?"

Arzosah lifted her chin to allow Salamander to relieve her of the message pouch.

"By the by, young Neb," Arzosah said, "I met your betrothed, and I was quite impressed."

"She's beautiful, isn't she?" Neb broke into a grin.

Arzosah rumbled with laughter. "Beautiful? Why would I care about that? She's fearless, is what I meant. There's a letter from her for you in that pouch."

Neb turned to Salamander and made a move toward the pouch that was more like a snake striking than a gesture of "give it to me." Salamander laughed and tossed him the leather sack.

"Find yours," Salamander said, "and then take the rest to the gwerbret."

"I will," Neb said. "My apologies for grabbing."

With the pouch cradled in his arms, Neb trotted back to the camp. Arzosah watched him go, then turned to Dallandra.

"Now that he's out of earshot," Arzosah said in Elvish, "I have a bone to pick with you, Dalla, and it's not inside that cow. It's mean of you to go around telling everyone my true name."

"What?" Dalla said. "I did no such thing!"

"Then how did Branna learn it?"

"She knew it?" Dallandra paused, thinking. "Ye gods! She must have remembered it, probably in one of her dweomer-dreams."

"She knew me in her last life?"

"Jill didn't truly know you, but she's the one who deciphered your name in the first place."

Arzosah gently laid her head upon the ground between her paws. "Another poor dragon felled by the blows of wyrd," Arzosah said. "I should have just thrown myself into a fire mountain and been done with it long years ago."

"Oh, by the Dark Sun herself!" Dallandra said. "What's so wrong?"

"To think that a dragon should be brought so low by the machinations of a lump of ectoplasm, a bit of etheric ooze, a gobbet of astral slime! That wretched Evandar, in other words. Curse him for writing my true name on rings, letting it fall into the hands of dweomermasters! It's the indignity of it all that hurts."

Dallandra set her hands on her hips and considered Arzosah for a long moment. "It's truly hard to feel pity for you," she said at last, "when you're larger than a banadar's tent."

Arzosah snarled, but she did lift her head and cross her paws in front of her chest.

"That's better," Dallandra said. "And speaking of the rose ring, it truly is time we had our little chat about Rori. What's happened? Something evil has, hasn't it?"

Arzosah groaned. "I suppose if I don't tell you," she said at last, "you'll only command me with my true name."

"I was thinking of that, truly, but I'd rather spare you the humiliation."

"Oh very well! There is one thing dragons hate above all else, and that's admitting we were wrong. We're so rarely wrong, of course, that we don't have much practice at it. Perhaps that's why we hate it so much."

"Perhaps," Dalla said. "Wrong about what?"

"I should have listened to you, there in Cerr Cawnen. You were right. I should have let Rhodry die and then gone off alone to mourn him. And—oh, yes—since I'm abasing myself, allow me to apologize for threatening to destroy the entire town. I was out of my mind with grief."

"I know you were. I was furious with you at the time, but I'd never hold it against you."

"My thanks, then. After he worked the transformation, I was almost ready to forgive Evandar. With Rori mine, I was no longer alone. Everything seemed splendid—for a while. But then, well, everything changed. Oh, bitter, bitter wyrd!"

"Would you please stop wallowing in self-pity and just tell us what happened?"

"Humph! You're certainly rude enough for two, but then, the dweomer seems to take people that way. Oh, very well! Rori went mad. It was the wound, you see. It's never healed."

"You can't mean the one that Raena gave him."

"Yes, I can. Just that."

"How—it shouldn't—it's been fifty years!"

"I know that, but it's never healed. It's not much of a wound, a mere scratch to a dragon, just as we said at the time, but it drips and oozes and keeps him awake. He licks it and licks it until I screech at him to stop, but he can't seem to just let it be. He goes about in a constant rage over it. Sometimes he just flies off, and I don't see him for months on end. Then he'll return, and all will be well for a little while, until that wretched, cursed wound drives him mad again."

Salamander grunted in disgust.

"It's a hard thing to hear," Dallandra said. "Arzosah, Rori could come to me. I might be able to do something for that cut now. Before there just wasn't enough time, since he was on the verge of bleeding to death and all."

"Oh, I suggested he find you years and years ago. He wouldn't hear of it." Arzosah paused, thinking. "He feels shamed, I suppose. He wouldn't listen to you either, that day in Cerr Cawnen, but now he knows that you were right."

"I'd never gloat or suchlike."

"I know that. You know that. He refuses to see it. The wound's never going to heal on its own, is it? It must have evil dweomer upon it."

"Not necessarily. The silver dagger punctured a lung, you see. That's why he was dying from such a small cut."

"How horrible! But it certainly doesn't run that deep now. It's probably because of the thickness of our skin."

"Yes, your scales must be quite solid."

"Indeed they are, and they're attached to still another layer of skin." Arzosah raised her head to expose her neck, a soft, pale gray-green. "You can see it under my chin, but it's thin there. On our sides, it's really quite substantial."

"That's probably why the wound hasn't killed him." Dallandra paused, struck by an ugly thought. "You know, if we do manage to transform him back into human form and that wound tears the lung again, he'll die. Oh, ye gods! I'm utterly perplexed by this."

"Don't say that!" Arzosah's voice rose high. "If you can't find a cure, what hope does he have?"

Dallandra merely sighed for an answer and glanced at Salamander, who'd gone pale.

"I don't know anything about physicking," Salamander said. "I never studied it, not even when I was in Bardek. Nevyn might have been able to help, but I don't suppose young Neb remembers medical lore."

"It's not the sort of thing one does remember from life to life," Dallandra said. "He's got a good mind for learning it, though. The herbwoman in Trev Hael taught him about some common herbs in return for his writing out labels and such things for her, and now I'm teaching him more, but he's still an apprentice. I wish Rori weren't being so stubborn. Until I see him and get a look at the wound, I won't know if I can help or not. It's too bad I can't summon him, but I don't know his true name."

"Maybe you don't, but maybe you do." Arzosah said. "My guess is that it's Rhodry tranDevaberiel. Or perhaps, Rhodry Aberwyn tranDevaberiel. I doubt if the Maelwaedd clan comes into it, but one never knows. I'd wager high on some combination of those names, I would."

"Oh, ye gods!" Dallandra felt like an utter fool. "I was thinking that he'd have a Dragonish true name now."

"No. Oh, no! You see, what I've come to realize is this: at root, in his soul and heart, he's still that elven half-breed. He's not a true dragon, Dalla, and he'll never be one. And that's the crux, the predicament, the quandary, as our prattling gerthddyn might say."

"I beg your pardon!" Salamander said. "I don't prattle."

"You should beg it, and you do too prattle. But Dalla, now Rori's driving me mad in turn. By all the holy flames of fire! If you could help, I'd—well, I don't know what I'd do, but it would be something good."

"I'll certainly do anything I can to help him, but I wonder. If he's not a true dragon, will his name have the same power over him?"

"Blasts of brimstone!" Arzosah thwacked her tail against the ground. "I hadn't thought of that. It doesn't seem likely."

"It's worth a try nonetheless."

"And I thank you for that." Arzosah hesitated, then clacked her jaws together several times. "I hope I'm not wrong about his true name. Having to admit I was wrong twice in a single day? I couldn't bear it."

Arzosah was spared that further humiliation. In an ordinary tone of voice, Dallandra spoke aloud a number of possible combinations of the names: Rhodry tranDevaberiel, Rori tranDevaberiel, Rhodry Aberwyn tranDevaberiel, and the like. Eventually she came to "Rhodry tranDevaberiel o'r Aberwyn." The moment she spoke it, she felt a little tremor of power, a slight burning in her mouth, and a delicate ripple of sensation around her lungs.

"That might be it," she said. "I'll try the summoning, but let's not get our hopes up too high." She glanced at the sun, low in the west, and allowed her mind to shift its focus away from the material plane. "The astral tides of Air are still running at the full. I'll wait till they've given way to Water."

Even though Branna's letter was short and simple, Neb read it through three times. From her sloppy scrawl, so different from Solla's precise hand, he could tell that she'd signed the letter herself. He kissed the signature several times, then rolled the letter up and put it into his saddlebags, where it would be handy when he wanted to read it again. While he waited for Dallandra to return, he wandered through the encampment until he found Tieryn Cadryc, who was pleased to learn that his wife and niece were faring well.

"Next letter you write," Cadryc said, "tell my lady that we've had no word from our daughter, but that I still have hope." He paused, chewing on the edge of his mustache. "I'm afraid that bastard's not going to let our Adranna go, but don't tell her that, of course."

Yet it was the very next morning, when the cool dawn was brightening into a hot day, that Lord Honelg's herald finally appeared again on his lord's walls. He blew three notes on his horn and waved his staff, making the bright ribands dance in the pale light. The shout went round Ridvar's camp to summon Indar.

Neb—and everyone else in the Westfolk camp—hurried up the hill to join the gwerbret's men, who had gathered some fifty yards from the entrance to the dun's earthworks to wait during the parley. Speculations multiplied in whispers and murmurs, ranging from the extravagant hope that Honelg would surrender to the grim thought that he was merely going to order the princes and the gwerbret off his lands once again.

In the event, the outcome fell between the two. When Indar returned, he sported a thin smile of satisfaction. He knelt before Ridvar, then spoke as loudly as he could to make his voice carry to all his anxious listeners.

"Lord Honelg wants to send the womenfolk out, Your Grace," Indar said. "He wishes to know if you'll guarantee their safety."

"The gall of the man!" Ridvar snarled. "As if I'd do aught else! Besides, Lady Adranna's father is here."

"Cursed right I am!" Cadryc shoved his way through the throng to join the gwerbret. "If anyone tries to harm my daughter or any of her women, then he'll have me to answer to."

"And that should provide all the reassurance he needs," Ridvar said.

Indar rose, bowed to the noble-born, and trotted back to the dun, his staff held high, to disappear into the maze of earthworks. While this second parley continued, Ridvar and Cadryc's men hurriedly armed, just in case Honelg was trying to work a ruse. In the past, a few dishonorable lords had used a call for parley to mount a surprise sally once the gates were open.

"Let's move closer," Salamander said to Neb. "I want to be right at hand when the lady comes out."

"I take it you think we'll be safe."

"I do. I truly can't see a devotee of Alshandra risking his women to trick an enemy."

With some fancy maneuvering and a bevy of apologies, Salamander and Neb managed to work their way forward till they could stand beside Gerran, who had put on his mail shirt, though he carried his pot helm tucked under his left arm. He acknowledged the pair with a nod, then went back to watching the dun.

Both heralds' horns rang out. Indar walked out of the maze, and right behind him came a woman who looked so much like Galla that Neb knew it had to be Adranna. She was leading a little girl along by the hand, and right behind her came three women wearing the stained and faded dresses that marked them as servants. The servants carried bundles wrapped in blankets, the lady's possessions, no doubt, as well as the few things they themselves owned.

"The lass is Treniffa," Salamander whispered to Neb. "I don't know the servants' names. My heart's beginning to be troubled, though, because I don't see Lady Varigga, Honelg's mother."

Tieryn Cadryc started forward to go meet them, but Ridvar caught his sleeve.

"You'd better stay back," Ridvar said, "in case one of those archers decides you're too valuable a target to ignore. They're commoners, after all. We can't expect them to behave honorably."

"True spoken, Your Grace." Cadryc stayed among his men.

Adranna hesitated at the sight of the army, then continued on, walking at a measured pace with her head held high across that last stretch of uneven ground. The servants trailed miserably after, and little Treniffa looked frankly terrified.

"Still no sign of Varigga," Salamander said. "I fear the worst. The gates are closing now."

"How can you tell?" Neb said. "I can't see a cursed thing from here."

Salamander gave him a weary smile, and Neb suddenly realized that the gerthddyn had just scryed out the dun. Adranna hesitated again, looking over the waiting men, then came straight for Salamander.

"You!" Adranna stopped in front of him and considered him for a long moment. "Raldd told us of your treachery. You—after we fed you at our table."

"It aches my heart," Salamander began, "but—"

Adranna spat full into his face. With a toss of her head she walked past him, head held high. Neb pulled an ink-stained rag out of his pocket and handed it to Salamander, who took it with a murmur of thanks.

Tieryn Cadryc was hurrying forward to meet Adranna when Treniffa spotted him. With a howl of "Gran, Gran!" she broke away from her mother's grasp and ran weeping to his outspread arms. At the sight Adranna began to weep as well. For a moment she stood trembling and alone, watching her father as if she feared a blow.

"Addi!" Cadryc bellowed. "Thanks be to every god! Er, or every goddess, I suppose I should say, eh? Your mother's been worried half out of her mind, and I don't mind admitting that I'm cursed glad to see you out of that dun."

"I—" Adranna was weeping too hard to finish. She ran the last few yards with the servants hurrying after. The Red Wolf warband closed around them all and swept them downhill to safety.

After a brief discussion with his daughter and his captain, Cadryc decided to send the women back to Cengarn immediately. Gerran picked out five men for an escort and gave them their orders—get the women to safety, then return to the army. Two of those he picked, Warryc and Daumyr, decided to argue about it.

"Your Grace, and you, too, Captain," Warryc said, "we respectfully request that you let us stay with the army and send someone else to Cengarn instead."

"Oh, do you now?" Cadryc sounded amused. "And why should the captain let you do that?"

"It was us that Honelg lied to, Your Grace, about there being illness in his dun, I mean. We don't want to miss the fight."

"So he did. I'd forgotten that." Cadryc glanced at Gerran. "You get the last word on this."

"What makes you think you're going to miss anything?" Gerran said. "We could be here for the rest of the summer."

"Well, true-spoken." Warryc paused to turn uphill and look at the dun. "But he's sent his women out, hasn't it? I'd wager that's a sign of change."

"Oh, very well, then." Gerran scowled at him, but he knew that the scowl couldn't hide his respect for them. "Turn those horses over to young Allo and Bryn and tell them to join the escort."

"My thanks!" Warryc made a bob of a bow in Cadryc's direction. "And my thanks to you, too, my lord."

Still grinning, the pair of them led the horses away.

"I hope five men will be enough," Cadryc said. "I keep wondering if Honelg has allies somewhere close by, someone who might want to take my daughter for a hostage."

"If he does have allies," Gerran said, "they're not Deverry men."

"That's what's troubling me the most."

"True spoken, but if Horsekin were lying in ambush, the dragon would have smelled them even if she couldn't see them."

"I keep forgetting about that blasted creature. Imph, I must be getting old, seeing enemies everywhere."

Yet the tieryn wasn't the only person who worried about Adranna's safety. With the escort settled, Gerran went out to the pasture where the Red Wolf horses were tethered to pick out the most tractable mounts for the women. Prince Daralanteriel and Dallandra came down to join him there.

"A request of you, Captain," the prince said. "The Wise One here has asked me to send four archers back to Cengarn with the escort."

"That's a generous offer, Your Highness," Gerran said. "I'll accept it gladly."

"You're going to ask me why," Dallandra said with a good-humored smile. "Not all the dragons in this part of the world are friendly, and so I thought archers might come in handy, as it were. I asked the prince to send some of our men along."

And what good, Gerran thought to himself, *are hunting bows going to be against dragons?* Yet he merely smiled and bowed to her, because he could guess that Dallandra in truth had another sort of enemy in mind. Of what sort, he had no idea, but he also had no doubt that she knew, and that was what mattered.

After he chose the horses, Gerran delegated servants to saddle them. There were provisions to be packed and loaded onto a mule, too, since the trip would take two days. During these preparations Lady Adranna sat on an empty barrel turned on its side, with Trenni sitting cross-legged in front of her to lean back between her mother's knees. The servants knelt on the grass behind them. Gerran wanted to say something comforting to the lady, but he could think of nothing. The army was here to kill her lord and husband, and she knew it as well as anyone.

Once everything was ready for the journey, Cadryc knelt down in front of his daughter. "What about Matto?" he said.

"What do you think?" Adranna said. "Honelg wouldn't let him go." Her voice snapped with rage like green wood hissing and sparking on a fire. "No matter how hard I begged."

"Imph." Cadryc paused for a long moment. "I see. Well, here, we'll do what we can to get him out alive for you. Matto, I mean."

"Da, if you could!" Adranna caught her breath with a gasp and choked back tears. "Mayhap my goddess—"

"Hush!" Cadryc snapped. "I'd have you keep silence about that lying demoness where the men can hear you."

Adranna crossed her arms over her chest, then set her jaw and stared him in the eye. "And I'd have you not call *her* that."

For a moment they glared at each other in silence. Adranna had never looked more like her father than at that moment, Gerran decided. Trenni sat stone-still between them, her pinched little face pale, her eyes wide. Abruptly, Adranna broke the impasse. She stroked her daughter's hair and bent forward to murmur to her until her stiff little shoulders relaxed.

"Oh, very well, Da," Adranna said. "I doubt me if I'd get anything but curses if I did say her name." She paused, drawing a long breath. "Soon enough I'll be a widow, anyway, and I'm minded to go to the temple of the Moon once I am, but I plan on going with a lying heart, to worship my own goddess under their guise."

"What? Ye gods, it's a bit soon to make that decision. This blasted siege could last for months."

"Nah nah nah! You don't understand us, and you don't understand *her* ways. Although—" Her voice turned hesitant. "Although I don't truly know what my lord will do. He's been so strange lately. When he sent us out, he was talking about bearing the last witness, but I don't know if he can go through with it or not."

"The what? What in the icy hells is that?"

Adranna shook her head and silently mouthed "not where the child can hear." Cadryc nodded to show he'd understood. "Ask that snake-tongued betrayer of a gerthddyn what it means," Adranna said. "He seems to know enough about us, judging from the way he's brought ruin upon us all."

When the women rode out, Cadryc rode with them, though he announced that he'd turn back after a mile or so. Gerran walked down to the road to see them off, then went to the Westfolk's encampment to look for Neb. He found him and Salamander both kneeling on the ground in front of Dallandra's tent. With a clean doeskin to lay their work upon, they were folding bandages out of linen rags. Gerran hunkered down across from them.

"Tell me somewhat," Gerran said. "Why did the prince give us those archers?"

"Swear to me you won't repeat a word of this," Neb said, "and I'll tell you."

"Done, then."

"Dalla thinks there may be a shape-changer dogging our heels, one who can fly. If she's right, he's up to no good."

Gerran had the distinct sensation that he was going to choke. He managed a cough, took a deep breath, and finally found his voice. "Shape-changer?" he said. "Ah by the black hairy arse of the Lord of Hell! There is such a thing, then?"

"There is." Neb sounded so grim that Gerran believed him without hesitation. "It's not just some fancy tale like Salamander tells in the marketplace."

"Indeed," Salamander put in. "Gerro, if you see a bird, particularly a raven, who looks far too big to be a normal bird, as it were, then come tell Dalla or me straightaway."

"I will. You can rest assured about that. Another question. Lady Adranna told her father that Honelg was planning on bearing the last witness. She said to ask you what that meant."

Salamander winced, then frowned down at the bandage in his hands. "I'm not absolutely sure," he said at last. "But I do know it bodes ill. 'Witnessing' to these people always seems to mean dying in some form or another. So I'd guess it means fighting to the death."

"Honelg would do that anyway," Gerran said. "He can hardly surrender. Ridvar will hang him if he does. Now that he's let Lady Adranna go, he's got naught to bargain with."

"What about the lives of his men?" Neb said. "And the men from his village, too."

"His men have sworn to die with him, if need be," Gerran said. "And they will. His villagers—I'd suppose that any who wanted to leave would have left with the women. Ridvar wouldn't have harmed them. In his eyes, they don't matter."

"Huh." Neb snorted profoundly. "No doubt."

When Cadryc returned, Gerran told him what Salamander had said about bearing the last witness, but he kept Neb's talk of shape-changers to himself. If Cadryc believed it, then he'd be sorely troubled about a threat he could do nothing to turn aside, and if he disbelieved, then he'd think that his scribe and his captain had both gone daft. Neither seemed like a reasonable risk to run, especially since the only two people in the encampment who could defeat that sort of enemy were already on their guard.

Late that night, Gerran was standing watch at the edge of the Red Wolf camp when he saw a dim light flickering in an upper window of the otherwise dark dun. Someone who couldn't sleep had lit a candle lantern, he supposed. In a moment the light disappeared, only to reappear briefly through an arrow-slit on the floor below, then disappear once more. In a short while he spotted the light again, and for a moment he thought the dun was on fire, because it gleamed through chinks in the loosely set stones of the outer wall.

The light, however, never spread further. *A lantern, then,* Gerran thought. *But why would someone be sitting outside next to the wall like that?* Any sentries should have been up on the catwalks, and indeed, occasionally in the starlight he could discern men, walking back and forth at the top of the walls. Eventually, toward the end of his watch, the lantern light disappeared and stayed gone.

In the morning Gerran mentioned the mysterious light to Dallandra, who thanked him but seemed untroubled by the news—much to Gerran's relief. He'd been afraid that the light meant some sort of evil dweomer at work.

"I doubt it," Dallandra said. "More likely Honelg just couldn't sleep, as you suspected. Salamander mentioned that he's got a shrine to his goddess somewhere in the dun, and he could well have gone there to pray."

"Ah," Gerran said. "That makes sense."

"I've been meaning to ask you," Dallandra continued, "if you think Honelg will sally soon—or at all."

"I've no idea, my lady. The man's obviously daft, and so who knows what he'll do? And that means we can do naught but sit and wait."

Those left behind in Cengarn were just as impatient for news of the siege, but their curiosity was the more easily slaked. The afternoon was just turning to a long summer evening when Arzosah appeared over Dun Cengarn for a second time. Branna was sitting in the women's hall working on Neb's wedding shirt. At the sound of shouting in the ward she laid the shirt into her workbasket just as Midda came rushing in.

"She's back," Midda said, gasping for breath. "The dragon, I mean. Lord Oth wants you to go talk with her."

"What?" Lady Galla practically bounced out of her chair. "How dare he! Branna, I don't want you doing any such thing."

"Aunt Galla, I'll be very careful, I promise," Branna said. "Since she knows me now, it'll be safer for me than anyone else."

"Apparently Oth thinks so." Galla paused for a scowl. "He obviously doesn't have the courage to go himself, and I shall tell him so at dinner tonight."

Branna made her escape from the women's hall before Galla could argue further and hurried upstairs. As she climbed the ladder to the roof, she could smell the dragon's spoilt-wine scent. She scrambled out onto the sunny roof where Arzosah sat comfortably coiled, waiting for her. Branna curtsied, a gesture that brought a rumble of approval from the wyrm.

"And a good evening to you," Arzosah said. "Is all well here?"

"It is, truly," Branna said. "I see you've brought us more messages."

"I have, and some good news. Your cousin and her daughter are safe and on their way here. They should arrive soon, in fact, well before sunset. I overflew them not long ago at all."

"Thank every true goddess for that!" Branna felt like howling in sheer joy. "I can't even say how much it gladdens my heart."

"I thought it might." Arzosah raised her head to reveal the dangling sack of messages. "If you could relieve me of this unseemly pouch, I'll be off to hunt."

"Gladly. Did you hear that Oth found Alshandra worshippers in the dun? We don't know, though, if there are any down in town."

"I did hear that. While I hunt and suchlike, I've been keeping an eye out for anyone who might have left town and ridden west." The dragon curled one paw and contemplated her claws. "The prince personally asked me to do so."

"Which one?"

"Voran. For a human being he's unusually clever. We don't want anyone trying to warn Zakh Gral."

Once she had the pouch, Branna tossed it through the trapdoor, then climbed down after it as fast as she could. From above, she could hear Arzosah take flight with the slap and drumming of her enormous wings. Branna scooped up the messages and ran downstairs. On the landing she hesitated, then decided that Oth could wait a moment or ten. With a fling of the heavy door, she burst into the women's hall.

"Aunt Galla!" Branna called out. "He's let her go. Honelg, I mean. Adranna and Trenni are nearly here."

Galla looked at her, smiled, hesitated, then wept in the flooding relief of tears, though she kept smiling the entire time. Solla hurried to her side and put an arm around her shoulders.

"I'll just take these messages to Lord Oth," Branna said. "I'll come back as soon as he gives me leave."

"Better yet," Drwmigga said, "we'll all go down to the great hall as soon as Galla's composed herself. We'll all want to go out to the ward to greet Lady Adranna."

Just as the dragon predicted, Adranna, Trenni, and their escort reached Cengarn well before sunset. A fort guard on duty above the north gate saw their tiny procession straggling down the road and shouted the news to one of his fellows, who ran up to the dun with it. With Drwmigga at their head, as befitted her rank as the lady of the dun, the women left the great hall and waited by the open gates. Thanks to the steepness of the hill and the twists in Cengarn's streets, they had something of a wait before they finally saw Adranna. She and little Treniffa were still on horseback, but the servant lasses and the men of the escort had dismounted to spare their horses during the steep climb up. Those pages left behind in the dun hurried forward to help the ladies, and the two remaining grooms came for the horses.

Once they'd dismounted, Adranna and Treniffa made no move to come forward. They stood together, Adranna's arm around her daughter's shoulders, as if they expected to be arrested rather than welcomed. The servant lasses huddled behind them. It was Drwmigga's place to say a few words, but she seemed to have forgotten this particular courtesy. Branna felt like kicking her, but instead she strode over to her cousins.

"It gladdens my heart to see you safe," Branna said. "Addi, you can't imagine how worried we've been."

At that Adranna managed a smile, but she was looking over Branna's shoulder at her mother. Lady Galla wiped a few tears away with the back of her hand.

"You've been very naughty, Addi," Galla said, "but I never wanted you to marry that awful man in the first place, and so it's no wonder, I suppose."

"Oh, Mama!" Adranna's reserve broke at last. She ran to Galla and threw her arms around her. "It gladdens my heart to see you." Her voice cracked, but she managed to choke back any tears. "I'm so tired."

"Let's all go inside," Drwmigga said, "and take you up to the women's hall. It will be nicer there."

The women ate in their own hall that night, leaving the great hall to the men of the fort guard under the command of Lord Oth. Everyone but Adranna talked bravely about all sorts of things, none of which truly mattered except for Branna's betrothal. Yet, even though her cousin did show some pleasure at the news and ask for some details about Neb, Branna changed the subject as soon as she could. Adranna was about to become a widow, and Branna refused to dwell on her own happiness. She did wonder, though, if Adranna would mourn her lord. She had accepted the marriage freely enough, Branna knew from the talk of the older women in her clan, but had she come to love him or hate him during those years shut up with him on the edge of the wild forest? Adranna gave no sign either way as the talk flowed around her like water around a rock in a stream.

It was late that evening before Branna had a moment alone with her niece. Since there were no other noble-born children in the dun, and thus no nursemaid, Treniffa would sleep on a trundle bed in her mother's chamber, but exhausted though she was, she was afraid to go to sleep alone. Branna lit candle lanterns, gave one to Trenni to carry and took the other, then led her up to the room. Midda had already laid clean linen sheets and a blanket on the narrow little bed's straw mattress. Branna set the lanterns down where there was no danger of tipping them onto the braided rushes covering the floor. Shadows danced in the curve of the wall and made Trenni flinch.

"It's too hot tonight for a blanket," Branna said, "so we'll fold that up and make you a pillow instead."

Trenni nodded. She was looking around the chamber wide-eyed, staring at the shadows and the flickering light. "You'll stay till I go to sleep?" she said at last.

"I will."

"Will you leave the candles burning?"

"I will indeed."

"Will Mama be up soon?"

"I'm sure of that. She's very tired too."

"Then will you stay till she comes?"

"I will, love. Don't you trouble your heart. You're safe now."

Branna helped her take off her dress, torn in places and filthy from the trip to Cengarn. Underneath she was wearing a thin shift of linen that was yellow and shiny with age.

"Do you have another dress with you?" Branna said.

"I don't," Trenni said. "We didn't bring much. Mama was afraid

Da would change his mind and not let us go. So we just grabbed some things and ran downstairs."

"I see. Well, on the morrow we can sew you a new one."

Trenni sat down on the edge of the bed. "Aunt Branna?" she said. "Will they kill Matto when they take our dun?"

Branna hesitated. She wanted to say neither the truth nor the lie. The truth would hurt the child now, but a lie would wound her more deeply later.

"They will, won't they?" Trenni's thin voice went flat. "I don't want him to die."

"Neither do I," Branna said. "My Neb promised me he'd try to save him, and he's got some very important friends there with him."

Trenni lay down and turned on her side to hide her face against the improvised pillow. Branna thought at first that she was weeping, but she'd fallen sleep without another word.

Adranna came up soon after and released Branna from guard duty, as Branna was thinking of it. Since the night had turned stifling, Branna took one of the lanterns up to the flat roof of the main broch tower. Clouds, coming up from the south, covered half the stars, and a soft wind blew some of the day's heat away. From the western quarter of the sky she heard what at first sounded like thunder, but instead of dying away, it strengthened into a regular drumlike sound, growing louder and closer. Arzosah, she assumed, and she looked up in hopes of seeing the great wyrm as she flew by.

While Branna did see a dragon flying from the west, the wyrm shone as silver and bright as a full moon against the gathering clouds. She could guess that it was Arzosah's mate, Rori, surrounded by Wildfolk of Aethyr. He flew hard and steadily, heading straight north, most likely to join the battle for Honelg's dun. She was reminded once again of her wretched stepmother, mocking her for thinking she'd seen a dragon, insisting it had only been a silver owl. *I'm well out of that dun!* she thought. *May the gods bless Aunt Galla forever!*

The greatest blessing that she could imagine now would be the safe return of young Matyc, but whether such could ever happen lay in the laps of the gods indeed.

Inside Dallandra's tent the air, stifling from the coming storm, weighed on Salamander like a wool cloak, but by staying inside they could talk about dweomer, or even work it, away from Deverry men with the exception, of course, of Neb. Dallandra had made a silver dweomer light to hang near the smoke hole. Gnats and moths swarmed around it, and a trio of sprites were amusing themselves by trying to catch the insects with their tiny fingers.

"I keep thinking about that dark dweomerman," Dallandra said. "My worst fear is that he's somehow or other gotten himself inside Honelg's dun."

"Now, that I doubt very much, O Princess of Powers Perilous," Salamander said. "He certainly wasn't there when I was."

"That's some reassurance, at least. Have you scried the dun out lately?"

"I have. No sign of him there."

"There's been none at the temple either. No one's ever rebuilt that astral construct, whatever it was. The priests seem to be devoting all their time and energy to keep the cattle safe from Arzosah. They've started bringing them into the temple grounds at night."

"Which must be a great disappointment to our wyrm."

"I suppose, but that's not my point. If they have time to worry about their precious cows, they're not likely to be working dark dweomer against us. Besides, that many animals give off a tremendous cloud of etheric magnetism. I'll have to be very careful if I go there again—go in the body of light, I mean."

"I hadn't thought of that, but you're quite right. A cloud of magnetic force like that could make a working very tricky."

"Have you seen anything suspicious at Zakh Gral?"

"I've not. I scry them out every time I think of them, but they keep a-building as if they don't have a care in the world. There's been no sign of the raven mazrak either."

"I hope he's not flying west to warn the fortress."

"He can't, oh mistress of mighty magicks. They'd kill him on the spot. Rocca made it abundantly clear that Alshandra abhors mazrakir above all other kinds of dweomer."

"Well and good, then. I wonder about Zaklof, though. You told me that his prophecy about Cadryc's son was genuine."

"It was, truly, but they see all and every sign of dweomer as a gift from their goddess. If Zaklof were here, no doubt he'd tell us solemnly that he'd only lent Alshandra his voice for a moment. A mazrak, however, couldn't claim any such thing."

For Neb's sake, they were speaking in Deverrian, because Neb and Meranaldar were working with wax tablets directly under the dweomer light. Neb was teaching his fellow scribe how to write in Deverrian. Although both their voices were pleasant enough, Salamander found himself growing profoundly irritated with what they were saying, tedious details such as "you've got to make the tail on this letter a little longer" or "try to make a true circle when you do that one."

"Ye gods," Salamander said. "I feel positively overwrought tonight. I keep brooding over Adranna's remark about bearing the last witness. You know, Gerran keeps saying that Honelg is daft, and I begin to think he's right. There's something oddly unclean about Alshandra's worship."

"Of course there is! She wasn't a goddess at all. Her cult's making their people die for a handful of lies and kill for a shabby handful more."

"Now that is a splendid way of putting it. Most tidy, pertinent, and apt."

From outside they heard men talking in Elvish. Calonderiel swept open the tent flap and stuck his head in. "The dragon wants to speak with you, beloved," he said in Elvish. "She says she's come up with an idea."

"About what?"

"She wouldn't tell me." Cal paused for a scowl. "I'm only a mere banadar, after all."

"She is temperamental, isn't she?" Dallandra rolled her eyes heavenward. "Where is she?"

"Down by that rivulet in the pasture. Follow your nose. The scent of rotting beef will guide you."

Mostly to get out of the stuffy tent, Salamander volunteered to escort her. With the rain clouds moving up from the south, the night had turned dark even for elven eyes. Once they were safely away from the main camp, Dallandra made another silver ball, a small one, this time, supplying just enough light for them to negotiate the rocky path down to Arzosah's temporary lair. They found her chewing thoughtfully on a white oxtail, hair and all, but she obligingly spat it out when they arrived.

"The banadar told me you wanted to speak with me," Dallandra said.

"Is that what he is, the actual banadar?" Arzosah said. "I might have been nicer to him if I'd known that, but then, he was awfully rude to me."

"He tends to lack tact, yes," Dalla said. "Not that you have a long supply of it yourself."

"I'm a dragon. I don't need tact. But be that as it may, I've had an idea about those archers. I was sitting here thinking that it looks like rain, and how much I hate being out in the rain. I wish, I was thinking, that we dragons could make our own weather. That's when the idea came to me."

"Um?" Dallandra said. "I don't quite follow—"

"That's because I'm not finished yet," Arzosah said. "Now, tell me something. The arrows, are they heavy? They look very slender and light."

"They have wooden shafts, yes. What makes them deadly is the force created by the snap of the bowstring and the bend of the bow."

"Good! That's what I thought, but I needed to make sure." Arzosah crossed her front paws and considered something for a mo-

ment. "Now, long ago, during the siege of Cengarn, when Rori was
still Rhodry, he told me that he couldn't shoot arrows from my back
because the wind stirred up by my wings knocked them off-course.
I remember him trying to throw javelins from my back as well, and
again, he couldn't, because of the wind."

Salamander laughed, one sharp crow of triumph.

"I think you follow my drift, as it were," Arzosah said. "Now,
suppose I flew around above the dun walls, flapping madly. How
many arrows do you think would reach their targets?"

"Very few." Dallandra broke into a grin. "What a splendid idea!"

"So I thought." Arzosah rumbled briefly. "The plan does have
one difficulty, though, namely, there's only one of me, and to make
turns I have to swing wide."

"So while you're on the one side of the broch, the arrows on the
other will fly true," Salamander joined in. "If Rori would only get
himself here!"

"There's no sign of him?" Arzosah said.

"I don't know if there is or not," Salamander said. "Every time I
scry him out, he's in some wild place. It's hard for me to tell one
wilderness from another."

Arzosah drew back her head in sincere surprise. "I suppose that's
because you don't hunt for your dinner," she said at last. "Well,
Dalla, I know you did your best to summon him, and your best effort has powerful dweomer behind it, so we can hope he'll come
soon."

The rain arrived in the middle of the night, a swift downpour
that hammered on the tent roof and woke Salamander. All around
him the archers of Calonderiel's warband slept, as silent and motionless as only those raised in the close quarters of a Westfolk alar's
tents could be. For some while Salamander lay awake, worrying
about his brother, the coming battle, and worst of all, the hypo-
thetical dark dweomermaster who might or might not be close by.
He considered scrying, but the etheric disturbance given off by the
falling rain made it impossible. Finally he fell back asleep to wake
suddenly at dawn.

The rain had stopped, but when he looked at the little patch of sky visible through the smokehole, he could see swirling clouds. Still, the air was dry enough for him to try scrying. This time he got a dim impression of the silver wyrm, flying over the temple of Bel, before the vision turned murky and disappeared into etheric water-mist. Salamander put on his boots and got up, slipping out of the tent without waking anyone else. He walked over to Dallandra's tent, where the tent flap hung open, a sign that he'd not be inter-rupting some intimate moment.

"Dalla?" he said softly. "Are you awake?"

He could hear blankets rustling; then Dallandra pulled back the flap and ducked out.

"I was just about to come out," she said softly. "Cal's still asleep, though. What is it?"

"Rori's on his way."

"A thousand thanks to the Star Goddesses! Here, wait for me. I'm going to wake Cal up and tell him."

Uphill, the human army was waking as well; Salamander could see servants trying to start fires with damp wood, and men stand-ing around yawning or talking in small groups. Something touched his mind, a feeling too weak to be an omen, but too strong for a mere guess. He looked up, studying the cloudy sky. Sure enough, off to the south he could see some creature flying, a very large crea-ture, coming fast with a flash of silver wings.

"Dalla!" Salamander called out. "He's here!"

Dallandra shoved back the tent flap and hurried out to watch with him. Salamander was expecting Rori to land down in Ar-zosah's pasture. Even though they stood a good quarter mile from her, everyone in camp could still hear her distant roar of greeting. As Salamander turned toward the sound, he saw the black dragon leap into the air and join Rori. Wingtip to wingtip, they flew off to the east, then spiraled down to land out of sight behind a distant copse.

"They must want a private word," Dallandra said. "Before they join us, I mean."

"Most likely," Salamander said.

But in only a little space of time Arzosah returned alone. She flew low over the Westfolk camp and shouted to Dallandra as she passed by, "Meet me in my lair."

"Oh, ye gods!" Salamander said. "I hope he's willing to join the battle."

"And when did Rhodry ever spurn a fight?"

"True spoken." Salamander's spirits rose again. "Let us go hear what her ladyship has to tell us."

Calonderiel came with them as they ran down to join Arzosah. She glanced his way, curled her upper lip in scorn, and spoke only to Dallandra.

"He's looking forward to joining the battle," Arzosah said. "And he thinks my plan a good one. He suggests that you tell that banadar person to go call a council of war, so all the men who are going to attack the dun will know what we plan to do about those arrows."

Calonderiel growled quite audibly. Arzosah pretended not to notice.

"Why won't he come talk to us?" Dallandra said.

"He feels too shamed," Arzosah said. "He was an honor-bound man before Evandar worked his dweomer, wasn't he? And a dragon after, and our pride matches that of the honor-bound, so there we are."

"I still don't understand. Shamed?" Salamander asked. "Why?"

"I don't know." Arzosah lifted her furled wings slightly in her equivalent of a shrug. "I see nothing shameful about being a dragon, and so I don't see why he should."

"Well, you were hatched a dragon," Dallandra said, "but he wasn't. I'd like to think that he wishes he'd listened to me, but somehow that doesn't seem like Rhodry."

"As stubborn as a lord should be," Arzosah said. "Isn't that the Deverry ideal for their wretched nobles? Stubborn in all things, harsh to their equals, but generous to those below them, and then nasty and vicious, or some such thing."

"Some such thing, yes." Dallandra turned to Calonderiel. "Well, banadar person, I think that calling a council of war seems like a good idea. Do you?"

"Very much so." Calonderiel shot the dragon a dark glance. "Even fools speak the truth now and then."

Arzosah opened her mouth to reply, but Dallandra shouted and stepped in between them. "Enough! Both of you! We'd better get back to the camp."

"That's true," Calonderiel said. "It's going to take all day for the princes and the gwerbret to hammer out a plan of attack. We'd better get started."

Until they were well away from the smell of dragon and dead cow both, Salamander followed Dallandra and Calonderiel, then let them go on ahead. When he used the wind-torn clouds to scry, he saw Lord Honelg, pacing back and forth in front of the honor hearth as usual. This time, however, his sworn men, his archers from the village, and the servants had all left him alone in his hall. Out in the ward the men milled around. A few stood in little groups and talked furiously. Some of them wept; others kneeled on the wet cobbles and lifted their arms in prayer.

Panic! Salamander thought. *Understandable, but why wait till now?* Eventually he noticed that every now and then, someone would point to the sky and the rest all fall silent to look up. *The dragons, of course, the two evil minions of our supposed dark lord Vandar!* One of the guards atop the dun wall must have seen Rori fly over and Arzosah join him. Salamander couldn't quite remember if their appearance meant that the end of the world was near or merely that Vandar himself was taking a hand in Honelg's destruction. Either way, those trapped inside the dun doubtless felt that their last hour had come.

"And they're right enough about that," Salamander said aloud. "I sincerely hope that the Great Ones have got hold of dear Alshandra. I want her to see just how much evil she's worked."

Salamander took a couple of strides in the direction of the encampment, but all at once he felt such grief overwhelm him that he

sank to his knees. For a long time he knelt in the wet grass, struggling with both pity and guilt for those souls he'd helped doom,
until at last Dallandra came looking for him.

"What's so wrong?" she said.

"I hardly know." Salamander scrambled to his feet. "Except I
wish I'd never ridden Honelg's way."

"What? We had to find out about Zakh Gral."

"Oh, of course. I just wish I'd done my spying some other way."

Visibly puzzled, Dallandra was watching him as if waiting for
him to do or say something more. Salamander thought of trying to
explain further, but he knew it would be futile. Her work for her
own kind had come to rule Dallandra's life, and she hated any who
were their enemies, no matter how piteous.

"Come have some breakfast," she said at last. "You're going to
need your strength."

With two dragons as allies, Gerran allowed himself a thin slice of
optimism, which took the form of his thinking ahead to the problem of reaching Zakh Gral once they'd disposed of the current
siege. The men in the army had their doubts. Rumors ran through
the entire encampment, in fact, that the dragons were only pre-
tending to support Ridvar's cause and in truth were spies for the
Horsekin, that they weren't dragons at all but dweomer illusions or
evil human sorcerers, and that they would demand human flesh as
payment for their aid. Since the noble-born spent the day in Prince
Voran's tent, wrangling over various plans for taking the dun, Gerran and Salamander were left with the job of calming everyone's
nerves.

"Ye gods," Salamander said, "if I had a silver coin for every time
I've said 'that's not true' today, I'd be as rich as Prince Voran."

"True spoken," Gerran said. "We've shoveled a lot of horseshit."

It was just at sunset, and they were taking a well-deserved rest by
the fire in the Red Wolf camp. A couple of servants were frying
chopped salt pork and big handfuls of sliced onions in an iron pan

while a kettle of barley porridge simmered nearby, dangling from a tripod. Clae and Coryn were taking turns stirring the porridge, which, judging from the effort it took to move the wooden paddle, seemed to be thickening up nicely.

"I suppose," Salamander said, "that eventually those cooks are going to dump the one pan into the other and call it the warband's dinner."

"Most likely," Gerran said. "You're welcome to join us if you'd like."

"Oh, I wasn't fishing for an invitation, I assure you!" Salamander looked faintly ill. "Just an idle wondering."

"What I'm wondering about is that council of war. You'd think it'd be over by now." Gerran stood and peered uphill through the twilight toward Ridvar's white pavilion. As he watched, men began leaving, a few at a time. "Huh! And it is."

Tieryn Cadryc was one of the first out. He came striding up to the fire and paused to sniff the greasy air. "Smells good, lads," he said. "There's nothing like the smell of frying onions when you're hungry."

Salamander opened his mouth as if to speak, then shut it again and merely smiled.

"Gerran!" Cadryc went on. "There you are, eh? Doubtless you want to know how the council went. Well, the plan comes down to letting the dragons counter the archers while we get our men through to the gates with the ram."

"Isn't that the plan you had in mind when the council started?" Salamander said.

"It is, truly. But the point of a council of war is to see if someone can come up with a better idea or find the weaknesses in the one you've got." Cadryc allowed himself a weary smile. "And with two princes and a gwerbret doing the arguing, these things take time. Now, Prince Voran thought we should wait until we got some sappers and miners here, but Prince Dar pointed out that the longer we sit here at this dun, the more likely it is that the Horsekin will finish their cursed stone wall around their dun before we get there. And so on and on it went."

Yet in the end, part of their plan, at least, turned out to be useless. Dawn broke in a sky half-obscured by clouds off to the north. Most of the men ate their breakfast rations standing up, staring at the sky, wondering about rain and dragons both. A troubled silence lay over the camp. Even Gerran succumbed to the mood. He couldn't shake the feeling that the day would see some momentous occurrence, maybe a defeat, maybe a victory—but something was about to happen at last.

Sure enough, the sun stood about halfway 'twixt dawn and noon when Honelg's herald appeared on the dun wall, waving his staff to ask for a parley. The shout went up for Indar, who came running with the ribands on his staff streaming out behind him. This time, rather than meet among Honelg's earthworks, the two heralds came down very nearly to the gwerbret's siege line. Gerran followed Cadryc as his lordship squeezed himself in behind Voran to hear the parley.

"I see no reason to stand upon ceremony, your highnesses and your grace," the herald said. "My lord Honelg has decided to open his gates. He welcomes you in, should you dare to try to reach them."

The herald turned and waved at the dun. When Gerran looked up he saw archers lining the catwalks between every pair of crenels.

"My lord further suggests," the herald continued, "that if you don't care to come visit him, you might quit his lands with all due speed." He bowed to the assembled lords, then turned and walked back, disappearing between the earthworks surrounding the dun's motte.

For a moment, a strange silence lay over both those defending and those attacking the dun, broken at last by the creaking squeak and grumble of a winch pulling open a pair of heavy gates. Up on the walls the archers began laughing, a rising tumble of noise somewhere between hysteria and mirth.

Ridvar and Voran turned to face one another and seemed to be about to speak, but neither said a word until the laughter died away. Prince Dar set his hands on his hips and stared up at the dun. From his alien face, so preternaturally handsome, it was impossible to tell what he might be feeling.

"They're all daft," Voran said. "They must be!"

"I'm not so sure of that," Daralanteriel said. "Daft, mayhap, but clever as well. How many of your men would live to reach the gates, my lords, if we lacked allies with wings?"

"A good point, Your Highness." Ridvar finally found his voice. "They would have made us pay high, more than they're worth, the bastards."

"I suggest we have our men arm and ready themselves." Voran bowed in Daralanteriel's direction. "If one of your people could alert the dragons?"

"Gladly," Daralanteriel said. "And may all of our gods favor us today."

While the men armed, Prince Voran and Gwerbret Ridvar squabbled but in an oddly amiable way about the order of the charge, if you could call the run ahead through a twisty maze a charge. Ridvar had the typical young lord's dream of glory, that he would lead his men personally through the gates, but both princes shouted him down.

"Until your wife gives you a son, Your Grace," Voran said, "the rhan needs you alive, and truly, it would be a pleasant thing if you survived a fair bit longer than that as well."

The person who ended up leading that charge turned out to be someone that the noble-born had never even considered. The sun had cleared the horizon and was turning the clouds a bright silver when the army assembled in a rough column, four men abreast, at the base of the hill. Since Honelg had been declared in rebellion against the gwerbret, Ridvar's men would take the lead, but Cadryc, Gerran, and their ten men from the Red Wolf warband had an honorable position near the front. Prince Voran's men would be the last in, as they were there as a courtesy to the gwerbret rather than out of need.

The Westfolk archers were the exception. They clustered off to one side, and besides the quivers at their hips and the bows over their backs, they carried coils of rope slung over their shoulders.

"For scaling the wall once Honelg's archers are off it," Warryc told Gerran. "I asked."

"My thanks," Gerran said. "I wondered."

"I was talking to the men in Ridvar's lead squad. They're cursed glad they won't have to carry a blasted ram up the hill." Warryc was grinning as he spoke.

"Oh, they'll have their day. Don't forget, Zakh Gral's waiting for us. Today's only the first skirmish in a long war."

Warryc's smile disappeared. Gerran put on his helm over his padded cap and twisted it slightly to settle the nasal bar in place. He drew his sword, then went back to watching Ridvar's captain, who held a silver horn at the ready. Before he could signal the charge, however, Gerran heard another sort of music, the drum beat of enormous wings, coming fast and steadily. With a roar the silver dragon swooped out of the cloudy sky and launched himself for the dun.

Honelg's men shouted, screamed, dodged this way and that on their catwalks. The dragon roared like a river in spate, a rumbling thunder that drowned out their panic. On huge silver wings he rose into the sky and turned in a wide swing for another pass. The archers on the wall steadied themselves. When he swooped again, a barrage of arrows sprang to meet him, but with a strong beat of his wings, he sent them tumbling every which way, harmless in the air.

Shouts of rage and shrieks of terror rose from the wall. The silver dragon swooped up high, disappearing into the brightness of the rising sun. At this seeming retreat Gerran felt sick with disappointment, but only for a moment. With a roar and a rush of wings like a winter storm, the dragon reappeared to stoop and plunge. Straight down he came, fast, faster, plummeting toward the dun. Just when it seemed he'd crash into the broch tower, he twisted, swooped over the outer wall, and rose with a screaming archer in his claws. A swarm of arrows rose from the battlements, fluttered, and fell short.

Not one man among the besiegers cheered or even called out a warcry. The archer may have been an enemy, but he was also a fellow human being, and he kept screaming and screaming in agony and terror as the silver dragon climbed the sky. With a quick banking of his wings, the dragon swooped over the dun once more—and let him go. With a last horrible shriek the archer fell, flailing his arms, till he disappeared from the besiegers' view behind the walls that had so badly failed to protect him. All at once the shriek died in mid-note. A brief hush fell over dun and siege lines both; then archers began disappearing from the walls as fast as they could climb down. Gerran could guess that they were running for the safety of the broch.

"Now!" Gerran yelled. "Let's go!"

Gerran took off running for the path up to the dun. Behind him he heard yells break out, warcries and howling as his men streamed after him, and an answering babble of warcries from the gwerbret's men. As he rounded the first bend in the path, he got a glimpse back and saw Ridvar's captain leading his men directly after. Silver horns rang out down at the foot of the motte. Another turn, and Gerran glanced behind to see the Westfolk archers not on the path but on the dirt banks bordering it. Like deer they leaped from one bank to another as they aimed for the dun walls. Gerran felt his breath begin to come hard, but one more turn brought him to the gates.

"They're open!" he screamed with what air he had left. "The bastards meant it."

Gerran paused to breathe and to let his men mass behind him. Through the gates he could see the silver wyrm making another pass, swooping low over the dun as if looking for stragglers. From the window-slits high in the broch, arrows flew and hissed through the air, but the dragon's wings were making such a strong wind that they twisted and fell. With a roar like a river in flood Arzosah swept down from the clouds and joined her mate. Round and round the broch they flew, and the gusts from their powerful wings knocked the flying arrows every which way. They clubbed the air like giants drumming, pounding, pounding, pounding as they flew.

"Now, lads!" Gerran shouted. "Before the wyrms tire!"

With a shriek of war cries rising behind him, Gerran charged into the ward. At first arrows dropped feebly around him, but the wooden rain died away fast. He could see that the door to the great hall stood open. He knew that the first man through would die, but he saw no way out of plunging in. If he flinched now, the men behind him would as well, and if they were milling around the ward leaderless, they'd be easy prey for a sally. His entire life had swept him to this last charge. For the first time in that life Gerran howled a war cry.

"For the Red Wolf!"

He ran toward the open door, but well before he could reach the broch, men poured out of it, Lord Honelg and his captain, Rhwn, at their head. They'd chosen not to cower inside but to make one last charge of their own. Behind them came the villagers, armed with clubs, threshing flails, improvised pikes, any weapon they could grab now that their bows had failed them. The only armor that any of them wore were leather jerkins, and not many of them had those. Gerran felt a brief moment of pity, a moment cut short by the charge.

"Falcon!" Rhwn was heading straight for him. "You're mine!"

The lines clashed in a crazed swirl of fighting. The poorly-armed villagers were slashing around them randomly, trying to get a clean strike on someone, anyone, while the swordsmen struggled to face off with an equal. Gerran ducked under a clumsy swing of a flail and managed to reach Rhwn. He got one solid strike on Rhwn's shield and parried the answering blow just as a man fell against Rhwn from behind and shoved him half to the ground. Gerran stepped back to let him gain his feet. Rhwn steadied himself, then lunged forward with a hard swing of his blade from below. Gerran dodged, slashed, and cut him hard across the throat. Blood welled as his knees buckled, and he fell onto the cobbles. Gerran spun around, looking for another enemy.

All at once the shouts turned to screams from the villagers. Arrows hissed past him, but these weren't coming down from the broch. The Westfolk archers had gained the walls. Gerran could hear Honelg's men shouting Alshandra's name in a last terrified chorus. He watched in something like horror as Westfolk arrows slithered through the air and struck home, bursting through good solid mail. Honelg's men fell clawing at the death piercing their chests.

With a last roar the two dragons flew off. The Westfolk loosed shaft after shaft. Villagers in their futile bits of leather armor dropped and died or fell screaming, wounded and writhing as their hayforks and scythes clattered on the cobbles of the ward. Gerran took two steps toward the slaughter, then found himself remembering the villagers mowed down by Horsekin raiders. For a terrible moment he wondered if he were any different from the raiders, bringing death to men who couldn't fight back, and he stayed where he was, merely watching.

Most of Honelg's riders had already followed their captain into the Otherlands. A few held out, backs to the broch wall, but Ridvar's men mobbed them and cut them down. Gerran turned back and knelt down next to Rhwn's body. Here, at least, was someone who'd been able to defend himself. As the battle fit left him, Gerran realized that he'd just killed a man whom he'd once considered an ally, if not a friend.

"I'm sorry," he said. "It wasn't even much of a fight, was it?" He wondered why he'd spoken aloud. Rhwn couldn't hear him. He stood up, sword still in his hand, and saw the man who'd rolled against the captain and made him stagger.

Warryc lay sprawled on the ground, killed by a stab in the back. Gerran knelt down beside his body and closed its eyes. One of his men, killed from behind.

"Gerro!" Neb ran over to him. "I'll help you carry him inside. That battle's over. The chirurgeons have taken over the great hall."

"That's of no use," Gerran said. "He's dead."

Neb let out his breath in a sharp puff. "May he find rest in the Otherlands," he said. "My heart aches over the losing of him. I'd hoped it was only a wound."

"So did I. Who gave it to him? Did anyone see?"

"One of Ridvar's men told me that it was Honelg himself."

"Where's Honelg's body? I want to spit on his corpse."

"I don't know."

Neither did anyone else, apparently, when Gerran set about searching the dun. None of the men he came across had seen Honelg, alive or dead, since the very start of the battle. The end result of havoc lay strewn over the ward. Gerran strode past wounded men, heard men weeping, stepped over dead men, kicked a litter of dropped or broken weapons out of his way as he walked. Eventually he met up with Prince Voran, who was searching for the lord as well with a squad of his own men.

"I want to give him a proper burial," Voran remarked, "but for his wife's sake, not his. No one's found his son either."

"His son's but seven summers old, Your Highness," Gerran said.

Voran winced. "Well, then, let's hope he's still alive. I begin to think his father must be."

"Indeed, Your Highness, since no one's found him. I want a word with his lordship, you see. He stabbed one of my men in the back."

"Perhaps we won't bother with the proper burial, then. I wonder where he's gone to earth?"

Gerran remembered the mysterious light he'd seen and Dallandra's talk of a shrine to Honelg's goddess. "I've got an idea about that, Your Highness," he said. "There's some sort of hidden chamber inside the dun walls. The gerthddyn will know where it is."

"Your Highness?" One of Voran's men spoke up. "I saw the gerthddyn helping carry the wounded. He's doubtless in the great hall."

Voran took the lead as they strode around the broch. They found Salamander just coming out. Some other man's blood soaked the front of his shirt.

"Gerro!" Salamander trotted over to him, then saw Prince Voran and started to kneel.

"Stay on your feet, man," Voran said. "This is no time to worry about courtesies."

"My humble thanks, Your Highness," Salamander said. "Gerro, Daumyr told me about Warryc. You must be hunting for Honelg."

"I am. How did you know?"

"The look on your face. Pure death and twice as cold."

"Oh. Do you know where the shrine is? I'd wager that he's in there."

"A good guess, but if you're right, getting him out again's not going to be an easy task. There's one narrow door, and it'll be shadowy inside."

"Just show me where it is. I'll get him out of it. The prince's men can handle the rest of the traitors, if there be any with him."

Salamander led them around the walls to a door made of rough wood planks. Gerran would have thought it the entrance to a storage shed if Salamander hadn't pointed to it and mouthed the words "in there."

Gerran strode up to the door and kicked it as hard as he could. With a groan it splintered down the middle. The pieces swung inside to a gloom lit by splinters of sunlight. At the far end, on what appeared to be a stone altar, a man lay sprawled on his back. *Honelg?* Gerran wondered. Someone else, however, knelt before it. When he stood and turned to face the door, Gerran recognized the lord. A pot helm dangled from his left hand.

"Honelg!" Gerran shouted. "I'm challenging you. If you think your lying whore of a goddess will protect you, you're wrong. Get out here!"

"I'll take your challenge, Falcon," Honelg called back, "if you'll promise me one thing on your word of honor."

"What it is?"

"That I won't be mobbed and killed before I can get clear of the door."

"Fair enough. You have my sworn word that you'll face me and me alone."

"Done, then!"

Gerran heard the men behind him begin moving back as Prince Voran gave orders to clear a combat ground. Honelg walked half the distance to the door. When he paused in a shaft of sunlight to toss his helm aside, Gerran could see that the lord was wearing only a linen shirt with his brigga.

"Ye gods!" Gerran said. "Where's your mail? If you've not got a hauberk at least, we'll lend you one."

Honelg laughed, and an oddly merry laugh at that. "I have Alshandra, and you have your armor," he said. "I declare this a fair fight."

"Well and good, then, but if you won't wear a helm, then I'll lay mine aside, too."

Behind him a babble rose, calling him daft, urging him to keep the helm on. Gerran took it off and held helm and shield both out in Salamander's general direction. The gerthddyn took them, then darted back out of the way.

"I warn you." Honelg sounded as calm as if he were discussing some tedious everyday detail. "You'll never gain this victory. My goddess will either see to it that you're slain, or else *she*'ll take me to my true home at last."

"Oh, will she now? Then let's not keep the lady waiting."

Honelg drew his sword with his right hand, then pulled his dagger from his belt with his left and walked to the door of the shrine. Gerran stepped back to let Honelg's eyes grow used to the sunlight.

"On the altar you'll find one of my servants," Honelg said. "He was going to surrender to your prince, so I slew him for *her* sake. Hang his corpse for the ravens, will you?"

"I'll see to it he's buried decently, more like." Gerran let his sword lie easy in his hand, point down, as if he were off his guard. "Get out here, you pisspoor excuse for a man!"

Honelg's face flushed red. With a howl of "Alshandra!" he flung up his sword and charged. Gerran stepped to one side and flicked his blade up, catching the lord high across the ribs. Blood spread through his shirt as Honelg turned, gasping, to face him, only to meet Gerran's blade on the back swing. Gerran cut him low, this time, splitting his belly like an overripe peach. The force of the blow spun the lord half-around.

Through the slice in Honelg's shirt guts bulged, blood-streaked gray membranes. Honelg dropped to his knees, and his sword slid from his hand as he clutched the pieces of his blood-soaked shirt to the wound. He threw his head back and gasped open-mouthed, in too much pain to even scream.

"The first was for your servant," Gerran said, "the second for Warryc. You're a mad dog, Honelg, not a man at all."

Gerran set one foot against Honelg's chest and shoved the dying lord so hard that Honelg buckled sideways, sprawling into the dirt with a twist that laid him on his back. Honelg moaned, and he seemed to be looking at the sky, his eyes flickering this way and that.

"Where are you?" Honelg whispered. "My lady! Too dark."

He caught his breath with one last ghastly rattle and died.

For a long moment no one moved or spoke. Prince Voran was the first to shudder; he cursed softly under his breath. As if at a signal the other men began to mutter among themselves, but not at the mere sight of death. Gerran turned to a white-faced Salamander and retrieved his helm and shield.

"Tell me somewhat, gerthddyn," Gerran said. "Was he calling for his lying whore of a demoness?"

"He was," Salamander said. "She's supposed to come meet her faithful when they die. I wish he'd seen the truth before he died, but then, if he'd seen the truth, he wouldn't have died."

"As if I give a pig's fart!" Gerran said. "The Lord of Hell's welcome to him."

Salamander looked inclined to argue. Rather than curse at the gerthddyn, Gerran turned away. Movement caught his gaze, and he glanced at the broch. Someone was standing on the roof, someone too short and slender to be a warrior from either side.

"Is that Honelg's son?" Gerran said, pointing with his sword.

"It looks like it, truly," Salamander said. "And it looks like others have seen the lad as well. Come on!" He took off running for the broch.

A little clot of Westfolk and Deverry men, Tieryn Cadryc and Gwerbret Ridvar among them, stood in the ward and craned their necks to look up. By the time that Gerran and Salamander joined them, the skinny little lad had gone over the side in a futile attempt to escape. He was clinging to the outer wall of the broch, a few feet down from the roof and a good long way above the ward.

"We've got him now," Ridvar said.

"Got him?" Prince Daralanteriel said. "It seems to me that he's a fair bit higher than we can reach."

"I meant, Your Highness, that one of the archers can strike the lad down easily enough."

"What?" Calonderiel stepped forward and set his hands on his hips. "Do I have this right? You want one of my men to kill a frightened child for you, and in cold blood? How old is he? Eight summers? Seven?"

"It's not his age that matters," Ridvar said. "He's Honelg's heir, the heir of a rebel against my rule. When he comes of age, he'll swear vengeance for this, and that makes him a threat. It's not like I want to kill him." Ridvar's voice carried little conviction on this last. "But I can't tolerate rebels and keep the respect of my men."

"Indeed?" Calonderiel paused to let his lip curl in contempt. "Well, if that matters so much to you, fetch him down yourself."

Ridvar's face flushed red, and he set his lips together hard. He turned his gaze to Daralanteriel and raised one eyebrow in a silent question.

"The banadar's men are his to command," Dar said, "not mine."

"Now here!" Cadryc shoved himself between Calonderiel and Ridvar. "Your Grace, that lad is my grandson."

Ridvar began to speak, then hesitated. Cadryc crossed his arms over his chest and stared the young gwerbret full in the face. For a long moment the impasse held.

"I can't have heard you a-right, Gwerbret Ridvar," Prince Voran came striding over. "Come now! If we can take the child alive, I can send him back to Dun Deverry as a hostage. He'll be no threat there."

"Not until he grows up, anyway," Ridvar said, "uh, Your Highness."

"I take it, Your Grace," Cadryc was speaking only to Ridvar, and his voice had grown tight as a strung bow, "that my word of honor's not enough for you. One of my men died in that fight, just by the by, and now you're insulting—"

"Naught of the sort!" Voran grabbed Cadryc's arm before he could finish speaking and start a second rebellion on the spot. "Think, man! Having bloodkin at court will be of great advantage to the Red Wolf."

Gerran had heard enough. He left them wrangling and ran into the broch. On tables in the middle of the great hall the chirurgeons were working frantically. Over by the honor hearth the dead were laid out, and the wounded or dying lay across from them on the commoners' side. The hall reeked of blood-soaked straw, vomit, and the excrement of the dying. At the foot of the staircase, Neb stood washing his red-stained hands in a bucket of water.

"Gerro!" Neb hailed him. "Has anyone found Honelg's son?"

"He's stuck partway down the outside of the broch," Gerran said, "and our ever so noble gwerbret wants one of the archers to kill the lad in cold blood. I thought I'd have a try at saving him."

"Oh, ye gods!" Dallandra turned from her work to join the talk. "Gerro, the archers aren't going to do it, are they?"

"Not while the banadar's there."

"Good. Please, do try to save the lad!"

"I will, my lady. If I can get onto the roof, maybe I can reach him."

"He's not going to trust you." Neb shook red-stained water from his hands, then wiped them on his shirt. "You're the man who killed his father."

"I—" Gerran paused in mid-sentence, struck by a thought as

painful as an arrow wound. *At least I didn't have to watch when the Horsekin killed my Da.*

"Let me try," Neb went on. "These stairs, do they go all the way up to the roof?"

"It looks that way." Gerran gladly turned away from his thoughts. "Here, I'll go ahead of you, just in case there's someone hiding up there, someone with a sword, I mean."

As he followed Gerran up to the top floor of the broch, Neb was hoping that any possible swordsmen were long gone, and his hope was realized. The trapdoor to the roof already stood open, with the ladder in readiness. As Neb climbed up and out, he heard the distant voices of the noble-born, loud and angry in two languages. Apparently the banadar was invoking Elvish gods as well as arguing with the gwerbret in Deverrian.

Above the clouds were thickening in the gray sky. He'd have to work fast, Neb realized. Once the stones were rain-slick, the boy could slip and fall to his death whether he wanted to die or not.

"There's some rope." Gerran was standing on the ladder with only his head and shoulders out of the trapdoor. "I figured there'd be a coil or two lying about up here, just in case the defenders had a chance to escape over the side. The lad probably didn't think to use it."

"Most likely," Neb said. "You'd best not be here when I get the lad to safety."

"True spoken. I'll go down and leave the broch."

Neb picked up the longest rope and walked across to the edge, some ten feet above Matto, who was clinging spread-eagled and trembling against the rough stones of his dead father's broch. Neb tied one end of the rope around a crenel and tested the strength of his knot with a good hard pull. It held, and he turned the other end into a noose.

"Matto!" Neb called out. "There's no use in dying. A royal prince is here, and he's offering you mercy."

The arguing far below suddenly stopped. Apparently the noble-born had heard him. What counted, however, was the lad's reaction, not theirs. When he leaned through the crenelation, Neb saw a dark-haired little boy looking back at him, his mouth half-open, his face streaked with tears.

"You're stuck, aren't you?" Neb said, and he smiled.

"Who are you?" Matto's young voice was steady, but just barely so. "You don't look like one of the prince's men."

"I'm a scribe who's been helping the chirurgeons. Look—I'm not armed."

Matto didn't answer, but neither did he throw himself down.

"Come to think of it," Neb went on. "I'm one of your kinfolk. I just got betrothed to your mother's cousin, Lady Branna."

For a moment Matto looked as if he'd speak, but he kept silent.

"I've come to get you up safely," Neb continued. "I'll swear it on my honor, I mean you no harm." With that he lowered the rope. "Slip that loop around you. Lift one arm at a time, then snug the rope up—under your shoulders, like. Then hang on for all you're worth."

"Matto!" Cadryc's shout drifted up to them. "Don't be a fool, lad. Do what he asks."

For a moment the rope and young Matyc's wyrd both dangled uselessly in front of the boy. Neb was just about to coax him further when Matyc reached out with one hand and caught the rope.

"Good lad!" Neb called down to him. "Now, over your head and under your arms, one at a time. Good—get a hold on a stone with that hand now and use the other to—right! Snug up that noose a bit. Splendid! Now, hang on, and up we go!"

Secured by the rope and Neb's weight above him, Matyc could push off and use his legs to clamber up the rough stonework. When the boy reached the top, Neb hauled him between the crenels over the edge to safety. Down below the watching Westfolk broke out in cheers. Matyc freed himself from the noose and flung the rope to the slates.

"Will I truly be safe?" he said.

"Of course," Neb said. "If anyone tries treachery, they'll have your grandfather to argue with."

Matto managed a brief smile. "No one argues with my gran and wins." He let the smile fade. "Is my mam safe?"

"She is, and your sister with her. They're at Cengarn with your grandmother."

"That's splendid." Matyc was staring down at the men in the ward so far below. "You have my thanks. I—" His voice broke suddenly, and he covered his face with both hands. He began sobbing so hard his shoulders heaved.

Neb found a reasonably clean rag in his brigga pocket and handed it to Matto. "Here," he said, "I know the world looks black and ugly now, but in a bit, it will brighten again."

"Never." His voice choked on phlegm and tears. "My da—"

"We all have to die sometime, Matto. Your father died fighting for the goddess he loved. He had an honorable death, far more honorable than most men."

"There's somewhat you don't know." Matto's tears continued to run as he stammered out the words. "Da wanted to kill me. He tried to kill me. He said it would be better than letting Vandar's spawn get hold of me. He drew his sword, and he tried to grab me, but I got away. I ran upstairs, and the battle started, and he didn't follow me. I didn't know where else to go, so I just hid."

"And then you came out onto the roof?"

"I did." Matto paused to choke back tears. "That's when I watched him die. I could see the fight."

"Did it sadden your heart when he died?"

Matto nodded. His tears had stopped at last; he wiped his face on the rag and blew his nose.

"I saw my father die, too," Neb went on. "He was very ill, you see, from a flux in his bowels."

"Oh. Then you do know what it feels like."

"I do."

"But he didn't try to kill you."

"He didn't. That's going to be a hard thing to think about. Tell your Gran and ask his help."

"I will, then. I'm so tired." Matto handed the rag back. "None of us could sleep last night, knowing what was coming."

"Well, tonight you'll sleep in your grandfather's tent and be safe. Come along now. We'll go down and speak with Prince Voran."

They found the prince still outside, talking with Tieryn Cadryc and Gwerbret Ridvar near the door to the broch. Neb hesitated, unwilling to disturb the noble-born, but Voran gave him a weary sort of smile and waved them over. Matyc ran to his grandfather, who laid a hand on his shoulder and pulled him close.

"Splendid!" the prince said. "It gladdens my heart that you could talk the lad down. You've done a good thing this day."

"My thanks, Your Highness," Neb said, "but it was Gerran who put me in mind to do it."

"Then he's done a good thing, too." Voran turned his attention to Matyc, who stood stiffly at Cadryc's side. Apparently he had no intention of kneeling to his captor.

"Very well, Lord Matyc," the prince said. "Do you forswear your father's rebellion against his rightful overlord?"

Matyc hesitated, but a glance at Cadryc seemed to make up the lad's mind. "I do, Your Highness," Matyc said.

"Do you give up all claim to this demesne, here before witnesses of your own rank and beyond?"

"I do. I'd rather be a silver dagger than keep it."

Neb glanced at Ridvar, standing nearby with his arms crossed tightly over his chest, and found the gwerbret's face utterly expressionless.

"I think we can make you some provision better than the long road," Voran said. "Very well, Lord Matyc. You're now my hostage with my personal vow of safety. The scribe here can write out a formal quitclaim to the demesne for you to sign or seal later. Does that suit you?"

"It does, Your Highness, but I don't think anyone's got the coin to ransom me out."

"We'll worry about all that later," Voran said. "For now, go with your grandfather. He'll stand surety for you."

"Coryn's here," Cadryc said, "and you've got a new cousin by marriage, young Clae, so you'll not lack for company. Here, do you realize it was your cousin's betrothed who just saved you?"

"I did, Gran." Matyc turned to Neb. "My thanks."

"You're quite welcome," Neb said.

Matyc bowed to Prince Voran; then with one last glance at the unspeaking Ridvar, he allowed Cadryc to lead him out of the dun.

With Matyc safe, there remained the question of Lord Honelg's mother, Lady Varigga. Salamander had expected her to take shelter in Alshandra's shrine. Since she hadn't, Salamander went into the broch to search for the lady. On an upper floor he found the chamber that must have been the women's hall, because it sported one faded tapestry and a threadbare Bardek carpet as well as a pair of embroidery frames with half-finished work still in them. Varigga, however, wasn't there.

With a cold feeling around his heart Salamander began to search the bed chambers. Sure enough, he found her at last in her little dowager's nest at the top of the tower. She was sprawled on the bed in a drying soak of blood, a red-streaked dagger lying beneath her flaccid right hand. She'd slit her wrists.

"Bearing the last witness." Salamander felt as if the words were choking him. "I think me we've discovered what that means." He walked over to the corpse and closed its eyes. "May you find peace, my lady. I beg you, forgive me for turning traitor to your hospitality."

Since none of the Westfolk had been wounded, Dallandra had been helping the chirurgeons with the Deverry men. She forced her mind to concentrate on the work, to see only the work, to stay stubbornly on the physical plane and never open up the Sight.

Yet despite her efforts, she was always aware of the dead. Their etheric doubles floated through the hall, or hovered over their bodies, or clung to those of their friends who still lived. They were desperate to be seen, to be recognized by the living in the vain hope that somehow or other, they would wake from a dream and find that they still lived themselves.

There was nothing she could do for them. She'd tried to help Deverry men before, after other battles, but none of the dead would believe what she told them or follow her up to the river of life and death and the meadows of pale white flowers along its shores. Eventually they would cross it whether they followed her or not, but they would have spared themselves much grief and panic if only they could have brought themselves to listen to a voice speaking from the center of a silver flame. At times she considered trying to build a second body of light, one in human form, but it would have taken her a great deal of effort and just possibly have made her first, preferred form unstable.

As well as Warryc, two of Ridvar's men were dead, and six others had suffered wounds or, in one case, a broken arm from slipping and falling on blood-soaked ground. The massive casualties came from Honelg's ranks. His sworn riders had all died as their vows demanded, but most of the servants and villagers had lived through the battle. Not all of the Westfolk archers had aimed to kill men who wore no armor and had barely a weapon to defend themselves. Dallandra knew how to cut an arrow out of a wound in a way that would minimize the damage rather than making it worse. She had an eager audience when she shared that knowledge.

The chirurgeons had finished doing what they could when Gwerbret Ridvar walked in. He found his own riders and spoke to each one, kneeling down from time to time to clasp their hands and thank them. When he saw the two dead riders, he raised his hands in the air and prayed over their bodies, just a few brief words, but it made the wounded smile in thanks to see their friends honored. Ridvar also came over to the chirurgeons to thank them personally for aiding his men.

"Tell me," the gwerbret said. "Do any of you recognize Raldd? He was a groom, and he's the traitor who rode ahead to warn this dun."

No one did—a groom was beneath the notice of learned men like chirurgeons and fighting men as well.

"One of the pages might," a chirurgeon said. "They were helping with the horses back at Dun Cengarn."

"Ask Clae," Dallandra said. "He's the one who spotted Raldd and gave us what warning we had."

"Indeed?" Ridvar said. "I never heard that. Well, I'll have to thank the lad. Who's his father?"

Dallandra considered the question—doubtless Ridvar was assuming that Clae was the usual sort of page, the son of a noble-born man. To tell the truth, that he was only a scribe's brother, would make Ridvar dismiss him. "He's a younger son, Your Grace, and his father's dead," she said. "Tieryn Cadryc took him in."

"Ah. I'll send someone to speak to Cadryc, then."

With a wave all round the young gwerbret strode out of the hall. Dallandra found a bucket of reasonably clean water and began washing the blood and bits of flesh off her hands and arms. She was almost done when Salamander came down the staircase to the great hall. He looked so ill that at first she feared he'd been wounded himself.

"No, no, fear not, O Princess of Powers Perilous," Salamander said in Elvish. "I just made another ghastly discovery. Lady Varigga killed herself upstairs. I don't know if she saw the combat twixt her son and Gerran. Did you know about that?"

"One of the chirurgeons told me."

In but a few moments they both heard more, when Neb and Clae came into the great hall together, shepherded by one of the gwerbret's riders. Clae clung to his brother's hand, and his face turned pale at the sight of the dead men, but otherwise he was surprisingly calm as he walked along, looking at each one.

"There he is." Clae pointed at the corpse of a sandy-haired lad who couldn't have been much older than Neb. An arrow had pierced his throat. "That's Raldd."

"Ah, horseshit!" the soldier said. "I'd been hoping we'd taken him alive. I wanted a word with the lad before the gwerbret hanged him."

"Can I leave now?" Clae said.

"Of course, lad," the soldier gave him a grim smile. "You've done well."

"Wait for me outside," Neb said. "We'll talk for a bit."

Clae walked slowly from the great hall, his head held high. *He's going to grow up into one of them,* Dallandra thought, and the thought brought her close to tears.

"I wanted to tell you somewhat quickly," Neb said. "Honelg tried to kill Matto before he took refuge in the shrine."

"He what?" Salamander said. "Oh, by the Black Sun herself!"

"It's ghastly, inn't?" Neb nodded in his direction. "He told the boy that death would be better than falling into the hands of Vandar's spawn."

"Oh." Salamander paused, and for a moment he looked aged as well as ill. "Apparently the pity I've been feeling for him is misplaced."

"I'd say it was." Neb turned to go, then glanced back. "I'd best go see how Clae fares. We can talk later."

Together, Salamander and Dallandra followed him outside to the cleaner air of the muddy ward. Here and there a few of Ridvar's men were picking up dropped weapons and tossing them onto a pile down near the gates. The Westfolk men were hunting for arrows that they could salvage, but they scorned the enemy's rough-made bows. Prince Voran's men were leading cows out of the stables, and servants staggered by with the sacks of grain and armloads of hay to feed this living booty. Later, she supposed, the servants would strip the dun of the rest of its livestock. The victors would eat well tonight.

"We should make sure that Arzosah and Rori get a couple of hogs," Salamander said. "Where are the dragons, by the by?"

"I don't know," Dallandra said. "I've not had a moment outside till now."

They left the dun and walked down the twisty maze of earthworks to the open ground below. The stink of a large encampment met them, but at least, Dallandra reflected, it didn't smell of fresh blood, unlike the great hall. Judging by the silver light behind the clouds, the sun hung past zenith but still well above the horizon.

"It's so odd," she said. "It was all over so quickly."

"Deverry battles tend to be like that," Salamander said. "I have this nasty feeling that Zakh Gral is going to be an entirely different affair."

"Me, too. Unfortunately."

"But let us leave opening that sack of troubles to another day."

"Yes. Tending the wounded is more than enough trouble for me for one afternoon."

"I meant to tell you," Salamander went on, "I heard that Ridvar is going to take the prisoners back to Cengarn and have them drawn and hanged as rebels."

"He what?" For a moment Dallandra couldn't speak. She took a deep breath. "Are you sure that's true?"

"I heard it from Ridvar's captain. The gwerbret wants to kill them publicly. He thinks that it will scare any of his townsfolk who believe in Alshandra into giving her up."

"May every god on this earth or above it blast Ridvar to the depths of his soul."

"Dalla!" Salamander caught her arm. "What—"

"I've been fighting to save the lives of those men, and now I see that I should have just let them die because it would have been kinder. And on top of that, that moon-calf lad of a gwerbret doesn't understand Alshandra's worshippers in the least."

"Here! You're the one who was just telling me that we had to be ruthless. What about those traitors in Cengarn?"

"I'll worry about them later. Where is he?"

"Who? The gwerbret—Dalla, you can't just go and—"

"Oh, can't I?" Dallandra pulled her arm free of his grasp.

With Salamander right behind, babbling words she didn't bother to comprehend, Dallandra strode through the camp. She found Ridvar standing in front of his tent with the two princes. A servant was just carrying away his mail and helm. Overhead hung the bright gold sun banner of Cengarn, matching the blazons on his shirt.

Dallandra marched up to Ridvar and grabbed him by the blazons with both hands. Distantly she heard men shouting that someone was laying hands on the gwerbret. Guards came running only to stop a few feet away when they saw that the interloper was a woman. One of them grabbed Salamander by the shirt collar and hauled him back. Dallandra ignored them.

"You!" she snarled. "I hear you're going to torture the prisoners to death."

Ridvar was too shocked to do more than gape at her. Prince Daralanteriel stepped forward, caught her hands, and pried them from the gwerbret's shirt.

"Dalla, you're exhausted," he said in Elvish, then switched to Deverrian. "My apologies, Your Grace. My healer—"

"Is not going to be put off so easily." Dallandra pulled her hands free. "Listen, you." She addressed this last to all three of them. "The chirurgeons and I have been slaving for hours to save the lives of men you're going to torture to death. I won't stand for it. I haven't studied healing for five hundred years to become an executioner."

"My dear woman," Ridvar recovered himself. "They're traitors to the—"

"Don't you condescend to me, you—" Dallandra stopped herself in the nick of time from calling him an ignorant child. "You don't see the obvious, do you? These cultists all want to die. They call it witnessing to their goddess. Why are you giving them exactly what they want? Seeing them go singing to their deaths is going to make converts, not deter them."

Once again Ridvar could only stare at her.

"You know," Prince Voran said, "she's quite right."

Prince Daralanteriel nodded his agreement. At these signs of

royal approval, the guards all moved away from Dallandra. Salamander's captor let him go with a murmured apology.

"I saw a grim truth today," Voran went on. "These Alshandra
worshippers are a different sort of man than we've ever seen before,
and my heart is sore troubled. Our people have always tended toward great passions and wild humors. Coupled with this set of peculiar beliefs—" He shook his head and shuddered. "Do we put out
a fire by throwing oil upon it?"

For a long moment Ridvar stood looking back and forth between
the two men of royal blood.

"Besides, Your Grace," Salamander stepped forward and knelt
smoothly in front of the gwerbret. "The prisoners are common-
born farmers. Where's the honor in killing them?"

Ridvar let out his breath in a sharp puff. "I'll take all this under
advisement," the gwerbret said, "but truly, I do see the truth in
what you're all saying."

Daralanteriel turned to Dallandra and spoke softly in Elvish.
"Go away and leave him to us."

It was a reasonable request, she supposed. Salamander got up
and slipped his arm companionably through hers.

"My humble thanks, Your Grace," Salamander said. Then he led
her firmly away.

This time Dallandra let him. Her fury had spent itself, leaving
her tired and a little dizzy. As they walked through the camps of the
Deverry men, they heard more gossip, that the gwerbret would also
leave men behind on fort guard, in case any Horsekin appeared to
visit their now-dead ally.

"And then there's that priestess, too," said one soldier. "If she
comes through here, she's in for a surprise. We're to arrest her and
bring her to Cengarn."

Salamander's face went dead-white, and he stopped walking, but
only briefly. With a catch of breath he nodded the man's way and
walked on faster. *Does he realize he's fallen in love with her?* Dallandra thought.

"What's wrong?" Dallandra waited to speak till they'd gone well past their informant.

"Naught, naught." Salamander smiled brightly. "It's just that I doubt if Rocca's a threat to the gwerbretrhyn."

"Of course she isn't. But she might make a good hostage to bargain with."

Again he went pale, and she noticed him shoving his hands into his brigga pockets as if to hide their trembling. *No, he doesn't realize it,* she thought. All at once she felt impossibly weary. "Ebañy, I've got to lie down. I've got to sleep. I hate battles so much, seeing men die, feeling their souls all around me, so bewildered."

She staggered, and for a moment lost her balance so badly that she nearly fell. The mass of tents below them on the hill seemed to rise up like a wave of filthy water. Salamander caught her arm and steadied her.

"Let's get you to your tent," he said. "You need to sleep."

"But I want to know about the dragons—"

"I'll scry for them, once you're resting."

In vision Salamander found the dragons among rocky hills and dark pines, a common type of terrain a good many miles to the north. Arzosah crouched on an outcrop of gray boulders, her wings tightly furled, her tail lashing in rage. Rori would settle near her, then suddenly leap into the air and fly in a wide circle, only to return and perch among the rocks for a brief while before flying again. Although Salamander could see that she was speaking, he couldn't hear her voice. He wondered if she were trying to persuade him to consult Dallandra about his wound. Whatever her subject was, Salamander could assume that Rori was refusing to listen.

Salamander broke the vision and turned to tell Dallandra what he'd seen, but she was already asleep, curled up in a nest of rumpled blankets. For a moment he stayed in the shelter of her tent and thought about Rocca. Would she come back only to blunder into a trap? There was no way he could warn her without betraying his own people—he was painfully aware of that. He opened his Sight again, though this time he thought of Rocca. He saw her standing outside the stone shrine, talking with two Horsekin men. All three were laughing, perhaps at a jest. Again, he could hear nothing. He watched her until she went inside the shrine, then looked around the fort.

The gates stood wide open, and two guards were sitting in the dirt between them, playing dice. A quick thought of Sidro brought her image to him. She was kneeling in the kitchen garden, weeding a row of cabbages with one of the Horsekin priestesses. In the sunlight her hair gleamed, as blue-black and shiny as a raven's feathers. She looked too untroubled to be someone who knew about the army of destruction assembling off to the east. He broke the vision. Apparently no one at Zakh Gral had the slightest idea that an attack was coming. Whoever the raven mazrak was, he certainly hadn't gone to the Horsekin with a warning.

Salamander got up without waking Dallandra and left to find Calonderiel. The banadar was standing in front of the prince's tent with his archers all around him to watch Daralanteriel divide up the Westfolk's share of the booty—scavenged arrows, blankets, live chickens, and the shoddy like—into equal little heaps, one for each man who'd fought that day.

"Dalla's in your tent," Salamander told Calonderiel. "She's exhausted."

"No doubt," Calonderiel said, "squandering her energies on the Roundears as she was. I'd better go make sure she's all right."

"I'd recommend it, truly." Salamander watched him hurry off, then turned back to consider the prizes of war. "You know, Dar, you might leave the dun's actual furnishings behind, like those pewter bowls, for instance. The gwerbret's going to attaint this dun and give it to some other lord."

"Too bad," Dar said cheerfully. "Ridvar gets plenty of coin and kind in taxes. He can just part with some of it. Let him furnish the dun all over again."

"I take it your heart is not warm with affection for the gwerbret."

Daralanteriel snorted loudly and went on sorting.

It was not long before everyone learned just whom the gwerbret would choose for the dun's new lord. Salamander changed his bloodstained shirt for one that was merely dirty, then wandered uphill to the Red Wolf camp. Servants had set up an iron spit over the central fire, braced by two green branches cut to their clefts. A young hog, his wyrd come upon him, was already roasting. The smell of food cooking made Salamander's stomach growl. For a moment he felt thoroughly disgusted with himself, that he'd be hungry after the things he'd just seen.

"Looking for Neb, are you, sir?" a servant said to him.

"I am, truly, and the captain as well."

"They're both down by the tieryn's tent. That big gray one over there."

"Have they buried Warryc yet?"

"They have, sir, but they gave him a grave of his own. I'm glad of it, because he was a decent man for a rider."

"I didn't care to think of him being dumped into a ditch with the rebels, truly."

"Did you hear the news about Raldd?" The servant glanced around, and then dropped his voice to a murmur. "They're going to draw him like a chicken and hang his corpse, trailing guts and all, out by the main gates for the ravens."

"Indeed? Well, he's dead and beyond caring."

Salamander walked on and found Neb sitting with Gerran on the ground in front of Tieryn Cadryc's tent. Gerran greeted him with a weary smile and a briefly raised hand. Salamander hunkered down to join them.

"His grace is inside with his grandson and the pages," Neb said. "Matyc's telling everyone about how his father tried to kill him."

"Again?" Gerran said.

"He's going to need to tell it over and over, and probably for a good long while."

"You're doubtless right, Neb," Salamander said. "How's your young brother taking all of this? The dead men and suchlike, I mean. I was impressed with the way he identified Raldd. I'll admit to being surprised when he didn't even weep."

"I was, too." Neb paused for a wry smile. "But don't forget, we lived through a plague back in Trev Hael. Death isn't a stranger to me and mine, alas."

"I had forgotten. My apologies."

"Well, a lot's happened since Clae and I came staggering out of the forest, hasn't it?" Neb shook his head in amazement. "It's hard to believe sometimes, when I think of it all."

"So it is," Salamander said. "This summer's been a true turning point in your life."

"In all our lives," Gerran said. "That fight this morning, it made me realize somewhat about the Westfolk and your longbows. Battle's never going to be the same. Now you can kill a man from a distance easier than you can kill him face-to-face." He turned his head and spat into the dirt. "Ye gods!"

"What?" Neb said. "I don't understand why it troubles your heart so much."

"Well, by the black hairy arse of the Lord of Hell! You stand on a wall, you loose an arrow, and your enemy dies before he has the least chance to fight back. Where's the glory in that?" Gerran paused to catch his breath. "Haven't men always praised me for my skill with a blade? Well, does it matter anymore how good a swordsman I am? Or anyone else either. Not if the enemy has archers."

"That's a good point, truly. I'd not thought—" Salamander broke off abruptly. "Look, here comes Prince Voran! On your knees, lads."

They all scrambled to kneel properly as, not merely the prince but Gwerbret Ridvar as well strode up, accompanied by their captains. Salamander was assuming that they wanted to speak with Tieryn Cadryc.

"There you are, Gerran," Prince Voran said instead. "I want to commend you on your part in the fighting today."

"Me, Your Highness?" Gerran blushed scarlet. "Truly, I was only doing my duty to my sworn lord."

At that Cadryc himself stuck his head out the tent flap, saw who his visitors were, and came out to bow to them.

"It's a good thing you're here, tieryn," Prince Voran said. "What I have to say to your captain concerns you, too."

"It does?" Cadryc said. "What's this, Gerro? Did they catch you looting Honelg's vast stores of gold and silver?"

Everyone laughed but Ridvar, who was glaring at nothing in particular off in the middle distance, his arms crossed tightly over his chest. Salamander noticed Cadryc glancing at the gwerbret, then looking away with a false smile stuck on his face like a smear of dirt. *Thank the gods the prince is here!* Salamander thought, *or we'd have a new war on our hands.*

"I found a couple of coppers on the ground, Your Highness," Gerran said, grinning. "I'll gladly hand them over if you'd like."

"Oh, I think me you can keep them," Voran said. "Though you deserve a better reward than that. You know, it would gladden my heart to have the letters patent written out right here to give you a demesne down in Deverry, but of course—" He paused to give Ridvar a significant look, "—of course, the gwerbret needs men like you on the border."

Ridvar roused himself from his sulk. He let his arms relax to his sides, glanced with a nod at the prince, then turned to Gerran. When he spoke, his voice held steady, though sounding gracious was apparently beyond him.

"Gerran, or should I say Lord Gerran?" he said. "I'd be honored if you'd take over Honelg's lands and dun. I think me you're one of the few men in the kingdom who can hold them loyal to me."

"Your Grace." Gerran swallowed heavily before he went on. "I'm honored beyond deserving."

"Not truly. Just as you deserve, I'd say. Get up, Lord Gerran."

Gerran never moved, merely stared open-mouthed.

"Excellent!" Voran rubbed his hands together like a merchant. "I'll send a messenger down to Dun Deverry with instructions for the College of Heralds. They'll draw up the necessary documents with the proper seals and suchlike. Um, you can get up now, Gerran."

"My thanks, Your Highness, for your excellent suggestion." Gwerbret Ridvar managed a smile at last. "I wager I can guess what name Gerran's going to choose for his new clan."

Still kneeling, Gerran stared at him with stunned eyes. Cadryc stepped forward to break the moment.

"We all can, eh?" Cadryc grabbed Gerran's hand to yank him up. "The Falcon, isn't it, lad?"

"It is." Gerran staggered to his feet, but he continued to look as dazed as if the gwerbret had struck him on the side of the head rather than ennobled him. "Unless there's already a clan by that name down in Deverry."

"You know, I think there was once," Prince Voran said, "and it came to some sort of bad end. The heralds will know, of course. But there's naught wrong with using the Red Falcon, for instance, or what about the Gold Falcon? The latter has a better ring to it."

"So it does," Gerran was whispering like a man who's just woken up from a sound sleep. "I—I—ye gods!"

"But curse it all!" Cadryc mugged a long face. "This means I'll have to get myself a new captain, doesn't it? Ah, well, there's no spring rain without mud, eh?"

This time even Ridvar joined in the general round of laughter. Salamander, however, found himself thinking of Lady Adranna. He was the only man there, he supposed, who was wondering how she'd take the news that she'd lost not only her husband, but her home.

Men on horseback instead of a dragon brought a report of the battle to Cengarn. When everyone had assembled in the great hall, Lord Oth told Drwmigga, and thus the other women as well, that apparently the dragons had gone off on some business of their own.

"They *are* beasts, after all," Oth said. "I'd imagine they've gone back to the wild. They may have a nest to tend or suchlike."

Perhaps, Branna thought, *but they're not as beastlike as all that.*

Besides the official reports, there were letters for Adranna and Branna, but while Branna pulled the seal off her note from Neb and read it eagerly, Adranna let hers lie unread in her lap and watched Oth, who was mumbling a word here and there as he scanned through a long missive from the gwerbret. Finally, he looked up with a smile.

"Good news, my lady!" he said to Adranna. "Your son is alive and well and riding home with your father."

Adranna allowed herself a quick smile and a flash of joy in her eyes. "And my husband?" she said calmly.

Oth arranged a solemn expression. "I'm afraid he's dead."

"And the dun?"

"Attainted and given to a new lord."

"Who is?"

"By the gods!" Oth was looking at the missive again. "Prince Voran's ennobled Gerran and made him the head of a new clan. It'll be the Gold Falcon!"

"Better him than some other man." Adranna shoved back her chair and stood up. "If you'll excuse me, my ladies?"

"Of course," Drwmigga said with a wave of her hand. "But wouldn't you—"

Adranna was already gone, striding across the hall toward the staircase.

"She can't have loved that horrid man." Galla stood, curtsied to Drwmigga, then ran after her daughter.

Branna dispensed with the curtsy and merely ran. She caught up with Galla and Adranna on the landing. The three of them went up to Adranna's chamber, where Midda was sitting with little Trenni, amusing the child with a game of Carnoic. When her mother came into the room, Trenni looked up from the board.

"Trenni, my love," Adranna said, "I've got the best news in the world. Matto's alive and coming home with Gran."

"That gladdens my heart," Trenni said, but she looked oddly solemn. "Is Da dead?"

"He is," Adranna said.

"Good." Trenni turned away and began to study the board with determined concentration.

Adranna had gone pale, and for a moment she swayed where she stood. Branna caught her cousin's elbow and steadied her. "Let's go to your mother's chamber," she murmured. A nod was the only answer Adranna had the strength to give.

Galla led the way to her chamber. Once inside, Branna barred the door. Adranna sank into a chair and covered her face with both hands. Her shoulders shook, and Branna assumed she was weeping, but in a moment she realized that Adranna was laughing and struggling to stop herself. Galla hovered near her but said nothing. Finally Adranna gave up the futile effort and looked up. Her face had gone dead-pale, and she laughed and laughed in a series of little choking chirps while her hands shook like those of an old woman with the palsy.

"Good, she said." Adranna forced out the words between coughs of laughter. "His own daughter. Good, she said."

On the little table stood a half-empty flask of Bardek wine. Branna grabbed the pottery cup from the washbasin and filled it with wine, then forced it between her cousin's shaking hands. Galla stood behind her daughter and began to rub her shoulders in a slow, soothing rhythm. Adranna managed to drink a few sips, and slowly her laughter stopped. She took one deep breath, then finished the wine in a long gulp.

"I don't suppose I ever truly loved him," Adranna said, "but I thought he was a better man than the others I might marry. Once we found our goddess, I felt I'd made the right choice for a certainty, and at times I thought I did love him. But if I ever did, I stopped when he wouldn't let Matto leave the dun with me and Trenni."

"In Neb's letter," Branna said, "it says that Honelg tried to kill Matto. He said it would be better than his being taken captive."

"What?" Galla went white around the mouth.

"I'm not surprised." Adranna held out the wine cup. "It gladdens my heart to know that he's dead and Matto alive."

Branna refilled the cup for her, then perched on the side of the bed. With a deep sigh of her own, Galla sat down in the other chair. Branna realized that they were both watching Adranna as if she were an invalid who might at any moment go into convulsions or manifest some other alarming symptom.

"What happened to that other letter?" Galla said. "The one Oth gave you."

"Here." Adranna pulled the silver tube from her kirtle and tossed it to Branna. "You can read it, if you would. I don't even recognize the seal."

"It's a rose," Branna said. "I'll wager it's from Prince Dar or Dallandra."

It was indeed from the Westfolk prince by the hand of his own scribe, whose letters were shaky, Branna noticed, not half as nice as her Neb's. The note, however, was the very soul of courtliness, expressing sympathy for the lady in her bereavement. He went on to say that he'd "taken charge of some jewelry which was found in the women's hall, the embroideries therein as well, and some clothing and a doll that seems to belong to your daughter. I shall bring it all with us to hand over to you in Dun Cengarn."

"What a decent man!" Adranna said, and for a moment a few tears ran. She irritably wiped them away on the back of her hand.

"He is that," Branna said. "It gladdens my heart that you'll get your jewelry back."

"Such as it is." Adranna smiled briefly. "But it has meaning for me."

Branna stopped herself from asking the question that nearly forced itself out of her mouth, *is it a symbol of your goddess?* So far they'd managed to avoid the subject of Alshandra, and Branna decided that they'd best continue to do so until Adranna had recovered further. She busied herself with rolling up the letter and slipping it back into its silver tube.

"Do you want to sleep, dearest?" Galla said.

"I do," Adranna said. "But, Mama, can I sleep here in your chamber?" Her voice sounded like a child's, high and weak.

"Of course you may! And I'll sit here with you, too."

Branna laid the message tube onto the table, then left them alone.

It was much later when Lady Galla came to Branna's chamber with the news that Adranna had woken from her nap and seemed more her old self again. She'd gone to her own chamber, where she and Trenni were having a long talk.

"That's the best thing for the child," Galla said. "There's little that you or I can do. Her comfort has to come from her mother."

"It seems to me, Aunt Galla," Branna said, "that Trenni doesn't truly need comforting."

"Not about her father, certainly. What a sensible child she is! But they did lose everything else they had, except, of course, for what dear Prince Daralanteriel is bringing them. How kind of him!"

"In his note Neb said that he'd snagged more of the booty, too. He's got a plate of colored glass and a silver cup he's bringing for Adranna."

"Excellent! If the plate is the one I think it is, that was a gift upon their wedding from the old gwerbret, Ridvar's father." Galla sighed, then suddenly smiled. "But I must say, the news about our Gerran warmed my heart!"

"All your scheming's finally borne fruit, has it?"

Galla laughed. "How perceptive you are, dear," she said. "So. There'll be a new clan, the Gold Falcon. Or wait, not a new one— there must have been another Falcon clan at one time, if Gerran needs to distinguish his with the 'gold' in the name."

"There was," Branna said. "My father's bard sang a ballad about them now and then. It's about a brother and sister who were far too fond of each other, if you take my meaning."

"There's rather a lot of ballads about that. In the old days duns were so far apart. I don't suppose you could find a lot of men of your own rank to fall in love with."

"Most likely not," Branna went on. "According to the ballad, this particular pair were named Brangwen and Gerraent. How odd! It almost sounds like me and Gerran, and here I never noticed that before! But anyway she was supposed to marry a prince of the realm. Her brother dishonored her first, so she drowned herself."

"What happened to the brother?"

"The prince killed him in single combat, and so the clan died for want of more heirs." All at once Branna felt oddly puzzled. "That's not right. I mean, I must be remembering some other song. I thought that Gerraent killed his friend over the sister, and then his friend's brother killed him. Or suchlike. Blast! These old songs all start sounding alike when you're trying to remember them."

"So many of them share the same tune, is why. Well, either way, let's hope that the new Falcon clan has a better wyrd than the old one did."

"Oh, I'm sure it will. That ghastly tale happened long long ago, after all. I'm just so pleased for our Gerran." Branna paused to give her aunt a grin. "Now we need to get him the right wife, and I think that she just might be your new serving woman."

"You know, how odd!" Galla returned the smile. "I was just thinking the same thing."

The army rode back to Dun Cengarn around noon on yet another rainy day. The summer storms so common in the northlands had returned with a vengeance. Despite the weather, Branna wanted to go down to the dun gates to welcome Neb home, but Aunt Galla bade her a very firm nay.

"I shan't have you hanging around the ward to wait for the men like a camp follower," Galla said.

"Well, truly," Branna said. "I suppose it wouldn't look very courtly of me."

All of the dun's women, from Drwmigga down to the lowest scullery lass, went to the great hall to wait. Lord Oth joined Drwmigga to consult with her about a victory feast. The wedding had quite literally eaten up an alarming share of the dun's stored provisions.

"One of the messages mentioned that they're bringing a couple of hogs with them," Oth said, "and some cows, so we'll have meat. Drink is another thing entirely. There's ale, and some Bardek wine, but not a drop of mead left in the dun."

"Then it will have to be meat and ale," Drwmigga said, "and what bread the cooks can bake at this late hour. I do wish my lord had sent off the messengers earlier."

"So do I," Oth said with a sigh. "Well, I'll go consult with the head cook right now."

It was some while before the women heard the army returning in a burst of shouting and the sound of a great many horses clattering into the ward. Drwmigga rose and beckoned to the others to follow her as she hurried out of the great hall to welcome home her lord and his royal guests. Branna noticed Adranna lingering behind, then turning and heading for the stairs.

"Let her go," Galla said. "There's no joy in this for her."

"There's not," Branna said. "And I'd just as soon she didn't have to see mine."

Branna had something of a wait, however, before she could greet Neb. The army filled the ward in waves—the royalty and their escorts first, then the noble-born, rode in, dismounted, turned their mounts over to the pages and servants, greeted their womenfolk and the yapping, milling dogs before the commoners could even gain the ward. At last she saw Neb, leading his horse in through the gates behind a slow-moving wagon. She waved madly; he didn't see her; her patience broke. She dodged through the horses, dogs, and men and ran to him. With a shout of wordless joy he dropped his horse's reins and flung his arms around her, drawing her so close she could barely breathe.

"It gladdens my heart to see you," Neb said, then kissed her.

They left Neb's horse to Clae and arm in arm strolled into the great hall. The gwerbret, his lady, and the two princes were sitting at the table of honor, while Cadryc and Galla had settled at their usual table with Solla and Salamander. There was no sign of any of the Westfolk but Prince Daralanteriel.

"Where's Dalla?" Branna said.

"The Westfolk are setting up camp down in the meadow," Neb said.

"What about Gerro? I want to congratulate him."

"I don't know." Neb paused, glancing around the great hall. "I saw him out in the ward when I rode in."

"Well, let's go join the others. He'll turn up sooner or later. Neb, my darling, I can't tell you how glad I am to have you back."

Branna wasn't the only woman wondering where Gerran might be. Once they'd greeted everyone at the table and sat down together toward the end, Branna noticed Solla looking around the great hall. Every time someone came down the stairs or entered the doorway, she would sit up a little straighter and watch till she could recognize them. Finally, when the serving lasses were already pouring what ale there was, Gerran did appear in the company of Lord Oth. Solla smiled and seemed poised to stand up to greet him, but Oth and Gerran headed up the stairs without ever glancing her way. She sat back in her chair with a sigh.

"I'll have to have a chat with our Gerran," Branna murmured to Neb. "He needs a wife now that he's a lord."

"Every man needs a wife," Neb said, smiling at her. "I learned that lesson well when I was off without you."

Branna caught his hand and squeezed it. "We could slip away in a bit," she said. "In all this confusion, no one will notice."

"True-spoken, so why wait? Let's go up to our chamber right now."

With the wedding guests and their escorts long gone, there was room in the barracks for the Red Wolf warband. Gerran had assumed that he would sleep there as well, but his sudden elevation in rank meant that Lord Oth gave him a chamber in the broch complex itself, one of the small chambers lacking a hearth and located up a great many stairs that were the lot of unmarried noble-born males, but a chamber none the less. Gerran dropped his saddlebags on the floor and his bedroll on the swaybacked mattress, then stood looking out of his narrow window at a view of the stables while he wondered what to do next. He was afraid to go down to the great hall, he realized, and sit with the noble-born, but he supposed it would be a breach of courtesy if he went and joined the Red Wolf warband at their tables.

Eventually, Clae solved the problem by appearing with a washbasin and a pitcher of water. Since the room lacked both table and storage chest, he set them on the stone sill of the unglazed window.

"Lord Oth sent me up with these," Clae said.

"Good," Gerran said. "I need to wash the dust off before I go back to the great hall."

While Gerran cleaned up, the lad set about untying the bedroll and spreading the blankets over the mattress. Gerran could remember doing the same thing for various lords when he'd been a page in this same dun. It occurred to him that as a noble lord, he was supposed to be supporting servants as well as a warband, not that he had the wherewithal to feed either.

"Here, Clae," he said, "do you want to be my page from now on?"

"I do. I'd be ever so honored, my lord. I was going to ask you, but Neb told me it would be discourteous."

"I suppose it would have been, not that I'd have cared. I'm not going to make much of a lord. You do realize, don't you, that it means leaving your brother behind."

"Neb told me that, too. I don't care. Well, I sort of care, but not enough to refuse your service."

"Consider it done, then."

"My thanks, my lord. And I've got a message for you. Calonderiel invited you to come down to his tent. He told me to tell anyone who asked that he wants to establish friendly relations with the Gold Falcon clan, but mostly he thought you'd like to have some mead, and he's got some."

"Splendid! Let's go. Maybe I can just sit with them at dinner tonight and figure out what I'm supposed to do later."

Although Branna and Neb would have liked to have stayed alone in their chamber forever, sheer hunger drove them out and down to the great hall. If anyone had missed them during the afternoon, no one mentioned it, and they returned to their places at Cadryc's table without so much as a smirk to greet them. Adranna had come down from the women's hall, bringing Trenni with her, to join Solla and Galla. Both children sat as close to their mother as they could get on the narrow bench. The tieryn was telling his assembled womenfolk how the prince had maneuvered Ridvar into offering Gerran the demesne.

"I've never seen our Falcon so surprised," Cadryc was saying. All at once he seemed to realize that some at the table would find the story painful. "Addi, my dear, I think me I'll finish the tale some other time."

"My thanks, Da." Adranna gave him a weary smile. "I'm not yet ready to hear—" She paused for a long moment. "To hear all of it."

"I thought not." Cadryc had a swallow of ale from his tankard and made a sour face. "Ye gods, this has been watered right down. I suppose the wedding drank the dun dry, eh? But as I was saying, those dragons were quite a marvel. Did I tell you yet about the priest of Bel's cows?"

Aunt Galla and Solla exchanged a glance, then murmured a cheerful, "You didn't and please do." *Anything to keep him from talking about Honelg and the attainder!* Branna thought, but once she heard the story, she did have to admit that it was a good one. She could imagine Arzosah's smug satisfaction at getting a good meal out of a particularly stingy priest. She joined in the general laughter, but Neb leaned close to whisper to her.

"There's a bit more to this tale than his grace knows," Neb said. "And it's not funny in the least. I'll tell you once we're alone."

"I wish you wouldn't tease like that." Branna dropped her voice as well. "Especially not here."

Lady Galla cleared her throat. She was looking at Neb with one eyebrow raised.

"My apologies," Neb said. "I shouldn't have been whispering. Just lover's drivel."

Everyone laughed, even Adranna, and the moment passed.

"I was just wondering about the other dragon," Branna said brightly. "Did he get any of the cows?"

"He might have," Cadryc said, "but he didn't stay around long enough for us to so much as thank him. They're strange beasts, dragons, and I think me that the silver one's the strangest of them all."

Branna could well believe it. Ever since she'd seen the silver wyrm fly over Cengarn, an odd feeling rose from deep in her mind every time she thought of the dragons, a nagging sort of irritation, such as a person feels when she forgets the name of someone she should know perfectly well. She'd been hoping that she'd have one of her memory-dreams to explain it, but so far at least, nothing had come to her. Now that Dallandra had returned, Branna was hoping that the dweomermaster would tell her more.

After dinner, Branna found Dallandra standing near the dragon hearth and waiting for a chance to speak with Lord Oth. They sat down together on a bench in a reasonably quiet spot near the door. Branna tried to tell her how the sight of the silver dragon had affected her, but she found herself stumbling over her words. It seemed to her that she was trying to say two things at once, or that two selves were trying to speak at once—*Jill*, she thought with a cold shudder. *That's who the other voice belongs to.*

"Have you dreamed about this?" Dallandra asked at length.

"I've not," Branna said, "In fact, I've not had any of those memory-dreams for many a night now. I hadn't realized just how much I've come to depend on them."

"The time's come for you to begin to remember your past lives consciously. That's why they've disappeared. Curse this wretched war! I shan't be able to start your training until it's over, one way or the other."

"You're not going to go west with the army, are you?"

"I am. The Westfolk need a healer along who understands them. We have our differences from Deverry men."

"I suppose you would, truly. But about the silver wyrm—"

For the first time since she'd met Dallandra, Branna felt the dweomermaster's mind shy away from a question. "Is somewhat wrong with my asking?" she said.

"Not wrong at all, merely difficult." But Dallandra hesitated for a long moment. "It's a very complicated thing."

"Did Jill know this dragon or suchlike?"

"She knew him before he was a dragon. Surely Salamander's told you that Rori started life as his brother."

"He did, but I'm not sure I believed him."

"It's quite true. Jill died before his transformation."

"Was he a mazrak, then? Did he get, well, stuck I suppose I mean?"

Dallandra laughed, but it was a nervous little bark, not true mirth. "He wasn't a mazrak. He was a silver dagger, just as Salamander told you. Well, I really don't think I can explain it to you in a way that will make sense. You really need to know more about the dweomer before I can make it clear."

Branna had never felt more bewildered. So—she'd known the dragon in her last life, but not in dragon form, and apparently he was something very strange indeed, a man who had become another creature without working dweomer to do so. The image that presented itself to her mind was of a butterfly emerging from a cocoon, the end result of some natural process.

"Very well," Branna said. "You know best."

"I just wish we had more time. We're leaving at dawn on the morrow."

"We'll be leaving for home as soon as we can, too."

"I heard that they'll be mustering the full army at your dun."

"Well, near it, I should say. We'd never fit everyone into our

ward." Branna felt suddenly uneasy. "If we get home safely, anyway. Should I stay on guard for mazrakir?"

"Did you see that raven while we were gone?"

"I didn't, and I'm glad of it, too."

"No doubt." Dallandra smiled at her. "Still, I'll remind Salamander to keep a watch for the wretched thing. I've been meaning
to tell you. He and Arzosah will be traveling with you."

"Now that's a great relief. No one's going to cause us trouble
with a dragon on guard."

"Indeed, which is why I asked her to go with you. Don't
worry about having to feed her. She prefers to hunt fresh game
for herself."

"That's good! Does she know more about Rori?"

"She does, but you'd best not ask her. Besides, she doubtless
won't tell you even if you do. It's a very sore subject with her. I
don't mean to put you off either." Dallandra looked away. "If it
weren't for this wretched war, I'd have time to explain things
properly."

And yet her words left Branna with the feeling that putting her
off was exactly what Dallandra had wanted to do.

allandra finally got her audience with Lord Oth only to find
that the princes Daralanteriel and Voran had done her work
for her. Oth listened to her plea for mercy upon those accused of
Alshandra worship, then interrupted with a smile.

"Indeed," Oth said, "I've had much time to think the matter
over, and I've talked with the two princes as well. I agree with all
of you, Lady Dallandra. I shall counsel his grace toward mercy, I
assure you. He does understand the reasons why that course would
be best."

"That gladdens my heart, Councillor," Dallandra said. "But
what exactly will he do to them?"

"I can promise nothing. The decision will have to be his grace's, but they owe a debt to the true gods that they cannot repay in coin, and so the laws do allow for them to be declared bondfolk and branded."

Dallandra winced.

"It's better than being drawn and hanged, I assure you," Oth said hastily. "I once saw a murderer punished that way, and truly, it's not a sight I long to see again."

"Well, true-spoken, I'm sure."

"Besides, Lord Gerran will need men to tend his new lands." Oth laid a finger alongside his nose and looked positively sly. "Most of the prisoners come from that village, not that I shall remind his grace of that. Debt-bound and branded they may be, but they'll return to their families."

"My lord, I'm sure the true gods will shower favor and fortune upon you for this! Someone mentioned that there was a child taken prisoner here in Cengarn. Surely he won't be subjected to a hot iron?"

"A kitchen lad, and truly, he's not very old. You know, some while ago Lady Branna begged me to release him. I think I may ask her if the Red Wolf will take him with them when they leave."

"That would be so splendid of you." Dallandra favored him with her best smile. "I thank you from the bottom of my heart." For good measure, she allowed Oth to kiss her hand as she was leaving.

As Dallandra walked across the ward toward the gates, she saw Gerran, a candle lantern in his hand, heading for the gwerbret's squat stone gaol. She hailed him, and he strolled over to greet her.

"Lord Oth spoke to me," Gerran said. "I'm on my way to get that kitchen lad out of gaol."

"That gladdens my heart," Dallandra said. "Oth kept his word, then."

"He generally does."

"Good. Do you know where Salamander is?"

"He went down to your encampment some while ago to fetch his horse and gear."

"I'll see him there, then. May you have a good journey home."

"My thanks, and the same to you, though we'll see you again at the muster."

Down in the meadow below Cengarn, the Westfolk had set up the bare bones of a camp. Dallandra's was the only tent they'd bothered to raise. Since the night was clear and warm, the men, even the prince, would sleep outside. Everyone wanted to pack up and leave as fast as possible on the morrow morning.

Dallandra found Salamander sitting at the campfire with Calonderiel and some of the archers. When he saw her, he got up and quirked an eyebrow.

"Yes," Dallandra said, "I do need to talk with you. Let's go down to the river."

The river was running low now that the summer was well advanced. The ford where Jill had died lay shallow, marked out with white stones that seemed to shimmer in the faint light of a quarter moon.

"Do you know where Rori and Arzosah are?" Dallandra said.

"More or less," Salamander said. "Arzosah's on her way here. Rori seems to be somewhere off to the west."

"I take it he's not going to come and let me look at that wound."

"Not soon, apparently. Arzosah will know more. I'll contact you through the fire when I know." Salamander stooped down and picked up a flat stone from the ground. He straightened again and tossed it with a snap of his wrist onto the surface of the ford. It only skipped twice before it sank into the water. "Not a good omen."

"It's a good thing that's only a children's game," Dalla said, smiling. "We've had enough genuine bad omens as it is."

"Yes, alas, alack, and welladay. Zakh Gral, I'm pleased to report, has apparently had no omens at all. Everything continues peaceful there."

"Good. Have you seen any sign of the raven mazrak?"

"I haven't, not a trace, track, or hint."

"I keep thinking about that wretched gate I closed. Why would he have left it open like that? It must have cost him a tremendous amount of power to build it, and why just leave it? You know, he might have been inside it at the time."

Salamander laughed in a long peal of delight. "Let us hope so, O Princess of Powers Perilous! That would answer the question, wouldn't it, of why he disappeared as soon as it was closed?"

"It certainly would, but stay on your guard. It's not a surety, and besides, anyone powerful enough to create that thing can doubtless find his way out again."

"Oh, most assuredly, but let us most devoutly pray it takes him a good long while."

Yet even as he spoke, Dallandra felt the frost of a danger-omen along her back. "Not long enough," she said. "Not long enough at all."

In the morning Branna woke early. She hurried downstairs, but a bleary-eyed servant told her that the Westfolk had already struck their tents and ridden away.

"The gerthddyn's still here, though," the lass told her. "I saw him badgering the cook for an early breakfast."

In but a few moments Branna saw him as well, when he came slouching into the great hall with a big chunk of bread in one hand and an apple in the other. He sat himself down on a bench in the curve of the wall over on the riders' side of hall. Branna decided to risk a lecture from Aunt Galla and went over to join him there.

"It gladdens my heart you'll be riding back with us," Branna said. "I've got ever so many questions to ask you."

"And here I'd hoped you were glad of my sterling character and splendid company," Salamander said with a grin.

"You're splendid company, sure enough, but I've got my doubts about your character."

"Wise of you." Salamander paused for a bite of bread.

"Tell me somewhat. Rori, the silver wyrm, he truly is your brother, isn't he?"

With his mouth full, Salamander nodded.

"I thought you were just making up one of your tales, but Dallandra said it was true. She didn't want to tell me how he got to be a dragon, though. She said I wouldn't understand. Why not?"

Salamander swallowed hastily. "Probably because you don't know enough about the dweomer yet. Tell me, do you know what an etheric double is? How about the body of light? Who are the Guardians?"

"Oh." Branna felt her disappointment like a weight across her shoulders. "I don't know any of that."

"The dweomer, my turtledove, is a very complex thing, more complex doubtless than anything you've ever tried to learn in your life. Like all things, you have to start at the beginning, not at the middle nor at the end."

"Blast! I was afraid of that."

"But there's one thing I can tell you about Rori, and that is, he's gone quite daft. Arzosah told me so, and she'd be the one to know. Although—" Salamander frowned down at his bread for a moment. "Although, to be honest, Rori was daft long before he got himself changed into a dragon."

The sensation of a double mind rose again to trouble her. She should know exactly what Salamander meant, or so she felt, and yet of course she'd not even known the dragon's name until a few weeks past.

When the other noble-born women came downstairs, Branna left Salamander's congenial company to join them on the honor side of the great hall. Drwmigga went to sit at Ridvar's right at the gwerbret's table. Although there was no sign of Adranna, Trenni walked down the stairs with her grandmother and sat at Cadryc's table. These days Solla always sat with the Red Wolf women, since she was about to leave Dun Cengarn and take up her new position as one of Galla's serving women. Branna took a chair next to Solla's, and Neb joined her there.

"Where's Gerran?" Lady Galla asked the tieryn.

"Oh, he asked my permission to eat with the men." Cadryc waved a hand in the direction of the commoners' side.

"I can see that, my dearest, but why?"

"Um, well, um." Cadryc considered for a moment, then shrugged. "He's not ready to face our Matto, he told me. The lad saw."

No one spoke, but Branna was aware of everyone at table, either glancing at Trenni or pointedly not looking her way.

"I know what he saw," Trenni said. "I don't care, and Matto shouldn't either."

"My dear, dear child." Galla made her voice soothing and soft. "You don't need to think about—"

"Granna, how can I not think about it?" Trenni gulped for breath, as if summoning courage. "Anyway, Matto won't eat in the great hall, he told me. He won't come down till we leave for home." She lowered her voice to a murmur. "It's because of his grace."

"And there's another tale for another day," Cadryc said firmly. "Let's all eat our blasted breakfast! We'll be leaving on the morrow, and that'll be an end to it."

Branna and Neb exchanged troubled glances. Since Neb had told her about the siege and its aftermath in detail, Branna knew that the gwerbret had wanted Matyc killed. *Ridvar's woven a nasty little trap around my uncle*, Branna thought. Ridvar had every right as gwerbret to dispose of the son of a traitor, but Cadryc had the duty as well as the desire to defend his grandson. Clan and overlord, overlord and clan—those were the two strands that bound a noble-born man's life, and often enough they pulled in opposite directions, or threatened to hang him. *If Prince Voran hadn't been there*—Branna refused to finish the thought, not on such a sunny morning, not with everyone she loved safe, at least for the nonce.

With the meal finished, Cadryc and Neb stayed in the great hall to allow Neb to write a letter to Mirryn, telling him the latest news and announcing that they'd all be home in a few days. The women went back to their hall. As they climbed the staircase, Solla lingered, looking back down toward the table where Gerran sat, unmistakably marked out by his red hair.

"I'll have to talk with Gerro," Branna said. "He really should start eating meals with us. And I'll wager that Aunt Galla seats him next to you."

"Why?" Solla said. "It was foolish of me, no doubt, to think he might—" she hesitated briefly, "—might find me of interest."

"Don't lose heart so easily! Gerran's learned to keep everything to himself, all these years. He doesn't part with words willingly."

"True-spoken." Solla looked away. "Alas."

Later that day, Branna was crossing the great hall when she saw Gerran sitting alone at the head of the warband's tables. He was leaning precariously back in his chair, his feet propped up on a nearby bench, and gazing into the servants' hearth while he nursed a tankard of ale. Branna decided that as a near-sister, she had the right to sound him out on the matter of his marriage. She marched over, and he hastily swung his feet off the bench and sat up straight.

"Tell me, Lord Gerran," she said, "why you're sitting here and not at one of the honor tables."

Gerran gave her a lopsided smile. "I don't know," he said. "Maybe it feels more like home here." He thought for a moment longer. "And I'm still your uncle's captain."

"True-spoken, that. I was wondering if you'd started thinking like a noble lord yet. Apparently not."

"And why were you wondering?"

"Because of Lady Solla."

His smile disappeared into a scowl.

"None of my affair, is it?" Branna said.

"It's not."

"But it is, because she's my friend, and you'll be staying in our dun till Uncle Cadryc finds another captain and those letters patent come back from Dun Deverry."

"She can't possibly want to marry me."

"Oh, don't be an ass, Gerro!" Branna had had quite enough of polite sparring. "Of course she does, and I'll wager you cursed well know it. You're not that doltish."

Gerran opened his mouth and shut it several times.

"Well?" Branna said.

"Here, I'll tell you the truth if you promise not to tell her. Or anyone, not even Neb."

He grinned so smugly at his proposed bargain that Branna felt like swearing at him. Honor and curiosity wrestled in her mind. Curiosity won.

"Oh, very well, I promise."

"I do want to marry her." Gerran lowered his voice to a near-whisper. "But if I ask her, and she agrees, what if I'm killed when we bring down Zakh Gral? She'll be betrothed to a dead man, a widow in everyone's eyes, and who's going to marry her then?"

Branna was so surprised at this decency that for a long moment she could find no words to respond. Gerran had a long swallow of ale and resumed staring at the ashy hearth.

"I do see," Branna said at last. "And truly, you're right. If you told Solla that, she'd say it wouldn't matter to her, and you'd probably end up announcing your betrothal—but it does matter. I shan't tell a soul. I'll just pray with all my heart that you ride home again from Zakh Gral."

That night, the last before the Red Wolf left Cengarn, the air inside the broch turned so humid and hot that Branna couldn't sleep. She slipped out of bed without waking Neb, threw on the first dress she found, and went barefoot up to the roof for the fresher air. A cool wind frayed a few stray clouds and sent them scudding off toward the east. The last-quarter moon seemed to sail with them, glimmering free, then disappearing again into cloud.

Distantly from the west Branna heard a sound like thunder, but by then she'd heard enough dragons in flight to recognize it for the beat of wings. She surveyed the sky, and at last she saw Rori, gleaming more silver than the moon with the Wildfolk of Aethyr clinging to him as he flew. She was expecting him to go on by, but he headed for the tower as if he might land.

Instead, at the last moment he lowered one wing and began to circle around the broch, as if to greet and salute her. As Branna stood on that particular tower with Cengarn spread out below her and watched a dragon circle in greeting, she suddenly remembered standing there long before and watching a man riding another dragon, waving as he passed by. The memory was so strong that she turned to speak to Dallandra, who had stood next to her at the time, only to find her, of course, not there.

For a moment Branna felt as if she might fall to her knees in a faint or trance. She started trembling, suddenly cold, as another vision came to her. Two times, two lives rose up before her, a shimmering memory, a clear view, one overlapping the other, then breaking free, as if they danced side by side inside her mind. She could see the silver wyrm flying over Dun Cengarn. She could see a man standing in a doorway with bright sun behind him, and over him the shadow of a pair of enormous wings, his dark wyrd. The two sights fused.

"Rhodry!" she called out. "Rhodry, I've come back! I'm here!"

It seemed the stupidest thing in the world to say, but the dragon tossed back his head and roared. She could hear joy in that greeting. He circled once more, then flew off due north. Branna watched him until he disappeared into the gloom of the horizon.

"Well and good, then, Jill," she said aloud. "It's going to take both of us, but you swore a vow that you'd pull him back from the brink of that wyrd, and by every god and goddess, I'm going to keep it."

GLOSSARY

Alar (Elvish) A group of elves, who may or may not be bloodkin, who choose to travel together for some indefinite period of time.

Alardan (Elv.) The meeting of several alarli, usually the occasion for a drunken party.

Astral The plane of existence directly "above" or "within" the etheric (q.v.). In other systems of magic, often referred to as the Akashic Record or the Treasure House of Images.

Banadar (Elv.) A warleader, equivalent to the Deverrian cadvridoc, q.v.

Blue Light Another name for the etheric plane (q.v.).

Body of Light An artificial thought-form (q.v.) constructed by a dweomermaster to allow him or her to travel through the inner planes.

Cadvridoc (Dev.) A war leader. Not a general in the modern sense, the cadvridoc is supposed to take the advice and counsel of the noble-born lords under him, but his is the right of final decision.

Captain (Dev. *pendaely.*) The second in command, after the lord himself, of a noble's warband. An interesting point is that the word *taely* (the root or unmutated form of -*daely,*) can mean either a warband or a family depending on context.

Deosil The direction in which the sun moves through the sky, clockwise. Most dweomer operations that involve a circular movement move deosil. The opposite, widdershins, is considered a sign of the dark dweomer and of the debased varieties of witchcraft.

Dweomer (trans. of Dev. *dwunddaevad.*) In its strict sense, a system of magic aimed at personal enlightenment through harmony with the natural universe in all its planes and manifestations; in the popular sense, magic, sorcery.

Ensorcel To produce an effect similar to hypnosis by direct manipulation of a person's aura. (True hypnosis manipulates the victim's consciousness only and thus is more easily resisted.)

Etheric The plane of existence directly "above" the physical. With its magnetic substance and currents, it holds physical matter in an invisible matrix and is the true source of what we call "life."

Etheric Double The true being of a person, the electromagnetic structure that holds the body together and that is the actual seat of consciousness.

Gerthddyn (Dev.) Literally, a "music man," a wandering minstrel and entertainer of much lower status than a true bard.

Gwerbret (Dev., The name derives from the Gaulish *vergobretes.*) The highest rank of nobility below the royal family itself. Gwerbrets (Dev. *gwerbretion*) function as the chief magistrates of their regions, and even kings hesitate to override their decisions because of their many ancient prerogatives.

Lwdd (Dev.) A blood-price; differs from wergild in that the amount of lwdd is negotiable in some circumstances, rather than being irrevocably set by law.

Malover (Dev.) A full, formal court of law with both a priest of Bel and either a gwerbret or a tieryn in attendance.

Rhan (Dev.) A political unit of land; thus, gwerbretrhyn, tierynrhyn, the area under the control of a given gwerbret or tieryn. The size of the various rhans (Dev. rhannau) varies widely, depending on the vagaries of inheritance and the fortunes of war rather than some legal definition.

Scrying The art of seeing distant people and places by magic.

Sigil An abstract magical figure, usually representing either a particular spirit or a particular kind of energy or power. These figures, which look a lot like geometrical scribbles, are derived by various rules from secret magical diagrams.

Tieryn (Dev.) An intermediate rank of the noble-born, below a gwerbret but above an ordinary lord (Dev. *arcloedd.*)

Wyrd (trans. of Dev. *tingedd.*) Fate, destiny; the inescapable problems carried over from a sentient being's last incarnation.

TABLE OF INCARNATIONS

643	696	718	773	835-843	918	980	1060s	1100s	1150s
Brangwen	Lyssa						Jill		Branna
Madoc		Addryc	Glyn	Caradoc			Blaen of Cwm Pecyl	Drwmyc	Voran
Blaen	Gweran		Ricyn	Maddyn	Maer	Meddry	Rhodry	Rhodry	Rori
Garraent	Tanyc	Cinvan	Dannyn	Owaen	Danry		Cullyn		Gerran
Rodda	Cabrylla		Dolyan				Lovyan		
Ysolla	Cadda		Macla	Clwna	Braedda		Seryan		Solla
Galrion	Nevyn	Nevyn	Nevyn	Nevyn	Nevyn	Nevyn	Nevyn		Neb
Rhegor							Caer		
Ylaena				Bellyra	Glaenara			Carramaena	Carramaena
Adoryc				Burcan			Sarcyn	Verrarc	
			Dagwyn	Aethan	Leomyr		Gwin		
			Saddar	Oggyn			Ogwern		Oth

TABLE OF INCARNATIONS

643	696	718	773	835-843	918	980	1060s	1100s	1150s
								Kiel	
				Anasyn					
				Lillorigga				Niffa	Niffa
				Bevyan				Dera	Galla
			Mael	Merodda			Mallona	Raena	Sidro
					Pertyc Maelwaedd		Rhodda	Lady Rhodda	
				Olaen				Jahdo	
				Maryn				Yraen	Clae
				Elyssa			Alaena	Marka	
							Rhys		Ridvar
							Sligyn	Erddyr	Cadryc
							Alastyr		Raven Mazrak